Jack O'Connell
Seattle
9 August 1996

Be Faithful Unto Death

Be Faithful Unto Death

Zsigmond Móricz

*Translated with an introduction
and notes by
Stephen Vizinczey*

C E U

CENTRAL EUROPEAN UNIVERSITY PRESS

Budapest   London   New York

This edition first published in 1995 by
Central European University Press
1051 Budapest
Nádor utca 9

First published in book form in Hungarian
as *Légy jó mindhalálig* in 1921.

Distributed by
Oxford University Press, Walton Street, Oxford OX2 6DP
Oxford New York Athens Auckland Bangkok Bombay
Calcutta Cape Town Dar-es-Salaam Delhi Florence Hong Kong
Istanbul Karachi Kuala Lumpur Madras Madrid Melbourne
Mexico City Nairobi Paris Singapore Taipei Tokyo Toronto
and associated companies in Berlin Ibadan
Distributed in the United States
by Oxford University Press Inc., New York

British Library Cataloguing in Publication Data
A CIP catalogue record for this book is available from the British Library

ISBN 1 85866 060 2

Library of Congress Cataloging in Publication Data
A CIP catalog record for this book is available from the Library of Congress

Typeset by Mayhew Typesetting, Rhayader, Powys
Printed and bound in Great Britain by Biddles of Guildford, Surrey

Contents

Introduction

A Portrait of the Artist as a Young Boy

JUST AS RICH people assume that they have nothing to learn from poor people, big nations assume that they have nothing to learn from small nations. This is not quite true in every field: the world is not ignorant of Albert Szentgyörgyi's discovery of vitamin C just because he discovered it in Szeged, a university town in southeastern Hungary, and Bartók and Kodály are listened to even if their country appears to be of no consequence. But when it comes to literature, it is assumed that nothing vitally important can originate in 'unimportant' places. While the achievements of Hungarian scientists and musicians are widely recognised, the riches of Hungarian literature are almost unknown in the English-speaking world. Yet it should be obvious that those scientists and musicians could have emerged in such great numbers only from a vigorous and inspiring cultural background.

Today the mass media – ignorance compounded by technology – are diminishing the audience for high culture in Hungary as everywhere else, but even so, in that country of ten million it is still possible to sell a hundred thousand copies of a book of poems by George Faludy, and practically the whole adult population has read *Be Faithful Unto Death*. From a literary point of view, Hungary is a big and important country.

Zsigmond Móricz (1879–1942), often called the Hungarian Balzac, began his literary career at the last turn of a century. He was one of the great stock-takers, and in most of his works he took stock of the treasures of a defeated people. 'The writer's job,' he said once, 'is to identify those truths we can survive by.' Few writers in world literature have so much to offer readers who want to know how to survive failure, poverty and despair and to learn what strengths they can draw on when they seem to have nothing. We are not worthless simply because we are powerless, we are not without riches even if we are poor – this was the idea that led Bartók and Kodály to wander the countryside collecting folk songs, and Zsigmond Móricz to go from village to village collecting old folk tales and ballads, gaining experiences which made him the most astute chronicler of quasi-feudal village life west of Turgenev and Tolstoy.

Móricz came from this background himself. Born in a village of sixty-four houses by the Tisza river, he was the oldest of five brothers. His mother was the daughter of a Protestant pastor, his father a struggling mechanic with six children to raise. They lived in a small house with an earthen floor. The snow came through the cracks in the door and the ceiling was so low that a boy could touch it with his up-stretched hands. Later Móricz described that cold, bare little house as paradise: they loved each other, they huddled together for heat and comfort, and they laughed a great deal. And they had – and read – the complete poems of Petőfi, which inspired poor people to raise themselves from the mud of resignation and small ambitions. Sándor (Alexander) Petőfi, a butcher's son, the poet of the 1848 war of independence, is to Hungarians what Abraham Lincoln is to Americans: proof that one can rise to greatness even from the bottom of society. It was Petőfi's poems which gave Móricz the confidence to decide that he would become a writer even before he left the village at the age of ten with a scholarship to the Calvinist College of Debrecen.

In 1889 Hungary was still an Austrian colony, and Debrecen, the country's 'Calvinist Rome', had been the main centre of opposition to the Catholic Habsburgs since the sixteenth century – a role acknowledged by the Austrian army, which sacked and burned the city on several occasions.

It was in the Great Church of Debrecen, which towers over *Be Faithful Unto Death*, that the lower and upper houses of the Hungarian parliament deposed the Habsburgs on 14 April 1849 and proclaimed Hungary an independent republic. However, the combined armies of Emperor Franz Joseph of Austria and Tsar Nicholas I crushed the independent state a few months later and the country was once again ruled from Vienna. ('The Austro-Hungarian Monarchy' was the same sort of political lie as 'The Kingdom of the Two Sicilies' for the Neapolitan kingdom or 'The Union of Soviet Socialist Republics' for the Russian empire.) The Calvinist College of Debrecen, which was and still is both a gymnasium (an élite secondary school similar to a French lycée) and a Protestant seminary, had a tradition of political defiance which conceived of all intellectual activity as a kind of priesthood. 'The greater a writer, the greater his responsibility to take a stand, to tell people what is true and where their duty lies,' Móricz said later, and for all the bitter fun he makes of it in this novel, the College of Debrecen must have had a good deal to do with his faith in literature as a source of truth and inner freedom. Móricz, like his alter ego Misi in *Be Faithful Unto Death*, 'was a rebel before he knew the word "rebel"; he didn't want to be a slave even before he knew what a slave was'. His first play, which he wrote at the age of sixteen, was about Sertorius, a Roman slave who raised an army against Rome. At twenty-one he returned to the College of Debrecen to study theology, but left after only one year, saying, 'I'm not going to serve a master who doesn't exist.'

He went in search of oral literature in the villages, he wrote articles, plays, translated from the French (he wanted to translate all of Molière's comedies), he got married, had two daughters, wrote a pulp novel, and finally, at the age of twenty-nine, it came to him that 'You can really write only about what hurts. What wounds you. And what is revenge.'

The result was 'Seven Kreutzers' (1909). The kreutzer was the penny of the Habsburg Empire, and the story is the game a mother plays with her son, trying to find seven kreutzers in the house so that they can buy soap. A beggar knocks on their door and asks for alms but, amazed at their poverty, gives them the seventh coin. This story and others by Móricz have been published by Corvina of Budapest in an excellent translation by George F. Cushing, under the title *Seven Pennies*. The first sentence could serve as an introduction to Móricz's whole oeuvre: 'What a good thing it was the gods decided that even the poor should be able to laugh!'

He never whines or bewails misfortune: the question he answers is always the same: how can we keep our spirits up in this miserable world? His account of the life of a poor worker, a distant relative, is called *The Happy Man* (1935), and his profoundly moving, shocking, yet inspiring short novel, *The Orphan* (*Árvácska*, 1936), is about an abused child, an intelligent, spirited little girl who is shipped from one callous pair of foster parents to the other. Not knowing any other lot, she somehow manages to find things to enjoy in a life which fills the reader with horror. As *Be Faithful Unto Death* amply demonstrates, few writers can match Móricz in portraying the consciousness of children.

The Orphan would make sense to readers everywhere; it is the kind of literary novel that could be a world bestseller, while several of the others, notably *An All-Night Party* and *The Gentry Amuse Themselves*, and many of his short stories would be most readily understood in Latin America, where similar semi-feudal conditions still prevail. One of these stories, 'The Barbarians' (1932), set on the Great Plain, is on a theme similar to Hemingway's 'The Killers' but is more powerful. Móricz portrays cruelty and misery with merciless objectivity, yet there is always sunlight in his work.

Among his novels about the life of the intelligentsia (teachers, students, doctors, lawyers, bureaucrats, writers), the best and most successful are *Be Faithful Unto Death* (1920) and *The Relatives* (1932). The relatives are city officials and municipal politicians who rob the taxpayers in various frauds and 'carry themselves as if no one saw through them'. The hero, a city auditor elected by mistake, is a decent man, but his infatuation with a society beauty and his own corrupt relatives bring him down. Throughout the novel his tormenting conscience is his wife, who adores him and wants him to live up to her image of him as a perfect man. Like many other loving but ferociously demanding wives in Móricz's novels, she was modelled on his wife Janka, with whom he had a stormy marriage for twenty years. She killed herself when he fell in love with an actress who played the lead in one of his plays. He wrote over a dozen original works for the theatre (apart from hundreds of playlets and sketches for cabaret), but he is a better dramatist in his stories and novels, and his best and most successful stage plays are his own dramatizations of *The Relatives* and *Be Faithful Unto Death*.

On the most obvious level, *Be Faithful Unto Death*, Móricz's tenth novel, is an exciting school story. The central character is an eleven-year-old scholarship student called Misi Nyilas who is unjustly accused of stealing a lottery prize. (Misi, pronounced Meeshee, is the diminutive of Mihály, the Hungarian for Michael.) A book for juveniles could have this simple plot, which would be easy to resolve, except that Misi Nyilas lives as much in his mind as in the world, and the two rarely connect. I imagine this is home ground for people in any country and they won't find anything exotically foreign about it; the constant hip-hop of consciousness brings the novel within every thinking reader's personal experience.

The most foreign thing in this novel, apart from the unpronounceable names, is not that it comes from Hungary but that it comes to us from the distant age of the written word. Misi Nyilas and his friend Orczy boast about the number of novels and poems they have read. Misi envies Orczy because, as a Catholic, he is excused from the Calvinist religion class and allowed to spend the whole hour in the library. 'My God, a room where there were only books! Misi couldn't imagine anything more glamorous.' He pines for a book of poetry which he has seen in the display window of a secondhand bookshop and which he cannot afford to buy.

One day he notices the shop assistant taking out the books and is terrified by the thought that they have been sold. 'Perhaps a rich man had passed by, noticed the display and said: "I'll buy them all!" His heart sank as if his brother had died . . .'

Misi Nyilas, who bears the surname of Móricz's grandmother, is the author's younger self, and apart from everything else, *Be Faithful Unto Death* is an autobiographical novel about the birth of a writer. As such, it belongs on the same shelf as Joyce's *A Portrait of the Artist as a Young Man*, Anthony Powell's *A Question of Upbringing*, Stendhal's *La Vie de Henry Brulard*, Balzac's *Louis Lambert* and Tolstoy's *Childhood*. Misi's memories evoke Móricz's own childhood and family circumstances; he boards in the College of Debrecen, just as Móricz did in the same year, and his most treasured possession is a bound book of empty pages. 'His stomach trembled from some inner fever when he looked at the book: it was waiting for him to write something so magnificent that no one had ever seen the like before. He didn't know what it would be, but he knew it would be very beautiful.' The story of the boy unjustly accused of stealing a winning lottery ticket is also the story of how he comes to write his first poem.

But if Misi Nyilas is a self-portrait and much of his story is autobiographical, it has nothing of the flattering self-image of adolescence about it, nothing of the glorification of a discerning youngster superior to the adult world – nothing, in short, of the kind of thing that makes *Catcher in the Rye* such a success with teenagers. Móricz wrote for grown-ups. 'I have been training myself constantly to write only what other writers are ashamed to touch,' he said once. Misi is seen from the perspective of adult wisdom and ironic judgment: the mostly diligent, timid, good little boy is not above pilfering a pocket knife and telling lies. The high-minded would-be writer doesn't like responsibility: whenever he does anything that anybody might notice and take objection to, he pretends that he *has to do it* because he was *ordered to*. He doesn't even want to hear about his friend's troubles: 'Misi guessed that there was some family secret behind their lives and was afraid that in his anger Gimesi would tell him about it.' At times he has a sensible idea, but always too late. And although he is an imaginative injustice-collector, constantly fighting (mainly in his head) real or fancied slurs on his dignity and honour, he is never troubled by his own misdeeds. When he lies, it is a *sacred lie*.

Móricz was fascinated by people's 'special sense which makes them unaware of anything which is less than glorious about them'. A common word for this sense of unawareness is sentimentality, the pleasant mode of the mind, and it is particularly prevalent in the portrayal of children, where sentimentality is practically irresistible. The recent Hungarian film of the novel, for instance, gives Misi a sick bird which he nurses back to health throughout the movie. Needless to say, there is no such bird in the novel itself. There is nothing in the book designed to elicit the reader's sympathy, to make soppy readers exclaim, 'What a darling boy!'

The child is a child, even if he shares his creator's history, his longing to write, his hypersensitivity, his frequent and sudden blushes, his readiness to laugh or cry — and his headaches and attacks of dizziness. Móricz died of a stroke at the age of sixty-three; the condition which eventually killed him may well have had something to do with the fact that he retained a child's powerful emotional responses all his life. It may be worth noting that Stendhal, who wrote with the same kind of controlled passion, kept a similarly 'childlike' intensity of feeling throughout adulthood and died of a stroke at the age of fifty-nine. In her biography of her father, Móricz's daughter Virág (Flora) writes that he used to laugh until tears came into his eyes and that she often saw him — a great and celebrated writer — cry so hard that his whole body shook. Whether or not a writer can touch us deeply depends a great deal on his emotional range, and the source of the magic here is that the eleven-year-old hero is not just a feat of memory: Móricz still had the child in him to draw on.

Misi never rests. His mind and body are always in motion;

he changes three times in one page; his thoughts, his moods and emotions are swift currents altering direction every other instant. He is one of the liveliest characters in literature, and it is impossible to read the book without recovering something of the intensity of one's own childhood emotions. The chief virtue of *Be Faithful Unto Death* is what needs the least elaboration: it is a rejuvenating experience.

The virtues of universality allow readers to enjoy this novel even if they relate it only to their own childhood, but it can also teach them a great deal about Hungary and Central Europe – a subject which may be of more than passing interest considering that two world wars started there. Facts are the least of it, but they are here too: Mr Nagy, one of the two senior students in Misi's dormitory, gives him a lively summary of two thousand years of Hungarian history. It took the Magyar tribes a millennium to leave the depths of Asia and ride to Europe, where they settled in the Carpathian Valley; as for the second thousand years, the first great calamity was the Mongol invasion of 1241. As Mr Nagy says to Misi:

> The Hungarians didn't surrender, didn't pay tribute like people to the east, and the whole nation was practically wiped out. But they achieved one thing: the Mongols didn't get past Hungary. That was always our destiny: we were the ones who had to stop the hordes from the east. Hungary was always the last battleground. It was the bastion where the Asiatic hordes had to stop. Isn't that amazing, that the Hungarians should have come here from the east to protect the west from the easterners? We bled away at that, fighting our eastern relatives to defend the alien westerners, who have remained strangers through a thousand years and always despised us.

As with the Mongols, so with the Turks. The Hungarians held up the armies of the Ottoman Empire at great cost for over a century; they were finally defeated in 1526 at Mohács, and the Turks ruled the middle third of the country for the next hundred and seventy-three years. Transylvania to the east, protected by its mountains, remained a free and independent principality, but the Habsburgs took western Hungary and after recapturing Buda in 1699 (with the help of Poland, Russia and the Venetian Republic) extended their power over the whole prostrate country. From then on Hungarian history consisted mainly of doomed uprisings against foreign rule, without any outside help.

Mr Nagy says to Misi:

Isn't it terrible that we are here in the middle of Europe, we live here, we work here, we suffer here, we sing and laugh here, when we can, and there isn't a single other nation in the whole wide world who understands our language . . . Neither our language nor our sentiments nor our lives. We are condemned to be on our own, we cannot count on anybody, we have only enemies in this world, no friends, no relatives anywhere . . .

This may sound melodramatic when read in safe countries, but Mr Nagy was speaking in 1892, at a time when Hungary's best and bravest had been hanged, imprisoned or driven into exile to secure Austrian control after the 1848–9 war of independence and the nation had subsided once again into lonely servitude. Móricz wrote *Be Faithful Unto Death* nearly thirty years later but Mr Nagy's cry of solitude in a friendless world struck an even deeper chord in 1920, the year of the Trianon Treaty, when it first appeared in serial form. (It was published as a book in 1921.) The Treaty cut off more than two-thirds of Hungary's territory and condemned almost half of her population to a life outside their country's borders. Hungarians and their yet unborn descendants were punished at Trianon because their perennial oppressors, the Habsburgs, had lost the war.

It is ironic that this novel, with its deeply felt reference to 'alien westerners . . . who have always despised us', was serialised in *West* (*Nyugat*), which was both the title and the political credo of the country's most significant literary and intellectual magazine. Móricz, the intelligentsia with its classical education, the merchant class, indeed the entire middle class, saw their only viable future in a Western-style democracy, but they were never allowed to have much of it.

The Western allies, whose only concern was to get some Hungarian to sign the Trianon Treaty, put in power Admiral Horthy of the 'Austro-Hungarian Monarchy' and the mainstays of the old Habsburg regime: the big landowners, the officer class, the gendarmerie. This is the world of Móricz's novels: the two boys in the dormitory talk about 'what hurts, what wounds' every generation of Hungarians.

When the communists took over after the Second World War they made Móricz's works widely available, assuming that they would teach people about the bad old days, but what Hungarians saw in Móricz was the unchanging destiny of their nation: to be occupied by foreign powers and ruled by quislings. The fright of Misi's mother when two gendarmes show up for what turns out to be a friendly call was all too familiar to people who were greeted by the blue-uniformed political police of the communist regime. After the 1956 revolution it dawned on the authorities that Móricz was not safely dead and continued to exercise a subversive influence, and along with other spirited poets and writers who wrote eloquently about old tyrannies he all but disappeared from the school curriculum. The new role models from the past were the literary and political figures who made their peace with the Habsburgs.

However, the 1956 revolution, the lack of any help from anywhere, the defeat, the terrible reprisals followed by despairing submission, were so eerily similar to what happened in the second half of the nineteenth century that *Be Faithful Unto Death* became timelier and even more popular.

Móricz, who always looked on the bright side of hopeless situations, voiced in this novel the inspiration that can come from powerlessness and isolation. 'We've got to be of some use,' says Mr Nagy, 'but what use, I have no idea . . . Wouldn't it be beautiful if we could all create something,

make something which could be useful to the whole world!'
It is a simple idea but not an obvious one, considering how
many people seek to right wrongs and secure their place under
the sun by blowing up shops and hijacking planes.

Churchill said that Central Europe had too much history.
There is certainly too much history here for an introduction to
a novel, but it may help to suggest why Móricz's work makes
sense to readers who live in more stable parts of the world.
When Mr Nagy spoke of Hungarian history 'tears came to
Misi's eyes. This was his own life.' Hungary's destiny has been
more precarious than most but the individual's fate is
precarious everywhere, and the struggle to survive and keep
our integrity is in such clear focus in Móricz's works because
his characters face the same problem both as individuals and as
a nation.

Readers will discover many examples of this for themselves;
here I just want to mention Misi's poem. It comes to life in a
most idiosyncratic way, like everything that our minds create.
It starts when Misi overhears an anecdote about a boy who
picks fledgling sparrows from their nest and puts them under
his shirt, then jumps from the church tower rather than submit
to his friends' taunts and demands. Later the closeness of a
beautiful girl suddenly brings out the lines, and still later Misi's
bitterness about being accused of theft and his fear of being
expelled from the College give the poem its final form. But
what emerges is the quintessential Hungarian belief in the
saving grace of inner freedom, which for most of the nation's
history was the only kind to be had. The poem has the
simplicity, melody, clarity, rhythm and rhyme of a folk song,
which I couldn't possibly reproduce in English, but it ends
with:

> He fears not the earth,
> he flies up to heaven,
> who has a hundred thousand wings
> beating in his heart.

Introduction

Be Faithful Unto Death is full of hidden echoes and symmetries which make the very form of it a pleasure: a hundred thousand sparrows appear in the first paragraph of the novel.

Stephen Vizinczey

Be Faithful Unto Death

I

The tribulations of a schoolboy at an age when losing your paint and your hat is a tragedy

THE COLLEGE was a big, sombre rectangular building constructed around an inner courtyard. In fact only the ancient façade opposite the historic Great Church of Debrecen was sombre; the sides and the back were simply bleak. But Misi Nyilas was overawed by every part of the building. Even in the dormitory, listening to the sharp clatter of hard little heels with metal cleats pounding along the bare stone corridors and to the chirping of a hundred thousand sparrows among the leaves of the immensely tall poplars in the courtyard, he felt a kind of religious awe, as if he were in church.

At this moment he was rummaging in one of the drawers of the big oblong table which stood in the middle of the room. There was only one table in the dormitory but each of the boys had his own drawer. The front of Mihály Nyilas's drawer was painted green like the rest of the table, but the tabletop was worn, its colour faded, whereas the drawer was still bright green. He was very fond of his green drawer; he only wished that its former owners hadn't scratched it all over with the key. Inside the drawer textbooks and exercise books were crammed in beautiful disorder. Misi was looking for Békési's Latin grammar; he wanted to take it to the botanical garden to study the mysterious chapter about gerunds and gerundives.

While searching for the book he cast a surreptitious look at Böszörményi, a classmate of his but a bigger boy, who was stretched out on his bed, even though this was strictly forbidden by the room prefect. Lying on his back with his right leg dangling over the edge of the bed, Böszörményi seemed to be totally preoccupied with the spider pottering about on the ceiling above him, so Misi decided it was safe to contemplate his treasures.

Hidden deep inside the drawer was a book about Mihály Csokonai Vitéz, the great eighteenth-century poet who was a student and master in this same college. Misi had bought it for thirty kreutzers from Harmathy's antiquarian bookshop, where it had spent the whole past year in the window. At that time he wasn't a boarder but a day boy and every morning on his way to school he looked in the window to check whether the book was still there. This is a slight exaggeration: he didn't pay any attention to the shop for months, and no wonder, back then he was an ignorant boy, hardly amounting to anything, scarcely even a child. However, by the end of his first year in the gymnasium he had become quite manly, and it was then, in early May, that he noticed Harmathy's display window and discovered Csokonai behind the glass.

But only when he was at home for the summer holidays did it occur to him that he should have bought the book. That thought ruined his whole summer. Every day he remembered the book and wondered whether it was still in the window or somebody had bought it. Even on the train going back to Debrecen, as he looked out at the Great Hungarian Plain, he kept thinking: Oh my God, is the Csokonai still there?

When he arrived at the college he was assigned to room nineteen on the second floor and got the last bed, which stood by itself at the door. There were seven beds in his dormitory, three of them standing against one long wall and three of them against the other, with the odd one placed sideways against the short wall by the door. That is to say, Misi got the bed which every schoolboy despised. But he was delighted with it. It seemed to him that this bed, standing all by itself, was like a castle. It wasn't stuck in a row like the others, just one among many; he had an independent, separate lair of his own. That was a good start.

After putting his things away he should have gone to the school office to register, but first he ran down to Harmathy's and looked in the window. Thank God, the Csokonai was still in its place! Its lovely pink cover had faded a little from the afternoon sun and it had a lot of dust on it, but the main thing was, it was there, it hadn't been sold.

He wanted to buy it but didn't dare to, because he didn't yet feel strong enough to squander his parents' money on something non-essential. However, he kept running down to the shop to check the display window.

One morning he had a terrible fright. He saw the shop assistant opening the window with a key, and watched from a distance, trembling, to see whether he was taking out the Csokonai. The assistant didn't pick up any particular book but gathered them all together into a pile and carried them inside.

Misi couldn't stay to see what the man was doing with the books because the bell rang for the first class, but during the ten-minute break at the end of the first hour he ran back to the street. By then the display window was totally empty and the assistant was languidly sweeping out the dirt with a brush and a dustpan.

Misi only took a quick look, then turned around and raced back to the college.

All morning he couldn't concentrate on what the teachers were saying; he kept wondering what was happening to those books that the assistant carried inside. Perhaps a rich man had passed by, noticed the display and said: 'I'll buy them all!'

His heart sank as if his brother had died, or somebody else whom he loved very much, and for a few days he didn't dare to go near the shop. When he finally summoned the courage to go and find out the terrible truth, he was amazed to see that the window was again filled with books – strange books that he had never seen before. The antiquarian bookshop was really a small grocery store with one corner and a display window reserved for the remainder stock of the City Press, and later that night Misi finally realised that the grocer, little old Mr Harmathy, was stuck with those old books. Ever since he bought them he had stood angrily in the doorway, putting on an amiable face only when someone came in to buy something. Now and then he changed the books on display, hoping that the new lot would be more to the liking of passers-by. But Harmathy's was on a quiet street where hardly anybody walked except housemaids carrying milk cans and one teacher from the college who went home that way.

By the middle of October Misi's longing for the book had become unbearable. With flaming cheeks he ventured into the shop and said to the surprised assistant: 'Please, sir, I used to see a book in the window. Csokonai. Would you be kind enough to look and see whether you still have it?'

The assistant went to look for the Csokonai and found it. He asked thirty kreutzers for it. The boy was amazed at this; he was prepared for the worst, for a whole forint, because that was all he had.

He ran away like a little dog whose master has thrown him a juicy morsel of meat. The dog chews bones under the table but when he gets a tasty mouthful of meat he runs away with it, because he is afraid his master will realise his mistake and take it back again.

But the book wasn't what Misi thought it was. It didn't have Csokonai's poems in it, just a lot of twaddle about his life.

When Misi opened the book and started reading it, he found he didn't understand a single word of the very first sentence. 'Psychology has already raised to the level of truth the hypothesis that the characteristics of the soul and its strength are transmitted to the children of the next generation in the same way as physical characteristics are transmitted, and Mihály Csokonai Vitéz is an interesting example of inherited spirituality.' No matter how many times he read this he couldn't understand it.

The whole book was like that, and after a while he no longer felt the same urgency about reading it. Still, he was

4

very happy that he had bought it and he owned it, and he often looked at the title page, on which he had written his name. He had written it in bold letters in the upper right-hand corner: Mihály Nyilas, 1892. On the lower half of the page there was a fancy stamp in blue ink which said: Ödön Spitz, Attorney-at-Law. Misi crossed this out mercilessly.

He experienced an extraordinary, indescribable pleasure from knowing that he had a real book of his own, a thick book which he had bought himself and which bore his name on the title page.

There were other treasures in the drawer. For five kreutzers he had bought a colour booklet in the series 'Historical Portrait Gallery', which one of his classmates had stolen from home and offered for sale during break, promising to obtain subsequent instalments as they appeared. That boy was called Imre Kelemen, and he was a bad student with a big appetite. He immediately bought two apples and a bun and ate the whole lot in front of Misi, finishing off the five kreutzers at one go, while Misi had exquisite lasting pleasure from knowing that crowned kings and heroes with comets above their heads lived in his drawer. And he got goose pimples from happiness if he just caught sight of the edge of the booklet. He decided that he was going to draw all the figures, and bought five sheets of drawing paper for the purpose.

But his latest and greatest treasure surpassed all of these. It was a book bound in sheepskin which he had found in the lumber room of the Töröks' house on Nagymester Street where he had boarded the previous year. When the Török sons were children they had used it as a football.

The moment Misi saw this book he decided he was going to steal it, not on account of the book itself (because as soon as he looked into it he saw that it was in Latin, and he had enough problems with the Latin he didn't know in school) but on account of the binding. He had a terrible craving for that binding. He went to visit the Töröks on two, no, three Sundays and finally in an unguarded moment his passion triumphed. He tore the book from its binding, left it in the lumber room and hid the binding under his coat. Hardly pausing to say goodbye, he ran back to the college.

He wouldn't show the binding to anybody, not for the whole world, but he couldn't sleep and couldn't study until he had bought fifty quires of paper. He took them to a binder on Darabos Street, who lived next to the house where Csokonai was born, and had them bound in the splendid sheepskin cover.

What endearments he whispered to that yellowish, delicate, soft leather book! How he polished it with his elbow, because there were still bits of earth on it from its time as a football . . .

He wanted to write everything into that book. He didn't yet know what he should write, but he was filled with excitement and tension at the thought that he was going to fill all those pages with his thoughts. His stomach trembled from some inner fever when he looked at the book: it was waiting for him to write something so magnificent that no one had ever seen the like before. He didn't know what it would be, but he knew it would be very beautiful.

He chose a simple word for the title: *Notes*. Above it, in the middle of the page, he drew his name in big, strong, slanted letters, in the same way as authors' names are printed on the title pages of books: *MIHÁLY NYILAS*. At the bottom of the page he wrote 'Debrecen' and the year, '1892'.

But then the days passed and he didn't write anything.

He was afraid.

What would happen if somebody looked into the book and read what he had written . . .? And criticised it, perhaps even denounced him for it. Or simply stole it, or laughed at him, ridiculed him for it. He himself was no longer satisfied with the title page. It wasn't right . . .

It looked all right considering that he was only in the second year of the gymnasium, but it wasn't worthy of the beautiful things he wanted to say. He was shocked to see that his lettering wasn't any better than the lettering in his school exercise books; and yet he had thought that when he wrote in this book, his lettering would be a hundred times better. So much better that anyone who saw it would be compelled to exclaim, 'Heavens!'

But it wasn't better, it was worse. It was ugly. In his school exercise books he had been obliged to write carefully, and here he had tried to write daringly. And what had come out was a childish scrawl.

This title page caused him a great deal of pain; it made him doubt his own strengths and abilities. Yet the pain was mixed with some joy, because he saw in this book a great task to be fulfilled: he saw what he had to do and what he would perform. That book was like a castle to be besieged, and he would achieve the greatest glory if he succeeded in conquering it.

As Böszörményi stirred in his bed, Misi turned red with alarm and looked at him. But Böszörményi didn't seem to be paying attention to him, so Misi calmed down a little. Then it occurred to him: why had Böszörményi stayed behind? The rest of the boys were down in the back courtyard playing ball, or in the Great Forest on the hill. He was frightened by the thought that Böszörményi was thinking about his paints again. He had bought a very fine carmine at Pongrác's the day before, for five kreutzers. Böszörményi had probably noticed it and now he was preparing to borrow it and never give it back. He would use up the whole thing, as he had done the other time. Misi decided to disappear quickly to the botanical gardens with his Latin grammar.

But when he closed the drawer Böszörményi broke the silence.

'Misi.'

Misi looked warily at his classmate, whose face didn't promise anything good. It was already certain that he wanted the paint.

'Tell me, do you have any paint?' asked Böszörményi.

Misi was dreading that word so much that it was not a surprise. 'What kind?' he mumbled.

'Sepia.'

'Sepia . . . I haven't got any.'

Then came a little pause and he began to breathe more easily, thinking that Böszörményi wanted nothing but sepia.

'Well . . . Do you have carmine?'

'Carmine? . . . Yes. I have some,' Misi said in a low voice, blinking nervously. His carmine was already finished; it was melting away.

'Really? You have some? That's great!' exclaimed Böszörményi. He jumped off his bed and came to the table.

Little Mihály Nyilas was so small that when they lined up for gym he was the fifth from the back. Without a word he reached deep into his drawer. He had hidden the carmine paint so well that no one else could have possibly found it. He had put it quite apart from the rest at the very back of the drawer, in the left corner, so that he had to put his whole arm in to reach it. He pulled it out and put it on the table.

'Beautiful!' said Böszörményi. He screwed up his eyes and studied the paint, then reached out his hand, scratched the paint with his fingernail, put it in the palm of his hand, threw it high in the air and caught it with his other hand. 'Beautiful!'

Little Mihály Nyilas looked at the flying carmine. He would never have dared to throw it up in the air. He would have been afraid that it might fall and break or that he might squeeze it so hard that it would melt in his fingers. He would have been afraid of many things, but what disgusted him was that paint should be used as a ball.

'Where did you buy it?' asked Böszörményi in a very serious voice.

'At Pongrác's.'

'For three kreutzers?'

This was the greatest insult, because you could buy carmine for three kreutzers, but that carmine was flat and dry. Even a blind man could see from a distance what you could get for three kreutzers. But his carmine had a fine, creamy, velvety feel; it was so rich, you didn't even need water for it; it stuck to your fingers right away. It was a magnificent fat little paint.

Böszörményi was the biggest dolt in the class, he didn't even know about paint. But he was very good at kicking and beating, so Misi didn't want to argue with him. 'For five,' he said simply.

Böszörményi stared and examined the paint so closely that he practically put it into his eye. 'It's all right! Good paint,' he said, and blushed a little. 'I will buy some too. I'm expecting some money from home.' And he put the paint down on the table in exactly the same spot from which he had taken it.

Misi cheered up, thinking that Böszörményi would restrain his passion for paint until he got some money from home.

But Böszörményi was too excited to drop the subject. 'My friend, once I get money from home,' he said proudly, 'I will buy six pieces of paint. Not even six. Ten! Fifty kreutzers' worth. So help me God!'

Misi felt a little ashamed that he had bought only one and that he couldn't brag about getting money from home. But Böszörményi's parents weren't very rich either, he had already heard that. Yet once he had seen the postman bringing him five crowns, and he got money a second time too. Misi didn't know how much and felt shy about asking; he didn't want people to think he was curious.

The two boys looked at each other without a word. Then Böszörményi picked up the paint again. He didn't simply pick it up by reaching out for it and taking it: first he leaned over it and looked at it with his left eye, then he closed his left eye and looked at it with his right eye. He looked at it as if he saw some dirt in it – a speck of dust or a little stone or a hair – or as if he didn't really like the mixture of the paint. Then he put it very carefully in the palm of his hand and with bent knees went to the window with it as if the paint were a little bird which he had to guard so that it wouldn't fly away.

Misi looked after him as if there really was a danger of the paint flying out the window. But Böszörményi went on studying the paint and it didn't move.

The afternoon sun poured through the window, along with the sour notes of a violin. The students of the teachers' college lived on the floor below them and scraped their violins so frightfully every day that Misi had come to loathe the violin for life. The scraping of the violin offended his ears even more than usual because his carmine paint was in danger. He didn't yet know for certain whether Böszörményi would take it or not, and he was particularly worried that the window was open.

'This paint is not bad,' said Böszörményi, turning from the window and coming back. On his way he threw the paint up to the ceiling again with his right hand and caught it with his left.

Misi would have liked to ask him not to throw it but didn't say anything because he didn't like to fight, especially with boys who were stronger than he was.

But in any case Böszörményi put the paint back on the table undamaged. 'Where are the others?' he asked.

Misi began to hope. 'They went down to the back courtyard to play ball,' he said promptly, thinking that this might distract Böszörményi's attention from the paint.

'To play ball?'

'Yes.'

'What are they playing?'

'Longameta.'

'Longameta?' asked Böszörményi thoughtfully.

'Yes,'

'Hmmm. Longameta. That's a good game. It takes lots of boys.'

'Yes, there will be lots of them, Mihály Sándor said so.'

'Why didn't you go?' asked Böszörményi.

Misi blushed. The boys never asked him, because to put it politely, he wasn't very adroit at catching balls. 'I'm going to the botanical garden to study.'

'So,' said Böszörményi, satisfied, having heard all he wanted to know. 'And I will paint.'

Misi said nothing; he submitted to his fate. He had his own opinion about Böszörményi's painting and couldn't understand why he would choose painting rather than playing ball. No

one would ever mistake him for Munkácsy.[1] It was really just
a waste of paint. What he really liked to do was put all sorts of
paint in a cup of water and stir it up. It satisfied him, turning
all the paint buttons into water. He didn't like drawing and
used the brush as a pencil. He would draw a flower in a pot,
the way it was done in elementary school, or big hooked
noses, but they all blurred into each other and then he just
threw the coloured water on the paper. He ruined the lovely
white paper, just as he had ruined the paint buttons. He had
the demon of destruction in his nerves, and of course he was
in his element when neither the paint nor the paper was his
own.

Misi gave up his paint in despair. He tucked the Latin
grammar under his arm and reached for his hat.

This stopped him for a moment. That hat was a great
wound in his soul. He hated it, because glued to the back of
it was a tuft of white pig bristles which were all black at the
bottom and spread out like a fan. It wasn't his kind of hat; it
was a hat for a bully who would push it back on the top of
his head and look everybody in the eye with a challenging
stare, asking: 'Well, brother, do you want a slap in the face?'
Misi would have liked a brown hat with a white brim that
curled upward: a serious little hat that he could pull down
over his forehead so that he could go about under it thinking
whatever he wished. That brutish hat with the pig bristles
burned his face. He didn't like its colour. It was green. And
it didn't have a wide band, just two narrow cords joined at
the end with a porcelain bead. Earlier he had skilfully
removed the bit of porcelain and tried gently to detach the
tuft of bristle, but then he saw that a big spot of glue would
be left under it which would make the hat even uglier . . .
And every time he picked up the hat, he looked to see
whether the tuft was coming away because of his meddling
with it.

As he was on his way out Böszörményi called after him.
'Nyilas!'

Misi turned.

'So you're leaving it?'

Misi looked at him helplessly.

'Terrific!' Böszörményi shouted jubilantly, and grabbed the paint.

Misi left the dormitory dragging his feet, thinking that he should have stood up for himself. The cloister was a big open corridor floored with red brick – the scarlet brick that can be found only in Debrecen. At home the bricks were yellow, sickly pale; here he always looked at the bricks of the cloister with pleasure, almost with admiration. Why were they so red? Did they have so much blood in them? He was really afraid to step hard on them: the colour stuck to his shoes, painting the ground for ten steps even after he left the cloister.

He looked down at the courtyard – he never failed to cast a glance from the great height into the dizzying depths below. There were no classes that afternoon; only a few boys were wandering about here and there. In the middle of the courtyard stood the well, in quiet solitude among a few dwarf trees. Its yellow brass wheel sparkled even at a distance, and so did the long brass tube which stuck out of the well. This long tube always stirred his imagination; it was like a mother ewe, with a dozen teats, lying on her back. If someone drew water from the well and placed the palm of his hand over the open end of the tube, the water would spurt from these little holes and the boys would bend over them to suck the water, which tasted of iron.

He should have denied that he had any paint! Nobody knew that he had bought new paint. And even if they had known, it was so well hidden that nobody could possibly find it. And even if they had found it, it was forbidden to put one's hand into someone else's drawer. And even if they had got into his drawer and used up his paint, the room prefect would have made them replace it . . . But this way, when he had *given* it away, there was nothing to be done . . .

He turned left in the cloister and began jumping down the dark wooden stairs, like a sparrow hopping from one branch to another. He was brooding and restless. When he got to the first floor he stopped in front of the student teachers' music room and looked at the keyhole. He would have liked to peek through it. The student teachers were having a music lesson, and for a moment he listened to the strange song which drifted out. They were painfully singing scales, but he didn't know that. He just listened for a moment like a faun in the woods stretching out his neck at a strange sound and then leaping away.

When he reached the ground floor he ran lickety-split out into the open like a bird freed from a cage.

He had been living in the College for only a month. The previous year his tuition had been free but he had boarded with the Töröks; this year he had won a free place in the college and had come to live in this big dark building, roped in from the wild.

Apart from that, he was very proud of his college. His younger brother was going to school in Patak, and Misi was also threatened by the danger that his parents would take him there next year, because it was nearer to them. But now he was filled with Debrecen pride and he was convinced that there was no college like it in the whole wide world. He looked up at the tall building with its columns topped by big heads carved out of stone. Even these stone heads filled his soul, with their swollen smooth-shaven faces or curly Greek beards. Beneath them stood the vendor's wicker stall. Misi looked at the little rolls and the buns with four horns, the pale apples, but didn't think of buying them; he never bought anything there. He held on to his little purse with the twisting clasp on top, which had only forty-five kreutzers in it. He had not the faintest idea how he was going to pay sixty kreutzers to Mrs Csigai the laundress in a week's time. Whenever he thought of it he nearly died of fright.

He skipped alongside the iron railing of the church garden, touching every rail with one finger, and looked at the enormous mass of the Great Church. He shouldn't have had the book bound. That was why he had no money! But then he thought, if he hadn't had the book bound, life wouldn't be worth living. It wouldn't be worthwhile studying; nothing would matter. He was seized by such an inexpressible fever that he couldn't control himself. It had been no small thing to walk by the vendor's stall every day for a whole month without buying a single apple or plum or a slice of melon or a bun or a crescent roll or a slice of marzipan, but it would have been simply impossible not to have his diary bound . . . Only now that Mrs Csigai was about to bring back his washed and ironed clothes, he had no idea what to do . . .

He went into the botanical garden, which was right beside the college. It wasn't a beautiful garden; he had never liked it. He seldom went there, because it bothered him that every plant had a little plaque stuck into the earth beside it. He would have liked to know the names of the plants but they were all in Latin and he hadn't learned a single one of them during his first year.

He tried to study Latin but he kept thinking of Mrs Csigai, the small, quiet, kindly washerwoman who always came with a soundless and wordless smile, bringing his clean white clothes. He couldn't get anywhere with the irregular verbs.

Tall theology students dressed in black walked back and forth with long steps: they were studying too. He was the only small boy there. The other boys were playing ball behind the college. Misi felt miserable, having to be in the garden all by himself. He was filled with sorrow; he couldn't pay any attention to the Latin. Böszörményi wasn't studying either; he was ruining his paint. That wound, that thorn in his side, couldn't be forgotten. Gimesi, his only friend, was faithless. He lived in Péterfia Street, outside the city on the edge of the forest, in such a strange home which was unlike anyone else's home. He lived over a big gate with his grandmother, in such a small room, such an incredibly small room – only they could have lived there, because the ceiling was too low for anybody else. But Gimesi was still a little boy, even shorter and thinner than Misi. He was recklessly brave, though; he fought with his head, just with his head, like a battering ram. He would attack anybody, hitting them in the stomach with his head, so that even the big boys ran from him. This Gimesi wrote his name as Ghimessy, but people still pronounced it Gimesi.

Gimesi was so much in Misi's heart that he couldn't be without him for a moment. Even if he didn't think about it he felt his friendship for him. He looked into the Latin grammar and mechanically repeated the following lines:

a.) From the root of the Present. Imp. Ind.: *ferebam*, etc. Past. Ind. *ferebar*, etc. Future I: *feram. feres*, etc. Future II: *ferar. fereris*, etc. Pres. Subj.: *feram. feras*, etc. Past Subj.: *ferar. feraris*, etc. Gerund: *ferendi*, etc. Gerundive: *ferendus. -a. -um.* b.) From the root of the Perf. Perf. Indicative: *tuli. tulisti*, etc. Pluperfect: *tulerum*, etc. Future II: *tulero*, etc. Perf. Subj.: *tulerim*, etc. Pluperfect: *tulissem*. Perf. Inf.: *tulisse.* c.) From the root of Sup. Pres. Perf. Ind. (Passive): *latus. -a. -um. sum*, etc. Pluperfect: *latus. -a. -um. eram*, etc.

He would have liked to memorise them all, but it was impossible. His heart, his mind, were filled with some great pain. He was thinking of his parents and tears came into his eyes. He couldn't ask them for money because they didn't have any either. Here in the college he was eating meat and all sorts of good things while at home they were living on thin potato soup, and he was overcome by shame as he repeated to himself the Latin conjugation. His face burned at the thought that he had had his book bound. At home his mother knew that on the first of the month he would have to pay Mrs Csigai sixty kreutzers, but she wasn't worried because she assumed that her son still had a forint or even more: she didn't know that he had bought the Csokonai for thirty kreutzers and the 'Historical Portraits' for five kreutzers. And the diary had cost fifteen kreutzers, and the binding of the book twenty. The paint and the drawing paper cost thirteen − that made altogether eighty-eight kreutzers. If he hadn't bought all those things he would be all right, he would be able to pay Mrs Csigai the sixty kreutzers and still be left with forty-five kreutzers to spend on apples or whatever.

If only he hadn't bought the Csokonai. If only he hadn't

bound the diary . . . But the Csokonai was such a thick book, and he had never before owned a real book of his own, only what he got as a prize at the end of term last year, *The Thousand and One Nights*. He had left it at home and he was in a state about that too, worrying that his brothers would tear it up or dirty it. At home he couldn't protect anything, because his second youngest brother Béla might open all the drawers and take out the book. Béla would promise to play with it very carefully, but for certain when Misi went home for vacation the book would be dirty and all the beautiful pictures would be torn out, because his fourth brother was just a baby, he couldn't read anything, all he could do was tear things up. Or perhaps *The Thousand and One Nights* would be gone for good, because Jóska Kocsis, who lived next door and stole everything, would steal it. When Misi's uncle was home the previous summer Jóska stole his fine tools for mending shoes, and when they recognised the tools Jóska's father answered them with the old proverb: 'The bird belongs to the one who catches it, not to the one who lets it go.'

Misi sat on the grass slope above the gravel path with his feet on the gravel. He was tired from all the walking he had done.

Now he would gladly have given his bound diary back. And yet, oh Lord, it was dearer to him than anything! Because the Csokonai, once he finished reading it, wasn't something he really had to have. And it was difficult to read, too. Though parts of it were quite good. When it said, for instance, that Csokonai was always sleepy and his teacher excused him from early morning classes . . . True, the writer of the book attacked the teacher for excusing him, but Misi did not agree with the author about this. He wished that he had such a teacher – not because he wanted to miss the early morning class (these days school started not at six but at eight in the morning, thank God) but because even now a good teacher could excuse a student from a lot of other things. For instance the irregular verbs or the verb roots of the supine. That was what he would have to learn now, but he couldn't do it, he couldn't even understand them in class . . . True, even during class he was wondering about Mrs Csigai, how he was going to pay her the sixty kreutzers, but he didn't understand a single word of the teacher's explanation. He must have missed something. Perhaps he missed something when he was thinking of his diary, how he would write *The Heart* in it, because he had decided he would write an account of everything he read, and the most beautiful thing he had read was *The Heart*. He thought how he should summarise the story. And there was *The Little Drummer* . . . No, he didn't like that so much, except the part about the little boy – he couldn't remember his name – who lived in Turin, Italy, a poor man's son, who would get up during the night when his father was asleep and address wrappers for him. And in the morning his father said, 'You see, my son, your father isn't such a weakling as you might think. During the night I wrote a hundred and fifty more addresses than I usually do.' The boy was very happy to hear that and it spurred him on to work harder to please his father. So he got up every night to write and his father didn't notice anything, except he said once, 'It's amazing how much oil we're using in the lamp lately.' The boy wanted to confess but then his father thought of something else and so he didn't say anything. At the end of the month his father came home in a cheerful mood, even bringing him presents, saying 'You see, my son, how I work to support you and your brothers. You just study diligently, because you know how we will need your help.' There were tears in the boy's heart and so he worked even longer during the night. But all this staying up at night had its harmful consequences, because he never got enough sleep and so he was sleepy and depressed and yawned all day. In the evening for the first time in his life he fell asleep while doing his homework, and his father woke him up. This happened almost every evening. The father watched his son suspiciously; he couldn't imagine what could be wrong with him, and often rebuked him and threatened him with his anger. The boy often resolved not to get up that night, but when the time came he felt that he would commit a great sin if he didn't get up . . .

As Misi relived the story in his mind he couldn't bear the sadness of it. His eyes filled with tears and then he broke into sobs.

What a bad, useless, reckless son he was! He did nothing to help his parents even though he knew that his father earned his bread with a hundred times more labour than the man who wrote the addresses. He had to wield a heavy axe from morning to night, had to cut huge trees to feed his family. Not like Misi, who could sit in a warm room, or in the cool shade, wielding a light pen. And yet he gave way to his wicked desires and his vanity and squandered the money entrusted to him. He had paid thirty-five kreutzers for the diary in which there was nothing but empty paper, when he could have bought the same amount of paper in single sheets for five kreutzers . . . And he wouldn't have needed to spend five kreutzers; for one kreutzer he could have bought three sheets, and even that would have been too much; he wouldn't be able to fill so much paper during the free study period . . .

Great sorrow was squeezing his heart but he was afraid that the theology students would notice it and ask why he was crying. Perhaps they would rebuke him or laugh at him, or perhaps they would denounce him and he would get punished for not paying attention to the irregular verbs. So he got up and went to the back of the garden, intending to cry behind the big bushes. But moving about he lost his desire to cry and was only sad. He resolved to make up for his sins by working hard; he would translate all the stories in the back of the Latin grammar book and write them into his diary. And then he would start another section in the diary, in which he would write his own compositions. He would write the story of the poor boy who copied out the address labels as well as the story of every other book he read. Then in a third section he would write miscellaneous notes. First of all he would write down the timetable, because for the life of him he couldn't keep it in his head. He never knew what classes there would be the next day . . . And in this section he would write how much money he had and what he bought . . .

Here he was taken aback. Because if he wrote down how much money he had brought from home and how much he had spent, then he would have to write down Csokonai and the 'Historical Portraits', and the diary too, and then everyone could see what an irresponsible spendthrift he was . . . So he gave up that idea and decided that in the future he would make a note of any further monies he received and how he spent them. If let's say he got some money from somewhere, then he would keep a proper account of it . . . For instance, if his father sent a forint from home he would husband it well, spending it only on things he should spend it on, which he could write into the book, because they would be honest outlays. To the washerwoman, for instance. For exercise books, for pencil, for paint – but only for as much as was absolutely necessary for school. And he would also write down exactly when he bought the pencil and how long it lasted . . .

Thus, treacherously, the paint came back to his mind, the carmine red button that Böszörményi had perhaps used up completely by now.

That made him terribly nervous, and without further thought he began to run back to the college. He closed the Latin grammar where he had kept his finger in it all this time, because he had been ready to start studying at any moment.

He ran back the same way he had come. He wanted to enter by the main gate where Csokonai's statue stood, forgetting in his hurry that by this time it would be locked. He almost hit his head against the big iron gate and then had to go around the whole building to go in by another entrance. He didn't like taking the long way, because the longer the road, the greater was the danger that he might meet somebody, an acquaintance or a classmate who might stare at him, possibly talk to him. Or perhaps he would meet a teacher who would stop him, look him over and say, 'What are you doing, running about for nothing?' Or he might meet a senior

student who would shout at him, 'Hey, shrimp, run and get
me two cigars. Here's half a kreutzer, don't lose it.' This was
the worst possibility, because a senior student was in the habit
of giving something to a junior for his services – perhaps even
a kreutzer for candy or something – or perhaps a peach. Misi
was faint from fear that he would run into a senior student. If
he had to run an errand for somebody, then as soon as he
returned and gave the change back he would run away, not
even giving the senior student time to say that it was all right.

Luckily he managed to get into the building without
meeting anybody. Only when he got to the manuscript library
did he have to melt into the wall, as the old librarian came out
and double-locked the door with a loud creaking noise. The
old man walked away, but at the end of the corridor he
stopped, turned around, hurried back and tried the handle to
make sure the door was locked. When the door withstood all
his shaking and pushing and he had satisfied himself that it
would not open, he went on his way without noticing Misi
and disappeared down the staircase. Misi had heard about this
peculiarity of the old librarian and knew that he would turn
back from the first floor as well, to come and check again
whether he had locked the door properly. And later as he
stepped from the courtyard into the street he would get
frightened again, turn around, go back into the building and
climb two flights of stairs to find out whether he had left
the library door open. Misi had often heard about this but he
had never seen it with his own eyes. Now he forgot about
everything else, even his paint, and waited in the dark
corridor, trembling with excitement, to see whether it was
true. He stood at the top of the stairs looking down, and his
heart stopped when he saw the old man on the first floor
landing, turning to take the stairs down to the ground floor.
But at the first step, with a nervous gesture, he turned around
and started up the stairs again. Misi couldn't have been more
frightened if he had seen a ghost; he couldn't move his legs; it
was as if they were made of wood. But once he felt his body
twitch, whoosh! he ran like a rabbit. By the time the old man

reached the second floor Misi was already far from the dark corridor. God forbid that the librarian should see him! Maybe he would think that Misi was spying on him to jeer at him like the other small boys. He might even recognise him and report him to the headmaster, 'Old Sergeant', who could roar like a lion. God forbid that anyone should be noticed by *him*! Misi's classroom was opposite the classroom where the head-master taught, and even through the closed door they could hear him roar. Then all the boys in Misi's class would start to laugh and the master would laugh too as he rapped on his desk: 'Pay attention!'

Misi was afraid of being called on the carpet by the roaring headmaster, but his curiosity was stronger and he came back surreptitiously and hid in a dark corner to watch the old librarian, who did indeed climb back upstairs from the ground floor and then yet again from the courtyard to check whether he had left the door of the library unlocked.

Only when it was clear that the old man wouldn't climb the stairs any more did Misi go back to the dormitory. Mr Lisznyai, the room prefect, was smoking, leaning out of the window to blow the smoke away; Mr Nagy, the other senior student in the dormitory, sat at the table rolling a cigarette. These two were eighteen-year-olds, in the eighth form of the gymnasium; the other five boys were second-formers aged eleven.

As Misi entered the dormitory, they all burst out laughing. Taken unawares, he looked at them with alarm.

Böszörményi was no longer painting; he was munching on a slice of brown bread and laughing louder than all the rest. 'What's on your head?' he roared.

Misi turned red as a lobster and touched his head, remembering that he had absent-mindedly stuck olive leaves into his hair while thinking about the translation of the Phaedrus fables: he had put the sweet-smelling leaves into his hair in the same way as he saw them drawn on the heads of the Latin poets. But then he had more to grow red about, when he remembered that he had left his hat in the botanical garden.

Without saying a word, he threw his Latin grammar on the table and ran out.

He ran as fast as he could, but by the time he got there the gate was closed. He gripped the long iron rails and looked into the garden despairingly. For a long time he stood there, holding on to the gate and crying. Above his head hung the long iron handle of the bell; he only had to pull it and someone would come and open the gate so that he could go in and find his hat, but he didn't dare to pull the handle. He didn't even dare to reach for it, and when he saw a gardener approaching he drew back, afraid that the man might see him and ask him what he wanted.

He walked away and stood behind some trees near the college and cried until the supper bell rang. When he heard it, he ran up to the dormitory. The boys had already gone down to the dining hall. He went to his bed, took his suitcase from under it and searched hurriedly for his old straw hat. It was a terrible hat; he didn't want to wear it any more, because a few days earlier when they had gone on a nature walk into the forest, it had got soaked in the rain and lost its shape. He put it on now none the less, pulled it down to his eyes, then ran like one possessed down to the dining room.

He was the last. The boys all stood by the long tables, and the master on duty was starting the prayer, but it was a warm early autumn day and the door had been left open to let in more air, so he managed to slip in and get to his place without being noticed. It would have been a pity to miss supper; it was a fine meal, one of his favourites: porridge with lots of sugar.

II

---

*Our hero receives a package from home which makes
him so famous that he has to get used to being stared at.
The lost hat helps him to his first paying job*

ONE DARK and gloomy day in the middle of October,
during the first break between classes, Misi ran, as he
always did, to scan the list of names on the black
notice board outside the porter's lodge and see who had
received letters. This time he saw his own name, and it gave
him a fright. Whenever he heard his name or saw it written his
heart started beating unbearably.

Two kreutzers had to be paid for every letter and he had the
money ready in his hand as he entered the porter's lodge. The
porter looked at all the letters, but there was none for him.

'What's your name again?'

'Mihály Nyilas, second form.'

The porter, who was small and wore big boots, shifted his
pipe from one side of his mouth to the other and looked
through the pile of letters once again.

'You say your name was on the list?'

'Yes.'

'András Nyilas?'

'Not András, *Mihály* Nyilas, second form.'

'I know, I know – well, I can't see any letter for you here.'

Then the porter smacked his forehead and pushed up his
small round hat, the sort worn by respectable citizens of the
town. 'I remember now – you didn't get a letter, you got a
parcel!'

A parcel! Little Misi's heart jumped with fright at this new joy. A parcel! His mother had sent him a parcel! He grew pale at the thought of it, then blushed. At home his mother had told him, 'Don't expect any parcels, my son, I can't send you delicacies like the other boys' parents so I would rather not send you anything. Why should we let them see how poor we are.'

Misi signed for his parcel, took the delivery slip and handed over the two kreutzers.

'Five,' said the porter offhandedly.

But Misi was so excited that he paid no attention.

'Didn't you hear? Five pieces of money.'

Only then did Misi listen, realising that the porter was growling at him. Completely flustered, he started to search his pockets. His coins fell to the floor and he had to get on his knees to retrieve them from under the table. He could have sunk into the ground with shame.

The bell rang for classes, so he started to run and dropped his coins again, thirty-six kreutzers, all he had left after paying the porter for the delivery slip, and he still hadn't paid Mrs Csigai.

When he entered the classroom Mr Gyéres the Latin master was already there but was still behind the desk writing in the day book.

Misi quickly slipped into his seat. 'Where were you?' his neighbour Gimesi whispered into his ear.

'I got a parcel.'

'A parcel?!'

Misi sensed that Gimesi was looking at him with envy, and smiled happily.

The Latin master stood up and looked around the class. It was a tense and painful moment: he was deciding which student he should question. Misi tried to look nondescript and indifferent so as not to attract the master's attention. Schoolboys understand about mimicry like no other mite in creation: Misi played the schoolboy who knew everything and wasn't thinking of anything. God forbid that the happiness

of the parcel should show on his face! If it did the master's
eyes would immediately fasten on him, and that would be the
end.

The master called a boy from one of the back rows and
Misi breathed more easily. Now he knew he was safe, because
Mr Gyéres's method was to attack one section of the class at a
time and question all the students who were at the same level.
They were seated according to their scholastic performance, so
today the good students could relax: it was the lazy boys' turn
to sweat.

Mr Gyéres was a young man and as he came down from
the platform and walked up and down the rows of benches,
he wafted clouds of cologne. At every step he leaned absent-
mindedly on the edge of the desk he was passing. His hands
had been scrubbed very thoroughly and his nails were smooth
and shiny. Misi was nervous when Mr Gyéres stood near him,
because you could never be sure that he wouldn't call the
person who happened to be under his hand. He had dazzling
white cuffs with glittering gold cufflinks and a dappled silk tie,
loosely knotted; he never wore a bow. He was a dandy,
extremely elegant, always dressed to the nines. His trousers
were exactly the right length to cover the top of his shoes, but
even so he always rolled them up to make sure that they
wouldn't get muddy. It was impossible to pay attention to
what he was saying because you could sense in every word he
said that the subject wasn't so important, what really mattered
was that his trousers had no wrinkles, the fit of his waistcoat
could not be faulted and not a speck of dust was allowed to
settle on him. The poor little schoolboys didn't understand,
because it is the luxury of the poor that they don't have to
worry about their appearance and can roll in the dust like
black piglets. They mocked the well-dressed, perfumed
masters and chalked rhymes about them on the walls where
everybody could see them:

> Gyéres, Báthori, Sarkadi,
> Three stinking coxcombs.

These three taught Latin, mathematics and drawing respectively. Latin wasn't the most important thing that Misi learned from Mr Gyéres. The Latin master's loving care for his appearance inspired the boys to emulate his wonderful self-confidence and ease of manner – though in Misi's case the result showed up only a decade later when he suddenly started worshipping his body and became brave and self-assured in company when bravery and self-assurance were called for.

'Did it come from home?'

'Uh-huh.'

Misi put in front of Gimesi the notice that had come with the parcel, with TO and FROM and space for a short message, all of these filled in by his mother in her small, thin, sloping hand. How his heart beat at the sight of her writing; he could almost see her pale white face, her scary big black eyes. He snatched the form back, quickly tore off the message, put it in his pocket and showed Gimesi only the part with the addresses.

Gimesi read the notice carefully. The parcel weighed 'three and a half kilos'.

'What is it?' whispered Orczy from Misi's other side. The boys were seated three to a bench according to their marks: Orczy was first in the class, Misi second and Gimesi third. Orczy was the Latin master's favourite; he didn't take his eyes off the master and was in a constant state of readiness to give the right answer if another student faltered. None the less he sensed that something momentous was going on beside him, so he leaned towards Misi to ask.

'It's a parcel,' said Misi.

Orczy was silent; he didn't know what that meant.

'Nyilas got a food parcel,' whispered Gimesi.

'Oh,' said Orczy, but it was apparent that he didn't understand. His father was the richest and most important man in the city, and Orczy Junior was like a young lord; what did he know about the hunger of poor boarders from the country who had to subsist on the college food? He only visited the school. The other boys made fun of him behind his back on account of his velvet jacket, his knickerbockers, his skinny legs and the way he walked, bending his knees and swaying as if he was rocking himself. In short he was an amazingly grand young gentleman; he didn't belong among young colts from the country.

Gimesi bent his head to be able to laugh without being noticed by the master; he was laughing at Orczy, who had no idea what a food parcel was. Gimesi knew because his grandmother sent parcels to her other relatives. He knew his life would be better if he could receive a parcel.

During break all the boys discussed the parcel. They tried to guess what was in it; they listed the things they would like to get in a parcel; everybody eyed little Mihály Nyilas with curiosity and envy.

The next hour was mathematics. Mr Báthori rushed into the room. He was a nervous, forceful man with clay-coloured hair which he combed upward, stern, flashing eyes and massive fists; rumour had it that he once hit a porter so hard that he dislocated the man's jaw. This impressed the boys, because they had a lot of trouble with the booted porters, but it wasn't true. Mr Báthori was engaged to be married and, like Mr Gyéres, spent a lot of time dressing, but at least he didn't make himself smell. Sometimes he hit the blackboard so hard with the chalk that it broke into bits which flew everywhere and threatened the eyes of boys as far back as the fifth row. He didn't care much for his subject; it didn't occur to him that he should help his students to focus their minds on the mysteries of mathematics and make them understand and love the laws of numbers, that he should open the doors of their little souls to the wonders of knowledge. The moment a boy closed his eyes in front of the fractions on the blackboard, Mr Báthori exploded with fury: 'You know nothing, you idiot!' and the four walls rang. Misi was ashamed for the boy and wished that he could whisper the answer to him, but it turned out that he didn't understand the fractions either . . .

At last the twelve o'clock bell rang to set them free. In less than two minutes Misi was up in the dormitory, resolved not to mention that he had got a parcel, because his mother had written on the delivery slip: 'Don't brag about it, little one; there is nothing to boast about.' So his first word was:

'Parcel!'

'What?' shouted the boys. 'Parcel?!'

'Nyilas got a parcel, Nyilas got a parcel!' cried Böszörményi. 'But I will get one too, they already wrote from home, I will get a whole roasted goose.'

Misi was already ashamed of his parcel. Now he would have to show it to everybody, put it on the table like all the others. He had never taken anything from the other boys' parcels, except for one small savoury scone from Mr Lisznyai the room prefect, who got more parcels than anyone else.

The bell rang for lunch and they all ran.

Later as they were leaving the dining hall Mihály Sándor asked him, 'Have you ever been to the post office?'

'No.'

'Then you won't be able to get your parcel.'

'You think I won't?'

'All right then, I will go with you.'

Misi was glad of the offer and they went away together.

They were back by two o'clock but by then the bell had rung for class and they had to run, leaving the parcel on top of Misi's trunk. There was no time to look at it, to open it and smell it. Things in parcels had a special smell.

As they were bounding down the stairs, Misi remembered his father coming home from a long trek one day and taking a good-smelling loaf from his knapsack, saying 'Here it is, bread seen by the birds!' It was one of Misi's happiest moments.

The afternoon dragged on even more painfully than the morning. First came religion, then Hungarian literature.

The religion master, Mr Valkai, was a big, fat, swarthy man with skin lined like corduroy and a small black moustache. He walked with great dignity and carried a stack of papers under his arm. He didn't put them on the desk but stopped in front of the class, looked the boys over and nodded to indicate that they could sit down.

'Now, boy,' he said, pointing to one of them, 'tell me, what was the lesson for today?'

The boy jumped up and started to hem and haw, groping for words. But Mr Valkai wasn't an ogre, he always helped the boys out with the answer, putting it as a question, saying 'Such-and-such a thing happened, didn't it . . .' He recited the lesson himself; they only had to answer with a yes or a no. And Mr Valkai asked the questions in such a way that it was impossible for a boy to say no when he should have said yes. 'Tell me, Jacob had twelve sons, didn't he? Very good, very good.'

Even in his old age Misi would remember the boredom of this class, because this blessed good man treated his subject with such deadly indifference, as if he was a day labourer shucking corn. Later in life when Misi tried to decide when he first started to think about things beyond this world, he never thought of Mr Valkai or his other teachers of religion, he thought of his mother. Sometimes on summer evenings they would sit on the ground under the mulberry tree, hugging their knees and waiting for his father, who did carpentry work on distant farms but came home every night. At such times they looked up at the sky and Misi's mother told him that those little stars were worlds just as big as the Earth . . . And beyond those there were other stars, and beyond those still more and more stars, and more and more, on and on, until Misi got dizzy, thinking of infinity, how vast the universe was and how many things were in it . . . And then his mother picked up a little bug from under their feet and they looked at it, at how beautiful it was, what fine little legs it had. There was a little parasite living inside this little bug, and even that was a living creature, and that too was perfect, and perhaps that parasite had an even smaller parasite inside it. But even if it didn't, what a fine invisible structure of blood and cells it had. Well! Who made it, who invented it? It exists. But why? For how long? What will become of it afterwards? And what was it before? When Misi thought of these things he always rolled himself up into a ball, hugging his knees as he did on those starry nights with his mother . . . That was his religion.

But when he thought of the religion classes he was weighed down by boredom and weariness. In the sixth form he had to wear dark glasses to protect his eyes, and then he slept through religion classes, because he never came across a teacher of religion capable of moving a child's soul with the most terrifying and most exciting mysteries.

'Thank God that's over,' sighed Gimesi, suppressing such a big yawn that the tears came to his eyes as the good and kind Mr Valkai walked out of the classroom. He was the most humane of all the masters. He even used to ask the children, 'How did you tear your coat?' or 'Why don't you wash your neck?' This was quite unusual, because the masters walked among the students as superior beings; they didn't try to bring them up properly, they just performed in front of them.

'Did you get your parcel?' asked Gimesi.

'Yes.'

'You did? What's in it?'

'I haven't had a chance to open it yet.'

'What does it look like?'

'It's sewn up in burlap.'

'In burlap? Why didn't you cut it open?'

'There was no time. We had to come to class.'

Mihály Sándor, who sat two benches farther back, asked the others, 'Did you know that Nyilas got a parcel?'

'Oh, boy, if I had got a parcel I wouldn't have come to class, I would have stayed in the dormitory to see what I got,' said Gimesi.

Orczy had just come in, because he was a Roman Catholic and was excused from religion classes. Now he too asked about the parcel. Misi had never been such a famous person.

The second class was Hungarian literature. It was taught by an assistant teacher who had already published a couple of poems in a Budapest magazine. Everybody said that he was a great poet. In fact he was a theology graduate who taught a few classes at the college and supervised the boarders. This teacher was a young man, he didn't even have a moustache, but he was the most absent-minded person Misi had ever seen. He mixed up words so that often his talk was a meaningless jumble, and then he blushed and looked around like a frightened little dog. When he entered the classroom the boys started laughing.

'What are you laughing at?' asked Misi.

'Don't you see?'

'What?'

'The lamb has been shorn.'

Misi didn't understand at first but then he looked at the teacher's head. He must have come straight from the barber. Misi thought he looked so funny that he nearly choked with laughter. He stuffed his fist in his mouth and when they sat down he tried to hide by putting his head on the desk. He laughed till the tears came.

The young assistant teacher couldn't imagine what had got into them but when with an habitual gesture he reached up to his head to comb his hair with his fingers, the laughter grew louder. So then he knew.

He turned beet-red and lowered his head but then he started laughing himself. 'I see you think it's funny,' he said, using the polite third person for 'you': he was the only master who addressed them as if they were adults. He did it even though the teachers were told they must use the familiar second person with pupils up to the fifth form. 'Well, you needn't be surprised that I got a haircut. I would rather wear it long, really long, but then people would stare at me in the street, so I always postpone having it cut for as long as I can, until I look like a caveman, and today I had bad luck too – the wind grabbed my hat.' This made the boys laugh even harder. 'I ran after it and the wind blew my long hair and everybody stared at me, so I went into the nearest barber-shop to get a haircut. It's terrible what that barber did to me. He cut my hair so short, I would have liked to tell him, For God's sake, master . . . ! But you can't argue with the barber, he cuts your head off with his clippers, doesn't he?'

That produced a tremendous gale of laughter.

'So that's how I have to wear my head now, until my hair grows back. It can't be helped . . . Everybody salutes with the hat he has — or rather, everybody has to wear the head the barber gives him, isn't that so?'

They laughed at that too, and the whole hour went for nothing. This was more irregular than it would be now, for in those days students weren't marked two or three times a year, they were tested every time they had to answer questions in class: those unfortunates who were called up by the teacher had to be able to demonstrate that they had learned the lesson assigned the previous day and were marked according to their performance. But this time there was no testing, no teaching, only laughing. The young assistant master begged them to stop and threatened them with bad marks. 'For God's sake, please stop laughing, or I'll give a 5 to each of you.'

This made the boys laugh even more, because there was no such mark; the worst mark was a 4. They knew that the assistant master also taught at the girls' school and tried to frighten the girls with fives.

That day Misi didn't learn much but he acquired a great deal of self-confidence and he went up to the dormitory with his heart full of pride in his parcel.

As he opened the door he saw that all the boys were standing around the table, eating. He didn't know what they were eating but he sensed trouble.

His parcel was open. That was what they were eating.

And they were laughing at his expense.

Mr Lisznyai the room prefect came in later. 'Who opened the parcel?' he asked sternly.

Nobody owned up to it. They claimed that when they came in the parcel was already open and the food laid out on the table. They thought Misi had put it out for them.

How could they lie like that? thought Misi. He had left the parcel unopened on his trunk. If only he had locked it inside! He felt awkward about saying anything. He was afraid there might have been something in the parcel that wasn't meant to be seen by anybody but him. He searched for his mother's letter. His mother would never send him a parcel without a letter.

'Here is your letter!' shouted Andrási, who was one of the thieves, although he was an outstanding student. He didn't have classes in the afternoon and had come up to the dormitory and opened the parcel with a boy from next door whose nickname was 'Pumpkin'.

The letter had been used to wrap up the savoury scones because it was forbidden to send letters in parcels. Misi went to the window with it, nibbling on a scone. 'Where is the liniment?' he asked when he had finished reading.

'What liniment?'

'My mother writes here that she made me some liniment to put on my hands when they get chapped. She said I should also put it on my shoes to keep the water out. It's written here.'

'Liniment!' exclaimed Böszörményi, growing pale. 'That was liniment?'

'What?'

'Well, what they spread on the bread . . .'

'Who spread it on the bread?' asked Andrási, turning red with indignation. 'You did it!'

'Look! He ate the shoe polish and now he wants to blame us!' said Pumpkin.

Böszörményi was not fazed. 'Well, didn't you have any of it? You spread it on the bread quite thickly, didn't you?'

'I did not! You didn't give me any, you barefaced liar, you pig, you dirty rascal. Didn't you say that you were taking it all for yourself?' shouted Pumpkin.

'Don't raise your voice here!' shouted the prefect.

'If I ate it, he ate it too.'

The others were amazed and then they laughed.

'I thought it was butter.'

'Oh, I'm glad I didn't eat any of it. I told you it was rancid, I said it stank!' shouted Andrási.

'Yes, it did stink, rather,' Böszörményi said.

'But you ate it just the same!'

'It stank a little but it was good, wasn't it?' jeered one of the other boys.

'It was all right for a strong stomach.'

'What will happen now?'

'They can throw it up.'

The boys thought it was very funny and some of them bent forward, clutched their stomachs, opened their mouths and gagged, pretending that they were in pain and about to vomit. Everybody laughed at Böszörményi because he had eaten most of the liniment; he didn't want to leave any for Misi.

Misi put what remained of his parcel into his trunk. That evening at the college nobody talked about anything but the shoe polish that Böszörményi and Pumpkin ate.

In the end those two somehow got hold of a bottle of brandy to get rid of the taste of the liniment. By late evening Böszörményi was roaring drunk and accused the whole dormitory of stealing his knife. 'You stole my knife!' he kept shouting.

'Who stole it?'

'It was here on the table, everybody ate with my knife, how would I know which one put it in his pocket?'

'Shut up!'

'Give me back my knife!'

'Give back the shoe polish!'

All discussion led to the shoe polish.

Even the theology students in the college learned that one of the young boarders had received a parcel and it was the boot-cleaning liniment that his roommates had devoured first.

Mr Lisznyai the room prefect was so upset about the whole affair that he swore he was going to resign from his post and move out of the college.

That night the boys went to bed very late and they were

already half-asleep when Mr Nagy from the eighth form, who was a very serious person but could also be very funny, woke them up saying: 'I think I hear the sound of boots being shined in somebody's stomach.'

Böszörményi panted loudly in his bed as the boys went off into another fit of laughter.

They tormented him until he stood up in his bed, rolled his blanket into a rope and fought them with it. 'You stole my knife, you low-down thieving bandits!' he shouted. 'And it was a lousy parcel, there wasn't anything good in it, it was a beggar's parcel. Wait till you see my parcel! I'll get a whole roasted goose!'

'It won't taste as good as a jar of good shoe polish!'

Though it was already past midnight the liniment business flared up in laughter again and again, and it continued the next day in class. Böszörményi became famous and went about in a rage like a bull cast out of the herd. The two other culprits were forgotten: the world always wants one pariah, the most noticeable one; the smaller ones are ignored, they disappear. There is always only one to get the stick, all the beating, all the anger and all the ridicule.

When Misi wasn't laughing he was thinking of his parents. He studied his mother's letter in the botanical garden because there weren't too many people there, and cried like a lamb, hidden among the bushes. Having had a good cry, he began running to get back to the college in time for the first afternoon class, but he had hardly started when he stopped abruptly and stood rooted to the ground.

A young man working in one of the flowerbeds was wearing on his head . . .

Yes, Misi recognised it, he could identify it without hesitation: the gardener was wearing his hat. He recognised it from the tuft of white pig bristles and from its colour too. It had the same greenish colour, and two narrow cords around it in place of a band, just like the hat he had lost. He looked at it for a long time; he would have liked to talk to the man but

35

was afraid. He was still wearing his shapeless straw hat and there was his good hat a few steps away, on somebody else's head! And it was ruined! It was dirty and crumpled as if it wasn't his hat at all.

But then he thought that perhaps the hat actually wasn't his. So he didn't dare to say, 'Please, would you be kind enough to give me back my hat?'

Hearing the school bell in the distance, he started to run. He got back in time for class but was sad all afternoon; he saw his whole life as sorrow and misery. He didn't dare to tell anyone about his hat, because he was ashamed of losing it. He didn't want to be a laughing-stock; he was sure the boys would jeer at him as they jeered at Böszörményi about his knife.

But that was another thing, Böszörményi's knife!

The previous evening when he went up to the dormitory he had found the caretaker putting logs into the stove, which was built into the wall and opened in the corridor. The boys sat around it before supper to keep warm, and sometimes the grown-up eighth-formers were joined by their classmates from other dormitories. Mr Lisznyai, the prefect, often received guests by the stove, such as Mr Páncél and Mr Haranghy, who was a poet and had published several poems in Debrecen newspapers. He was there now and as Misi came in he was telling a story about Colonel Simonyi. When this bravest of all Hungarian hussars was a boy, he climbed up a red church tower with his friends to catch sparrows. He noticed a nest in a crack on the outside wall of the tower, and the boys put out a plank and held one end of it so that he could walk out on it to get to the nest. He took the nestlings under his shirt and when the other boys asked him, 'Will you give us some?' he said 'No!' They got angry. 'If you don't give us some we will let go of the plank.' 'I won't give you any.' They let go of the plank and he fell from the top of the red tower. No sooner had he hit the ground than he jumped up and snapped his fingers at them. 'You still won't get any!'

Misi loved this story and marvelled at it. As he listened he was busy making order in his trunk, laying out his new underwear that had come in the parcel and brushing the crumbs from it.

As he worked away in the semi-darkness, he found Böszörményi's knife.

His heart stopped.

First he wanted to cry out, 'I found the knife!' Then he got scared that Böszörményi would start shouting, 'You stole my knife, you wanted to steal it, how else would it have got into your trunk?' and suchlike. So without saying anything he put the knife aside and continued rummaging in the trunk, touching the knife again from time to time. It was a very elegant little knife: its handle was made of horn and mother-of-pearl and was shaped like a fish; the fish even had eyes.

Then he reflected that they had eaten his whole parcel, leaving hardly anything for him. And the young gardener was wearing his hat. He was entitled to some compensation. He would not give back the knife but would take it home and show it to his little brothers. What a wonderful thing it would be when they gaped at the knife that he had got himself in Debrecen!

He was nearly fainting from the excitement. He hid the knife in the secret compartment of his old wooden trunk, passed on to him from his mother's father, who had travelled with it as a boy when he went to the college in Sárospatak. The left-hand drawer had a false bottom where you could conceal money and other small valuables. You could lock this hidden compartment by moving two little sticks which were concealed in the inside frame of the trunk so that no one would see them who didn't know about them. After putting the knife in the compartment Misi moved the sticks to left and right to lock it. He knew that he wouldn't open it until he was safely home again.

Nobody was paying any attention to him but still he hurried as he moved his things from his bed to the trunk, afraid that somebody would ask, 'What are you doing there in the dark?'

It was the rule that they didn't light the lamps before supper; that was the time for conversation, until a quarter past six, when the bell rang for the first group to go down to the dining hall. Misi's dormitory was in the first group.

He thought a great deal about the knife during the night and felt that it was the good Lord's doing. That was how it had to be: he had to get a present to make up for all his losses and sufferings. He was very happy; he was immensely pleased with the handle made of horn and mother-of-pearl. Anyway, it wasn't Böszörményi's knife. Where would Böszörményi have got such a knife? He must have stolen it somewhere, perhaps from his father or one of his relatives, or somebody else, but he must have stolen it, because he had thieving hands.

He thought a great deal about the knife during classes the next day and the day after that, and he didn't let the key to the trunk leave his pocket for a moment. He had bouts of panic thinking what would happen if somebody opened his trunk. What if he hadn't locked it? Once he ran up to the dormitory during break; it was forbidden, but he had to check. He became like the old librarian: he didn't trust himself and began to count all the times when he had forgotten something. Once at home, for instance, when he went to the priest's house for milk he had left his hat there, that worn straw hat which he was wearing now.

On the 18th of October it started to snow.

The day of the first snowfall was an important date and every year the boys carved it into the white-painted frame of the dormitory window. A week later the snow melted and they didn't get real snow until the end of February, but the important thing was the first snowfall.

That afternoon Misi went for water with two clay jugs. Usually he went to the well in the back courtyard, because the water from that well didn't taste so much of iron, and it was a few steps nearer to the back staircase. But now he felt like walking in the falling snow, so he went to the great courtyard at the front. Mr Valkai, wearing his black hat and a long black coat, was there and saw the boy with the straw hat. 'My dear little fellow, come here, come here.'

Misi looked at him aghast. What had he done?

'Why are you still wearing a straw hat?'

Misi didn't know what to say. He just stared ahead obstinately.

'Don't you have a felt hat?'

Misi shook his head.

'You never had one?'

Misi nodded that he did.

'Well, what happened to it? Did somebody steal it?'

Misi nodded again.

'Hmmmm . . . Hmmmm.' The giant master was hemming for some time. 'What is your name, my little fellow?'

Misi told his name.

'What is it? Speak up!'

Misi said his name again and blushed. Mr Valkai always gave him top marks and still didn't recognise him!

'What dormitory are you in?'

'I'm in nineteen, sir.'

The big man nodded and walked away and Misi, shivering and shaking from an inner fever, went to fill the jugs at the well. By the time he reached the second floor the two heavy jugs were almost pulling his arms from their sockets and his hands were practically frozen to the handles. Before going into the dormitory he warmed his hands at the gas lamp in the corridor, which had just been lit.

Mr Páncél was visiting, telling a story in his sharp, high-pitched voice. Misi put the jugs in their place and withdrew to his bed in the warm room. Feeling weak and sad, sickly and weary, he listened to the conversation until the bell rang for supper.

They had dumplings with curd cheese. The others complained that the curd cheese was thin and watery and stuck like glue, while Misi scarcely noticed what he ate: he was thinking that his parents would be in despair about his hat.

When they got back to the dormitory they lit the lamp, took out their books and started to study. At the upper end of the big table, opposite each other, sat the two grown-up eighth-formers, Mr Lisznyai the room prefect and Mr Nagy. This Mr Nagy was slightly crippled in his left shoulder and even had a little hump, but he was very bright, the brightest student in the whole college. He was always reading when the rest were playing ball or skating; he couldn't go with them, so he stretched out on his bed and read or studied. He knew everything and he could talk about anything in the world. That was what Misi admired the most, because he too liked reading but he immediately forgot what he read and didn't have the courage to express an opinion on any subject.

The five small schoolboys of the dormitory (all of them in the second form, although Böszörményi and Andrási were in a different classroom from the other three) were sitting around the table too.

Lázár Andrási was a strong freckled boy who never studied but came first in his class because he had a memory like a pantry: whatever was put there stayed there. What he once heard, he knew, and he was never weighed down by the burden of studying. When he read a poem once or twice, he could recite it by heart, no matter how long it was. When they came out of chapel on Sunday he could repeat the sermon word for word. This boy became a parson in a small village and could recite six hundred lines of Ovid even at the age of sixty. If he got stuck in *The Iliad* he grumbled that he was losing his memory.

Little Nyilas wasn't such a brave fellow. He couldn't learn anything by heart; he couldn't force his mind to concentrate on the word order. Later in Sárospatak he had to learn ten lines of Virgil and was called up to recite it in five successive classes, and he failed every time. He didn't like studying either, especially not when he had worries; he couldn't wait to go to bed. At nine the bell rang in the courtyard, which meant that everybody had to be in bed and all the lamps in the dormitories had to be out.

Misi was very tired and fell asleep right away, but around midnight he woke up thinking of his hat. Why had he said that it was *stolen*? The whole college would be searched. They would check every trunk, and they would find the knife! That would be the end of everything. He was so cold that his teeth were chattering.

If only he hadn't told everybody at the beginning of the year that he had a secret compartment in his trunk! But Mihály Sándor had the same sort of trunk, which he got from his father, a village teacher, and he bragged that his trunk was in better shape than Misi's. So Misi had to say that his trunk had a secret compartment and showed it to everybody to prove it. All the boys tried out the lock of the secret compartment; boys even came over from the other dormitories to look at it. At the time he was very proud that he had such a famous trunk, but now he could foresee that, just for the fun of it, they would move the sticks which locked the compartment and out would come Böszörményi's knife. He didn't fall asleep until dawn but by then he had figured out what he had to do. In the morning he was going to put the knife in his pocket, walk out to the street and drop it through the grating where they pushed down melon skins in the autumn.

In the morning he was so tired and so pale that everybody noticed it.

'What's wrong with you, little Nyilas?' asked Mr Nagy.

'Nothing.'

'You look as if you've been whitewashed,' said Mr Lisznyai the room prefect. 'Go to the doctor.'

Later he noticed that Misi was still around. 'What? Haven't you gone? You must go. I won't allow anybody to get sick here.'

Misi just looked ahead with a frozen stare. 'Do you want me to bring your breakfast, Mr Lisznyai?' he asked.

'Devil take the breakfast! Go to the doctor! Dress warmly and be there at nine o'clock. Csicsó will bring the breakfast.'

Misi saw that his plan was spoiled; now the question was only whether they came to search the dormitory at eight o'clock or later. He didn't dare to leave the trunk while the boys were in the room; he would rather volunteer to go to the doctor at nine.

When the rest of the boys left for classes at eight o'clock he stayed behind and took the knife out of the trunk and put it in his pocket. Then he put on his winter coat, wound a scarf around his neck and started out for the doctor.

He went down the wooden steps by the Csokonai statue, musing how nice it would be if he didn't have to throw away the knife but could hide it instead, some place where he could find it before going home for the summer. If only he could think of a place to hide it! He was squeezing the knife in his pocket and hanging his head as he walked towards the doctor's house.

The doctor was a very old gentleman. The boys had to address him as Excellency and had to kiss his hand. He had rosy skin like a doughnut and prescribed only two medicines, almond milk and a laxative. Imre Csicsó had whispered into Misi's ear before going down to classes, 'If he gives you almond milk, I will drink it for you.' Misi was pleased with the offer, because he hated almond milk; it nauseated him.

Finally he was in the doctor's surgery, which had a low ceiling. His Excellency lived in a tiny house next to the Bishop's mansion, but he had beautiful furniture and a great many books, as well as a lot of strange medical instruments.

Misi was very excited; he could hardly see for tears. Without a word the old doctor took his pulse, looked at his tongue and wrote a prescription. He handed the prescription to Misi, patted his cheek and sent him to the pharmacy.

The pharmacy was right across the street. They had strange, strong smells there, and big fat worm candies, the kind that his grandmother used to get when she had worms in her stomach. He was very fond of these snail-shaped, red and white coloured candies but they were expensive so he just devoured them with his eyes. There was another kind of candy there, pasty ones that were bitter inside; he liked them too. He got a lot of them from his uncle the engineer, who never brought any other candy to the children: he said this kind was good for them. Misi sat in the pharmacy like a condemned man, overawed by the strong smells, the churchlike silence; he felt that he was in death's waiting room.

The horse-drawn tram arrived in front of the pharmacy. The driver unhitched the horses and hitched them to the other end. All this time passed, and Misi still didn't know what to do with the knife.

When he got his medicine, which he didn't have to pay for (it was charged to the college), he started homeward, walking as slowly as he could. But even so he couldn't think of anything. He passed by three grilles in the street and stopped at each one of them but didn't have the heart to throw in the knife. In the end he decided he would hide it somewhere in the college. As he was climbing up the steps to the dormitory he thought he would hide it in one of the cracks in the wooden joists of the stairway. But then how would he get it out?

Then on the first-floor landing he saw a big oak rubbish bin that stood against the wall. With an impulsive gesture he grabbed the knife and let it slide down the space between the wooden bin and the wall. Only when he heard it hit the floor did he think, My God, there's no way to get it back! For the next seventy years his thoughts would be tied to that place, knowing that he had a secret there.

He went into the dormitory. He would have liked to join the boys in class – he didn't feel ill – but it was religion so he decided against it. He stayed in the dormitory, took his spoon out of his trunk and swallowed a spoonful of laxative. My God, it was terrible! Then he had an idea. Every time the bell rang downstairs he threw a spoonful of laxative out of the window. Between bells he read his 'Historical Portrait Gallery' book.

At noon the boys came back one by one, and they were all curious.

'What did the doctor prescribe?'

'Laxative.'

'Brrrrhh. You can drink that!'

'Did you take it?'

'Well, you can see for yourselves, three spoonfuls are missing.'

The room prefect came in, looking very gloomy. 'Nyilas, listen to me, where is your hat?'

Misi knew he was in trouble. He said nothing.

'What sort of nonsense is that, still wearing a straw hat in winter?'

But then the bell rang for lunch. Nothing more was said about the hat, and Misi ate everything that was put in front of him. When they went back to the dormitory the prefect called him again.

'Don't tell me you had lunch?'

'Yes, sir.'

'If you had laxative, how could you eat? Didn't the doctor tell you not to eat anything?'

'No, sir.'

'Then your problem is something else, it's the hat. That's what upset your stomach.'

The boys laughed.

'All right, out with it, where is your hat?'

'I don't know.'

'You don't know! Who ever heard of such a thing, somebody not knowing where his hat has got to. Valkai stopped me in the courtyard and asked me "Where is Nyilas's hat?" How should I know where your hat is? Why should I be lectured about it? I'm nobody's wet-nurse. If I can take care of my hat, the rest of you can do the same.'

This outburst roused Misi's spirit. He felt that the prefect was treating him as an equal. Now he wasn't ashamed to say it. 'Somebody stole my hat.'

The whole dormitory fell silent.

'Are you saying that I stole it?' cried Böszörményi, quite beside himself. 'What a swinish thing to say! I won't let

44

you say it! I didn't steal anybody's hat. I want you to with-
draw it.'

'I didn't say . . .'

'To accuse me like that! You can search my trunk. Let's
search everybody's trunk,' he shouted as loudly as he could.

The prefect had had enough. 'Don't shout. Nobody
said that you stole it. What a way to behave! Get hold of
yourself.'

'You must prove it. Prove it!' shrieked Böszörményi. 'You
can spit in my eyes if you find the hat in my trunk.'

All the trunks were searched and Misi congratulated himself
that he had disposed of the knife. Now he didn't care if he
never saw it again. The main thing was that it wasn't in his
trunk. He even opened the secret compartment to show them
that he hadn't hidden his own hat in it. Everybody's things
were turned upside down, but the hat wasn't found.

Since it was Saturday, there were no classes after lunch and
the whole afternoon was devoted to the hat. Misi sat on his
bed, crying quietly.

In the evening when there were only the two of them in
the room, Mr Nagy came over to him. 'Listen, little Nyilas, I
want to tell you something.'

Thinking that Mr Nagy wanted to ask him to fetch
something, Misi jumped off his bed and followed Mr Nagy to
the window.

Mr Nagy sat down and took hold of one of the buttons on
the boy's jacket. 'Listen, for the last three years I've been
reading aloud every day to a blind gentleman. I read the
newspaper to him from five to six and he pays ten kreutzers
an hour.'

Misi looked at him expectantly.

'I have too much studying to do this year. Would you like
to take over from me?'

The boy turned beet-red and couldn't say anything, only
nodded vehemently to say yes.

'There is only one thing that is terribly important. You have
to start exactly at five o'clock and you have to stop exactly at

six. The old gentleman is crazy about punctuality. It's three forints a month!'

Misi's eyes filled with tears. 'Thank you very much, Mr Nagy.'

'All right, I will tell him tonight that from tomorrow you will be coming to read to him. You will already get a forint at the end of the month.'

'Yes, sir.'

Misi felt that his heart would jump out and tear his narrow jacket. He became a grown-up from one minute to the next, a real grown-up, a man who earned his bread. He had to hide somewhere so that he could cry to his heart's content.

III

*The schoolboy works diligently, studies, earns top
marks and finds two friends*

RESOLVED TO BE diligent and punctual right from the
start, Misi presented himself at the blind gentleman's
place half an hour ahead of time. Mr Pósalaky lived
just past the pharmacy, in a smart little wooden house at the
back of a courtyard behind a yellow mansion, and his doors
were left unlocked to allow visitors to enter unhindered. He
sat in a wicker armchair, all alone, warmed by a lively fire
crackling in the stove. He was so strange, this blind old man,
dressed neatly and sitting by the fire in his bright orderly
room, smoking a cigar. The lamp on the table was lit.

'Good evening, sir.'

'Good evening. Who is it?'

'It's me, I came to read for you.'

'Fine. Just sit down, my boy.'

Misi sat down at the table covered with newspapers. 'Which
paper do you want me to read, sir?'

'It's not time yet. You start at five.'

Misi wished that he hadn't come so early. He was too
eager, that was not polite. He was giving the wrong impression of himself. The gentleman would think that he was a
disorganised sort of person who didn't even know what time
it was. He blushed and didn't dare to utter a word. He sat in
his chair silently, listening to the ticking of the clock.

On a waxed and polished brown cupboard stood a clock on
four alabaster legs. It wasn't like the clock at the Töröks' place

47

where Misi had boarded the year before. The Töröks' clock had a golden hussar riding on top of it and was covered with a glass case; here there was no glass case and the top of the clock looked like the top of a Greek temple. Misi thought this was much more dignified, and anyway, the glass case over the Töröks' clock was cracked and patched up with glue and paper.

The clock slowly sounded the seconds; he was practically counting them. It took an impossibly long time before the clock's hand moved, and the old gentleman didn't say a word. He must have been thinking of something, because he sat there smoking his cigar, very calm and relaxed.

Misi began to study him. He had quite a ruddy face and a thick white moustache, very thick and wavy, like rosemary covered with frost. A beautiful moustache. And he wasn't all that old: he looked like a healthy man with a happy disposition. His blue eyes looked so clear that Misi became embarrassed. He wouldn't have believed that the gentleman couldn't see if he hadn't worn a green silk visor on his forehead.

Misi would have liked to say something but didn't know what. After a while he spoke. 'In our village the snow doesn't come so early.'

The old gentleman didn't respond.

Misi lost heart. He wasn't going to disturb the old man's peace again. Who knew what he was thinking – and to say something so childish! What did the old gentleman care when the snow fell in Misi's village? The snow was falling here, now. Misi would have liked to take back his remark; he wished that he hadn't said it. He shifted about in his chair, biting his lips.

He would have liked to ask, 'Is it true that you don't see anything, Mr Pósalaky? Don't you even see the light? Don't you know when the sun rises and when it gets dark?'

But the old gentleman just smoked his cigar, slowly and comfortably. He was a heavy man; he filled the wicker armchair. His hands were soft and pink, his face was freshly shaven, and he was bursting with good health. He must have been cheerful and good-humoured because he was always smiling.

So passed a quarter of an hour.

The clock started to strike. First it struck three times, slowly, with a high-pitched sound, then again four times with a deeper, quicker sound, as if it was chuckling at Misi. Then he was left on his own once again. There was no more noise and all Misi could do was listen to the tick-tock marking the seconds.

Finally he stole a glance at the newspaper lying nearest to him on the table. He would have liked to read the paper but was worried that the old gentleman wasn't completely blind and would notice, and would think that he had come to read for himself. So he just read the name of the paper and the beginning of a leader on the front page. When he had read it he wanted to turn the paper over (it was folded in two), but he was afraid that the rustling of the paper would alert the old gentleman, so he started to read the top of the second column. The editorial said that the horse-drawn trams in the city were to be replaced everywhere by steam-driven trams, and this was all thanks to the efforts and vision of the mayor, who had already done so much for the development of the city. He was the most outstanding mayor Debrecen had ever had. Misi found this interesting because he had great respect for eminent persons. He had heard that Mr Pósalaky was a town councillor before he lost his sight, and would have liked to ask him when they first started the horse-drawn trams, and what they used in Debrecen before that. Watching from the pharmacy, he had seen the drivers unhitch the horses from the tram and lead them around to the other end to hitch them up for the return journey. Then the ticket collector climbed up to the box at the back and blew his brass horn, and lo and behold, the tram started! The narrow-gauge railway went out of the city into the Great Forest, but Misi had never been on it, because you had to pay, which was why he walked from the station with his trunk and walked out to the forest with the other boys to collect crabapples. How he would have liked to ride on the narrow-gauge railway! It seemed to him a fine, grand thing to do.

He was startled by the Great Church clock outside as it struck the hour. The hammer struck the bell in a slow, stately manner but struck it hard, and the strokes were so far apart that he could count to five between them. Then it started to hit the great bell and gave it five strokes too. It sounded so near, as if it was calling through the window: *You see? This is the time you should have come!*

At that even the small alabaster clock in the room stirred itself and began to strike five, marking the past four hours in a thin, high sound and the present hour in a deep, resonant tone.

Then Misi bravely picked up the newspaper and read aloud the heading of the front-page leader: 'The Future of Debrecen'. 'Now, as our city marches forward with giant steps into the modern age, the council has decided that the last two horse-drawn trams are to be withdrawn from service . . .' He read quickly, so quickly that he didn't take in a single word. He just read clearly and intelligibly, taking care that the words didn't run into each other, performing acrobatics with his mouth and tongue to enunciate clearly the high and low sounds. He put his whole soul into the reading, so that every word should be pronounced perfectly.

He flew over the lines. After one article came another. When the old gentleman didn't want to hear something he said, 'Skip.' Then Misi skipped, but he had to read all the headings. He wasn't allowed to leave out a single one, not even the heading of the smallest notice, though the old gentleman said 'Skip' to most of them.

When the clock struck six Misi was in the middle of an article which he was reading more slowly because it interested him. It was about the people who tilled the soil in the forest owned by the city. The land they cultivated between the trees amounted in all to ten thousand acres. They struggled with Nature in marshes and on sandy hillocks, forcing the soil to yield rye one year, corn the next. 'The centuries-old oak trees which survive this kind of farming seem to weep for their comrades who have disappeared, as they look down on these poor withered stalks,' Misi read. 'The peasants plant not for themselves but for their animals, and since transporting the forage would take too much time and would cost more than it was worth, they bring their animals into the forest to feed them . . .'

The clock struck right there and the old man stopped him, saying: 'Well, let's leave something for tomorrow, too.'

Misi put down the newspaper and stood up. He noticed that the old gentleman was about to say something and he blushed, expecting to be told that he shouldn't come so early. But that was not what the old gentleman said.

'Well, you know,' he said, 'the snow doesn't usually come so early to Debrecen either . . . I can't recall a time when we had snow as early as this year.'

Misi said nothing, just stood there, but the old gentleman stopped and didn't look as though he intended to say anything more, so Misi wished him good night.

The old gentleman nodded in a friendly fashion. 'Good evening.'

Outside the wind blew snow into Misi's eyes. He raised his collar and hunched his shoulders and ran across the courtyard. He was afraid there might be a dog and that it would rush at him. He didn't like dogs. They had many dogs in his village and they all bit people. He had been bitten twice when going for the milk.

In the college he was safe from the wind. Soon it was time for supper. Again they had porridge with sugar: it was his favourite dish, but the other boys were furious; some proposed that they should throw it against the wall. 'Into the cook's face, you mean!'

In the evening as they sat around the table studying, Misi was thinking of the centuries-old oak trees in the Great Forest looking down at the shrivelled cornstalks and sickly ears of rye and waving their branches sadly, grieving that their good comrades should be cut down for such measly things as these.

Outside the wind was roaring, rattling the windows and shaking the eaves, but the stove was hot and the warmth of the room made the small boys sleepy.

Since he had received a parcel Misi counted for a little more among his schoolmates. The subject of the shoe polish came up only when the others wanted to make Böszörményi angry, so even this injured party became less hostile towards Misi. He was no longer a stranger among the boys; once they even asked him to play ball with them, and he wasn't as awkward as he expected. However, because of the bad weather there would probably be no more ball-playing until the spring.

These were good days. He got a new hat from home, a small brown hat with a wide brim and a band around it, not a braid, and no pig bristles. It was the right sort of hat for a student, for a serious person. It didn't make anybody look twice at him. As always, he cried a great deal over his mother's letter; as soon as he saw her slanted writing his heart twisted and, he didn't know why, the tears came.

He was called up in class every day, and he recited the lessons without making mistakes. He understood everything and all the masters were satisfied with him.

He never again showed up early at the old gentleman's place; he lingered in front of the yellow mansion until the clock of the Great Church began to strike. Having noticed that the hammer touched the bell five minutes before it began to strike, he waited until he heard that quiet solitary sound and then went into the courtyard. By the time he reached the little house at the back of the courtyard the clock was beginning to strike, and when he sat down in his chair by the table the clock with the alabaster legs started its cheerful chime.

One day Orczy said to Misi: 'Look here, Nyilas, today is Saturday and my mother says I should invite you. Come and see us this afternoon.'

'Me?'

'Yes.'

'Why?'

'Well, no special reason.'

'There has to be a reason!' Misi said.

Orczy laughed. 'It's just a visit. Will you come?'

Misi couldn't get over his surprise. The two of them had sat beside each other in class for a whole year, but Orczy had never before invited him to his home. Nobody else invited him either, except Gimesi who sat on his other side. He had visited Gimesi's place several times, mostly the year before.

The three of them were still the best students in the class and occupied the front bench. They all got a poor 3 in physical training but 1 in everything else, except that Orczy got a 2 in penmanship. Some of the boys thought it was unfair that Orczy should be top student when he had only a 2 mark in penmanship, but Misi didn't mind: Orczy really knew more than he did. For instance in one of the Latin texts there was a reference to Julius Caesar. Mr Gyéres asked the class who Julius Caesar was: had anybody heard of him? Nobody could answer. Then Orczy got up and said that Julius Caesar was a play, he had seen it in Budapest, and Julius Caesar was killed.

'Who killed him?'

That Orczy didn't know. He had forgotten.

'That's all right, you can sit down,' said the master with a smile, and patted Orczy's cheek. Orczy was his favourite.

Misi was impressed by all the things Orczy knew. There was something in almost every class that Orczy knew and the rest of them didn't. True, he wasn't really good at memorising things, but Misi wasn't that good at it either. Anyway, he knew that by merit neither of them belonged to the first bench; the best student in the class was K. Sánta, officially number four. Sánta wore high boots and came from a poor family in Debrecen; his father was a woodcutter, they said. He hardly spoke but he knew everything – that is, everything that was taught at school. Misi knew about things that weren't taught in school; he had learned a lot from his mother. But K. Sánta was the only one in the class who knew the conjugations and he came fourth only because he was unjustly given two 2's. Gimesi, who came third, was also a good student, but all his exercise books had spots on them and he was always carving bits of wood in class. If he was called up unexpectedly he rarely knew what to say, but if the question was repeated he would give a brilliant answer.

Misi leaned over to Gimesi during class and whispered, 'I have something to tell you later.'

'What?'

'I will tell you.'

When the class ended at midday Orczy packed his books into a piece of black oilcloth, tied them up with a yellow strap which had a steel handle, put on his winter coat, turned to Misi and bowed from the waist: 'I'll be expecting you.'

Misi didn't respond. He was offended that Orczy used such a high-flown expression. 'I'll be expecting you.' What did Orczy mean, *expecting* him? He wouldn't have dreamed of saying such a thing.

'What's your news?' asked Gimesi, tying up his books with a very ordinary strap. He always packed up in a hurry and in a slapdash way, not carefully like Orczy.

'Listen . . .'

'Go on.'

'Orczy invited me to his house.'

'To his house?'

'Yes.'

'God Almighty!'

'He didn't invite you?'

'No he didn't.'

'Then I won't go either,' said Misi.

Gimesi thought about it. He looked at Misi. His eyes were sparkling with tears. 'Don't be crazy.'

'I won't go.'

'You're an ass!' said Gimesi, and butted him with his head. That was his way; he always fought with his head.

Misi fell back on the bench laughing, and his books fell on the floor. He had neither a strap nor oilcloth; he carried his books in his hand.

'I won't go,' he said as he stood up.

Gimesi shrugged. 'If you are such a fool . . .'

As the boys crowded through the door Orczy pushed his way back into the room. He had been running: his face was red and he was out of breath. 'Nyilas!'

Misi looked at him and blushed, thinking that Orczy already knew he didn't want to go to their house.

'Come here,' said Orczy, drawing him aside and whispering. Gimesi watched them for a while and then ran away.

'I forgot to tell you how to get to our place,' said Orczy.

'I . . .' Misi wanted to say that he wouldn't go but then stopped. It was hard to say it, because he very much wanted to go now that Gimesi wasn't there.

Orczy gave detailed instructions, explained that they lived in Kossuth Street next to the theatre, told him the number and said he had to go up to the first floor; that was where they lived. 'My mother said that I absolutely must invite you because Mr Gyéres told her about you.'

Misi was speechless. The Latin master!

Orczy nodded in a friendly manner and then ran off. He wanted to make up for the delay.

Misi ran out to the courtyard to catch up with Gimesi and tell him he had no choice: he had to go; the Latin master said so. But he couldn't see his friend, although he ran after him as far as the Csokonai garden. He lingered there to catch his breath and then, when the bell rang for lunch, he ran back to the college and up to the dormitory with his books. By then the other boys had gone to lunch. He ran back down to the dining hall but was late.

They had *gulyás* soup and semolina pudding. He ate heartily and the clatter of the spoons and the plates had a soothing effect on him. When the head prefect got up to say prayers Misi was still eating: his mouth was full of pudding. And he finished on the way out what was left on his plate.

In the dormitory he started to dress.

'What is he dressing up for?'

'Look, Nyilas is washing himself!' the boys shouted.

'He's putting on a clean shirt!'

'Aren't you going to wash your feet?'

'Where is he going?' wondered the boys.

Misi didn't say. He just shrugged. 'I have to go out. Mr Gyéres said so.'

That was his justification. Without it he wouldn't have dared to make such a fuss.

Misi knew where the theatre was and when he passed it he stopped to look at the playbill. They were doing *The Scamp*. He would have loved to see it. He decided he would buy a ticket, because you could get one at the college for ten kreutzers. But you also had to ask permission from your class teacher and in his case that was the Latin master. That was the only reason why he hadn't bought a ticket before; he wouldn't have minded spending money on a play. He lingered at the theatre, looking at it from every angle, but then ran away because a smooth-shaven man with a top hat and a big round cape came along, humming something to himself.

It was a fine day. The snow had disappeared from the street; only some remained under the bushes in the gardens and some on the bushes themselves. The sun was shining but the air was cold.

When he found the building where the Orczys lived he walked to and fro in front of it until he managed to muster the courage to go inside. Then he rushed in. He climbed the stairs, holding on to the wrought iron railing, and found himself in front of a big white door without a handle. He didn't know what to do. It was impossible to enter such a door: it had no handle! He stood there for a long time, growing quite dispirited, until the door opened suddenly and a maid rushed out as if she was being chased. She nearly ran him down.

'I'm looking for Orczy.'

'For Bébuci? He's here, just go in. Go on!'

Misi was annoyed that a maid should talk to him in such a way and so he didn't say anything, he just went in.

He found himself in a beautiful room with shining white cupboards. Looking around, he saw four doors. Which one should he take? He heard laughter behind his back and turned to look. The maid was being impertinent again, laughing at him.

'You go in there, to the left. No, not that way, to the left! Not that way, I'm telling you, to the left!' Then, still laughing, she pointed to the door on the right. 'To the right, I meant.' With that she went out and closed the door behind her.

Misi reached up to turn the handle of the door on the right and entered a dark little room with a bright shaft of light running through it from another door which stood open. He stopped in the dark and looked through the open door into a large room filled with sunlight. Over a big table there hung a big round sparkling glittering something, another sun! It dazzled him. A beautiful blonde lady was sitting at the table, laughing.

He heard Orczy's voice. 'I'm moving my knight. My knight defies you.'

They didn't notice him and he didn't want to disturb them. They were playing chess. He could play chess too; Uncle Török[1] had taught him the previous winter. Then as time passed and it seemed that they would never notice him, he said softly, 'Orczy!'

They heard him and looked around. He stepped forward a little, clutched the edge of the door frame and said again, in a whisper, 'Orczy.'

Orczy turned around and saw him. The blonde woman, too, saw the little boy standing there in his winter coat, clutching the door frame and whispering into the room, and she was seized by a fit of laughter.

Orczy came out to greet Misi and said, '*Servus*, Nyilas. I was playing chess with my mother.'

They shook hands awkwardly.

Misi's face was burning from the wind; there is always a strong wind blowing around the college and the theatre in Debrecen, and he had lingered a long time in both places.

'Take off your coat.'

He took off his coat. His mother had made that coat; she had padded it with cotton wool and it was as warm as an eiderdown, but it didn't look very elegant. The two boys took the coat out to the hall and hung it up, and also hung up the new felt hat. Even the wall where they hung up the clothes was covered with green cloth and decorated with antlers and swords. Then they went back to the room; Orczy looked around but his mother was gone.

'Please sit down. Make yourself comfortable.'

Orczy always spoke in this detestable manner, saying things like *make yourself comfortable.*

Misi sat down and asked, 'Is this where you study?'

'Yes, this is my room.'

This annoyed Misi. *My room!* Why was it his room? Did he build it?

'Here are my books, there are my toys, gym gear . . .'

Misi didn't see much because there was no direct light in the den, only what came in through the open doorway. He looked up at the ceiling and was amazed at how high it was. He thought only classrooms and the other rooms in the college had such high ceilings. At home the ceilings were so low that when his father raised his axe it hit the beams, and the main beam was so low that even he, Misi, could reach it if he raised his arm. It would be nice if their house was a little higher, because when his father carved sledge-runners in the house the wood shavings flew about and his mother kept shouting, 'Watch the lamp! Watch the lamp!' This made his father furious and he shouted until the whole house shook. 'Blast the lamp. You seem to care about nothing but the lamp! If it breaks, we'll buy another one.'

But Misi wouldn't have dared to breathe a word about any of this here. He felt it would shame him if they knew that his father carved sledge-runners in the house. It was fun, though; Misi liked the wood shavings, they looked nice and smelled nice. He and his brothers could play with them, carve drawings in the earthen floor with them. They didn't have to worry about breaking or scratching anything; the lamp was the only thing to watch. Here at Orczy's everything seemed so fragile and delicate; he wouldn't have dared to play with his younger brothers here.

'Do you have any brothers or sisters?' he asked Orczy.

'I have an older brother,' Orczy said offhandedly as he brought a stack of magazines to the table. They all had a red cover and the same title, *Youth Journal*. Orczy opened one of them and showed Misi an article which he had written himself. It was entitled 'The Joys of Summer' and was about his holiday on his parents' estate, the thrill of riding on a horse, and his dog Hector: that dog was his greatest joy.

Misi's heart beat faster as he read the article, wide-eyed and envious. 'Did you really write this?'

'I did.'

'You wrote it yourself?'

'Yes, of course.'

'So help you God?'

'Yes.'

Misi was thinking, how was it possible when Orczy had only 2 in penmanship? 'Swear!'

'So help me God.'

It was true, then. Misi had to accept it.

He kept staring at Orczy's name under the article: Vilmos Orczy, Vilmos Orczy, Vilmos Orczy. He repeated the name to himself over and over, studying the typeface in which the magazine printed the name: Vilmos Orczy. If only he could turn the page and see his own name, Mihály Nyilas!

He was so churned up inside that he couldn't pay attention to anything else. He had bought special paper, he had paid to have it bound, he had copied out poems, 'The Foolish Farmer' and others, making his letters very small, like fly-specks, so as to have room for more poems. But to write something like 'The Joys of Summer' and see it printed in a magazine and have his name printed under it . . . !

He just couldn't believe that Orczy had written something

that got printed, something that became a *printed work* like Csokonai's poems, something that he, Misi, might copy into his book.

'They gave me an album for it, specially bound,' said Orczy when he saw that Misi was interested. He showed him a big red book with gilded edges: it was the 'Historical Portrait Gallery'! Not just one instalment, like the one Misi had bought for five kreutzers, but the whole series, bound in one volume. The whole history of Hungary was in that book. All the Hungarian kings, all the heroes, all the great lords . . . It hurt Misi, because he knew that he would never, ever have such a wonderful book, he would never, ever have enough money to buy it.

He was petrified; he just stared at the book and Orczy's name printed in the magazine, until he was distracted by a woman's voice calling from the other room.

'Bébuci!'

'Come, Nyilas, Mama calls,' whispered Orczy.

Misi got up as if waking from a dream. They went into the other room to see the beautiful blonde lady.

'Misi Nyilas,' said Orczy, pointing at him.

The room was so bright, with the sun shining through the window, that Misi just stood there dazzled without saying a word.

Orczy's mother sat down at a small table by the window. He looked at her with wonder, because she was so beautiful, she was like a fairy, like an angel; her hair was flaxen blonde, like her son's. Only later did it occur to Misi that he should have kissed her hand.

'Well, so you are little Misi Nyilas.' Her voice was so light, it was as if a bird had spoken. Misi's mother had a similar voice; when she sang it was like someone playing a tune on crystal glasses. But her hair was black and thick and long; when she let it down to comb it, it covered her face, her shoulders, her breasts; you could hardly see anything of her.

'So you're my son's little friend.'

Misi was embarrassed. He didn't know that they were friends. 'We sit on the same bench. He is the first in class, I'm the second.'

The lady began to laugh. She laughed in such a strange way: first she looked grave and solemn, then her eyes widened, then all of a sudden, quite unexpectedly, she started to laugh.

Now she didn't know what to say to the boy. 'Do you like my son?'

Misi looked at Orczy, trying to decide whether he liked him or not.

As he said nothing, the lady asked another question. 'Do you fight? Do you hit each other?'

Misi's eyes widened. He was quite flabbergasted. Why should she ask him such a question? He had never fought with anyone. Was she mistaking him for someone else?

And what a dress she was wearing! His mother made dresses for the whole village, for all the young girls and women, but such a dress as this blonde lady was wearing he couldn't have even imagined. It was as if she wasn't a woman but a painting, a living picture.

'So . . . do you scratch each other?' she asked.

That really embarrassed Misi; he grew red and hot. Now he was certain that she didn't know who he was. 'It was Láng, not me!' he burst out suddenly.

'Who?'

'It was Láng who threw him on the ground,' Misi said.

The lady was taken aback. She looked concerned.

'He didn't throw me on the ground!' shouted Orczy, flustered, fearful, blushing. 'Mama, darling, it was just horse-play.'

Misi grew pale, realising that he had said something he shouldn't have. 'I don't really know what happened,' he stammered, 'there were so many boys on top of him that I couldn't see.'

'It was just a game,' shouted Orczy. 'We were just piling on top of each other, playing building-a-woodpile. Nyilas knows nothing about it! He doesn't play, he doesn't fight, he couldn't tell one from the other.'

Then there was silence. All three of them felt very awkward.

'Does my son fight a lot?' the lady finally asked Misi, seeming worried.

'No, Orczy doesn't fight either,' Misi said.

The lady looked grave and solemn again, then burst out laughing. 'Who? Orczy?!'

'Yes, Orczy doesn't fight either.'

'Orczy! Papa! Papa, come here!' She couldn't stop laughing.

The door of the neighbouring room opened and a tall bearded gentleman came in, a dignified personage, like a president.

'I have news for you,' she announced. 'Your son is already a man of consequence, he is called Orczy!'

The tall gentleman looked at Misi sternly. 'What's your name?'

But the boy felt that they were all his enemies. He drew in his thin cheeks, creased his eyebrows and said nothing.

'I remember now, you're my son's friend!' The tall gentleman smiled and put his hand on the boy's head. 'Is he the one Mr Gyéres talked about?'

'Yes, papa.'

'Bravo! . . . A brave little fellow!'

'My dear, are you aware that your son gets thrashed at school?' the lady asked the gentleman.

'But no, mama, darling, no, it isn't true!'

'Not a word, *Orczy!*' she cried, laughing.

The father laughed, too. 'Let them thrash him, it will make him stronger! A boy who doesn't fight won't amount to anything.'

Misi thought that strange.

'Just be careful, Orczy,' the father said, 'make sure they don't hurt your head . . . All right, boys, go on playing.'

Then the parents left the room.

Misi had heard that Orczy's father was a president; he knew

that had to be something very important and mysterious, a frightening eminence, But until then he had had no idea what a great personage Mr Orczy was, that they had an estate and horses and a dog, Hector . . .

Orczy had a toy which Misi liked very much. It was called Statue Foundry, and it consisted of a big lump of wax and various moulds. Orczy went to the kitchen to soften the wax, then brought it back and used one of the moulds to make a statue. 'It's Goethe,' he said.

Little Nyilas laughed. 'Gőte?'

'Yes. You know, the German.'

'He's not German, he's Hungarian and he doesn't know a word of German.'

'Who? Goethe?'

'Yes.' Misi laughed mischievously.

'Hey!' said Orczy, taken aback. 'He's the greatest German poet.'

'No he isn't, he's our gravedigger. Old Gőte is the grave-digger in our village,' and he laughed at his joke, thinking of drunken old Gőte. It took some time to explain it to Orczy but when he understood he laughed too.

'Now I will make Schiller.'

'Schiller? You mean you will make Shiller wine? Well, if you make the wine Gőte will drink it.'

They laughed. They were both very pleased with the joke.

Orczy ran out to tell it to his mother so she could laugh too.

'You know whom you should make?' Misi asked when Orczy came back.

'Who?'

'Petőfi.'[2]

'I can't. I don't have a mould for him.'

Later on Orczy said, 'We have the complete poems of Petőfi. Do you want to see it?'

'We have it too. And I've read them all.'

'What?'

'Petőfi.'

Orczy went back to moulding Schiller, then stopped and looked at Misi. 'You read every poem?'

'Yes.'

Orczy looked at him doubtfully and went on with his work.

Orczy's brother came into the room. Misi had seen him once at the college, talking with Mr Lisznyai in the courtyard. He was a very impressive young man, this Mr Henry Orczy.

'Henry,' his younger brother told him, 'do you know that Gőte drinks Shiller?'

'Good joke,' said Mr Orczy with a smile, and went out.

It was fun messing around with the wax but it stank and soon the table was covered with it.

'Did you read all of Petőfi?'

'Yes. I read every one of them to my mother last summer. And then I read them all to myself.'

Orczy didn't look at him. He crumbled the wax statue he had made.

Misi was thinking of 'The Joys of Summer'.

'Did you really write that article yourself?'

'Yes . . . Well, my brother wrote a bit of it.'

'Your brother?'

'Yes. But Papa said that I wrote the good parts. You can laugh at them, he said.'

Misi was amazed. Was it possible to write things to make people laugh?

The maid came to call them to tea. The table was set just for the two of them. They were given chocolate, which he had never had before. He found it nauseatingly sweet; he could hardly eat it. He did eat it, though; he was afraid that if he left it there they would think he had no manners. They were given coffee to drink. He usually drank coffee with half a lump of sugar; this had too much sugar in it. The coffee cake, however, was excellent. He could have eaten twelve slices of it, and he was very cheerful and carefree, but when Orczy's mother came in and sat down beside them he wouldn't touch another morsel. 'Thank you very much, I don't want any.'

'Of course you do. They don't make coffee cake at the college. Have another slice, my little friend.'

'Thank you very much, I've had enough.'

'Then put a piece in your pocket. Two pieces. You can have them in the college.'

'No, thank you very much.' He was not someone to trifle with. Once he had said that he didn't want any, then he didn't want any. It happened once at home during Sunday lunch: after the macaroni he got up, followed by his younger brothers, and they all went around the table, kissed their elders' hands, thanking them for the meal – and that was when the roasted chicken was brought in. His younger brothers cheered and rushed back to the table but he did not. He wouldn't have had another bite to save his life. Not after he had said his thanks for the meal.

'Well, all right, then, but you will have compote?'

That was different. His mother used to make it too – five or six jars every summer and sometimes ten, depending on how much sugar there was.

The lady's compote tasted very good. It was so good that he had two helpings.

'Don't you want any, Bébuci? Why don't you eat?'

Bébuci! Misi was glad nobody had called him by some silly nickname like that.

Guests arrived. What a fright that was: they were all girls. They were little girls dressed like the drawings of girls in *Girls' Journal*; he wouldn't have believed that real girls would go about dressed like that. They greeted him, too, but he just stood there, silently – not like Bébuci, who shook hands with all of them. One was a plump girl with yellow hair: her face was extremely white and red, and her hair glittered like real gold. She looked at Misi with her grey eyes; she had very big eyes, and the longer she looked at him the more he blushed. His whole body grew weak, his knees trembled, he couldn't have said a word. Only after he noticed that the girl had freckles around her nose was he able to rouse himself and whisper into Orczy's ear that he was leaving.

'You want to go back to the college?'

'Yes.'

'Then I'll see you out,' said Orczy.

As they got to the hallway, Misi remembered that he hadn't kissed Mrs Orczy's hand. He didn't do it when he arrived, and he forgot to do it when he was leaving. He went back, braving all the company, to kiss her hand; he didn't want her to think badly of him. Unfortunately, Mrs Orczy happened to be embracing the girl with the yellow hair and the grey eyes, so he turned around quickly and ran out to the hallway.

'Why are you running?' asked Orczy.

Misi pulled his winter coat from the hook with such force that he tore the loop.

'Are you afraid of girls?'

'I'm not afraid of anything.'

'I tell them jokes.'

Misi scowled.

'Don't you have girls in your family? Cousins?'

'No, we don't have any.'

'Don't you have a brother?'

'Brother?'

'Yes.'

'Of course I have brothers. There are five of us.'

'But girls?'

'Girls . . . no.'

'When will you come again?'

Misi looked at him, and wanted to say, Next time you come to my place, but visitors were forbidden to come up to the dormitories; only the prefects could have visitors. To prevent pilfering and thievery the college had closed the doors of the living quarters to everyone who did not belong there. Misi shrugged, thinking he would never come to Orczy's again. 'I don't know when I'll come,' he said, and shook Orczy's hand.

'*Servus.*'
'*Servus.*'

Orczy's mother came out to the hallway with a little parcel in her hand.

'Is our little friend running away?' she asked her son, laughing. She put the little parcel in Misi's hand. 'Here, take this with you, you can open it only when you get home. I hope you go straight to the college.'

'No, I don't.'

'Where are you going?'

'I'm going to read aloud.'

'Where?'

'I read to an old blind gentleman for an hour every day.'

The beautiful blonde lady looked impressed. 'And is he . . . paying you for it, or . . .'

'Oh, yes, I get paid ten kreutzers!'

'For a month?'

'For an hour!'

And she looked at the little boy with absolute amazement.

Misi hadn't mentioned his job at school, and so Orczy was surprised too.

'Do you hear that, Orczy?' she asked her son, laughing, but tears spilled out of her eyes.

Misi sensed that she wasn't laughing at him, so he laughed, too, pleased that he was such a wonder. Then he remembered that he should kiss Mrs Orczy's hand, but couldn't muster the courage. He always kissed the hand of Mrs Török, and Mrs Vásárhelyi, but this was such an elegant fine lady, he didn't dare . . . He blushed, thinking that she saw that he was a coward.

He lingered in the streets. He waited for five o'clock to come, reliving every minute of the visit in his mind. When he thought of the girl with the grey eyes and the yellow hair, he started to run as fast as a rabbit, he didn't know where.

IV

Something surprising happens. This is how we live:
things always turn out differently from the way
we expected

MISI RAN FROM the Orczys', but the farther he got from their place the worse he felt. His face burned as if he were near a big fire. He felt humiliated, small, foolish. He was so angry with himself that he bit his fist. What a stupid way to behave! Why hadn't he kissed Mrs Orczy's hand? And then he had run away! They must all be talking about him. They would tell the yellow-haired girl that when he arrived he said 'Orczy' instead of 'Hello'. And then he betrayed Orczy, telling his parents that he was beaten at school.

Misi tried to salvage his sinking self-respect by denigrating his friend. How Orczy had bragged! *His* room! And saying they had a complete Petőfi! That made him feel better, remembering that his friend talked about the complete Petőfi as the most valuable book they had. Well, his parents had that too. But these were just skirmishes in his mind. His face was still burning at the thought that they were talking about him. He could see Orczy making fun of him in front of the girls. Because Orczy knew how to make people laugh. What fun he made of their music teacher, imitating the way he marked time wearing white gloves.

He ran and ran, thinking that they were laughing at him at Orczy's house because he fled from the girls.

It was very early, only four o'clock, so he couldn't go to the old gentleman yet. He could have stayed at Orczy's for another three-quarters of an hour. Now Orczy was talking with the yellow-haired girl about him. And when she looked at him she had such clear grey eyes! But why were they so big?

When he thought of the girl he ran even faster, like one possessed. Eventually he had to slow down because he was out of breath, and then he could think more clearly.

Suddenly he heard somebody shouting at him. 'Where are you running to?'

It was Láng. Misi ran a couple of lengths more and then stopped. What was Láng doing there? 'I have to run to Mr Gyéres,' he lied.

'The Latin master?'

'Yes.'

They looked into each other's eyes. Láng always looked as though he wanted to hit him. Misi stared back.

Láng finally made a gesture indicating that he understood: it was all right. He had studied Misi's clothes, his shoes, his hat: he would have liked to ask why he was so dressed up for calling on Mr Gyéres but he decided not to, because he was a poor student and didn't like to talk about the teachers. He nodded and they parted, going in different directions.

But what did Láng want? They had never exchanged a single word before, and today of all days Láng had to stop him in the street . . . He should have asked Láng why he beat up Orczy! How they were hitting each other! Orczy got a proper beating, all right. And how he had lied to his mother about it, saying they were 'building a woodpile'. His mother, that little blonde lady, how could she know that her son was fighting? How could she know that he was beaten ignominiously? How could she know that her son was making a fool of her? She believed everything he told her, the poor woman. It was easy to deceive a mother. Misi's eyes filled with tears as he thought of his own mother, and he took out his handkerchief. He happened to be passing the Great Church, so he ran into the church garden and sat down on a bench next to a weeping willow, where he started to sob in earnest.

He cried for a long time; the tears poured down his cheeks. He sat on the bench, turning his back to the college so that no one would recognise him, and cried to his heart's content. Afterwards he felt as soft as butter. He had needed a good cry for a long time. He had so much trouble. But there was no place to cry, there was no place to be really alone; somebody was always staring at him.

The clock struck twice. He thought it would be three-quarters soon. But five o'clock still seemed so far away! He put spit on his handkerchief to wash his eyes and started out slowly for Mr Pósalaky's house. He was freezing cold and it was getting dark. The street lamps were lit; the narrow gas flames fluttered like butterflies.

When he entered the old gentleman's house he was chilled to the bone and shivering so much that his teeth chattered. He couldn't read; his tongue kept tripping over the words, and he started crying again.

'Now, now,' said the old gentleman. 'What is it? What is it?'

'Nothing.'

Since it was nothing, the old gentleman asked nothing about it.

However, since he couldn't go on reading, Misi had to say something. 'This afternoon I was visiting one of my classmates.'

The old gentleman listened attentively.

'And there . . . and there . . .'

'Did they say something to hurt you?'

'No, they didn't, only I . . . They are very grand people.'

'Grand people? Who are they?'

'They weren't mean to me, they were very nice, it's only that I . . . Their name is Orczy and they live next to the theatre. Mr Orczy is a president.'

There was a long pause and finally the old gentleman asked quietly, 'And what does your father do?'

'He is a carpenter.'

'Well . . .' The old gentleman thought about it and added, 'That is a good profession.'

Misi was cheered by that. He himself thought it was a good profession.

'Do you have a house?'

'A small one.'

'Do you have a cow?'

'A cow? No, we don't.'

'How about a pig?'

'We have a young pig.'

'How many children do your parents have?'

'Five. I'm the oldest.'

'Five? Boys or girls?'

'We are five boys.'

'That's serious . . . Then your father is a great man. With five boys you can turn the country upside down.'

'Before, when we lived in another village, we had a big stone house and several cows. Once when I was small we had a whole herd in our courtyard. My father took me out and put me on the back of a young bullock, and I said, *'Hey hey! Go go!'* . . . We had a combine harvester then, but it exploded and then we had to move to another village and my father became a carpenter.'

Misi had to go on; he didn't want the old gentleman to think that they were nobodies. 'We have an uncle who is a professor in Pozsony. He's my mother's brother. My father paid for his education.'

There was a long silence. He would have liked to say more but felt awkward about it. Finally the old gentleman said, 'Well . . . Go ahead. Read on.'

The little boy was relieved. His heart swung happily to and fro. The old man's voice had carried a note of respect. Misi decided that he would never again mention to anyone that his father was a carpenter. It was lucky that Orczy's mother hadn't asked him what his father did, because he would have told her. Until that day he had been proud that his father was a carpenter. They were on good terms with everybody in the village; his father discussed the world with the minister and the teacher; he even talked to the circuit judge, like this: 'Well, Your Honour, your moustache is quite perky today!' And: 'Take off those gaiters, Your Honour, there isn't any mud on the roads.' The stone house was a lie, though. Misi had heard that at school: one of the boys had said his parents had a stone house and it made a deep impression on him. Misi's family owned their own house and it wasn't a bad one, only it wasn't built from stone. But what did that matter, what difference did it make to a blind man whether it was stone or not?

He read the newspapers quickly, brightly and confidently. He rolled on as steadily as a grinder; he did not stop once until six.

When the clock started to strike six, the old gentleman said: 'Let's leave some for tomorrow.'

Misi felt that he had read less than he ought to have done. 'Please, Mr Pósalaky, I'd gladly read some more.'

'No, no. You should be getting back to the college, I don't want you to be late.'

'I won't be late. They don't ring the bell for supper until a quarter past.'

'Run along, you've already wasted five minutes.'

'Let me read just a minute more.'

But the old man wasn't in the mood to listen, he fidgeted in his chair restlessly. 'If you read any more I might have a foolish dream again, like the one I had last night.'

'What did you dream?'

The old man shook his head, smiled and relaxed again. 'I dreamed that a cat caught me. I was a little mouse in her mouth. The cat swam across some water, then she became a large cloud, and I looked up to see her drift away. I ate noodles with cottage cheese, and then I was looking over the Great Plain, and it was all planted with peas as far as the eye could see. I was a big ox and had to graze among the peas. I never could stand peas! Well, that is what I dreamed. I can hardly ever remember my dreams, but I couldn't forget those cursed peas. When I woke in the morning, I had an upset stomach.'

Misi had a good laugh, and the old gentleman laughed too. 'I told my dream to the cleaning woman and she interpreted it for me. She said the cat is 85, the cloud is 73, the noodles with cottage cheese are 39, the ox is 45 . . . Oh, oh, I left out something. The water. The water is 22. It's a bad number. It's bad to dream about water. It means a death in the family.'

'Everything has a number?'

'Yes. For the lottery.'

The lottery! Misi had heard about the lottery in the village. When somebody had any kind of luck, the peasants said, 'Your numbers came up.'

'Listen, I thought of something,' said the old man. 'Let's play these numbers. Why not? The worst that can happen is that we lose a coin. Let God have it. There's a silver piece on the table. Take it to the tobacconist tomorrow and put it on these numbers. Write them down. If we win, half is yours. Why shouldn't we be rich! What was that you said about the Orczys? Grand people?' He shook with laughter; his big stomach moved up and down. 'Well, let us be grand people ourselves!' The old man's portly belly shook as he chuckled.

The boy liked the idea of gambling. He took out a pencil and wrote down the numbers. The old man dictated them but again he left out the water. 'I always forget it,' he sighed. 'It wants to be left out of the list. We won't win.'

'Shall I take the coin from the table, Mr Pósalaky?'

'No, on second thoughts, leave that coin, that's there for my breakfast coffee. Here is a banknote. Let's put down a whole forint. If it's a goose, let it be a fat goose.'

Misi took the money and while he was putting on his coat the old gentleman said, after giving the matter some thought: 'They are not grand, those people. In Debrecen you're not an important person if you weren't born on this side of Basahalmán. So they own a few properties here and there . . . President? You're not a grand person because you are president of the Society for the Regulation of the Tisza River.'

The boy bent his head. Reminded of his behaviour at the Orczys', he was overwhelmed once again by black shame.

It wasn't until Misi got back to the college that he thought of the little parcel he was carrying, the parcel Mrs Orczy had given him. Then he had to open it right away, in the dark corridor. It contained coffee cake and biscuits.

If he took those up to the dormitory . . . The very thought frightened him, and he ate the whole lot then and there, in the dark corridor. By the time he finished, the bell was ringing for supper. He didn't even go upstairs but went straight to the dining hall.

Supper was frankfurters with peas. He laughed when it was served.

'What are you laughing at?' asked Mihály Sándor, who sat beside him.

'The whole Great Plain was planted with peas.'

'What are you talking about?'

'Nothing.'

'Nothing? That's not much.'

'I'm going to play the lottery tomorrow,' Misi said recklessly.

Mihály Sándor stared at him. 'What do you mean?'

'Here's a forint. Tomorrow I'm going to put it on the lottery.'

'He's talking rubbish,' Mihály Sándor said to the others. By then they were envying the little boy who was earning money, when lots of grown-ups didn't earn any.

Misi sensed it and blushed. 'It's not mine. I was told to put it on the lottery.'

'For whom?'

'For the old gentleman.'

'A forint on the lottery?'

'Yes.'

'Well, then. Why didn't you say so?'

They started to eat. For the first time Misi thought the peas were too thin, but the frankfurters on top of them were very good. The bread wasn't good, though; it was sour and tasted mouldy. He had to tell the whole story of the lottery numbers, but by then he didn't have his heart in it.

'Why is this bread so mouldy?' he asked Mihály Sándor to make peace with him.

'It's mouldy because they make it from mouldy flour.'

That evening Misi wasn't in the mood for studying. He was looking at the book but he was seeing the girl with yellow hair. If he closed his eyes he could see her gazing at him. He had a headache and the heat of the room was making him drowsy. To wake himself up he went out to the corridor. When he wanted to hide from the others he always went to the WC and closed the door on himself. There he was as completely alone as if he wasn't even in Debrecen. The whole cubicle was drenched with pink-coloured carbolic; it had a strange, strong smell, a piercing, unpleasant smell. Still, it was better to be there by himself than with the others in the dormitory . . . He sat there for so long that another boy started banging on the door. 'What is it?' Misi asked, startled.

'Did you fall asleep in there?'

'No I did not!'

'Nyilas fell asleep in the privy!'

It was true, he had fallen asleep, and now he was afraid they would jeer at him for it . . .

He hurried back to the dormitory and sat down at the table in front of his open textbook and exercise book, but he was so sleepy that he could have cried.

It was salvation when the bell rang at nine o'clock. He threw off his clothes so quickly that he didn't know how. He tore off his jacket and vest at one go and was under the blanket in a second. He was dizzy; the bed was flying with him. The girl's big grey eyes were watching him; he couldn't hide from them, but he didn't even want to. It felt good looking into her eyes. And he raised his hand; he would have liked to grab her hair. Then he fell asleep. He had a strange dream. He was running with the grey-eyed girl in a garden near the river and they ran about so much that when he woke up he was sweating. One night – a long time ago when he was still in the first form – he had had a similar dream about Zsuzsi and never mentioned it to anybody.

Misi's strange state lasted for days. On Monday Orczy was very attentive and friendly: Misi expected him to say that the girls were very sorry he had left and so was Mrs Orczy, but Orczy didn't say anything like that. Misi would have liked to ask him who those girl 'cousins' were but didn't even dare to hint at the subject; he didn't want Orczy to think that he was interested.

During break Orczy went out to buy two crescent rolls. He was eating one of them as he came back and offered the other to Misi. 'Here, take it.'

Misi was offended that Orczy, already eating, should try to toss him something as if he were a dog, so he said he didn't want it.

'Why not?'

'I'm not hungry.'

Orczy shrugged and ate the other crescent roll as well. That was the end of the matter. It never came up again.

'Did you go to their place?' Gimesi asked him during Latin class.

Misi reddened and nodded yes.

Gimesi looked at him expectantly. Evidently he would have liked to hear something about it, but Misi said nothing. He only whispered at the end of the class, 'Mr Gyéres said I had to go.'

'Mr Gyéres?' asked Gimesi, looking wide-eyed at the Latin master.

'Yes,' persisted Misi, growing redder.

They didn't talk any more about it but Misi felt he owed something to Gimesi. The following day, as there was a commemoration ceremony in the morning to honour a man who had left ten thousand forints to the college, afternoon classes were cancelled. He said to Gimesi, 'Can I come and see you this afternoon?'

'Of course.'

Misi went to Gimesi's after lunch. He hadn't been there for a long time. He kissed the grandmother's hand. Gimesi was standing at the big window, painting birds, and they painted all afternoon.

'You can make statues at Orczy's.'

'Statues?'

'From wax.' And he explained how.

Gimesi wanted a statue kit too. He said he was going to write to his mother and ask her to send him one.

Misi had never heard about Gimesi's mother. Gimesi and his grandmother lived as if they were all alone in the world. Misi was quite surprised that Gimesi would mention his mother so offhandedly. But he didn't want to ask. He only thought what a good boy this Gimesi was, better than himself, a true friend. He was very fond of him. He was smaller and weaker than Misi and he didn't know the lessons as well, he was only third in the class, and probably his mother wasn't a blonde fairy but a normal serious brown-haired woman . . . He would have liked to kiss Gimesi as if they were brothers and tell him, 'We are friends'.

'Was it nice at the Orczys'?' asked Gimesi while stirring new paint in the saucer.

'Well . . . Uppity . . . Not really uppity, I guess . . .' He didn't know what to say, he just twisted his mouth this way and that.

Gimesi was a delicate boy. He had small slanting black eyes with hardly any eyebrows or eyelashes, and a very small and very beautiful mouth, as small as a girl's, but he was a very manly and brave fellow. He wasn't as handsome as Orczy, who was bigger than both of them and looked better, with his white skin and blond hair and straight nose, and his velvet suit; he was like a fine, fragrant, budding flower. Compared to him Gimesi and Misi were two poor, small, skinny bodies. Especially Misi; he knew it himself. He was very scrawny and he had a sickly yellow complexion. He had a deep voice, a big mouth and big teeth; he tried to stop himself laughing when he remembered that his teeth were yellow. Gimesi's were long and narrow. Orczy's teeth were like pearls. They said that he washed them every day. Misi could not imagine how it was possible to wash teeth. With soap, in a washbasin? The idea disgusted him.

'It went to Orczy's head.'

'What?'

Misi would have liked to say something bad about Orczy: that he entered a competition and won. But why should he say anything bad about Orczy? Orczy was always good to him. And he sensed that Orczy knew he didn't merit the first place in class: that was why he was so attentive. Misi didn't really know what he had against him, he just wished he could have been superior to Orczy also in his clothes, in his room, in his books, in his girl relatives, grey-eyed and yellow-haired . . .

'There were a lot of ugly girls at the Orczys',' he said quickly, because he was afraid that Gimesi would guess the truth.

'You don't say!' exclaimed Gimesi, and the brush stopped in his hand. 'Girls?'

'Yes.'

'Young girls? Girls of my age?'

'Yes.'

'Many?'

'Many, many.'

'How many? Thirty?' They both burst out laughing at that.

'No, there weren't as many as thirty, but there were a lot.'

'Oh, boy!' said Gimesi.

'I left, though.'

'You didn't stay when the girls came?'

'No.'

'You're crazy!'

Misi laughed, feeling flattered. 'You wouldn't have left?'

'Not in a million years!'

'What would you have done with them?'

Gimesi straightened himself and looked at Misi thoughtfully. God only knew what he was thinking, but he grew all excited, and laughed. 'I would have fought them!'

Misi laughed, too. 'You mean, the way you fight, with your head?'

'With my head, naturally!'

Gimesi came out from behind the table and ran around the room with his head bent forward as if he were a bull, then turned around suddenly and gored Misi.

Misi fell down on his back and kept laughing as Gimesi jumped on him and they wrestled.

Hearing the noise, the grandmother came in. 'What's going on? What are you doing?'

Gimesi stopped wrestling, leaped up and went back to his paints. Misi, too, got up from the floor, looking sheepish.

'I don't like that kind of rough play,' Grandmother said severely. 'My little Lajos isn't used to that sort of thing.'

Gimesi said nothing and Nyilas turned pale, then red. It seemed the grandmother was making him responsible, as if he was corrupting her grandson.

Grandmother looked very stern and moved things about angrily. The little woman was yellow with age, her big nose was pitted with black dots and there wasn't another face in the world with so many wrinkles. 'Don't let me catch you at it again!' she said. 'Do you hear me?'

Gimesi bent over the saucer with the paint, blushing. Misi grew quite dark in the face with shame and indignation.

'Young gentlemen don't roll on the floor, they don't fight with their host,' Grandmother went on, getting more and more cross. 'When young gentlemen go to visit their friends, they behave themselves.'

Gimesi looked up at his grandmother, working up his courage. 'I started it, I pushed him down on the floor.'

'All the worse, then, I hope you're ashamed of yourself. I've told you often enough. You're not a baby any more, you should know what you owe to your name. Wild little hooligans will never amount to anything. Do you want to end up a good-for-nothing gallows-bird like . . . Don't let it happen again!' she said as she went out.

The boys were quiet for a while. Misi was terribly offended. They didn't deserve that – they hadn't done anything . . . Gimesi, painting a parrot, grumbled in a low voice, 'Her brain's dried up, don't pay any attention to her.'

That shocked Misi even more, because he too had a grandmother and he wouldn't have dreamed of making such a remark about her. Every word his grandmother uttered was sacred to him, and however unjust she might be, he would have suffered it in silence. 'Don't talk that way,' he said quietly and nervously.

'But I will. I will tell her too.' Gimesi turned red as paprika and his eyes became moist and glowed like amber. He flung out every word until he ran out of breath. 'I'm not a little snot like I was last year. She could scold me for no reason when I was in the first form, but not now! Now I know what's what!'

Misi guessed that there was some family secret behind their lives and was afraid that in his anger Gimesi would tell him about it. So he wanted to distract him. 'Look at this.'

With his eyes still moist, Gimesi looked at the piece of paper that Misi was holding out to him. 'What is it?' he asked, puzzled and surly.

'A lottery ticket!'

Gimesi's eyes widened. 'What?' he asked, and his mouth remained open.

'I'm betting on these five numbers.'

Gimesi burst out laughing. He threw his head back, put his hands on his stomach and laughed soundlessly. 'You're playing the lottery?'

'Yes.'

'Oh, boy, I never laughed so much in my life. You put money on the lottery?'

Misi laughed too. He laughed until he choked; he had to cough afterwards. Suddenly he too found it very strange that he was a gambler.

'And you think you'll win?'

'I don't know.'

'If you win ten forints, what will you buy with it?'

'What will I buy? . . . Well . . . I'll buy a knife.'

'What kind?'

'What kind?' He thought of Böszörményi's knife behind the rubbish bin. Perhaps he would never be able to retrieve it! 'I'll buy a pocket knife shaped like a fish . . . with a pearl handle . . .'

'Oh boy, if I had ten forints!'

'What would you buy?'

'I'd send five forints to my mother.'

That hit Misi hard. He hadn't thought of his mother.

'And I'd spend the other five in the pastry shop,' said Gimesi.

Misi said nothing. He wouldn't have done that. Pastry, what was that? He had passed the pastry shop the day before, on his way from the Orczys', but it hadn't entered his head to buy a cake. What for? Theatre was different. He would spend on that. 'If I win, only half of it will be mine. The other half belongs to the old blind gentleman.'

'To that doddering old man?'

'He's not doddering,' said Misi, offended.

'All right, all right. It's just that I call all old people doddering. If they're old they're doddering.' And Gimesi laughed aloud, because he still couldn't get it into his head that anybody would waste money playing the lottery. 'Did he give you the money?'

'Yes.'

'A silver coin?'

'No.'

'Two silver coins?'

'No.'

'More?'

'Paper money. A whole forint.'

'One forint!' Gimesi was flabbergasted. 'My friend, one forint would be enough even for prize money!' He started to laugh again. 'I've never had a forint. My grandmother doesn't give me two kreutzers to spend for myself.'

'I have twenty-six kreutzers.'

'Twenty-six?'

'Well, it's gone down to twenty-one. I had to pay five kreutzers for the parcel and the letter.'

'If I had twenty coins I would buy six cream pastries, one for you, one for Orczy, one for Tannenbaum, one for Grandmother and two for me.'

That, too, was good for a laugh.

'Orczy won an album, the "Historical Portrait Gallery". He won it with an article about his holiday "The Joys of Summer" which was printed in the *Youth Journal*.'

'They printed it?'

'Yes.'

'They printed what Orczy wrote?'

'Yes.'

Gimesi started to laugh soundlessly again, but it turned into hiccups. 'They printed his spelling mistakes, too?'

'His brother corrected those.'

'His brother? That tall boy?'

'Yes. Orczy wrote the article and his brother corrected it, and added a few things.'

Gimesi looked at Misi suspiciously.

'Oh, boy, you're so good at it!'

'What do you mean?' asked Misi, and reddened because he felt that it was wrong of him to mention the brother.

'You're so good at talking someone down behind his back.'

Misi was silent.

'I'm just curious what you'll say about us when you leave.'

All the blood rushed to Misi's heart and he got so dizzy that he had to sit down. He looked at Gimesi despairingly.

Misi's silence, his terrible look, bothered his friend. 'You can say whatever you want, I don't mind,' Gimesi said, with a shrug.

Misi would have liked to shout, to scream: I wouldn't ever

say anything bad about you, even if they cut me to pieces, because I love you. But he only said: 'Do you really think that I could say anything bad about you?'

Gimesi didn't reply. There was a painful silence.

Misi sat by the table and Gimesi, flustered and embarrassed, went on painting. 'How do you know about Orczy's brother helping with the article?' he asked under his breath.

Misi looked out of the window. He would have liked to say defiantly that he had invented it. Let Gimesi believe that he was capable of such a thing.

'Did you make it up?'

Misi shook his head.

'Well, go on, tell me, don't make me mad or I'll butt you with my head again.'

Misi put his head down on the table and started to cry. 'And your grandmother blamed me for that too,' he gasped between sobs.

It made Gimesi nervous. He shifted from one foot to the other, played with his paintbrush, put it in his mouth and got some carmine on his lips. 'You're crazy,' he said, and his eyes began to glow.

'When did I ever say anything bad about you? Could you say anything bad about me?'

'Well, you did it to Orczy.'

'Because I had to go there. Mr Gyéres ordered me to. And he also told Orczy's parents that I should go there. They just wanted to look me over so they could laugh at me. They put coffee cake in my pocket as if I was a child. And . . . And that's why I came here, to tell you that I will never go there again.'

Gimesi looked at him with amazement, in the same way as he had looked at his grandmother, and went back to his painting. 'Well, go on crying, I don't care.' Then he put down his brush, went to the jug, poured a glass of water and brought it to Misi. 'Here, drink.'

Misi was moved; he hadn't expected so much goodness. He drank the water.

'Wash your eyes, because if my grandmother comes in and sees you crying she'll bite your head off.'

Misi dipped his hand in the glass and put some water on his eyes. Then, looking at his friend, he saw the paint on his lip. Gimesi had red paint right down to his chin. Misi started to laugh. 'You'd better wash yourself!'

'What for?'

'Look at your mouth.'

Gimesi went to the mirror and looked at himself. 'Hey! I look like a clown!'

He went back to his paints and painted his upper lip green. 'Now I look even better.' And he started to jump around like a clown. They had a great time.

Misi sobered up when he noticed how dark it was outside. It was time for him to go and read.

Next day at school he had a private laugh with Gimesi because in Hungarian literature class they got back their compositions and Orczy's was marked with a 2. Orczy was insulted and kept throwing the exercise book about as if it didn't belong to him. In those days marks were a serious matter. Anyone who failed had to repeat the year, and at the end of every quarter bad students were given a warning notice which said, in effect, if you carry on the way you are going, you will fail. This was the time for the issuing of the warning notices. Misi didn't feel it concerned him but at noon, back in the dormitory, he learned that Böszörményi had received warning notices in two subjects.

Misi was quite pleased with the news. He felt that Böszörményi deserved it; he resented him on account of the knife. Strangely, he never thought of what the bigger boy had done to him; he no longer remembered what Böszörményi had taken from him, but every time he saw him he thought of the knife behind the big wooden rubbish bin and couldn't talk to him, couldn't be friends with him, couldn't forgive him. Böszörményi tried to make up, because he still hadn't received any parcel or any money and would have liked Misi to buy him something from the vendors in front of the college.

That afternoon they gave out the warning notices in Misi's class too. The local boys had to take theirs home and get them signed by their parents; the others were just read out in class and then posted to the parents. Misi felt a tightening in his chest when he heard the names of boys who had been good students the year before. What if he got a notice too? He had better watch it. He got a piercing sensation when he remembered that he still didn't understand the supine . . .

Thank God his name wasn't read out! A few days later in Latin class he observed something that bothered him. Mr Gyéres, according to his custom, stroked Orczy's hair when he passed by him, and now he also looked at Misi several times. Misi had disliked the way the Latin master favoured Orczy, but now that he knew he was a constant guest at the Orczys' home, he disliked it that Mr Gyéres was so reserved with Orczy. He didn't think it was right that the Latin master should speak to Orczy in the same tone as he used with the other boys, when at home he called him Bébuci! Was he Bébuci or was he Orczy? Misi felt that there couldn't be two kinds of relationships between two people. If you were friends with somebody then you should always be friends. If by chance his uncle who was a professor in Pozsony should come to Debrecen and teach him, would he call him Nyilas?

What Misi wanted was that the Latin master should be friends with Orczy, not treat him as a stranger, and should be friends with him too because he had been at Orczy's. And he should be friends also with Gimesi, who was Misi's good brother, and also with K. Sánta, who was in truth the best student in the class. He paused at Tannenbaum; that was an exceptional case. Back in the village the Jews didn't belong but in the college the boys were all one family, and Tannenbaum was actually cleverer than all the rest.

Misi was thinking of such things when the Latin master called him up. 'Nyilas!' He jumped up, frightened, because he hadn't been paying attention and had no idea what they were talking about. 'Come to the masters' room at the end of the class.'

Misi waited a little but as Mr Gyéres said nothing more he sat down. The class began to whisper. Everybody was whispering and watching him. It was perhaps the first time that he had noticed the whole class. Up to now he had been preoccupied with his relationship with a few of the boys, as if only they were at the school. His bench was at the front of the room right by the door, and when he came in he immediately sat down. He paid no more attention to the boys at the back than he paid to grass and bushes in the country.

When the bell rang Misi's heart contracted again and, forgetting his hat and coat, he ran after the Latin master. He had to wait a long time in the hall.

Thinking of the warning notices, he nearly fainted. He was going to fail! Perhaps they had already notified his father. They would demote him from the first bench to somewhere in the back, and he wouldn't sit beside Orczy and wouldn't be able to be friends with Gimesi either . . . The Orczys hadn't invited him to their home because he was a good boy, this sort of person or that sort of person, but because of his scholastic standing, and now they would never invite him again. And Gimesi's grandmother would never allow him to be friends with a bad student . . .

Misi felt that this was a terrible injustice. Seeing himself demoted from his place as Number Two, he had a profound sense of the cruelty of existence. Whatever he had been given wasn't for him, it was for the place where he sat in the class. It made no difference what the person who sat there was like; whoever sat there got the free room and board, the scholarship, the room prefect's special attention, the interest of the masters, Mr Nagy's consideration; that person got the job to read to the blind gentleman . . . His heart cried out; he couldn't bear to part from his position.

He was quite dizzy standing in the hallway. He was pale; his heart was beating very fast. When the door of the masters' room opened he could see Mr Gyéres in his elegant light suit, smoking a cigar, bending forward, talking attentively with someone – and he didn't call him!

Of course what could he expect, a ruined backsliding student who was waiting for his warning notice?

Mr Báthori, in a fitted brown jacket, came by and pounced on him. 'Whom are you waiting for?'

Shaken by the stern voice, Misi moved his mouth but no sounds came out. 'I'm waiting for Mr Gyéres,' he finally stammered.

Without replying, Mr Báthori went into the masters' room. His harsh voice made Misi pull himself together a bit. If it was a warning notice, let it be a warning notice! He thought of his father; his father was brave, he wouldn't be scared even by a greater danger. Defiance stirred in his soul: if he was to be the last, let him be the last! It made no difference. Whatever marks they gave him, he knew what he knew. And if they took away his scholarship then he would go home and hoe the ground.

He heaved a deep sigh, because the previous summer he had fainted once when he was hoeing. It wasn't an honest faint because he was just a bit dizzy, but he was very relieved when the blood went from his face and he broke out in a sweat so they could see that he wasn't play-acting. They just had to send him to school in Debrecen, because he would never amount to much in the fields.

Mr Gyéres came out of the masters' room, still holding his cigar, stopped in front of him, looking quite cheerful, and even leaned a bit towards him. 'Well, little Nyilas . . .' He took a puff from his cigar. His suit, his cigar, smelled very good and little Nyilas watched him, trying to look as obliging as he could.

'Well, tell me, would you take on the teaching of a boy?'

Misi didn't reply. The world turned around. He thought he would fly up into the air. All his anxieties drifted away like fog. He stood straight, motionless, and said nothing. After a while he nodded that he would take it on.

'Every Wednesday and Saturday afternoon you would have

to teach Latin and mathematics to that no-good Doroghy boy.'

'Yes, sir.'

'His aunt works for me. They are poor. They are good people but it's a big family and this little frog is just amusing himself, doesn't concentrate on anything.'

'Yes, sir.'

The master stopped and looked at the door of the Head's study. Somebody was coming out. 'Well, that's all. Talk with the boy and start this afternoon.'

'Yes, sir.'

'Oh, yes, you will be paid two forints a month.'

With that he turned his back on Misi and returned to the masters' room.

Misi ran from the place of his ordeal with shaking legs. The boys were waiting for him in the class. He could hardly speak, just threw himself on the bench.

'Well, what is it?' asked Gimesi. Barta and Tannenbaum joined them.

'Mr Gyéres told me that I have to teach Doroghy.'

'You're going to teach?'

'I have to. I'm ordered to.'

'And what will they pay?'

'Two forints!'

'Two forints?'

'Yes.'

'My friend,' said Gimesi, 'you'll be rich. You'll be making five forints a month.'

Tannenbaum shook his head with a grave expression. 'You can't teach for so little, for two forints.'

'Every day?' asked János Varga.

'No, only twice a week, Wednesdays and Saturdays.'

'Then it's enough,' said Varga.

Misi looked at Varga: this was the boy, always in clean clothes, who said that his family's house was built from stone. He was always doing deals, exchanging buttons for glass beads and chocolate for pens.

Tannenbaum looked at Varga. 'No, it's too little. He may be going there only twice a week, but he is expected to make sure that the boy knows enough to pass. And what's two forints for that? These days, when a button of paint costs five kreutzers!'

'That's very good pay,' argued Varga. 'I know a student in the fifth form, he gets two forints for teaching two hours a week, and he's a fifth-former!'

'But Misi won't be teaching for two hours, he'll be teaching two afternoons.'

Varga grew quite excited about the issue. 'He couldn't teach more than two hours at a time, because he has to go to read to the blind man at five. He starts out after lunch, he gets there by two and at four he has to leave.'

'That's still four hours a week,' said Tannenbaum.

'That's true,' agreed Imre Barta, who was the strongest boy in the class. 'Tannenbaum's right!' he added, clenching his fist.

Three more boys got involved in the argument. Orczy already had his overcoat on, because the next class was psalm-singing and Catholics were excused. 'For my part,' he said lightly, 'I believe if I were capable of earning two forints a month, my father would be so pleased that he would give me a hundred-forint colt as a present.' He laughed aloud, but kindly, so nobody resented it; it wasn't his fault that they were rich.

Misi was exhausted. He listened to the others, too tired to think. He had no idea who was right, whether two forints was too much or too little, whether he would be capable of teaching or whether he would even have the time, with his commitment to the old gentleman, and with all the studying that he had to do himself. He only knew that he had to lie down and sleep; otherwise he would fall asleep on the bench.

Mr Csoknyai, the singing master, came in; the boys stood up to greet him, and then everybody ran to his bench. When everybody sat down again, Misi remembered the boy he had to teach, Sándor Doroghy, and turned his head towards the boys in the back rows, wondering which one was Doroghy.

He thought he would recognise him, picking him out from the faces near the back wall, but he wasn't able to.

'Which one is Doroghy?'

Gimesi turned his head, too. 'That dumb kid? He's the one by the window, second bench from the back.'

When the master turned to face the blackboard Misi stood up to see Doroghy better. Now he recognised him and remembered the strange answer he had given in geography class. The master had told him that he was going to ask him an easy question, so he should be able to give the right answer for once: where was Constantinople? And Doroghy said Constantinople was in Africa. But now he seemed a nice-looking good little boy, sitting in the light by the window.

'He isn't dumb,' Misi whispered to Gimesi.

'He is dumb,' said Gimesi in a quiet, merciless voice. 'Anybody who sits that far back is dumb. They're all dumb, back there.'

Mr Csoknyai finished questioning the boys and started teaching. He was a peculiar character, perhaps the most peculiar of all the teachers. As if he wasn't a master but a guest. He was always very polite; when he addressed a boy he always said, would you be so kind, and when the boy gave his answer, he thanked him for it – thank you, thank you. And he lisped a little.

Misi understood nothing about music. He couldn't read or write a score. He knew just one thing: he knew how to write a violin key on an empty score sheet. He drew the most elegant violin keys in the whole class. He could sing E. F. E. D. – F. E. D. C. and D. D. G. F. – E. E. D. C. – *tam*. He especially liked the *tam*, but he didn't know what it meant.

'Please, be silent. Silence, I beg you, please!' said the little fat ruddy-faced singing master to end Misi's and Gimesi's argument. Then he started to talk about the scale or something. It was no disgrace not to understand it, because nobody in the class understood it except Orczy. Orczy laughed at the others when they complained that it was silly and stupid, because he played the piano and a score was as legible to him as a printed page.

They all cheered up when they got to the psalm-singing. Misi knew a lot of psalms, more than the others, because in the village school they did nothing but sing psalms. He couldn't carry a tune and this was a great sorrow to his mother, because the poor woman sang beautifully and his father was the best singer in every village they moved to, always the first man in the choir, leading all the others with his clear, strong voice. Misi learned to sing a little in the summer, in the flour mill where he ground the wheat for the family. It wasn't a watermill or a windmill, it was a 'dry mill' where the big stone wheel was driven by a horse walking in circles. Misi sat on the hub in the middle of the big millstone as it was turned around, and his job was to keep the borrowed horse moving by flicking it now and then with a whip. He was alone in the mill all afternoon and the solitude and the dull sound of the wheel turning gave him confidence to try his voice. He started to sing a song and suddenly – he himself didn't know how – he sang it in tune. The horse plodded around peacefully and Misi sat dreamily on the stone and sang:

> The young fisherman in his boat,
> tossed by the waves of Lake Balaton,
> thinks of his cruel sweetheart
> as he spreads his net.
> The fish get away, his sweetheart runs off,
> he is left alone, all alone.

By sheer accident, he sang in tune, and he was so pleased about it that he sang the same song over and over again, until late in the evening when his father came and stopped the merry-go-round by unhitching the horse.

Later his father built a new hayloft and when it was finished, one beautiful evening that same summer, Misi climbed to the top of the haystack and sang:

Red, white, green – red, white, green –
these are your nation's colours,
they show that you are a Magyar,
and they tell you, do not rest,
raise the tricolour, raise your spirits,
raise yourself, gain your freedom!

His mother came out to the barn and looked up. 'Why, the boy can sing!' she cried, clapping her hands. She called him down from the hayloft to hug him and cover him with kisses.

But that was the high point of his career as a singer. In class he couldn't cope with the half-beat or the quarter-beat, let alone the one-eighth note; he couldn't make them out in the score and he couldn't sing them, though he had to be part of the choir as an alto: he had the deepest voice in the whole class. Poor Mr Csoknyai did his best, he didn't want to spoil Misi's report card by giving him a 3 or 4 in music when he had 1 in every other subject, but with the best will in the world he could only give him a top mark for the report card, he couldn't provide him with an aptitude for music.

Only towards the end of the class did Misi realise that he couldn't possibly go to his pupil's house that day; he had to have lunch, classes started again at two o'clock, after classes he had to go to the old gentleman to read, then rush back to the college for supper, and after that they couldn't leave the college. So at the noon break he called after Doroghy, who was hurrying away.

'Doroghy!'

'Doroghy, Doroghy!' Varga shouted.

Misi's neighbours, wearing their overcoats and holding their books, formed a council and decided jointly that Misi could go and see his *pupil* only the following Wednesday afternoon.

Little Doroghy felt very awkward; he hardly dared to address his *tutor*. Misi felt similarly uneasy, doubting that he would have the ability to help anyone learn anything.

True, back in the village, in elementary school, the teacher had picked him to help some of the poorer students. The teacher was an angry, explosive man, and once he hit Misi over the head with a stick because Károly Drofti, one of the boys Misi was supposed to coach, didn't know his lesson. The stick was a thick one, used for carrying heavy buckets, and Misi's head swelled up until it was as big as a watermelon. His mother was very upset and sent Misi's younger brother for the doctor.

On his way to the doctor, the younger Nyilas had to walk past the school and the teacher, who happened to be standing in front of the school, asked him where he was going. Misi's younger brother gave a straight answer: his mother was sending him to fetch the doctor because Misi's head had swelled up, it had got as big as a watermelon.

'What does your mother know about it?!' the teacher said angrily, grabbing the boy's arm. He wouldn't let him go any farther and went to tend the sick himself.

Misi still remembered how upset he was when the teacher showed up with his younger brother. He wasn't afraid that the teacher would hit him again but he was ashamed that the teacher would think they wanted to denounce him.

The teacher made himself at home, sat down and started chatting amicably, and they never did send for the doctor. Misi's parents became friends with the teacher once they got to know him. He was impressed to hear that Misi's mother, even if only a carpenter's wife, was a minister's daughter, and he said that he himself had wanted to be a priest and had become a teacher only because he had fallen in love and got married.

Misi was somewhat apprehensive about tutoring a poor student, wondering whether he would be hit over the head again.

V

Misi gets involved with strange families, and sees and hears things which are outside the school curriculum

THE DOROGHYS LIVED in the front part of an old peasant house made of baked clay; the owners lived in the back. The house was whitewashed on the outside but the inside walls were painted, which made it look more like a city home.

They had two rooms. The front room had three windows, two facing the street and one facing the courtyard; the room behind had two windows opening to the verandah at the side of the house. Misi and his pupil worked in the front room at a large oval table, mostly by lamplight. It was December and darkness came early.

There were a lot of people in the house; he didn't like having so many people about. There were two grown-up girls and a younger one who was always giggling; he despised her for it.

Doroghy, who was called Alex at home, couldn't spell, didn't know the multiplication table and couldn't even read Latin. Misi was in despair. How could he possibly teach that boy anything?

The sensible thing would have been to tell the parents or Mr Gyéres that it was totally hopeless. But at the time Misi didn't think of it. He felt that he had been put in charge of the boy not to belittle him but to teach him what he didn't know.

But how?

If Doroghy didn't know something Misi went back a step. If Doroghy couldn't conjugate the subjunctive, then Misi would try the indicative; if Doroghy didn't know the future tense, then Misi tried the present tense. However, it turned out that Doroghy didn't even know the difference between the past and the present. So then Misi tried to make him understand that every action happened in one of three regions of time. Yes, but then he realised that not only did Doroghy know nothing about conjugating verbs, he didn't even know what to do with nouns. So Misi discovered that he had to backtrack a whole year, and in fact start with the very first Latin lesson. Doroghy couldn't even translate *alauda volat* or *rana coaxat*, yet both were on the very first page of the first-form Latin book.

But how could Misi teach the boy first-form Latin, starting with the very first lesson, when he also had to prepare him for the next day's lesson which required advanced knowledge? This tutoring turned out to be sheer torture. A born teacher, Misi preferred asking twenty questions to making one statement; he wanted his pupil to see the logic of the language, to reason things out for himself, step by step. But there was not enough time and neither of them had the strength for it.

'What were you doing in class when we studied this?' he asked the boy once, exasperated.

Alex didn't know the answer to that question either. But Misi was curious. How was it possible for Alex to be totally ignorant of lessons which the master had taken special care to explain and which the whole class had to recite aloud *ad nauseam*. So Misi kept asking, what were you doing when this or that was taught?

Alex scratched his head, and once he happened to remember. 'At that time I was harnessing a four-in-hand.'

'What?'

'A four-in-hand.'

'What's that?'

'It's a marvellous game and it's very simple. You catch four flies and tie them together with thread, and then they plough.'

The young tutor listened to this with open mouth. 'The flies plough?'

'Sure. All you have to do is pour a bit of ink on the desk, and when the flies go through the ink they leave furrows behind them.'

Misi couldn't help laughing and it encouraged the rascal to tell him more. 'Do you know what's a great game to play during maths? . . . You catch a spider, pull out its legs, and count how many times they can still move! There are lots of spiders in the courtyard, we'll never run out of them.'

'And what do you play during geography?'

'Geography?' asked Alex sleepily. 'There's no time to play then. I have to pay attention.'

'Pay attention?'

'Old Nazo does so many funny things, I don't want to miss a chance to laugh at him.'

Nyilas laughed, then collected himself, resolved to go on chopping wood, trying to force some knowledge on his pupil.

Alex was a quiet, handsome, clean boy. He was so tall that during physical education class, where they were lined up according to height, he was ten paces ahead of Misi, but he didn't seem taller in other classes. There he was all modesty, bowing his head and hunching his shoulders, trying to be invisible, and to a great extent he succeeded, because the teachers seemed hardly aware of his existence. Nothing else could explain the fact that he hadn't failed in every subject the year before.

After about two weeks one of the girls, the middle one, joined Alex and Misi in the front room where they were studying. The little tutor was embarrassed at first: it bothered him that a third person was listening; he felt that she was checking on him. But she didn't interrupt them; she was doing needlework. 'There is more light here than in the back room,' she said.

So they tried to ignore her, though Misi talked in a lower voice than when he was alone with Alex.

However, on one occasion, just a month after Misi started teaching, the girl remarked: 'I never in my life knew anyone as stupid as Alex. I don't think there is another boy in the world quite so dumb.'

Misi looked up, shocked by this spot-on observation.

The girl blushed and buried her face in the embroidery. She was wondrously beautiful. She had black shiny almond-shaped eyes that glittered as if they had little lamps inside them. Her face was pink but at the edges of her mouth it was white, and when she spoke Misi could see a lot of gleaming white teeth.

Alex scowled and made himself smaller; he even pursed his lips to make his mouth smaller.

Misi said nothing; he just marvelled at the beauty of the girl.

'You are killing yourself with this idiot,' she exclaimed. 'I wouldn't teach him if they gave me St Stephen's Cathedral in Vienna with buttons on.' As she laughed her teeth sparkled in the lamplight and her voice sounded like the song of a little bird in a cage. 'I would never have the patience. He'll never even know two plus two makes four.'

Misi, as was his habit, blushed terribly, becoming far more embarrassed than Alex. 'His problem is that he also has to study last year's work,' he said, trying to excuse his pupil.

'You mean he has to repeat the whole curriculum, starting with the first grade of elementary school.'

'No, I don't mean to . . .'

The girl smiled at him. 'Who taught you to teach?'

The little tutor had another attack of blushing. He felt what a reckless thing it had been for him to take on the task of tutoring. 'I'm only giving Alex a hand, trying to help him to remember. He knows exactly what I know, he just forgets it.'

'I couldn't possibly teach anybody,' said the girl, combing her hair with her fingers. She had long dark-brown hair, free and loose and tousled; it suited her very well.

'It's fun,' said Misi enthusiastically.

'What? Teaching?' The girl was bubbling with laughter, amused and amazed.

'Yes . . . I think it's the greatest joy to teach someone

something he didn't know. It's the greatest thing we can do for one another.' Misi became embarrassed that he had said something so portentous. He wasn't yet used to making statements; this was perhaps the first time in his life that he had told a stranger something which he thought was important and true.

'I couldn't teach,' repeated the girl, and turned down the corners of her mouth. Then she laughed again. 'And I had no patience to study either. But when I was at Dóczy I knew everything, though I never opened a book.'

'Where did you go to school?' Misi asked curiously, because he hadn't heard of the girls' gymnasium.

'At Dóczy.'

'What's that?'

The girl laughed. 'You never heard of it?'

Misi was embarrassed. He thought he was expected to know everything.

'Never mind,' she said, smiling mischievously and giving him a peculiar look. 'You will know all about it in a couple of years.'

Overcome with shyness, sensing that this had something to do with men and women, the sort of thing boys talked about among themselves when they talked about girls, Misi became so confused that he could hardly find his way back to his book. God forbid that he should look at her again!

Laughing quietly to herself, the girl picked up her embroidery. They sat in silence for a while because Misi didn't know how to continue the lesson. Now he was ashamed and didn't dare to talk in front of the girl.

Then the girl spoke again. 'I simply cannot imagine any other boy being as stupid as Alex.'

Alex raised his eyes and Misi noted that he had exactly the same eyes as his sister, black and glittering. He too had long eyelashes.

'Stupid!' Alex jeered. 'It would be better if you hadn't bought that Japanese fan.'

The girl turned scarlet; her face nearly exploded, and Misi, stealing a sidelong glance at her, saw that she was finding it difficult to talk. Yet when she finally spoke she sounded cool. 'He isn't too stupid for that, the insolent little brat, he can make snide remarks all right.'

The little tutor felt very uncomfortable between the sparring brother and sister, and tried to call Alex to order with his eyes.

'Sixty kreutzers,' Alex muttered pointedly.

The girl lost her temper. 'That's the limit! Imagine a snotty brat like you criticising anybody!'

'Snotty yourself! Wipe your nose!'

Misi lost his head completely. He had never witnessed such a scene between a brother and sister . . . Perhaps at home between him and his younger brothers, but that didn't count, because it was at home, there were no outsiders there, and they were all boys.

'I'll wipe your nose for you, you insolent little brat,' cried the girl and jumped up. 'How dare you talk to me like that? You should learn your seven times eight, you disgrace!'

At that instant the door flew open and the oldest daughter Viola appeared in the doorway. Dressed all in black and full of rage, she looked like a fury. She had been listening in the other room, wondering with growing resentment what Bella was doing interrupting the boy's lesson, and when she couldn't stand it any longer she burst in with murder in her eyes.

As soon as Alex saw his oldest sister he started whining. 'She doesn't let me work. Why does she have to come in here when I'm studying?'

Viola spoke sternly to her younger sister, her voice as sharp as a knife. 'Would you be kind enough to come out, please.'

'She always interrupts us!' wailed Alex.

'Was there ever such a liar?' shouted Bella.

'Excuse me, Miss Bella never interrupted us,' said Misi.

'She just said I'm stupid,' Alex complained.

'Don't be so sensitive, my little Alex,' Viola said sweetening her voice to smooth things over. 'You just concentrate on your lessons, my darling. That's all you have to do and then you'll get a good report card.'

'How can I study when they don't let me?'

'Of course they let you. I would like to see anyone try to disturb you in your studies!'

The other sister packed her needlework together. 'The shameless liar, having the brazenness to say that *I* keep him from studying! My heart broke to see how this poor tutor has to struggle against Alex's ignorance. He doesn't even know his seven times eight.'

'He won't learn it any sooner if you upset him,' said Viola.

'She always distracts me!'

'Now, now, we will ask Bella not to come into the room again while you are studying. Isn't that right, my dear Nyilas?'

Dear Nyilas would have preferred Bella to remain in the room. He regretted that he wouldn't see her again, because she was truly a wondrously beautiful girl, especially beside her older sister, who looked like a scrawny old spinster, always dressed in black and with her eyebrows completely grown together.

'I let him study. The point is, he doesn't *want* to study!' said Bella.

'Be quiet, that's your fault too,' the spinster rebuked her. 'If you had spent some time helping him when he was younger, he would be further ahead.'

'I would rather hang myself,' Bella burst out. 'Is it possible to help that idiot?'

'It is not only possible, it is absolutely necessary,' said Viola with merciless emphasis. 'He *must* study, this boy . . . The whole purpose of his life is to study! If he studies, he will have a *position*, he will have an *income*, he will have a *future*.'

Her words appalled the untutored mind of the little tutor. He looked at her aghast. It was such a strange thought! A boy would become a man and walk up and down on his estate with a big pipe in his mouth because he studied the ablative absolute! And the maid would come rushing in saying, 'Master, master, the sow gave birth to piglets.' Or he would walk into

an office in a smart black suit . . . It had never before occurred
to Misi that the lessons they had to learn day after day were
just a series of hurdles which they had to jump over so that
they could end up in a good, peaceful, lordly position . . . If
he had thought of that, the whole business of studying would
have been intolerable. This was why he should learn fractions
– and not because they were interesting? . . . That was what
he had always tried to say to Alex: Look at this, how strange,
how fascinating! Fascinating because true . . .

Now Viola turned to the little tutor as if he were a judge who
would deliver his verdict on this family scene. She appealed
to him, speaking passionately, forcefully, with an orator's
eloquence: 'Don't think that we were always such beggars, my
dear. Thank God, we are not poor even now, not as poor as
we may appear. My grandfather still had a great estate, ten,
twelve thousand acres. It was swept away by horse races, clubs
in Vienna and cards. When they were building the railways he
rented the first train so that nobody should sit in it but
himself. He wanted to ride alone, just as in his four-in-hand.
It cost a hundred and seventy thousand forints. It would be
nice if we had a hundred and seventy forints from that . . .'

Misi thought all this was grand and wonderful. He was
amazed but he also felt awkward that the girl should talk to
him about such things. It was not necessary, it was unseemly.
But he was also a little proud, as he had been one evening
back in the village when his mother sent him to the postmistress's house with a letter to make sure that it wouldn't
miss the next day's mail. That evening the postmistress talked
to him as if he was a grown-up and told him everything, even
about her husband's hernia, how a piece of his belly hung out
like a sausage and they had to press it back every night, and
this was why he couldn't work. Misi listened to her very
attentively because he felt that the poor, wretched postmistress
took him for a serious person, for a young gentleman, almost.

Viola couldn't stop herself: 'But none of that matters. This
boy can get back all we had. I've already settled my accounts

with life, I will be a servant for the rest of my days. My sisters'
and my brother's maid. You can look at my hands, see how
chapped they are. And look at my dress and my shoes. But
none of that hurts, because ever since I was a little girl I've
known that I had to sacrifice myself for the family. My dear
mother is sickly and my dear father is unhappy and I have to
be the maid of all work in the house because there are so
many things that somebody simply has to do. Isn't that so? . . .
There is always need for a beast of burden who gets up at
dawn and goes to bed at midnight, and that's me. Our house
is a hospital and a boarding school; one is lying in bed, the
other is a young lady, I am the only horse pulling our cart. If I
can just carry on. But how long can I carry on? These peasants
here who were born for it, they don't understand, they think
that everybody's like them. But my legs are already ruined;
when I come back from the market carrying ten kilos I just
faint into the bed. But that's all nothing . . .'

The poor girl took a deep breath and pointed at Alex as if
to a Winged Victory. 'The main thing is that I've brought him
up this far . . . He can put everything right if only he gets a
good report card.'

She sighed bitterly. 'It was no use for *me* to study. I had a
brain like fire and I had willpower. Anyone seeing me now
can't even imagine who I was . . . But what could I do with
report cards or degrees? All I could be was a postmistress, and I
am a postmistress . . . Or take this young lady, my sister. I put
her right through gymnasium, she matriculated too, and where
does it get her? The more a poor girl studies, the worse off she
is – her expectations grow but she can't do anything. This
boy, if he matriculates, whatever the difficulties, then he can
go to Budapest . . . Then he already has a career. The
moment he has his diploma he is exactly where the family was
forty years ago, he is again a Nagytárkányi-Bertóthi-Doroghy,
all the relatives' palaces will be open to him, the casino, the
clubs . . . The university will be child's play, by then he will
have so much money from the uncles and aunts that he can
amuse himself in any way he likes . . . But *now*, only now,

only for the next seven years, he has to pull himself together. And so do we. We have to be like Cinderella. We have to somehow struggle through this poverty, each from her own strength . . . Look at my sister. How could this poor girl marry? Where is the man for her? There isn't another girl in this town as beautiful as she is. She has the blood of two great noble families, she has Bertóthi and Mieskieviczky blood flowing in her veins, and she will wither away in a thatched cottage . . . But what can I do? Where could I take her without dresses, shoes, hats, gloves? I can't take her to a ball! And do you think I've ever been to a ball? . . . Who would marry her? Whom can I give her to? She will be nobody, she will be a drudge, she'll have no one to send out to buy her food, yes, my poor Bella, it's no use laughing, you'll end up carrying heavy baskets just as I do.'

She heaved a deep sigh and squeezed her forehead with her red hand. 'But this boy? He can marry an Odeschalchi girl, an Esterházy girl, a Károlyi girl, whichever takes his fancy.'

Misi looked at the spinster and her beautiful sister with horror: they were sacrificing themselves for a terrible, merciless future.

The spinster began to stroke her little Alex's head. 'Study, my love, study, study, my darling little angel, my baby, study, my treasure, study, don't you worry about anything, you will always have everything, only study, you will have clothes, shoes, exercise books, drawing paper, you can write, you can draw as much as you want to. You'll learn French, you'll learn to play the piano, and then you'll see, you'll remember your crotchety old sister with gratitude . . . Only try to learn what you have to learn, God forbid that we should disturb you, neither I, nor Bella nor anybody . . . Do you understand?'

And she hugged the boy's head with inexpressible love.

Somebody came into the other room. They stopped to listen: they could hear a man's voice. Misi guessed that it must be the father, because both sisters seemed embarrassed. Viola opened the door. A huge man with a splendid beard, wearing a fur coat, stood in the doorway.

Misi was overawed: he had never seen such a man. He looked like one of the heroes in the 'Historical Portrait Gallery'. Like Petneházy, a hero of the liberation of Buda from the Turks, or Miklós Bercsényi, one of Prince Rákóczi's generals in the war of liberation against Austria. He looked like a historic figure, especially in this old historic town of Debrecen, the city of heavy, cheerful men, smiles and big twisted moustaches. Misi stood up respectfully.

Alex jumped up and ran to his father with strange, trusting courage, kissed his hand and then kissed him on the mouth.

The girls greeted him with the peculiarly Central European greeting of loving respect, 'I kiss your hand'.

'Our friend, Misi Nyilas,' Viola said, introducing the little tutor. 'You know, Papa, the boy who is doing his homework with Alex.'

The father, smiling serenely, nodded towards the children, then sat down. Without a word he lowered himself into a chair and just sat there, smiling pleasantly. 'Did you catch a cold, Papa?' asked Viola.

He didn't reply, didn't nod; only his mouth moved under his big moustache. 'It's so hot in here that one could get apoplexy,' he complained after a while, propping his elbow on the table and stroking his forehead.

'Let me take your coat, Papa,' said Bella, and peeled his big thick fur coat off him. It was worn but it had fur on the inside as well as the outside.

His son sat on his lap.

'What are you studying?' asked the father.

The boy shrugged.

The big man looked at Misi, who responded obligingly. 'It's mathematics. We're practising the four basic operations with simple fractions.'

The father moved his eyebrows and took a closer look at Misi. 'From this?' he asked, absent-mindedly fingering the thin textbook.

'Yes.'

'Is that all? Are you such a donkey that you can't even learn that much?' He pronounced the word donkey as if he were caressing his son, though it was evident that he wanted to rebuke him. Amazingly, the boy wasn't at all afraid of him. He hid himself in his father's beard and stroked it with his fingers.

'Yes, yes, give him a talking-to, Papa,' said Bella sharply. 'He's so stupid he doesn't even know the multiplication tables.'

The father was silent. Misi was afraid that if this big man moved something would break.

'Stupid . . . Perhaps he isn't stupid, he's . . . just a donkey.' Once more he smiled strangely and bent his head forward.

'Papa, Bella bought a Japanese fan for sixty kreutzers,' Alex said slyly.

'What?' grunted the father, waking up.

'She calls me stupid because I told on her.'

'I'd throw her out with her fan,' growled the father.

'Don't be such a blabbermouth or I'll bash your head in,' snapped Bella.

'Boy, you really scare me.'

'Just wait, you'll get it soon.'

'And you'll get it from Papa, I promise you.'

Misi was dumbfounded, listening to all this. The most amazing thing was that the father didn't say anything. He didn't get angry, he wasn't outraged, he didn't laugh, he just gazed ahead with his small, fixed, unchanging smile. If Misi and his brothers ever talked to each other that way in front of their father, by then they would have already flown out of the window. They had a continuous tug-of-war at home because the little ones were always misbehaving and never wanted to do what they were told; they were always squealing and shrieking – but not in front of strangers, and never, ever, in the presence of their parents.

'Will he fail?' the father asked and looked at Misi.

Misi was frightened. He began to tremble, expecting the big

man to reach across the table, pick him up and break him in two like a piece of honey cake.

'I hope not, God forbid.'

'He will be all right as a shoemaker's apprentice,' the father said softly.

'Papa, you're taking this very lightly,' said Bella. 'You make a joke of it instead of grabbing him and shaking him to make him realise that something important is at stake. A child who is not beaten will never be a man.'

'Bring in the supper,' said the father.

That silenced them.

Now a pale woman, the mother, sidled in, supported by the youngest daughter, who was giggling and bending her head to hide her giggles. The mother was afraid that there would be trouble; that was why she had dragged herself out of bed. She sat down at the table. She was as white as a sheet and terribly thin.

The youngest daughter ran back and leaned against the door frame, giggling quietly. Whatever anyone said, she giggled.

For a while there was peace and quiet out of respect for the mother. Then Viola burst out, 'Does he study for my sake? Certainly not.' (The youngest daughter laughed aloud but covered her mouth with her hand.) 'Does he study for his father's sake? For his mother, for Bella or for little Ili?' (Hearing her name, the youngest daughter exploded with laughter and ran out of the room.) 'He's studying for himself. What he learns is his, his alone.'

There was silence again and then little Ili, who was a thirteen-year-old with black hair and instant blushes, slipped back into the doorway, because she was very curious and didn't want to miss a word.

Finally the mother spoke in a low voice. 'Yes, indeed, he's studying for his own sake.'

Viola grasped at this. 'If only I could have studied! I would have worked at it, I would have learned everything.' (Little Ili's stifled laughter from the doorway was like a mockingbird chirping.) 'Oh my God, I would have just finished university!'

(Now Ili laughed out loud again.) 'Well, what are you sniggering at? You, you wicked soul, what is so funny?' (Little Ili shrieked and stuffed her fist in her mouth.) 'You can study. I was just saying what an injustice it is that a girl remains a servant even if her mind can reach the stars. But this one, if we can just push him up to university, will become a nobleman right away.'

Little Ili burst out again and ran from the room, then from the other room into the courtyard, with her shrieking laughter.

The father leaned back in his chair and began to hum a song.

> Little dog, big dog,
> you bark too late . . .

As he hummed the song his breath wafted across the table and Misi was horrified and repelled by the smell of wine. He looked at the splendid man as if he were seeing a snake or a dragon. His father drank too, when he made contracts with the peasants, but those were special occasions, hellish times when his mother and the boys went through seventy-seven torments.

Misi remembered that it was almost five o'clock, so he stood up, said goodbye and left. Outside there was a strong wind blowing; it nearly picked him up and carried him away.

He was tired and absent-minded at the old gentleman's and read haltingly; the afternoon weighed on his mind.

He couldn't make out those people. He liked every one of them and was angry with every one of them. He was angriest with Alex. Why didn't he study? He had nothing else to do. And it would have paid him to study. Misi respected the oldest girl because her hands were so red and she sacrificed herself, but still, she was too rude. Bella, my God, what a beautiful girl, a princess. He didn't understand the little giggler, why no one gave her a good beating. Even as he left the house she was hiding in the corridor, giggling. And about what? That her sister could have finished university? When he thought of this he started to laugh himself, even while reading. He could hardly swallow his laughter. What a fool that little girl was! She was the stupidest among all those stupid people. And he could have laughed at that too.

This happened to be the end of the month, the 30th of November, and the old gentleman had put three silver forints out for him. 'Thank you very much,' said Misi, and put it in his little purse, which had contained only four kreutzers. For the past month he had lived on four kreutzers; luckily he hadn't had to buy anything, but now he had three whole forints, in a good place beside the lottery ticket in his purse. He went home skipping happily; he wasn't troubled now by the Doroghys' problems, the wind or the future: he had three forints in his pocket.

He was only sorry that he couldn't show his big coins to everybody in the dormitory. The boys would have wanted him to treat them.

Now he would be able to pay Mrs Csigai the one forint twenty kreutzers he owed for his laundry. He was quite looking forward to seeing her the next day; let her come! He would be left with one forint eighty for the next month; with some of that he would buy four paint buttons, including a gold one and a silver one; the gold one was fifteen kreutzers and the silver was ten.

And he would buy a pencil and a theatre ticket.

The next day was Sunday, the 1st of December.

December: the name gave him a mysterious holiday feeling. As if the start of December was the beginning of great things. There would be Christmas, and New Year's Eve too. December, Christmas, New Year's Eve – these were all magnificent words.

He wanted to celebrate the 1st of December by visiting someone, and he thought of the Töröks with whom he had boarded the previous year. He hadn't been at their place for a long time; not once since he had been busy reading and tutoring. Yet he was going home for Christmas and would have to take messages from them.

As soon as lunch was over he hurried off to Nagymester Street. When he saw the big white house at the corner it seemed older, more dignified than the other houses on the street. His heart gave an extra beat. He had been happy living there; he was still an innocent child in those days.

The gate was as rickety as ever. It couldn't be closed properly; they still hadn't fixed the latch. The trees in the courtyard were bare; they stretched their black fingers towards the sky, missing the beautiful rich foliage they had in the summer when little girls ran around chasing each other in their shade. At the back of the courtyard was the sty where Uncle Török fed his pigs with corn winter and summer, wearing his many-coloured woollen cap, which also served as a nightcap, and sucking his long-stemmed pipe. There were piglets in the spring, beautiful little white creatures; the veins showed through their transparent skin. They drank milk and some of them ventured into the trough and ate the swill with their mothers.

The steps were whitewashed and the ceiling of the verandah was vaulted, as in an old castle.

His heart beat faster at the familiar sights and he ran up the four steps as if he were coming home. He wished he had come sooner. Why hadn't he? He had just too much to do. Not like last year.

Auntie Török and Miss Ilonka were sitting in the kitchen, as always, talking. They never ran out of things to say to each other. The kitchen was a big spacious room; it was not only the kitchen but also the sitting room and the dining room. It had a big china cabinet, a sideboard and a dining table; that was where they ate and lived during the day.

'Heavens, it's our little scholar!' shouted Auntie Török and opened her big arms. She was a huge, strong woman, almost a giant, but her kindness and goodness were even more gigantic, and her face shone like a full moon.

'Good Lord, who is here?' cried Miss Ilonka, who unlike her mother was a very pretty little woman.

They hugged him and practically devoured him; they stroked him and measured him: how he had grown! Had he gained weight or lost weight? 'Skin and bone!' Auntie Török said. 'That miserable college food!' Miss Ilonka said: 'He looks fine to me. He's a strong wiry boy.'

'Tell me, what did you have for lunch?' they asked simultaneously, with extraordinary curiosity. They never forgot to ask it. He tried to remember what he had eaten for lunch but he had forgotten that they would ask him; next time he would write it down so that he would able to tell them. Apart from porridge with sugar and semolina pudding he didn't care that much what he ate, so long as there was enough of it. The boys ran into the dining hall like little piglets, gobbled up everything they were given and ran from the trough. But Auntie Török and Miss Ilonka wouldn't drop the subject, so he had to invent lunch.

'We had beef broth and noodles.'

'Soup with no meat in it! The villains! Where did they put the good boiled meat? Very clever, I must say. They give you only the water they boil it in!'

'No, no, we also had boiled meat with sauce.'

'Hmmm. And what kind of sauce did they give you?'

'What kind of sauce? . . . Tomato sauce.'

'Of course. Why do you ask, Mother? As if they had any other kind of sauce except onion and tomato.'

'And was it good?'

'Yes.'

'I can't say I put much trust in your opinion. What do you know? You would eat sawdust. You would like that too. You wouldn't know the difference . . . And what did you have with the noodles?'

'What . . . What was in the noodles? . . . Jam.'

'Of course it was jam! . . . Clear broth, some old cow's meat with tomato sauce, and noodles with jam. Do you expect those people to think of something different? I bet it

was old mouldy plum jam. They think anything is good
enough for the poor little students.'

'It wasn't mouldy, Miss Ilonka.'

'What do you know. I'm sure you think mould is sugar.'

'No, Miss Ilonka, I know the difference. The bread is
musty, yes, a bit mouldy. No, not mouldy, just musty.'

'Good Lord, how musty does it have to be that even this
one notices it!'

'But really, Auntie Török, please believe me, they cook
very well.'

'What do they cook well?'

'Come on, tell us, what do you like best?' asked Miss
Ilonka, and pinched his cheek.

'Porridge with sugar.'

At that both women clapped their hands in despair. They
gave up on the little scholar. They saw that he would never
amount to anything.

'He likes best what we wouldn't give to the pigs.'

'Now he loves the college food. But he didn't like Auntie
Török's cooking,' said the mother.

Misi was silent. He thought that he should pay some clever
and beautiful compliment to Auntie Török's cooking, but
nothing occurred to him.

'Don't embarrass him, Mother. It's not words that count but
how he looks. How he looked last year and how he looks
now.' Now it was Miss Ilonka's turn to commiserate over him,
saying how thin he was, while her mother took Misi's side.

'He looks all right to me,' said Mrs Török. 'He was thin last
year too. It was no use for me to feed him raisins.'

Miss Ilonka laughed in a kindly way; her voice was thin as
thread, just as it had been the year before. But Misi remembered his bad days with them, when his father didn't send the
ten forints punctually on the first of the month . . . He never
could send it punctually. At home people weren't like city
folk who worked in offices and got paid on the first of the
month rain or shine. His father first had to search for work
and take it on, do the work and then wait to get paid. At the

end nothing was left because by the time he got paid he had to hand it over straight away to pay what they owed to everybody in the village.

'And how goes the school?'

Miss Ilonka answered for him. 'From the way he's shifting about I can see that he's on top of things. I can see it from his nose.'

Misi smiled.

'Your Uncle Géza will be pleased. When did you hear from your uncle?'

'Oh, he hasn't written for a long time.'

They always talked about his uncle because he, too, had boarded with Auntie Török and had tutored their sons, and Miss Ilonka was especially interested in any news from him. In fact it was only for the sake of his Uncle Géza that they had given him room and full board for ten forints a month. And the love they had for his Uncle Géza shone a bit on him too . . .

This afternoon in the kitchen was so pleasant, so friendly. The mother sat in a wicker armchair made by the shepherds of the province; every house in Debrecen had one or two wicker chairs. Sitting on a little stool as always, Misi answered every question faithfully and laughed to his heart's content, relaxed as he was nowhere else. Compared to this, how soulless life in the college was! And it wasn't easy even with Mr Pósalaky, reading steadily for an hour. As for the Doroghys – what an ugly afternoon that had been! Here there was no crisis, here people were loving, here everything was as before. Not a piece of furniture had been moved; these were happy and good people.

This is how everybody should live always, Misi decided. Why didn't they?

'I have a pupil,' he announced, surprising them. He had wanted to say it for a long time but was shy about it; he was afraid they would think he was bragging.

The two women clapped their hands again and cried in unison: 'Who ever heard of such a thing?'

'He has a pupil!' said Auntie Török.

'Well, he's like his uncle, he's all brains,' said Miss Ilonka, and laced together her delicate fingers, as fine as a bird's. 'Good Lord, what a family! What heads they have! A twelve-year-old boy and he has a pupil!'

'Well! And what do they pay you for it?' asked Auntie Török.

'Two forints a month.'

'That's nice,' commented Miss Ilonka with less enthusiasm. She calmed down, seeing that it wasn't such a big thing after all. 'Good for you! Even two forints is nice. It's a big help these days. It's a joy to a father, having children like that . . . Oh, this little frog, imagine him having a pupil. Oh you green plum. I guess now I will have to call you Mr Nyilas!'

Misi was quiet and smiled happily, he even laughed until he remembered how often Auntie Török had told him, 'Pull the skin over your teeth'. Then he quickly pressed his lips together.

Uncle Török came in from the courtyard wearing his eternal multicoloured Bosnian hat with the pom-pom hanging from it. He was greyer than the previous year, and quieter, and was sucking his clay pipe, unlit as ever.

'Look, Papa, see who's here!'

'Ho ho ho!' cried the old man. He took his clay pipe out of his mouth, raised it high in the air by way of greeting, put it back again and stroked the boy's head with his freed hand. 'Good, good.'

They loved each other because the previous winter they had read together in the other room. Old Török, a retired teacher, read novels while Misi read old copies of *Home and Abroad* magazine. He also borrowed Uncle Török's novels, *The Man with Two Horns* and *Old Hungarian Legends*. And they played chess together. He didn't get along so well with anybody as he did with Uncle Török. And old Török, too, treated him quite differently from anybody else. He never talked with his wife or children; if they talked they always started to argue, but with Misi he had peaceful conversations.

'Papa, did you hear that Misi has become a teacher?' asked Miss Ilonka, who talked with her father only about other people. 'Imagine, he has a pupil!'

'Well done,' said Uncle Török, nodding his head emphatically. 'Is your charge in the same class as you?'

'Yes.' Misi felt awkward, he felt he was unmasked, because you couldn't really call it teaching when you were helping a classmate.

'That's very good. It helps you with your own studies. You will remember your subjects better if you also have to teach them,' said Török.

There was so much goodwill and wisdom in this remark that Misi suddenly felt he ought to be grateful to Alex because he could tutor him and in so doing could revise his own Latin and mathematics, which were his weakest subjects. And he vowed that he would never again use the word 'pupil'; he would only say that he was studying with Alex.

'They pay him two forints for it,' said Miss Ilonka. 'Other people have children like that, and ours have never ever brought two forints into the house.'

Misi's feeling that he was in a happy home began to evaporate. He remembered their troubles. The eldest son Mr Antal was a big dolt; Mr Imre did nothing but drink and run after girls. And Mr János was an even bigger disaster; that was how they always referred to him. The previous year he had visited them only twice, and poor Mr and Mrs Török used to shout at each other on his account.

Looking up at the kitchen wall, Misi was surprised to see that a charcoal drawing of János was no longer there. It had originally hung in the inner room but Uncle Török had thrown it out, saying 'Put it on the fire', so Mrs Török had put it up on the kitchen wall. But it was no longer there. What had become of it?

Misi had heard that János was a big practical joker who used to throw his weight around in the college and was a drunkard even then. Last year he was not even in Debrecen. He hadn't lived at home for years because his father wouldn't tolerate him. Once his mother paid his debts in secret and when Uncle Török found out about it he became unrecognisable.

Of course nobody talked to Misi about all this but he figured it out from all the shouting. Not that he cared much about it. What was he last year? Just a little donkey.

Now there was a painful silence in the kitchen: they were listening to footsteps on the verandah. Someone was coming. Uncle Török looked for a bit of an ember in the ashes to put in his pipe, and then – Good Lord! – the door opened and János came in. Casually, with his winter coat draped around his shoulders. Misi was sorry for having bad thoughts about him and stood up respectfully.

'Well, come in,' said Miss Ilonka, and pointed at Misi. 'A teacher. He is Géza Isaák's nephew. He is twelve years old and he is a teacher.'

János looked at Misi, jabbed his thumb into the top of his head, pressed it down hard and gave it a painful twist. 'Grow up, boy! D'you hear? Let your ears grow long and floppy.'

Misi's eyes filled with tears. His head hurt, but being humiliated hurt even more. He tried to hide it; he didn't want it to be noticed. He would have liked to run away; he no longer felt happy there. Why had he come? If he had known that Mr János was at home he wouldn't have come.

'Look what a bully you are! You beast!' said Miss Ilonka, and stroked Misi's head.

But Misi didn't want to be stroked either. He drew away. He didn't want them to touch him. He swallowed his tears. To treat him like that! I will show you, he thought. 'I also read to an old blind gentleman,' he said. 'I read to him for an hour every afternoon. I'm getting three forints for it.'

'What do I hear?' cried Miss Ilonka. 'I will faint! Five forints a month! You can buy two piglets for that, give one to a farmer and he'll fatten up the other for you. And by Christmas you could send huge hams to your father. The whole family could chew on it all winter.'

Misi was offended by this remark. His father didn't need

him to buy a piglet. 'I will win on the lottery,' he said defiantly. But then added in a low voice, 'Old Mr Pósalaky had a dream and he made me play his numbers on the lottery. If we win half of it is mine.'

Miss Ilonka didn't understand; she just gaped. 'Lottery! Now that's all that was needed. You too turned into a gambler. You should be ashamed of yourself. You aren't an honest person either,' she cried.

But János just laughed. 'No, no, he's a clever chap. Do you have the lottery ticket? Show me.'

'Good, good, all you need is advice from him. Then your poor father can give up on his son's earnings.'

Misi vaguely remembered hearing some wailing about the lottery when he lived with them. It must have been János who played and lost money on it. Now he was ashamed of the lottery ticket. He would have given a lot not to have it in his pocket; he took the ticket out of his little purse and handed it to Mr János.

Mr János examined it with the eyes of an expert. 'A one-forint ticket!' he exclaimed. 'That's serious business! I thought you put ten kreutzers on it.'

'No, Mr János, I didn't put anything on it,' the boy protested, and wished he hadn't been involved in it at all. It bothered him very much that he was mixed up in something that János approved of. It had to be a shameful thing. 'Mr Pósalaky put the money down. He only sent me to the tobacconist with it and told me to keep the ticket because he doesn't see. And he promised me half of what he wins.' But he had already half resolved not to accept that dirty money; he was disgusted with it. Good thing that there wasn't much chance of winning; not winning anything would be the best. Having decided that he wanted nothing to do with the whole business, he forgot about the ticket.

'Which Pósalaky are you talking about?' asked Mr János. 'The one who was a member of the city council?'

'Yes. He's blind now.'

'That's the one.'

There was silence. The women seemed sad, thinking of
János. Some repressed and heavy feeling descended on the
company.

'So what child do you teach?' asked János, who for some
unknown reason became interested in the young tutor.

'Alex Doroghy.'

'Doroghy?' János seemed surprised. 'Doroghy?'

'Yes.'

'He has sisters, doesn't he?'

'Yes. Three.'

'Three sisters. Isn't one of them a tall beautiful girl.'

'Yes,' replied Misi, reviving.

Ilonka looked up, roused from her musings. 'Oh, well, if
there is a girl in the family János knows her.'

'I don't know her *yet*,' replied János, laughing. 'But we will
get acquainted.'

'I can't wait.'

'You can relax, sister, you won't have to wait long.'

'I wish my other wishes would be fulfilled so promptly.'

'An angel's wishes are always fulfilled.'

Misi sat hunched up on the stool and it struck him as
strange that Mrs Török didn't say a single word to her son,
when last year it had been Mr Török who wouldn't talk to
him.

János started to whistle.

Outside there was the bustling and shuffling sound of
people coming up the steps to the verandah. Misi was pleased.
For once he wasn't afraid of strangers. He couldn't stand this
fight between brother and sister.

The Szikszays arrived.

These Szikszays were the Töröks' best friends. It was a rare
Sunday that they didn't come together. The whole family was
coming. First the father, a big, red-faced man who hummed
all the time; he would walk on the street singing aloud;
he radiated good cheer and contentment. Behind him came
his wife, who was as thin as a rail, carrying a baby whom Misi
had never seen. Beside her came two skinny bad boys who

were always playing loudly and destructively. The older one wouldn't eat anything but chocolate; he had already lost several teeth and the rest were rotting on both sides. Misi drew back; he didn't want to be the subject of conversation, and after kissing Mr and Mrs Szikszay's hands he stole into the other room to read. He still had an hour and a half and wanted to see what they had in their bookcase that he didn't already know.

They forgot about him and when he was leaving Mr János came up to him and whispered: 'My Misi, Misi . . .'

Misi blushed. Few people had ever addressed him in such a familiar way, and Mr János never.

'All right, my little friend, here is a letter. Take it to the Doroghy girl – to the beautiful one, mind!'

Misi was flabbergasted.

'But don't you dare to open it, because I swear to God I would write about it to your Uncle Géza.'

Misi took the letter dejectedly. This man was certainly capable of blackening him to his uncle.

He felt miserable to be given such a commission but didn't dare to refuse.

VI

Misi discovers the city's most ancient historic monument, which is not a ruined castle, not a palace, not marble or bronze, but a big three-hundred-year-old bush growing through a window

MONDAY MORNING was always a bad time; Misi dragged himself to the classroom tired and half-asleep. The first hour was Latin, and of course Mr Gyéres wasn't there when the bell rang.

'Sentry, sentry!' shouted the boys. 'Let Orczy go!'

Orczy laughed and jumped up from his bench. He was pleased to be entrusted with the task. His fine blond hair was brushed smooth and shone like gold. He was so healthy, brave and cheerful that Misi's morning drowsiness vanished and he finally woke up.

Since Mr Gyéres always slept late on Monday morning, a sentry was despatched to watch his window and report when he raised his roller blind. He lived near the college in a building owned by the church commissioners. During the winter most of the boys didn't want to be sentry because it meant having to put on their overcoats, but Orczy didn't seem to mind; he was cheerful and willing.

'You should come too, Nyilas.'

Misi was taken aback. 'Me?'

'Oh, come on, don't be a sissy.' Orczy laughed as he put on his overcoat.

Misi stirred but didn't move.

'Come on, don't be such a lazybones.'

At that Misi slid off the bench and threw on his winter coat. He wasn't a lazybones and he wasn't a sissy, but standing sentry was against the rules and he didn't like doing things that were forbidden. Secretly, yes. For instance, he read when he should have been studying. But to actually go outside the college when he was supposed to be in the classroom . . .

His heart was pounding, the class was buzzing. All the boys watched them as they walked out and the noise and the looks made Misi feel like a hero – Miklós Zrínyi[1] at Szigetvár, charging out of his castle to attack the besieging Turks . . .

Their steps echoed in the long empty corridor. They passed by Petőfi and Misi looked up at the beautiful statue with its bronze arm holding up a scroll with the poem which sparked off the 1848 revolution against the Austrians:

> Get on your feet, Magyar!
> It's now or never . . .

Then came the most difficult, most dangerous part. They had to pass the Headmaster's door. Here Misi was really frightened, because if one of the masters – or the old sergeant-major himself – came out and shouted at him he would be sure to faint.

But they passed the Head's door safely and turned the corner of the corridor where the 1-A classroom was. There they were startled by another sentry, from the first-year class. They frightened each other like two lambs meeting in a bush.

But Orczy was very brave and ran on. Misi ran after him, getting more and more afraid. After the 1-A and 1-B class-rooms there was a side door leading to the gingerbread stalls. There they ran out of the building, and as Misi looked back he saw the fat master of the fifth form, a threatening figure with his bristling moustache and his heavy stick. Luckily he didn't notice them.

On the street Misi calmed down a little. They turned towards the Great Church, walking briskly on the brick sidewalk. Misi kept his head down; if Mr Gyéres came towards them he would simply run into him with his head. But Orczy was in his element, cheerful and joking, laughing, looking around, as if they weren't on a forbidden mission but were going somewhere on the orders of the Latin master himself.

They stopped by the iron railings of the Memorial Garden. 'Do you see it?'

'No I don't.'

'You don't see it?'

'What?'

'It's down.'

'What?'

'The roller blind.'

Across the street there was a three-storey building. Misi strained his eyes looking at the windows, but he didn't know which one belonged to Mr Gyéres. Up to then he hadn't cared where the Latin master lived.

'Let's go into the garden.'

They went into the Memorial Garden and watched the Latin master's bedroom window from behind a bush. Now Misi knew which window to watch, because it was the only one at the front of the building which had its blind down. The first window on the ground floor.

'Will we wait for him?'

'Sure. When he rolls up the blind, he will start to wash himself. Then he will pour cologne all over himself. Then he will comb his moustache. Then he will dress. After that he will leave. We have plenty of time.'

Misi had goose pimples from the excitement. He had never imagined such an extraordinary adventure. He was laughing all the time, shifting from one foot to the other, and kept pulling his hands from his pockets and putting them back again. To have come so far from the classroom! He was thrilled even by the thought of it.

'Nyilas, do you know what is the most famous thing in this city?'

'No I don't.'

'That bush across the street.'

'Where?'

'Right there. Don't you see? Under the window of that little house. It was planted by Prince Rákóczi.'[2] This was a sacred name. Prince Rákóczi was one of the great tragic heroes of Hungarian history.

'The other day Uncle Lórinc was at our place,' Orczy went on, 'and he said that Jókai[3] asked him whether we still had that thorn bush. He warned him that Debrecen must never uproot it. Don't be as careless with it as with the Simonyi trees, he said.'

'What Simonyi trees?' asked Misi.

'Well, out at the edge of the Great Forest, where the villas end, Colonel Simonyi planted a beautiful row of giant poplars, three hundred trees, and they were all cut down last year. When Jókai heard about it he cried. He said he would never come to Debrecen again. There is nothing beautiful here any more, he said. Even back in 1848 the Simonyi trees were the only beautiful thing. Those trees and this thorn bush, because this is older. Three hundred years old. Prince Rákóczi planted it and you can see, it's grown into the window. Come on, let's look at it, the blind is still down.'

They went out to the street again, Misi running after Orczy with a dreaming, wondering heart.

They went right up to the low green-painted house which, though it had already sunk halfway into the earth, was preserved because of Rákóczi's bush. The window was covered by a heavy iron grille and a twisted tree had grown through the bars. It didn't look like a bush; it looked more like a very thick rope. It went in and out, back and forth, twisting around the iron bars, and then stuck up its head, which had long thin tendrils hanging from it. They had many such miserable bushes at the bottom of their garden at home, Misi thought.

'Well, what do you say?' asked Orczy enthusiastically.

'Prince Rákóczi planted this?' Misi was amazed. He would never have thought that it could be so famous. He had seen it many times and had often wondered why that ugly bush was left there. But now he was worried that something might happen to it. He knew that the city council couldn't be trusted. Now he remembered that the Töröks had cursed the mayor the previous year for cutting down the beautiful tall Simonyi trees. 'Jókai said that it was Rákóczi's bush?'

'Yes.'

'Mór Jókai?'

'Yes, he wrote lots of books. He was the greatest novelist.'

'I've already read some Jókai.'

'Me too.'

'What have you read?'

'I have two books of his,' said Orczy. *'Hungary under the Turks* and *The Little Decameron.'*

'I read those and I also read the one about a knight who was scalped by the Turks, and they put the headskin of a billy-goat on his head, and it worked and he became a man with horns.'

Orczy was impressed and laughed. 'That's what it said?'

'The Count of Fools was even better.'

They were startled by a man's voice.

'Hohoho . . . Playing hookey, eh? What are you up to?'

Misi looked up. It was Mr János, going to the office. Misi had heard the Töröks talking about it the previous day: Mr János had a job in an office now and should have been at work by eight, but he always arrived after nine. Misi blushed as the man put his hand on his shoulder. 'What are you doing here?'

'Mr Gyéres sent us to . . .' said Misi but couldn't go on, he was ashamed to lie in front of Orczy.

'Yeah. You should be on your way somewhere, and you just loiter in the street.' He drew Misi aside. 'Did you give it to her?'

Misi looked up at him, puzzled.

'My letter, my letter.'

'The letter? I don't go to the Doroghys' until Wednesday.'

'The devil take you . . . Not until Wednesday?'

'Yes.'

Mr János seemed to be pondering something. 'Oh, well, what can you do, if it's Wednesday it's Wednesday. But listen to me. You tell her that I beg the young lady not to burden her lovely hands with writing, just send a message with you, and just one word: *gladly*. Or *never*. Do you understand?'

'Yes.'

'So: *gladly* or *never*. And don't you forget!'

'I won't.'

'May God turn you into a crying gypsy if you forget it. If you make a mess of it I'll write a letter to your Uncle Géza and then you'll kick the bucket in your misery.'

Misi scowled and said nothing.

'All right, all right, boy, here's a six-kreutzer,' said Mr János, and put his hand in his pocket.

'I don't want it, thank you very much, I don't need it,' said Misi and drew away from him.

Mr János sized him up with a look. 'Well, well, I see you've become a big shot. Can you change a kreutzer?' Then he waved his hand dismissively. 'Never mind. If our grandfather hadn't died he would still be alive. So just do what you were told and you won't regret it.' He took the boy's hand and shook it, and pointed at a passing cart. 'I see they're collecting.' With that he hurried on.

There were too many things going on in the street for the boys to keep their eyes glued to the Latin master's window. The cart was advancing in the middle of the road, followed on the sidewalk by two tall theology students in black suits. As the sun suddenly emerged from behind a cloud it became very bright. Orczy watched the cart curiously.

'They are collecting,' Misi told him.

'What's that?' asked Orczy.

Misi knew, because in the dormitory they had talked about it for days, how late the college had left the collecting that year.

'What do you mean, collecting?'

'They're collecting for the boarders at the college.'

'And what are they collecting?'

'Whatever they get. Corn, wheat, flour, bacon, ham.'

Orczy gaped. 'The students? They are begging?!'

Misi blushed. 'It's no shame, it's collecting.'

Orczy laughed. 'I'd like to get on the cart and see what they've got.'

'Pumpkin did that.'

'Who is Pumpkin?'

'Marci Tajthy. In the dormitory we call him Pumpkin.'

The two theology students were just passing. The boys fell silent to hear what they were saying.

'It's a disgrace. These peasants try to fob us off with two cobs of corn or a few kreutzers.'

'I don't know why we're still doing this. They should call it off for good.'

They passed out of earshot, and Misi blushed. He no longer saw the thing as collecting, only as begging, and he felt ashamed.

'Come on, let's go,' Orczy nudged him.

They ran back to the other side of the street to watch Mr Gyéres's window.

The blind was up. Not only was the blind up but the window was open. Mr Gyéres was standing there all dressed and opened his eyes wide when he saw them. 'What are you doing there, you rascals?' he shouted. 'Came to watch my window? Spying on me! Instead of sitting in your classroom going over your lesson!'

The boys stood there as if someone had poured boiling water over them. 'Get back to the school! Just you wait, I'll teach you today!'

The boys started to run and this time they didn't try to hide; they pounded along the corridor, making an echo every time their shoes hit the stone floor, and arrived in the classroom gasping for breath.

'Quiet, quiet, quiet!' panted Orczy, and his fear infected the whole class. They fell silent and sat still.

For a few moments there was the silence of the grave, but then as the Latin master still hadn't arrived, they regained their spirits and began talking again. There was a kind of low steady buzzing as in a busy beehive.

Only Misi sat quiet and depressed. He lined up his books in front of him and prepared for the worst. He was certain that the Latin master would call him first to ask him all the questions about the day's lesson, searching for something he didn't know, and he knew he would just hem and haw. And then he wouldn't be tutoring Doroghy any more. This made him remember the letter that he had to pass on to the beautiful sister. He went hot and cold at the thought that he had such a terrible dirty thing to do. He bent his head and opened his Latin exercise book and read over his homework, looking for what the Latin master would ask him, looking for the words he didn't know. But he knew every word, understood everything.

He looked up from the book only when all the boys stood up; he hadn't even heard the door open. The master was already on the platform. Misi looked at him as if he were a ghost, he appeared so suddenly.

'I don't want this to happen again,' said the young master in a stern voice, and raised his close-cropped head with its two flapping sideburns, looking at the boys like a wild dog ready to bite them. 'It is not done, sending out sentries to watch for the teachers. If I ever see such wicked misbehaviour, it will end in expulsions! . . . All right, sit down . . . Orczy!' The master pointed to the pile of exercise books on his desk. These were the students' Latin compositions which he had taken away with him to read and mark. 'Hand everybody his composition.'

Orczy jumped up again. Misi heaved a sigh of relief. They would be correcting the previous day's work; they wouldn't be questioned. Orczy, fresh-faced and elegant, picked up the exercise books, put them first under his arm, then in his hands, and walked with light steps along the rows of benches, handing each student his own exercise book.

'Nyilas!'

Misi jumped up, ghastly pale.

'Translate this sentence into Latin: *He who robs men's trust is also a thief.* Well, go on, hurry up!' said Mr Gyéres, drumming on the desk with his pencil. 'What is the Latin for thief?'

'*Fur, furis.*'

'All right. What kind of sentence is that? Repeat the sentence.'

Misi repeated it and added: 'A compound sentence with two clauses. He is also a thief is one clause; who robs men's trust is the other clause.'

'Which is the principal clause?'

'He is also a thief.'

'Go on, go on, do I have to drag every word out of you? What is the other clause?'

'The other . . . Who robs men's trust.'

'What kind of clause is that?'

'It is the subordinate clause.'

'What kind of subordinate clause?'

'A modifying clause.'

'All right, get on with it. Translate.'

'*Etiam ille est fur . . .*'

'Go on, go on.'

'*Qui . . .*'

'Which is the word you don't know? Man?'

'*Homo, hominis*: man.'

'Trust?'

Misi was silent.

'All right. Trust is *fidutia*. Now translate the whole sentence.'

'*Etiam ille est fur, qui . . . fidutiam . . . hominum . . . furat.*'

'*Furat?* Don't make me furious! And don't start making up new words, especially in Latin. It's *rapit.*'

'*Etiam ille est fur, qui fidutiam hominum rapit.*'

'Well, write it down in your exercise book and try to think what it means.'

Misi's face was burning. He understood what the teacher

meant and was terribly frightened. He stared wide-eyed and his face sagged.

The Latin master paid him no more attention. He took some of the exercise books from Orczy and distributed them. Misi, still standing, just stared at the blackboard, which hadn't been properly cleaned. There were big patches of chalk on it. He felt as if he were in the stocks and everybody was staring at him. His face was now waxen and red by turns; the blood rushed to his head, to his feet; he felt dizzy standing on his two weak legs. He had stolen the Latin master's trust. Mr Gyéres couldn't have supposed that he would sink so low, when he had promoted him to a tutor. Now he was sure to take away his pupil. And that would be such a disgrace, he would never be able to go home to his parents. And what would his Uncle Géza say when he learned about it? . . . He grew so dizzy that he couldn't see clearly, couldn't think clearly, and would have fainted if Gimesi hadn't tugged at his jacket sleeve.

'Misi, sit down!'

Misi sat down. But he got scared about that too, because the Latin master hadn't said he should sit down. What should he do now? He was afraid to get up again, so he just slumped on the bench and felt inexpressibly sick at heart.

'Show me your composition! What did you get?' whispered Gimesi, who was very bitter because he had got a 2 minus for his.

Misi didn't have the strength to move his little finger. He only looked exhausted. The whole room was churning in front of him in a fog, and the letters were every colour of the rainbow.

'You got a 1!' said Gimesi, and left Misi's exercise book open. Then he also took Orczy's exercise book and opened it. '2 minus,' he said when he looked at it. 'And you got a 1! Misi, I'm going to hit you over the head.'

Misi smiled at this, a little. He would have liked to hug Gimesi, to press himself against him. He would have liked to lie down beside him and put his head in his lap and fall asleep and forget everything. Oh, if he could only sleep and never waken.

The time until the bell rang was spent in analysing the students' compositions. Misi didn't hear any of it. He heard only when the Latin master said, 'Well, I must allow that it was a very difficult composition, none of you could do it without mistakes, only Mihály Nyilas . . . But that my class could scribble so much nonsense! . . . I wouldn't have believed it. You made quite a spectacle of yourselves. Fourteen of you failed. Absurd!'

Instead of feeling proud and happy, Misi hung his head and was embarrassed. He felt that this special praise did him no good. Everybody was looking at him with envy. He would have preferred to get a 2 minus; he wanted to be like the others. He hated his name being singled out. He shivered at the thought of it. He didn't want to be singled out, he didn't want to be looked at; he would have liked to be invisible so that nobody could ever see him, so that he could kick his heels and write and draw and play without having to worry about what the others would say. He never asked anybody for anything, he didn't want anything, and they never left him alone. Now they believed that he had written a flawless composition to make them look foolish. And he hadn't. He hadn't realised that he wasn't making any mistakes. He thought he would get a 2 minus like Gimesi and Orczy . . .

When the bell rang the Latin master still hadn't finished analysing all their compositions, but he stopped, and before leaving he called Orczy.

'Orczy! For the next lesson translate what I dictate.'

Orczy, who was already on his feet, picked up a pencil and, bending slightly over the desk, looked expectantly at the teacher. Confident, sincere, shining, blond and cheerful, he began to write as Mr Gyéres dictated.

'The law . . . No, no. The lines of the law must never be crossed . . . You will translate this for the next lesson. No, that's not enough. You have to write an essay about it.'

With that the Latin master took his smart soft hat from the

peg on the wall and, surrounded by clouds of cologne, went away in a good humour.

During break the boys were discussing their marks; there were many passionate, noisy arguments. They all wanted to see Nyilas's work and were amazed that he didn't have a single mistake. Only one hyphen was missing. And it was marked with a 1. The next best compositions, even of the best students, got 2 minus. Even K. Sánta's.

Misi felt weak and sad all day.

He would have preferred to throw away the letter which was hidden in the inside pocket of his jacket. It burned his body. But then he would be stealing Mr János's trust. Mr János had put his trust in him . . . Still, he felt that something wasn't right about it. He thought that the correct thing to do would be either to destroy the letter or to give it back to Mr János. But he didn't dare. He was like a glass marble which somebody had thrown and he knew that he would just have to roll and roll until he came to a stop.

On Wednesday afternoon as he was studying with Doroghy he got up from the table and said to the boy: 'Do this exercise the way we started it.' And with that he left the room.

In the back room the sick mother was sitting in a wheel-chair. Misi passed through without speaking to her. Then came the kitchen; there was nobody there. Beyond that, to the right, he heard Bella humming. Following the sound, he entered a pantry lined with shelves of crockery and foodstuffs.

Bella looked at him with surprise. She was beautiful. The sleeves of her blouse were rolled back quite high and her dazzling white arms shone in the semi-darkness. She wore a long white apron and was putting flour into a big bowl. Her hair was caught up under a kerchief with only two black locks showing. She bent forward and smiled at Misi with her gleaming white teeth. She didn't say anything, just looked at him questioningly. Abashed, Misi said quickly and haltingly at the same time, 'Miss Bella, please, Mr János Török sent this letter to Miss Bella.'

Bella raised her eyebrows and looked surprised and puzzled. 'János Török, who is he?' She took the letter hesitatingly.

'The son of the people I boarded with last year.'

The beautiful girl had already opened the envelope. Then she stopped, wondering whether she should read the letter. But she glanced at it and once she had read the first line she burst out laughing. As she couldn't read very well in the dark she stepped to the doorway, where there was more light, leaving Misi stuck in the pantry behind her.

He saw that the letter was only five or six lines, yet the girl read it for as long as if it had been a whole volume, and the longer she read it the more she laughed. But after a while she suppressed her laughter and began to bite her lips. She was so beautiful, her neck was round and white and smooth like the ivory statues in the museum, and her chin and mouth . . . ! The kerchief tying up her hair was so becoming to her, and her black eyes were so brilliant, they threw off sparks. And her white arms – Misi had never seen such soft white naked arms. He hadn't known that such things existed. Her long coarse linen apron fell forward as she bent and he could see her slim waist and how her blouse rounded out above it. She was so strange and Misi didn't understand why she should be shaped in such a way when boys weren't like that. As he backed into the flour bin in the pantry he started to laugh too and a warmth came over him as if he was in a fairy tale. He felt so strange and he forgot everything, the Latin lessons, the boys, the studying, carrying the water up to the dormitory in the cold, as if everything had happened in order that he should stand in this cold pantry and look and watch how this marvellously beautiful cursed fairy princess from fairyland read the letter over and over again.

'What sort of man is this János Török?' she asked and looked at Misi with a gleam of suppressed laughter.

'He's a big good-for-nothing,' Misi said angrily without thinking.

The girl's mouth widened. She stared at him with surprise. Then she laughed. She leaned against the doorway and laughed with her eyes closed. It was a very strange sound, not a loud cheerful outburst but an inner laughter shaking her from inside. 'Well, you gave him a good recommendation,' she said warmly and looked at the thin mouse-like little boy with affection. 'János Török of Edelény,' she said sarcastically, glancing at the letter. 'He must be a practised roué.'

'He said that you should send him a message. Just one word. *Gladly* . . . or *never.*'

The girl frowned and looked searchingly at the little boy.

He sensed what that look meant: had he or had he not read the letter. He said hurriedly, 'On Monday morning Mr János saw me in the street . . .' Then he remembered that it happened under Mr Gyéres's window and swallowed hard, thinking of all the trouble that came from it. 'And Mr János said I should tell Miss Bella that she should say just one word, either *gladly* or *never.*'

'This János Török of Edelény must be a sly dog!' Bella threw her head back and laughed soundlessly again with her body shaking and her white slender neck shining in the semi-darkness. 'Well, tell him . . .' She raised her finger and waved it from side to side as if conducting a choir. 'Tell him – now don't forget, Misi . . . – it's Misi, isn't it? – my dear little friend Misuka, right? – tell him – don't tell him anything else, just tell him – *gladly never*! You understand? Or you can put it this way – *never gladly.* Just as you please. *Gladly never* or *never gladly.* You understand?'

The little boy understood and was flooded with pure joy and relief. It was so funny that he too began to laugh soundlessly. He was so glad that she made fun of Mr János. That would teach him to write letters!

They exchanged glances in the semi-darkness of the pantry like two children plotting a practical joke.

Misi had never felt so happy, proud and marvellous.

At that instant Bella quickly hid the letter in her bodice and, motioning to him to be quiet, stepped out into the kitchen. Someone was coming. Misi was horrified to realise that it was

Miss Viola, the eldest daughter, the terror of them all. There was such visible fear and confusion on Bella's beautiful face that he was afraid to step out of the pantry. He himself didn't know why but he didn't dare to reveal that he was there.

'All these dishes are still unwashed?' shouted the oldest sister. 'This is really too much!'

'Why is it too much?' asked Bella sharply.

'It's too much because it's too much,' Miss Viola rebuked her in an even sharper voice. 'It's too much that you don't want to do any work.'

'I was getting flour from the pantry.'

'Yes, of course, that is the important thing, getting the flour. You're going to make the bread in the evening and you get the flour now? What kind of logic is that? The dishes stand here unwashed all day, the water grows cold, it can't be used again, and you're playing in the pantry getting flour from the bin . . . It's easy to get flour when you have a bin full of it.'

'Well it has to be done too.'

'But not now. Later on when there is time . . .' A moment later the spinsterish sister snapped again. 'I just don't know what's going on here, you're all playing the fool, amusing yourselves, doing whatever comes into your head. But work? None of you is interested in serious work. I don't know what will become of us. If I rent that plot of land, do I rent it for myself? Why is it that nobody wants to work here?'

'I won't ruin my hands,' Bella countered nervously.

'Your hands!' Viola was horrified. 'What do you think your hands are for? You won't work?! You aren't going to ruin them? Of course you will. If I ruined my hands you will ruin yours too. The little princess is afraid to put her delicate soft fingers into the soapy water . . . You won't worry about them when they are black and coarse and hopelessly ruined like mine . . . I'm telling you once and for all, I'm warning you that I've had enough of going hungry and I'm not going to leave myself without a pig for the winter for anybody's sake. I've decided to rent this piece of land and that's the end of it.

I've made my decision, I'm resolved, and whatever I take into my head will happen. There won't be ten forints to waste on Japanese fans, little princess. There won't be eighty kreutzers to throw onto the rubbish heap . . . I was two weeks late with the rent for the land because of you. I could have put down the ten forints if you hadn't stolen from it. Once it was changed, the coins went everywhere. Well, I won't allow it to happen again. Now I have ten *pengő* in my hand again and I'm going to take it to the farmer right away and pay it down. In the spring I will go and turn up the soil. Afterwards we will plant and I will work there all summer, and the little princess will be here washing dishes, yes, and cooking, yes, and shopping, yes, yes. She will go to the market, indeed she will. If I could go to the market so can others . . . Others who are stronger and can carry heavy loads more easily. Yes. Because I can't tear myself into a hundred pieces. Because it's not possible to hoe the land with one hand and carry baskets from the market with the other, with a third hand stirring the pot and a fourth hand darning a hole in the princess's stocking.'

Misi stood in the pantry. He would have liked to be out of there. The longer he delayed it the more awkward it was. What would be the end of it? What if this spinster stepped into the pantry and saw him there? He would have to sink into the earth! So he took a deep breath and stepped out into the kitchen.

Miss Viola practically turned into a pillar of salt.

Bella clapped her hands together and said, 'Oh, my Lord Jesus, I quite forgot about you!' She turned towards her sister. 'He just came out to ask me for some hot water to melt some gum arabic and I left him in the pantry. I forgot all about him.' She started to laugh loudly and winked at Misi.

This helped him to recover from his confusion and he was grateful to Miss Bella for the lie. He felt that they were partners in crime and allies for life.

Miss Viola looked at the boy suspiciously. She wanted to ask him why he had hidden in the pantry but then said, 'Well, if you heard it anyway, let you be the judge. You tell me, my dear Nyilas, am I not right?' And she became quite voluble, telling him her plans for the next year, that she was going to grow corn and beside it other vegetables, cabbages and carrots and parsnips and everything that was needed in the kitchen, but the other two girls must take charge of the cooking and housekeeping. 'Am I not doing the right thing? Don't I sacrifice myself? Now we have to scramble for money and run to the market even for a sprig of parsley. If I have the land we will have sacks full of carrots and won't have to pay for them. Am I not right?'

'You are right, Miss Viola,' said Misi, 'but please don't grow carrots, they taste terrible. They are the most terrible food. Last autumn the Töröks bought two or three sacks of carrots and they gave me goose pimples. I hate them. I can eat them raw if I have to, but creamed carrot mash is the most horrible thing there is.'

Bella burst out in nervous, choking, happy laughter. The joke was on her sister.

The poor spinster looked from one to the other not knowing what to make of it. 'Well, I've had enough of you as well,' she said with her habitual rough sincerity. 'You two could be tied to the same bush. Well, Misi, you just go and study with your pupil. Go and eat gum arabic if you don't like carrots.'

Bella laughed even louder. The sound of it made Misi happy, but he pressed his lips together and ducked his head to hide his smile, and quickly left the kitchen.

The mother sitting in her wheelchair greeted him with her big dark eyes. This look took away his desire to laugh. He was very much afraid of this silent, pale woman, who sometimes seemed as if she wasn't alive any more and rarely looked at anybody. She looked out but she was sunken into herself. Now Misi sensed that her eyes were following him into the other room and even as he closed the door behind him and sat down at the table next to Alex, he felt her eyes stabbing into him, so much that he had to turn around to assure himself that she wasn't there but beyond the wall in the other room.

Doroghy had a big surprise waiting for him. He hadn't finished the exercise but sat above it and gazed into space, playing with his pen. 'Why didn't you finish it?' Misi asked him despairingly.

Alex replied with the innocence of an angel. 'I couldn't decide whether you have to start multiplying with the last number or the first one.'

Misi tore his hair. 'Oh my God, this is terrible. How often have I told you that it makes no difference. Don't you understand? It makes no difference. The only difference is that if you start multiplying from the right, then you write the result one column ahead. If you start multiplying from the left, then you write the result one column behind.'

'All right, then where do you want me to start, from the right or the left?'

'I just told you, it makes no difference.'

'If it's all the same, then where should I start?'

'All right, start from the right.'

'That's all I wanted to know. You're getting to be like Viola, always quarrelling.'

Misi opened his eyes wide and watched how Alex was multiplying. He thought that Alex should resemble Bella, and was quite sad to see that he looked like Viola. That he should have to torture himself with such people! He felt that his struggles with Alex were totally pointless, totally hopeless. He could see that no matter how hard he tried to teach him, Alex would fail, and there would be nothing but disgrace at the end of it.

While they were doing their Latin prep Bella came in. Though she was banned from the room she came in cheerfully and casually as though it was the most natural thing in the world. She didn't say anything for some time, just shifted things about in the cupboard as if she was paying no attention to them, then she stepped suddenly to the table, stood beside Misi and reached for Alex's exercise book.

Alex tried to grab it back. 'Hey!'

Bella lifted the book high in the air. 'I won't eat it.'

'Give it back.'

'Oh, how secretive you are!' And while holding it up in the air out of Alex's reach, she opened the exercise book. 'You got a 4?' She grimaced. 'A 4!'

Alex snatched the exercise book, which got a bit creased. 'Now how am I going to hand it to the Latin master?' he whined. 'You crumpled it.'

'First of all, it was you who crumpled it when you grabbed it. Secondly, however crumpled or smooth it is, you got a 4. You should be ashamed of yourself.'

'It's no shame. It was a very difficult exercise. Fourteen boys failed, and nobody had a better mark than 2 minus.'

'Not even Nyilas?'

'Well, he got a 1, I forgot.'

Bella laughed. 'You forgot? Good you remembered. Oh, you . . .' Stretching her arm past Misi she pushed her brother's head and as she drew back her arm, she gently stroked Misi's face.

Misi reddened and bowed his head and started to tremble. He sensed that she hadn't touched him by accident and that she wanted to express some fine and secret gratitude, affection, friendship.

'Get out of the room,' said Alex.

Bella laughed. 'Oh you toad.'

'I will tell on you that you were in the room again disturbing us, not letting me study.'

Bella looked at him thoughtfully, then laughed. 'Listen, Alex, I am going to tell you something. Let's make peace . . . You won't tell on me and I won't tell on you.'

Alex looked at her out of the corner of his eye.

'I know a few things about the young gentleman that I didn't tell. Like who smoked with the landlord's son.'

Alex stuck out his lower lip in a hostile manner.

'It happened a week ago. I would have had lots of opportunities to talk about it – isn't that so? Are we silent? And there are several other little stories . . . The pantry, and the button, you remember? . . . Well, do we make peace?' And she reached out her hand towards Alex. Once more she passed her arm in front of Misi and put her hand on their textbooks and notebooks. Her hand was so round and so white. She had a thin gold ring on one of her fingers, with a very tiny blue stone in it, the colour of forget-me-nots. Misi trembled, wondering whether she might stroke his face again.

'All right,' Alex mumbled and slapped her hand.

She laughed but didn't move; she left her hand in front of them. The sleeves of her blue blouse were not rolled back to her shoulder now, as in the pantry, but Misi sensed her lovely white arms and was afraid that she would move and bend her arms and embrace him.

'Do we have peace?'

'All right, if you stop being cheeky I won't say anything,' said Alex.

'Well, you little hamster, give me your paw.'

Alex stuck out his tongue and slapped her hand quickly, afraid that she was planning to trick him. She seized his grubby paw and it remained in the hollow of her white, smooth hand.

'Oofff – a pig's paw!' exclaimed Bella, laughing. 'There is no need for Viola to buy a pig, we have one right here.' She winked at Misi.

Misi laughed out loud. Oh, he liked that! It was such an unexpected and fitting remark and the reference to the conversation in the kitchen tickled him.

'All right, go on studying,' said Bella. 'As far as I am concerned you can bring home sixteen fail marks.' With that she shook her brother's hand, not in a manly way, palm against palm, but shaking it by the wrist.

Misi didn't dare to look at the girl leaning forward on the table right in front of him: every bit of her body in her soft dress was so strange, so alien; his right cheek which was next to her burned as if it was near a fire.

That afternoon's study wasn't worth a kreutzer. He had a profound sense that he was wasting his time with Alex. He was so confused, so upset, that he was nearly late for the old blind gentleman. He had to run.

As he was about to pass through the gate of the yellow house, Mr János suddenly appeared in front of him, barring his way.

'Well, which is it? Fire or water?'

First Misi couldn't think what he was talking about but when he remembered he gained courage and said in a clear loud voice. 'Yes!'

'Well, then, what did she say?'

'She said *gladly never.*'

'You seem to be confused, my boy.'

'No, I'm not. That's what she said. She said either that or *never gladly.*'

'Oh, you imbecile! You forgot. You don't know!'

'I do know. She said, tell him *gladly never* or *never gladly*, you can put it either way. That's what she said.'

'It's impossible!'

'It's the truth.'

'On your word?'

Misi would have liked to run because the clock was striking five.

'Come on, do you dare to swear to it?'

'Yes, but I don't like to swear about foolish things.'

'That's foolishness to you?' Mr János laughed. 'You rascal, I'll gobble you up!' He tried to press his thumb down on the boy's cap and give it a painful twist, but Misi ran away, so for once the trick didn't succeed.

In Misi's hectic life his daily reading aloud had become his hour of peace and calm. He enjoyed timing his arrival to the striking of the clocks; he liked sitting in the wicker armchair, finding everything clean and in order: the newspapers were always waiting for him on the table, in a neat pile, and it felt good to know that he was doing honest work. By then he read so clearly, so smoothly, that the blind old gentleman no longer had to ask, 'What was that?'

It was a nice place, that warm wooden cottage, and the ruddy-faced, white-haired old man was so kindly and so reliable, he never said a word to startle him . . .

When he returned to the dormitory it was filled with the smell of toast.

The boys were sitting around the stove listening to Mr Nagy, who was talking about student life in the old days. Misi pricked up his ears; he didn't want to miss a word.

'. . . Do you know why you are still called *lance boys*? Because in the old days the younger students used to carry the meal in cauldrons on long lances, poles, resting on their shoulders. You didn't just wait for the bell and run to the dining hall to eat at a well-laid table with a cloth and white porcelain plates.'

'You had stoneware plates and wooden spoons,' interjected Mr Lisznyai.

'The food was sent to the school by the parents, and it was eaten right here in the dormitory. Imagine, we sit here, the seven of us, and each day of the week one of the parents would send a loaf of bread and a potful of food. Beans or cabbage or noodles with cottage cheese – but not three-course meals like we have now, just a good potful. And the boys sat around it and everyone took his earthenware plate and wooden spoon and his pocket knife, and that's how they ate.'

'And they ate the same thing in the evening?'

'If there was any left. If not, they swallowed.'

'And that little potful had to be carried in a cauldron on poles?'

'No, that was something else. Families who lived far away couldn't send food every week, they had neither post nor trains in those days, so when a farmer sent his son to the city the young man arrived in an oxcart bringing with him ten bushels of wheat, peas, lentils, ham, and they hired a cook who cooked one dish every day. They called it *semper*, which as you know is Latin for always.'

'That's interesting,' commented Böszörményi.

'Well, you wouldn't find it so interesting,' said Mr Nagy. 'Because boys who were neither rich nor good students got nothing from the college but a bed. Some kind-hearted towns- folk took turns sending them a potful of porridge, that was all.'

This caused great hilarity.

'That's how collecting came about. In November the students went from house to house begging for food.'

'Boy, that was a rotten life!'

'Well, I'm sure in those days the townsfolk gave more willingly. They were proud of the students, who had choirs and gave concerts for them and danced with the young wives and daughters. And if there was a fire, they razed the houses. What are you laughing at? Don't think that they had firemen with water wagons to put out a fire. They went with beams and staves – you can still see them in the main library – and beat down the roofs of the neighbouring houses so they couldn't catch fire.'

'That's ridiculous!'

'Don't you know that Debrecen never had water? Do you have any idea how many years they've been drilling that artesian well? They're down to eight hundred and seventy metres and they still have no water. What they have is rock which breaks every drill. That's why they say of our city on the plain that Debrecen too has mountains, only they're under the ground.'

Misi laughed. He had heard that the previous year at the Töröks' but thought it was just a joke.

'The water for cooking had to be brought in barrels. In those days you had to flatter not the masters but the water women. You flattered them by giving them a whole big ham every year.'

As they sat in the good, warm, comfortable room it was a marvellous thing to listen to Mr Nagy and try to imagine what it was like in the old days.

'And how did they study?'

'The boys made their own instruments for maths and their own equipment for chemistry. They made their own drypoint needles for engravings – they did more engraving than drawing in those days.'

'It was a lovely art,' said Mr Lisznyai.

Then the bell rang for supper, which Misi had dreaded for

some time, as he so enjoyed listening. He was very upset that he hadn't heard all of it, that he had just arrived for the end of the talk. He would have liked always to be with the boys and listen to good talk.

It was a very good supper: noodles with cottage cheese made from ewe's milk. They filled their bellies. When it was over Mihály Sándor put in front of Misi a piece of paper with numbers.

'Nyilas! Look at this. Did your numbers come up?'

Misi stared at the five numbers on the paper. He reached in his pocket for his purse, opened it to take out the lottery ticket and got so scared that his heart stopped. The ticket wasn't there.

He searched for it among the coins but he couldn't find it. He moved his hands nervously, searching his pockets, while his eyes remained fixed on the piece of paper. He read the five numbers:

17, 85, 39, 73, 45.

Everybody stood up so he stood up too and put his purse in his pocket.

Mihály Sándor nudged him. 'Well, did any of your numbers come up?'

Misi was unable to speak.

Luckily as all the boys were leaving he managed to get away from Mihály Sándor and ran to be alone. He couldn't bear to be with the others. He thought he would choke among his cheerful laughing comrades. He ran to the little courtyard, where there was nobody.

Later he went up to the second floor but didn't dare to enter the dormitory. He hid in the corridor; his whole body was shaking.

He wasn't absolutely certain that these were Mr Pósalaky's numbers, but they seemed so frighteningly familiar!

VII

It is amazing how carefree and cheerful people can be around a suffering person. Is life worth living if the world takes so little account of heartache?

M ISI TOSSED ABOUT all night, unable to sleep. If he dozed off for a moment he was stung awake again by his restless conscience. He couldn't imagine what had happened to the lottery ticket. The morning found him dazed, exhausted; he felt he was the unluckiest person in the world. He could hardly move. Only the fresh ice-cold water in the wash-basin revived him a little.

Geography was not taught in their usual classroom but in the natural sciences room on the second floor, so even though Misi arrived a couple of minutes after the bell rang, he was still ahead of the master. The rest of the class was already there, buzzing away merrily. He sat down in his place on the front bench and, without making a sound, cowered there hoping that no one would notice him. He had got thin from the agonies of the night and was as pale as mould. How could he think of the lesson when he was half dead? He hardly knew what books he had brought with him.

Sitting on top of the desk with his back to the masters' room, facing the class, Orczy was giving a command perform-ance, impersonating the geography master. The boys watched him open-mouthed and laughed quietly at every word.

'You are a manly little fella . . .' said Orczy, mimicking the old man, whose nickname was Nazo and who was the butt of the whole school. Everybody jeered at him and mocked him and all the students learned to imitate his way of speaking, but not as well as Orczy, who bent his head sideways and managed to speak in a strange guttural voice while also blinking his eyelashes just like the old man. 'You are a manly little fella, my dear boy.'

There was a chorus of laughter and some of the other boys also tried to speak like Nazo. Many of them could not actually hear Orczy, but they saw how he imitated the geography master's bearing and gestures, and it was a funny and brave thing to do, because the old man could have come in at any moment.

Then Orczy started to mock one of Nazo's well-known anecdotes. As the tutor of a young count he had travelled in Egypt, and in every class he managed to mention the mysterious country of the Nile. 'When I was travelling in Egypt,' Orczy said in the old man's guttural voice, 'I saw two big frightful birds on top of a crocodile.' Orczy's act brought the house down. 'Well, the crocodile birds opened their beaks, so I picked up my gun, which had only one bullet, and blinded them both.'

The boys were shrieking. Not wishing to miss a word in spite of the noise they were making, the students sitting near the front bent forward, while the ones farther back stretched themselves right over the benches to get nearer to Orczy. So Orczy lowered his voice but his gestures became wilder. 'Well, the bullet went into the crocodile bird's right eye. From there it jumped over to the other crocodile bird's left eye. From there it ricocheted back to the first crocodile bird's left eye, and from there it ricocheted to the other bird's right eye. So, my dear son, I blinded both birds!'

The boys laughed so hard it was a wonder that they didn't burst, and those in the back rows came forward to crowd around Orczy. Then he dropped Egypt and said cantankerously, still imitating the old geography master, 'Oh, my dear sons, you are impudent fellas, pushing your way forward. What impudence!'

This made the biggest impact, because impudence was the

old geography master's favourite word. He never took a class without saying it several times.

'Sir, did you dream that story about the crocodile birds?' asked a boy from the back.

Orczy swooped down on him with his voice. 'You impudent fella . . . You don't belong back there among honest people. Come up here and stand beside me.'

Even Misi had to laugh at that. He leaned backward on his bench, opened his mouth, closed his eyes, threw his head back and laughed for a long time, half-asleep.

In the meantime the little old geography master came in and shuffled to the platform. All the boys were in their places in an instant, sitting up straight with their heads high and their mouths closed, while Misi sat as before, laughing with his head back, his eyes closed and his mouth open. He was vaguely aware of some stirring in the room but he was so exhausted from tossing and crying all night, so weak from his empty belly hurting, that he remained as he was, laughing. Then there was such quiet that even he came to himself and rubbed his face, scratched his head and his neck and yawned so hard that tears came to his eyes.

Then he heard the master's voice – the real one this time – saying, 'Mihály Nyilas'.

Misi thought that lightning had struck beside him. He didn't want to get up; it was impossible. He remained seated for so long that the whole class became restless and stared at him. Finally he stood up, pale and haggard, and gave the master a piercing look with his black eyes. He scowled and his hard, dark eyebrows were aimed stubbornly at the old man like arrows drawn.

The procedure was that the student who was called had to walk up to the blackboard, where they now had the map of France, and answer the master's questions, but Misi didn't move, he just stared at the old master with hatred. His neighbours Orczy and Gimesi looked at him, uncomprehending, alarmed, wondering what he was doing. After a while

Gimesi stood up to give him room to pass, so with wavering
steps Misi walked up to the blackboard, practically bumping
into the map of France.

'Well, my dear boy, what was the lesson for today?'

Misi was silent. He closed his eyes and the world turned
around. Then he forced his eyes open again so that he
wouldn't fall. He looked at the map. He could vaguely see the
image of France spread out like a colourful kerchief with its
lacy edges floating in the sea and brown lines of mountains
flowing down to the Mediterranean.

'Well, let us see, now, France!' the master said softly. 'What
kind of country is France? As you see, it shows you two faces.
In the east it is mostly mountains; in the west it is mostly
plains . . . And in the south, what do we have in the south?
What do they call that thick mountain range there?'

The class watched tensely. Nobody understood Nyilas, who
stood there like a deaf-mute, not saying a word. He might
have spoken before but not now; he resolved not to open his
mouth. Slowly he began to remember the last class, because
although he hadn't paid much attention then either, he
recognised the Pyrenees on the map and recalled the
Roncesvalles Pass. 'Roncesvalles, Roncesvalles,' he kept saying
to himself.

'These mountains completely cut off France from Spain.
There is only one place where you can pass through them.
What do they call that pass? . . . The Ron . . . The Ron . . .
The Roncesvalles Pass.'

'Roncesvalles, it's Roncesvalles,' said Misi to himself.

The little old teacher, who had shiny red skin and white
hair and was as shrunken as if he had been dried out in life's
oven, got angry suddenly, as was his custom. 'Ah, my dear
boy, you are an impudent fella!' Then he changed his mind,
taking account of who was standing in front of him, a boy
from the first bench, the second-best student in the class. So
he regretted his outburst and, wishing to make up for it, got
up from his chair, trotted to the map and began to explain the
whole lesson word for word as he had given it in the previous

day's class. He talked for about a quarter of an hour, while Misi said the place-names to himself before the old man managed to get them out. The Jura Mountains, the plains of the Côte d'Or and Langres – Misi remembered them all. But he stubbornly pressed his lips together; even if they beat him to death, he wouldn't say a word.

'Here is Aurignac,' the little old man continued, 'where in our own day, in 1852, a man working on the road came upon a graveyard from prehistoric times. They found in that graveyard, you know, not only human bones but the skeletons of extinct animals from the beginning of time – cave bears, hyenas, lions, mammoths, the woolly rhinoceros . . . And that proves that men were around even then . . .'

Misi looked at him with wonder. The geography master had already talked about Neanderthal Man but the story had never struck him so much as it did today. The old master said 'in our own day, in 1852' so naturally, as if it had been last year, as if they had both been alive at that time, though it was thirty years before Misi was born. It made prehistoric times seem closer to him and suddenly he fancied that he could see the obscure image of a prehistoric man going into his cave where there was already a bear, a lion and a mammoth.

But how could the mammoth get into the cave?

Misi's face seemed to open and there was a flash of awareness and attention in his eyes which inspired the old teacher, who leaned closer and went on talking to him. 'Of course all this was in prehistoric times. History is not familiar with this way of life. But then history started only the day before yesterday. The Egyptians built the Pyramids only four to five thousand years ago, but they found at – where was that place? – near Düsseldorf – ahhh, how often we've said it . . .'

The old man was struggling painfully with his memory, so Misi blurted out, 'the Neanderthal'.

'That's it, that's it, yes!' said Nazo, and touched the little boy's shoulder with his thin small hand. 'They found the skull of Neanderthal Man in the diluvial strata, which means that he lived two to three hundred thousand years ago. Now . . . If this skull is three hundred thousand years old – it may be more, but let's just say three hundred thousand years old – how many generations later came the people who carried the stones to the Pyramids? So we mustn't use lightly such words as "ancient times" and "a long time ago" . . . Whatever happened in your childhood was a long time ago to you but to me it was just yesterday, because when you were born I had already been a teacher for thirty years . . . And what was a long time ago to me is the present in the history of the Hungarian nation, since the Hungarian state has been here for a thousand years . . . And to look at it from the point of view of history, Árpád,[1] who brought the Hungarians to the Carpathian valley, was a long time ago for us, but it wasn't that long ago if you think of the Peloponnesian Wars or the building of Babylon. And that's where history begins. The whole story is only four to five thousand years. That's all we can trace back with the help of written or carved inscriptions. And yet there is the Florida peninsula, a coral formation which according to the estimates of Agassiz began to take shape one hundred and thirty-five thousand years ago. And the human jaw found in it is about ten thousand years old, judging by how deep it lay in the coral. That jaw is already the fully formed human jaw just like the one we have today. So human beings were complete ten thousand years ago; only their circumstances were different. Your Neanderthal skull, that is something else, that is still close to the ape's head . . . Think of what a difference it makes whether you have three hundred forints or just three forints. Well, that is how little we know of the history of man – three forints' worth.'

Down in the class there was laughter and buzzing and pushing, but Misi was mesmerised. His eyes brightened up as he listened to the little old man, whose soft, pink, dried-out skin, with scattered blue veins showing, clung gently to the bones of his forehead. His hands, too, were weak and trembling. After all this talking he was exhausted and had to sit down. They said of him that he was a friend of János Arany.[2]

As Misi looked at the old man he thought of the legendary poet; when János Arany shook old Nazo's hand, Nazo was still young Nazo.

The teacher shuffled back to his seat with bent head and sat down, looking into space, resting.

A boy stood up in the middle of the class.

'Sir.'

Startled, the old man looked up. 'What . . . what is it?' He put his hand to one of his big floppy ears shaped like a bat's wings, because he was hard of hearing. 'What do you want?'

'Sir, you didn't note the absentees.'

'What?'

'You didn't record the absentees' names in the class register,' shouted the boy as loudly as he could.

The old gentleman groped for the class register, drew it towards him with a trembling hand and opened it. He did this obediently like a man who knew that he must abide by the rules, only he didn't have the strength for them. He picked up his pen to write. 'What day is it today?'

'Thursday,' the boys roared in unison.

The master wrote everything that was necessary in his shaky handwriting and continued with bowed head:

'This much is beyond doubt: the human race had a history of which we have no trace, either in writing or in legends. Many hundreds of thousands of years had to pass before human beings, the last important members of the animal world, could develop an intellect to leave lasting marks of their existence . . . The first certain marks are those stone and bone implements which manifestly were made by human hands, and crude clay dishes and trinkets which were evidently baked not in ovens but over open fires . . . And there are the ancient burial grounds we talked about earlier. These ancient burial grounds teach us two things with absolute certainty: that the survival instinct and morality are inborn in people and they are just as much part of our biological nature as they are part of the nature of bees and ants. Moral instincts precede human beings, let alone human laws, which means that moral laws are an older and stronger basis of our existence than human laws.'

He propped his head on his hand and for a long time there was a kind of quiet buzz in the classroom which he didn't even notice. He had completely forgotten Misi, France, the class; he was inside his own thoughts, because he was working on a study of the prehistory of Debrecen.

'There are no clear-cut divisions between different periods of Man's existence. People in Debrecen still use implements from the Stone Age. The shepherds of the Great Plain still use implements made from a sheep's legbone.' He described a few of them but the boys were busy with private matters, exchanging buttons, carrying on quiet conversations, looking at each other's written compositions or preparing themselves for the next class, which was mathematics.

'You've got to be careful about using ancient objects to divide ages. In the islands of Malaya they still use stone and bone implements, though there are industrial products cheaply available. The razor, for instance, is universal now, yet I myself observed in Egypt (there was whispering and shuffling about) that the barbers in the public baths shaved their clients not with razors but with obsidian stone knives, using dolomite mud as shaving cream (quiet guffawing from the class). That kind of obsidian stone knife can be found also in Hungary, not far from Debrecen. In the Kovács Valley, which they call the Cursed Earth . . .'

'My parents have land there,' shouted one of the boys. 'It's a place where . . .'

The master tried to continue but another boy stood up and shouted, 'Please, sir . . .'

'What? What is it?' asked the old man, and again he cupped his hand behind his ear.

'Please, sir, Lajos Ondodi says that his parents have land in the Cursed Earth.'

The old man waved his hand impatiently to make the boy sit down. 'When they built the road there it loosened the soil and the wind licked all the sand off a hillside . . .'

There was such hilarity that he couldn't be heard. Several students started shouting: 'Who licked what off? What did they lick off?'

'What? What is it?' asked the old master, and again cupped his large ear in his hand, bending it forward comically. But no one responded; they just shook with laughter. The old man broke his chain of thought to say, 'Yes, it's funny, the origin of the name Cursed Earth. It was common grazing land but in the eighteen-fifties the city council divided it up and sold it. The poor people of Debrecen who were left without land to graze their animals cursed the land and cursed the people who bought it. So that is why it is called the Cursed Earth.'

The master went on talking as if he were speaking to his intellectual equals but the boys weren't interested. Those who listened were only looking for opportunities to make fun of him. One of them stood up and his strong clear voice rose above the general hubbub. 'Please, sir, we didn't understand *who did the licking.*'

The old man stared and again he got angry very suddenly. He got up and shrieked at the boy, 'You are an impudent fella, my boy, an impudent fella. You don't belong among honest people. Come up here and stand beside me.'

The whole class bowed its head and there was a storm of laughter. Only Orczy, sitting on the front bench, remained serious and shook his head with solemn disapproval.

The old teacher became confused. He understood that the boys didn't care about what he wanted to say, and he fell silent. But then, collecting himself, he turned to Misi, who was still standing by the map of France, and continued to explain to him how the wind blowing away the sand uncovered objects from the Stone Age. 'This proves that the Debrecen area was inhabited by human beings even in the Neolithic period.'

Misi was happy that the geography master was talking only to him. He was deeply moved and understood everything he heard, and feeling that he was absorbing profound and lasting knowledge, his soul reached out with gratitude towards the little old man.

Orczy stood up. 'Excuse me, sir, may I ask a question?'

'Yes, what?' asked the master. He cupped his ear again and twisted his mouth. His big nose, which stuck out from his face, was so thin that the sunlight coming through the window made it seem almost transparent.

'Please, sir, how many years before Christ did we have the Stone Age in Debrecen?'

'How many years before Christ?' sighed the geography master. 'We're talking about the Neolithic Age – I am unaware of any evidence that anything has been found in our country from the earlier Palaeolithic Age. The Neolithic Age was already the age of ground and polished stone weapons and implements.'

'Yes, sir, but excuse me, was the Neolithic Age before Christ?'

The teacher raised his arm. 'Where was Christ then! Christ was here only yesterday! We had passed through the Stone Age, the Bronze Age, the Copper Age, and we were in the Iron Age by the time Christ was born. Man is such a backward creature that just to make a change in the way he chiselled a stone implement took him thousands of years. How then can we talk about dates, my dear boy?'

He took a bunch of keys from his pocket and opened a drawer in the desk.

'Here is this piece of stone . . . It's a hammer broken in two. It broke where the hole is; that's where the handle fitted in. This is the head. That is such a beautiful finely chiselled piece that it must be from the Neolithic Age. So it is at most three or four thousand years old. But how far was this from the beginning of the Stone Age, when they just worked with pieces of stone more or less as they found them? . . . There is at least a hundred thousand years between the two. We can think of the Stone Age as lasting a hundred or a hundred and fifty or perhaps two hundred thousand years.'

'Before or after Christ?' asked Orczy stubbornly.

The teacher grew red in his sudden anger. 'You are an idiot, my dear boy, just like your father before you. Come, stand here beside me.'

Briskly and obligingly Orczy hurried up to the platform, followed by the laughter of the other schoolboys. He motioned to them gravely that they should leave off laughing, that it was no time for merriment.

'Look at this stone. Do you see it?'

'Yes, sir.'

'Do you observe how fine and smooth it is? This was ground and polished with some other implement. Well, just to have an idea of historical time, think of this. So little time has passed from the birth of Christ to our own day that in the Stone Age that length of time wasn't sufficient for people even to think of shaping a stone. Here is another piece of stone with a hole in it so small that a man could only have put his finger in it and used it to chisel stone knives. The hole was useful because it gave him a stronger grip on the stone. The time it took for people to think of making this tiny hole in a stone was twenty times more than the time that has passed from the birth of Christ until now. So your question makes absolutely no sense. If I think of two or three thousand years I'm not thinking of it from the birth of Christ, nor from today's date in the class register, but . . .'

'From the day of the Creation,' interrupted Orczy.

'From your Granddad's death!' shouted the teacher. 'What do I count it from?' he asked, turning to Misi, who still stood in front of the map of France, listening attentively.

'Not from any particular date, just approximately,' said Misi. 'We can only guess,' he added with a little shrug.

'Right!' cried the teacher, and raised his arms. 'We can only guess, all the numbers and all the dates we say can only be approximate . . . All right, Orczy, you may go back to your seat.'

Offended and very much annoyed, Orczy bit his lips. Before he sat down he looked back and, seeing that the master wasn't looking, he made a face and cupped his ear with his hand. This produced a ripple of laughter.

The bell rang.

'Very good, my dear boy,' the master said to Misi. 'You may go.' He took his notebook from his pocket, licked the two-centimetre pencil attached to it and marked a big 1 beside Mihály Nyilas's name. Imre Barta stood up to watch it.

As soon as the master left pandemonium broke loose.

'That's really outrageous,' said Feri Szegedi. 'Misi didn't say a single word and he still got a 1. I could have recited the whole lesson and Nazo would still have given me a 3. That old fool should be kicked by God's horse.'

Some of the boys laughed but most of them were already on their way out, making their way downstairs to their own classroom.

Szegedi meant to insult Misi with his remark and gave him a sidelong glance. Misi heard him but didn't argue; in his heart he thought Szegedi was right, though he knew the master had sensed that he was paying attention and understood.

Tannenbaum came to Misi's defence. 'Yes, Misi acquitted himself well. He may not have known today's lesson, but he said that . . . what d'you call it? . . .' Tannenbaum put down his things, opened his geography text where he had marked it on the map, and wrote 'Neanderthal' in his exercise book with a pencil.

'All Misi did was shrug his shoulders!' shouted Szegedi.

Gimesi turned into a red-hot pepper. 'If you shrug you get a 4 and fail. If Nyilas shrugs he gets the best mark. That's the way of the world.'

'You honour students stick together,' screamed Szegedi, and spat.

Gimesi, who already had his books under his arm, ran at him like a little dog, or rather like a little goat, with head down, and pushed Szegedi so hard that he fell against the master's desk. Then they started to punch each other. Gimesi's books flew in all directions and he scratched Szegedi with his small white hands. Szegedi hammered Gimesi's head with his fists and, as Gimesi's hair was always close-cropped, the pounding made a big noise. However, it was well known that Gimesi had a thick skull and this didn't hurt him. But he succeeded in scratching Szegedi so badly that his face was bleeding. Then Imre Barta leaped over the benches and separated them. 'Hey, hey, hey!'

'You'll pay for this, you'll see,' shouted Szegedi, spraying blood and saliva from his mouth. 'Misi, you just come to our part of town!'

Misi remembered that Szegedi lived not far from his pupil. 'What did I do?' he asked, and began to cry.

'If I can grab that dirty pig's ear I'm going to pull it off,' shouted Gimesi, still full of his victory, and picked up his books.

'Neanderthal, Neanderthal, Neanderthal,' Tannenbaum kept repeating.

Gimesi was first to enter the downstairs classroom, with Tannenbaum at his side; lately they had become good friends. Misi dragged himself after them, silent and dejected.

When they came in, one of the boys shouted, 'Bravo Gimesi!' There followed a whole outburst of hurrahs. 'Long live Little Spittle!' they cried. 'Hurrah!' Nobody knew why Gimesi had got so angry, but there was no question that he had attacked a boy bigger than himself and emerged the undisputed victor.

'Stop fooling!' said Gimesi, but he smiled. He was pleased by the ovation, though he didn't like to be called Little Spittle. At first they had called him Tom Thumb and he had protested, objecting that the people of his village in Transylvania had a different name for Tom Thumb. Then he had said a name that sounded like Little Spittle, which the boys adopted enthusiastically, so he ended up worse off.

Misi was worried about Latin class. If Mr Gyéres called him up, he wouldn't escape as easily as in geography. When Orczy and Mihály Sándor started whispering together, he suspected that they were plotting against him, and he was right, because afterwards Orczy came to him and asked in a very determined voice, 'Misi, did your numbers win in the lottery?'

Misi bowed his head and said nothing.

'You can tell me. Our old cook, who is a real expert, buys a ticket for six kreutzers every week, and we fret about it together, wondering whether she has won or not. So I'm an expert on the lottery, it's no use lying to me, I see through you as if you were made of glass.'

The bell rang and the Latin master came in. The boys were still standing in little groups, discussing the fight in the natural sciences classroom, and no one was in his place. Mr Gyéres stopped and faced them. He had his gloves in his hand and flicked them irritably, as if to say, What are you lot up to? What's happening? . . . They all scrambled to their seats.

The master went up to the platform, sat down at the desk and opened the class register. 'Is this your first class today?'

'No, no, sir . . . we had geography, sir!' came from all parts of the room.

'Are you sure?'

Although it wasn't his job to report, Orczy jumped up and said loud and clear: 'Excuse me, sir . . .' He managed to grab all the attention; some of the boys protested, but Gyéres signalled them to be quiet and looked at Orczy.

'We had geography, sir.'

'Didn't the master make a note of it in the class register?'

'He wrote it in. I saw it.'

Mr Gyéres flipped over the page for that day in the register. Orczy hurried up to the platform and, bowing to ask permission, turned the pages himself to look for the geography master's note. He found it two pages further on.

Mr Gyéres smiled, thanked Orczy for his help and motioned him back to his seat, but couldn't resist making a joke at his colleague's expense. 'I suppose your geography master thinks that it won't matter a bean in a hundred years time.'

This remark was greeted with a tremendous uproar, but Orczy managed to outshout them all: 'In a hundred thousand years time!'

This was so strange that Mr Gyéres became curious. 'What do you mean?'

Orczy jumped up. 'Please, sir, our geography master counts humanity's . . . humanity's whatsit . . . in hundreds of thousands of years . . . the stone implements changed only once in a hundred thousand years. It took people a hundred thousand years to think of polishing them.'

Mr Gyéres tilted his chair backwards and looked at Orczy. The muscles in his face kept dancing around as he tried to restrain his laughter. Surprised by Orczy's sharp remark, he only said. 'Very good. Excellent.'

He waved Orczy back to his seat, flicked his hand again to order silence and called up Szent, a boy on the very last bench who never did anything but make spitballs. He got stuck at the third sentence and Mr Gyéres had to get down from the platform to help him. In the end he spent the whole hour down at the back with the bad students, analysing the structure of the Latin sentence with them. Up at the front it was possible to talk a little.

'Where is your lottery ticket?' asked Orczy.

'I gave it back to the old man.'

'Don't you remember the numbers?'

'No, I don't.'

'You're a donkey, the numbers are everything!' Orczy fell silent; it was difficult to hold a conversation in Mr Gyéres's class. After a while, when it seemed safe, he turned back to Misi. 'You do realise, don't you, that you can win a fortune on the lottery? When I told my brother that I was going to bet six kreutzers and would buy a pair of nickel-plated skates with the four kreutzers I would win, he said I was a child. When he played the lottery, he said, he would win a lot more than that. Not four forints, not even a thousand forints, but real money. Misi, you don't understand, you may have won a fortune!'

More than a thousand forints! That was all that Misi needed, the thought that he might have lost a fortune with the ticket. He didn't say anything, he drew back into himself like a hedgehog . . . And why was Orczy bothering him now? He should have told him that the ticket could be worth a lot while he still had it! Misi drew away from Orczy, nearer to Gimesi whom he loved more than ever: Tom Thumb had fought on his account.

Gimesi kept touching his head.

'Does it hurt?' Misi asked.

'I don't mind a bit. If they make me angry, I'll plaster the wall with them!' But Gimesi was in a very bad mood; Misi felt sorry for him. Afraid that Gimesi would be wounded by his pity, he drew away a little and embraced his friend only in his soul.

After class Orczy went to Gimesi, knowing that Misi was better friends with Gimesi than with him. 'Gimesi, get Misi to tell you what numbers he played on the lottery. Box it out of him!'

'Why? Did he win?'

'He doesn't know! He doesn't know what numbers he played!'

'You don't know?' asked Gimesi, turning towards Misi and raising his thin eyebrows and opening his small, moist, slanted black eyes to gaze at him with trustful affection. 'Well, I'll pound him and then he will know. Nobody can get anywhere with Misi because he's stubborn as a wild donkey, but I know how to loosen him up. I will trip him, he will fall, and then I will pound him until he softens up.'

Misi just sat on the bench, smiled and didn't say anything. He would have given a great deal if nobody mentioned lottery to him ever again.

'All right, are you going to tell me or not?!' asked Gimesi.

'Leave me alone.'

'Hey, I'm not old Nazo, you know,' said Gimesi, getting more excited, raising his voice. 'Did you win or didn't you?'

'I didn't win.'

'Tell me the numbers! . . . Come on, tell me. You're not going to tell me? I will shake the numbers out of you, they'll fall out of you!' He put his hands around Misi's neck and began to shake him. He was still playful but his eyes were already burning.

'Stop, don't be silly,' said Misi, so moved by his friend's concern that he almost cried.

'Will you tell me or won't you?!'

'No.'

Getting really angry, Gimesi grabbed Misi's head and knocked it against the bench as hard as he could.

Misi was so surprised that he couldn't breathe.

'So you won't tell, you won't tell!' As if he had gone mad, Gimesi began banging Misi's head against the bench. Misi's head was the most sensitive part of his body; his head always hurt from the slightest touch. He jumped up and elbowed Gimesi away with such force that Gimesi flew out of the bench and landed on the floor. He lay there for a little, gasping for breath. Misi was afraid for his friend and, pale and trembling, leaned over him to help him up. But at that same instant Gimesi jumped up and leaped at Misi like an angry hamster, and began to box him with his head as he had done with Szegedi.

The other boys surrounded them. Misi didn't want to take the fight seriously and lost his temper only when Gimesi had boxed him three or four times. When his blood began to boil he jumped at Gimesi, hit him in the face with his fists, then grabbed him by the waist and pulled him down to the floor. He grabbed Gimesi's thin little neck, pressed it against the floor and squeezed it so hard he thought it would snap. True, Gimesi was hitting him and scratching him at the same time but it was nothing. In the end Misi knelt on his friend's neck and when he saw Gimesi's little face writhing in his grip, full of terrible anger and hatred, without goodness or forgiveness, he jumped up, went back to his place, slumped in his seat with his face down on the desk and sobbed.

Mortally humiliated and panting for revenge, Gimesi raised himself from the floor. The other boys had stood around them and watched the fight without saying a word, except for

Orczy, who kept shouting, 'They've gone mad, they're out of their minds!'

But most of the well-off town boys, who had never fought, surrounded the combatants with divine indifference; they weren't even laughing.

'Don't cry,' Gimesi said to Misi. There was blood on his face, but he didn't cry.

Misi got hold of himself and stopped crying.

'But what on earth was it all about?' Tannenbaum kept asking despairingly. 'Why did they fight? Why would they fight like that?'

'Who knows!' said K. Sánta, and went back to his place, preparing his books and notebooks for the next hour, which was mathematics. Nothing fazed him.

János Varga, who sat on the second bench, asked Gimesi: 'But really, what happened? What did Misi do?'

'He's just a dirty peasant,' said Gimesi, pressing his handkerchief against the bruises under his eyes.

The insult twisted Misi's insides, burned his heart to cinders. He resolved never to say another word to Gimesi.

Little by little the boys went wild. Fighting broke out all over the classroom. They were slapping each other without any reason whatsoever, laughing and cursing. It was a mad day, a fools' day.

Mr Báthori, the mathematics master, came in. His eyes flashed when he saw his students hitting each other on top of their desks. He carried a thick walnut stick, and he hit the master's desk with it so hard that the boys turned into gentle lambs. In an instant they were all in their seats and wouldn't have dreamt of stirring. They were more afraid of Mr Báthori than of flood or fire.

'Hands down!' shouted the master and there was a rapid fire of hands being slapped on benches. Mr Báthori looked them over like a hungry lion. 'We'll see whether you can behave yourselves!'

He sat down and noted the subject of the hour in the class

register. Then he got up, took a piece of chalk, wrapped it in a scrap of paper, put it between his thumb and index finger and walked to the blackboard. 'All right, today it is the rule of three. We learn how to find a number in the same ratio to a given number as exists between two other given numbers.'

There was helpful tension and order all through the hour. The boys were reined in by the energy of the master, who talked the whole time like a sergeant-major, briefly, incisively, harshly . . .

The last hour was physical training. Shrieking with joy, they ran down to the gym. This was a big hall on the ground floor with windows to the courtyard. Half of the floor was covered with wonderful wood shavings; it was fun jumping up and down in them, and if someone fell from one of the vaulting-horses he wouldn't hurt himself.

Misi didn't like gym. Just as he was among the first in other classes, here he was the last. It was painful when they were lined up according to height; he was the fifth from the back. After him came Gimesi and Gyuri Tikos, a little boy who wore high boots, a real *civis* boy, the son of rich peasants living in town, who was always grave and never laughed on his own, a little brown child, as old for his age as he was undersized. You could never have a fight with him; if you told him, 'I'll slap you,' he reported it to the teacher, not because he was a coward or wanted to hurt you but simply because it was his nature to place himself under the protection of the powerful. Misi was good friends with him in the gym; he liked it that Gyuri could wear high boots and a black-braided grey jacket, which Misi himself couldn't wear, because his father was neither a landowner nor a peasant: Misi was a half-breed, neither peasantry nor gentry, or rather he was beginning to think that he belonged to both classes. He was sorry now that he had made Tikos change places with Gimesi. At the start of the year the physical training instructor put Gimesi behind Tikos and Tikos behind Misi, but in those days Misi was in love with his dear Gimesi − that vicious boxing machine whom he couldn't even look at now − so when the instructor turned his back he grabbed Gimesi and pulled him forward, ahead of Tikos. At first Tikos was angry and they were afraid that he would denounce them to the instructor, but then Tikos came to like the change of place because it put him just ahead of the mayor's cousin Pista Simonffy, and of all the boys Tikos liked best being near him.

Pista was another marvellous little fellow, such a busybody that he was mixed up in everything, running back and forth all the time like an excitable little dog. He had several older brothers in the school and during breaks he ran from one class to another to visit them. Now he was in the fifth form, now in the seventh, now the fourth; he had a place everywhere. He was so small, he was babied in every class. When he went to visit, the older boys picked him up, put him on their shoulders, gave him cigarettes and teased him affectionately.

He was ideally suited to carry gossip from one class to another. 'Do you know what the Head said in the fourth form?'

A circle immediately formed around him. 'What?'

'Fish was doodling on the blackboard when the Head came in. "Who are you, you good-for-nothing?" asked the Head. "Fish" . . . "I can see that from the shape of your mouth," said the Head. "What's your name?"'

Orczy ran to the group to laugh with them, but didn't ask what they were laughing about. Pista wanted to please Orczy, because he knew more than any of the others what important people the Orczys were, so he started to tell the story again. 'The Head went to the fourth form and gave Fish a swipe on the backside with his stick for doodling on the blackboard. He asked his name and . . .'

'I can see that from your mouth,' Orczy interjected with a wave of his hand to signal that he knew the story. 'Sándor Nagy takes all the Head's sayings down in shorthand, and since we walk home together as far as Kossuth Street he quotes them to me every day. But never mind that, tell me, Pista, you must know – is it true that Mr Gyéres is courting Magda Margitai?'

Pista looked thoughtful. 'Well, he visits them.'

'Right,' said Orczy. 'But when?'

'I will tell you exactly. I will go there tonight and smell it out.'

Orczy laughed. 'Sándor Nagy told me about it yesterday. He's very jealous.'

'Who? Sándor Nagy?'

'Yes. Sándor wrote a poem to her yesterday and gave it to her at the skating rink. He's recited it to me so often, I can tell you the first verse. *I listened to your voice / And I could not hear you. / I looked into your eyes / And I could not see you . . .* He said he's going to challenge Mr Gyéres to a duel.'

'Sándor Nagy will challenge the Latin master to a duel?'

Orczy chuckled.

Misi listened open-mouthed.

A powerful voice blared forth. 'Line up!'

The physical training instructor entered from a small room at the side of the gym and the boys scrambled into their lines. 'I want these lines straight! What's that there? Who has such a big belly? . . . Ten . . . shun!'

The boys stood to attention. 'All right, walk the circle. One! Two! One! Two! One, two, one-two, come on, you slackers, all right, trot! Run-run-run.'

When they had run twice around the gym the instructor bellowed: 'Halt! . . .' They stopped instantly. They were now back in their places. 'At ease.'

That was how it always started.

Misi was terribly bored. He thought physical training was stupid. Now they had to march to the vaulting-horse and leap over it in turn. It wasn't high and it was easy for the tall boys who had long legs, but the short ones got stuck on top of it and they could feel the instructor's contempt.

The physical training instructor was a short thickset man with a little black moustache, a harsh voice and a haughty bearing, a fat man with thick shoulders and arms bursting out of his jacket who never demonstrated what he wanted the boys to do. He was fond of the strong ones and exercised them separately. For him a good gymnast was one who came from home with bulging muscles; he didn't even look at the weaklings. Out of a sense of duty he let them use the vaulting-horse and parallel bars but he felt that they were only dirtying the equipment. The good gymnasts were different: not only did he form them into a separate group and let them excel themselves in various exercises, he even talked and laughed with them. He paid so little attention to the weaklings that even after eight years he didn't know their names. He had wanted to be a pastor but, as often happens, he got a wife before he got a parish and as he had been an excellent student and theologian at the college for twelve years, he was given the job of physical training instructor when old Zábráczky retired. Zábráczky had taught penmanship and physical training because these two subjects required no special qualification or talent; he was still a man of the old world: he got this grace and favour post from a bishop . . .

In his sorrow about the lost lottery ticket and his fight with Gimesi, Misi didn't have the heart to run at the vaulting horse and couldn't even jump on it.

'Well, what happened? Are you afraid your pants will fall down?' bellowed the instructor.

Misi tried just to walk past the vaulting-horse but the instructor shouted at him. 'Come on, try again, once more!'

Misi had to go back and run at the horse again but he couldn't get into his stride and stopped short of it.

'Once more!'

With his head hanging Misi trudged back for the third time. 'Run!'

Misi started then slowed down and braced himself to stop. He walked to the side without even going near the horse.

The instructor's jaw dropped. 'Come back, come back!' he beckoned with his finger. 'Well, what kind of *virtus* is that? Let me see you run again.'

Exhausted from all the excitement of the day, Misi turned as obstinate as a mule and would not budge.

The instructor stamped his foot. 'One-two!'

Misi did not speak, he did not move a muscle.

'Someone give this boy a push, because if I give him a push he will fly over the tower of the Great Church.' The instructor's eyes were aflame, and he began to stretch his immense arms and legs, ready to move and grind Misi into the ground.

But Misi clenched his teeth and did not stir.

'You refuse to obey? Insubordination! . . . Rebellion!' screamed the instructor and took a step towards Misi. The boys waited in fear and trembling to see what would happen next.

Then Orczy stepped out of the line, came forward and said in a clear voice: 'Please, sir, Mihály Nyilas is sick.'

'I didn't ask you!'

Orczy of course was overconfident, thinking that as the first student of the class he was entitled to be the protector of the weak and helpless. Instead of withdrawing he began to argue. 'Excuse me, sir, but it's the truth, it's a fact.'

But here he was not the first student; this was gymnastics, and with his long awkward legs he impressed the instructor no more than Misi Nyilas. The instructor stared at him, dumbfounded, beside himself, panting like a wild boar. He noticed that the boy had a finer shirt and a finer haircut than the others, in short, was *a gentry monkey*, and that enraged him as the red cloth enrages the bull. The gentry monkey dared to talk back to him! He took it as a personal insult, a criticism of his lack of qualifications, his peasant origins and his secret drinking, and now all his anger turned on Orczy.

'Come here,' he said hoarsely, purple-faced from the rush of blood to his head.

Orczy walked towards the instructor bravely with head high. 'Here!' roared the instructor and pointed to his feet.

Now Orczy started to walk a little more carefully, realising that the instructor wanted to hit him. He was frightened, surprised and outraged. He didn't want to be hit . . . But it was too late. He had no choice but to go on walking, erect, rigid and brave, looking straight into the instructor's eyes.

The class watched with bated breath. Orczy grew pale and he knew it, but he would not retreat. The instructor, however, was having second thoughts, reflecting that the boy had done nothing wrong except to be born a weakling, a worm . . . It was the last moment: he had already raised his hand to knock off the boy's head, saying, 'Well, to teach you never to meddle in what doesn't concern you, my young gentleman . . .' Yes, his hand was raised to box Orczy's ears, but midway it changed direction and he twirled his moustache – it was the customary village gesture to frighten someone with a blow and then turn it into a joke by twirling one's moustache. 'Well, you worm . . . That one there is out – if he's sick let him go to the devil. But you will jump, and you'll jump for him too. *Ein, zwei.*'

To tell the truth, Orczy would have preferred a slap in the face to stumbling over the horse, but he stopped in time, he couldn't jump. He ended up the same way as Misi. Anyway, it wasn't becoming for an honours student to be good at gymnastics as well.

'Congratulations!' exclaimed the instructor. 'Why in God's name do they send me worms like that?'

Orczy bowed his head as if in shame, but when he turned towards the boys he raised his head again and grinned.

Then the instructor noticed Misi, who had gone back to his place in the line. 'What are you doing there? Get out of the line!'

Misi didn't move. He wanted to say that he wasn't sick but, suddenly feeling dizzy, he staggered to the wall for support, leaned against it with the palms of his hands, fainted and fell to the floor.

The instructor was surprised. 'Pour a glass of water on his face. Hey, Pista!' he shouted. Simonffy, who stood nearest to him, was a skilled gymnast in spite of his smallness and therefore the instructor knew him. 'There is some water on the table in my room. Go and fetch it.'

Pista ran into the little room and returned straight away with a half-filled glass. He put his hand in it and began to sprinkle Misi's face. Misi regained consciousness with disgust. He smelled some horrible stink. The liquid in the glass was not water but clear plum brandy.

The instructor reddened and castigated his stupid head for forgetting about it. In time the boys too smelled the brandy and began to titter. The instructor roared at them: 'Attenshun!' That was his medicine for everything. 'Barta! Keleman! Pick up that little worm and set him on that coil of rope.'

Barta was quite moved. He felt sorry for Misi; he had respect for him in class, and for the first time in his life he made a cutting remark about the instructor. 'He drinks brandy from a water glass, the animal.'

Misi finally calmed down. He felt weak and it was good to slump on the coil of rope, leaning his back against the cool wall. The gym was swirling in front of his eyes and it made him dizzy. He kept yawning and shivering. At one point when he saw Orczy and Gimesi talking his eyes filled with tears. How good they were to him! They had both fought for him that morning.

'I know what's wrong with him . . . He lost his lottery ticket and his numbers came out,' said Gimesi.

Orczy was shocked. 'You don't mean it!'

'I know because he wrote down his numbers at our place and I just asked Mihály Sándor – he knows the winning numbers. And my friend, the only number that didn't come out was the 22. The other four came out.'

'But what if it was stolen?' Orczy asked. 'It's not impossible, you know.'

Gimesi was surprised. He hadn't thought of that.

The instructor noticed them standing out of line and whispering. That was against the rules. They were all supposed to stand silently in their places and wait for their turn. He looked hard and steadily at Orczy and Gimesi, and even when the two boys slipped back to their places he continued to glare at them, whipping them with his eyes.

Misi remembered that he had beaten dear good Gimesi who took his part. That was the way he showed his gratitude! He was sure he would be base to Orczy too, because he was just a base peasant.

The tears rolled down into his mouth through his nose and he swallowed them and sniffled. He felt faint and dizzy and would have liked to put his head in his mother's lap. But she wasn't there, the poor woman!

VIII

Misi doesn't like people to fuss about him, particularly when he is in trouble. He wants to be left alone to think of home and contemplate the fate of humanity in peace, · to forget his little catastrophe by thinking of big ones

AFTER THE MIDDAY meal Misi sat down at the table, telling himself that he ought to study. The dormitory was empty; only Mr Nagy was there, lying on his bed reading. As Misi pulled out his drawer he was reminded of the letter that he had started to write to his parents. It had been lying in the drawer for at least a week. He quickly took it out along with his ink bottle and steel-nibbed pen.

My dear good parents! Don't be angry with me, my dear good parents, that I wrote so long ago to my dear good parents, but . . .[1]

That was all he had written. He looked at it, studied it. If only the 'but' weren't there he could easily continue. What should he say? Why hadn't he written? He was afraid of lying, because his mother's words were constantly in front of him; he could almost feel them burning his skin: 'My son, always behave as if I could see you; just tell yourself that my eyes can see you and then you will never do anything that is not right.'

He could feel her eyes on him and fear tickled his throat. He looked at his letter dejectedly. Mr Nagy stirred on the bed, and Misi quickly dipped the pen into the inkpot and started to write.

> . . . I had no time, because every day I read aloud to an old gentleman who is blind and pays ten kreutzers for an hour's reading, I read for him from five to six in the afternoon, but I have to start out half-an-hour before, because he is a very punctual gentleman and won't tolerate people being late. And by the time I get home we have to go to the dining hall for supper, and after supper I have to study. And Wednesday and Saturday afternoon I cannot write because I am tutoring a classmate in Latin and mathematics. That's why I couldn't write to my dear good parents.

He stopped there and rested. He had solved the problem: he hadn't lied and he had also managed not to tell them about the trouble he was in. He even smiled a little, thinking how clever he was. Not even his mother could fault that letter.

The wind was blowing outside, splashing slush against the window pane. It reminded him of the swill his mother fed to the pigs; he pictured her carrying the pail with her bare arms. He put his elbow on the table and rested his head on his hand and examined his writing, watched it until the letters blurred in front of his eyes.

He thought of his mother's brother András, who repaired tractors and combine harvesters. He was a good, upright man who talked in a very melodious way as if he were preaching a sermon. He had wanted to be a pastor but didn't have the chance to finish his schooling. He had a beautiful resonant voice, could shout louder than anybody, and always spoke about beautiful and good things as if addressing the faithful from the pulpit. He spent the whole winter with Misi's parents because he had no job. He read all winter – novels and newspapers and books on mechanics – and Misi's mother had to cook better on his account because he wouldn't eat just anything. He even drank wine and would send Misi to the tavern for half a litre. Sometimes he invited Misi's father to drink with him. 'Bertalan, come, have a glass!' But Misi's father declined. 'I won't drink. If I drink I can't work.' Misi's father spent the whole winter making sledge-runners. Once on a nasty sleety winter day like this one Misi looked through the window and saw his father in the courtyard trying to split a big tree trunk with a spike. When Misi's mother, leaving the house, saw how he was struggling and sweating in the freezing cold, how he had to suffer to support them all, she turned around, went back into the house and said to her brother, 'András, do you have a soul? How can you lie there and ignore that poor man struggling with that big tree trunk? Go and give him a hand!' At that Uncle András stirred with visible reluctance, looked up from his book and said in a surly voice, 'I'm not going, I wouldn't think of it.' With that he lay back with his book and read on. However, after a few minutes he got up angrily and went away somewhere.

Misi's mother was speechless. She just sat down and cried, and Misi sniffled beside her. How he would have liked to help! He went out to the courtyard to watch his father, at least. He stood there for a while, blue with cold, with his teeth chattering, until his father noticed him and shouted, 'What are you shivering here for? Get back to the house!' But Misi just stood there. To tell the truth he would have loved to go into the house; it was monstrously cold outside, and cold always hurt him. But nobody understood his sacrifice, neither his father nor his mother, and that hurt more than the cold. So when he finally went in he started to quarrel with his younger brothers, who were making a racket in the room. 'Be quiet!' he told them, and he even shook little Feri.

Tears rolled down Misi's cheeks as he sat in the warm dormitory, and he put his head down on his fists to hide them. How was the family at home? Did they have firewood, bread, food? And did his grandmother still buy her kilo of coffee, even now? His father's mother, who lived with them, wouldn't drink plain milk and she wouldn't eat caraway-seed soup either. She always had her separate coffee which no one else was allowed to touch; she roasted the beans herself, then she ground them and the whole house was filled with the smell of the ground coffee, which none of them could stand because they got none of it. Misi's grandmother also ordered meat, because she had trouble with her stomach; she couldn't exist on that wretched food the children ate. And none of them dared to say a word to her. They treated her with reverence, because it was Misi's father who had ruined her: she lost her farm because of a bad speculation that he made. So that was why they had to keep quiet. God forbid that she should be offended! . . .

Misi's father wore himself out working but never seemed to be sad. He was either cheerful or angry. But his anger never lasted, because he got rid of it with a string of curses.

The only person who suffered was Misi's mother, who had to work for the whole family, though her thin, weak, sad little body wasn't made for work; only poverty forced her to it. She would have liked to study and read and go to plays and concerts, but instead she had to wash and cook and clean and sew for all the children. And she sewed for the village girls as well: the whole house was filled with the smell of fresh cotton . . . She would have liked to rest, too, and eat good things, bu . she always had the worst of everything. She ate when her husband slammed the door saying: 'It's pig swill, you cooked it, you eat it.' And then they could eat, the small, hungry, thin children and their thin, worn-out mother . . .

Misi sat a long while over his letter and became very drowsy. He could hardly sit up and would have liked to go to bed, but it was forbidden. He had suffered so much that day, he was so exhausted that it hurt him to sit up, so he put his arm on the table and rested his head on it. He tried to keep his eyes open but a minute later they closed. He decided he would think about the letter for a while. Then he fell asleep.

He dreamed of his father. 'All right, give me the lottery ticket,' his father said. 'I will go and pick up the money.' Misi was relieved to hear that, because he couldn't have gone for the money himself. But then he got frightened, because he knew that he had lost the ticket. He pretended to look for it, jumped about, opened every drawer, ran around his parents' little house, while his father watched him, getting more and more angry. 'You lost it, you villain.'

Misi was afraid that his father would start to curse, because he could curse without mercy when he got angry. So Misi jumped about all the more and flew around the house like a sparrow. He could feel himself brushing against things. His body had no weight; he beat his wings frantically; he bumped into every piece of furniture. But he couldn't find the ticket. 'What are you jumping about for? I'm not going to bite your nose off. Just tell me where you put it.'

Misi finally stopped and stood trembling in front of his father, who turned his ruddy face and broad, wise forehead towards him and looked at him with his beautiful, serious blue eyes.

Then Misi bent his head and confessed. 'I haven't got it.'

'What happened to it? Who stole it?'

'Böszörményi,' Misi said almost inaudibly.

'Böszörményi?'

'Yes. He accused me of stealing his pocket-knife. He said I threw it behind the rubbish bin on the first floor. So now, out of revenge, just to make trouble for me, he stole the lottery ticket and tore it up. I even saw him tearing it up but I didn't know what it was. And now he just laughs at me.'

His father looked thoughtful then averted his eyes and said, 'Ah, good. Now I will go and sharpen the axe. Come and turn the grindstone for me.'

In the next instant Misi was turning the grindstone as fast as the wind blew. He heard the cry of the axe as the grindstone caught it.

He was terrified that his father would cut Böszörményi in two; he knew that was why the axe was being sharpened. His body was shaking with cold and he could see Böszörményi, with a fur cap on his head, crossing the main Market Square in Debrecen, laughing, not knowing that he would be cut into two. Then Misi's father raised his axe, raised it as high as the golden ball on top of the tower of the Great Church, to strike Böszörményi down, and Misi grabbed his arm and shouted with all his might, 'Dear Father, Faaaaaaather!'

Misi was so terrified that he woke up. He was afraid that Mr Nagy would notice something, but he was reading on his bed. Misi looked at him but couldn't quite see him; his vision was blurred and he felt feverish. He understood that he had been dreaming, but everything in the dream was so real that he thought it had really happened. He stared at Mr Nagy for so long that Mr Nagy felt it and stirred. Misi was afraid that he might talk to him, so he quickly bent his head and looked at his letter to his parents. But that bothered him too. It was upsetting to see words in his own writing, marks of his restless, hectic life.

Mr Nagy sat up on his bed. 'Listen, little Nyilas, this is terrible. Do you know what I'm reading? I'm reading the ancient history of the Hungarian nation – about the people who went in search of the place we came from.'

Misi looked up eagerly. This was the only subject which could have distracted him from his misery. He was overcome with a hungry desire to hear what Mr Nagy could tell him.

'We live in the middle of Europe like a foundling, like an abandoned illegitimate child. You may not know what that means and I'm not going to explain it to you, but it means a child who is ashamed of his birth, who doesn't know his parents and doesn't dare to search for them. Yet he is consumed by curiosity and a longing to know them.'

Misi took this personally. He never dared to tell anybody about his parents, about their poverty and their troubles, that his father was a carpenter and his mother had a little hump on her back, or what his Uncle András was like, or that they were ruined. Not a word. There was nothing in their lives worth bragging about. Their good fortune didn't amount to as much as a single word.

'You see, we live at the heart of Europe, in this Hungary shaped like a heart. Even the two chambers of the heart, two ventricles and two auricles, are drawn on it by the two big rivers, the Danube and the Tisza.'

Misi found this very true and very moving. He didn't yet know the anatomy of the heart but he thought that *heart* was the most beautiful word in the language and he was very pleased that Hungary resembled a heart. His own life, he thought, with all its trouble and misery, deserved the name of heart, because his heart was alive and he felt that his family's whole life was one great sick heart.

'Isn't it terrible that we are here in the middle of Europe, we live here, we work here, we suffer here, we sing and laugh here, when we can, and there isn't a single other nation in the whole wide world who understands our language . . . Neither our language nor our sentiments nor our lives. We are condemned to be on our own, we cannot count on anybody, we have only enemies in this world, no friends, no relatives anywhere.'

Tears came to Misi's eyes. This was his own life, his own destiny. He was condemned to live in Debrecen, in this big alien city, in this big college, and there wasn't anyone anywhere who would help him. Whatever happened to him, nobody would ever defend him.

'It wasn't always so,' continued Mr Nagy, 'there was once a Magna Ungaria, a Great Hungary, in the distant Urals along the shores of the Volga. At the time when we moved to this place we kept in constant touch with the Old Country. The Greek emperor Constantine wrote in the tenth century that the Hungarians used to send ambassadors to their brothers who had remained in the east. They exchanged visits and constantly enquired after them, and frequently received news from them.'

Misi strained his mind to understand. He hadn't yet studied history in Debrecen; that would come the following year. But even in elementary school he had learned a little about the history of the Hungarian people. He had learned all that most peasant boys would ever learn; they would grow up in the village and never again hear any news of history. But he had no images in his mind of what he had learned, only words which didn't mean anything special. He remembered only that our ancestors came to this beautiful land from Asia, led by their chieftain Árpád. But now in an instant the nation's life became a human story for him. From old Nazo in geography class that morning he had acquired a sense of prehistoric men, and now from Mr Nagy he was acquiring a notion of the ancient Hungarians, who raised Árpád on a shield when they elected him their leader.

'The contacts became less frequent as time passed but in the thirteenth century they still had some awareness of their eastern relatives. Have you ever heard of Brother Julian? No? At the time of King Béla IV this Julian set out with four other monks of his order to convert the Hungarians in the Old Country, who were of course still pagans. After enduring a great deal of hardship they got there − they went by way of Constantinople on foot, an appalling journey − from there to the Caucasus − take out the map, I will show you.'

Misi quickly found the world atlas and together they looked at the map of Russia.

'Probably starting from Székesfehérvár, they went across country to the Danube, took a boat down to Belgrade, from there they walked to Constantinople, there they got on a boat which took them across the Black Sea, and from the Crimea they walked to the Volga. But three of them turned back at the Crimea; they couldn't stand the misery, the hunger and the persecution. Julian and one of the other monks went on. When they reached the Volga, Julian's comrade died too, in some epidemic. So Brother Julian walked alone through the Tartar lands up to Kazan. The people of the steppes lived then in leather tents minding their herds of cattle; they lived the same way as herdsmen lived here on the Great Plain. There Brother Julian encountered a woman who spoke Hungarian, and she explained to him how he could get to the Old Country. He followed her directions and two days later he reached the Hungarian tribes. They were very pleased to see him; they took him from house to house, they plied him with food and drink and asked him about their long-lost brothers. "Where do you live? Where do you suffer? We know that you gained Attila's inheritance. Take good care of it." And that sort of thing.

'But Brother Julian couldn't stay long. "Return to your country, my blood," the old Hungarian chieftain told him, "and tell your king, my brother, that I, the chieftain of the Old Hungarians, greet him, embrace him, kiss him. And I send him word that he should prepare for a great danger. The Mongols are coming from the east and they will destroy the world. I have already received my orders from them, they say I have to join them with all my armed men. And that is an order I cannot disobey. Let my brother collect his allies and be ready to withstand the Mongol invasion." So poor Brother Julian started on his return journey on the 21st of June, not the way he had come but by a shorter route the Old Hungarians advised him to take. He took a barge down the Volga, then cut across Russian and Moldovan territory to reach Transylvania. Though his strength was failing he reached Székesfehérvár on the third day of Christmas and, already on the point of death, gave the message to King Béla IV . . .

'And that was how it came to pass. Four years later, in 1241, the Mongols reached Hungary. The Hungarians didn't surrender, didn't pay tribute like people to the east, and the whole nation was practically wiped out. But they achieved one thing: the Mongols didn't get past Hungary. That was always our destiny: we were the ones who had to stop the hordes from the east. Hungary was always the last battleground. It was the bastion where the Asiatic hordes had to stop. Isn't that amazing, that the Hungarians should have come here from the east to protect the west from the easterners? We bled away at that, fighting our eastern relatives to defend the alien westerners, who have remained strangers through a thousand years and always despised us.'

The senior and the junior student looked at the map for a while in silence.

Now Mr Nagy turned to the map of Asia. 'Look, most likely that was our nation's cradle where Hungarians lived in prehistoric times.'

With his index finger he drew a circle around the southwestern part of Siberia, from the Aral Sea in the south to the Urals in the west to the Ob in the north and to the Altai Mountains in the east. 'This was the home of many related tribes – the Finns, the Ugors, the Ostyaks, the Magyars, the Huns and the Avars. It was a time of peace. You had great empires, powerful kings. It must have been a couple of thousand years since the last great migration when whole nations moved – you mustn't think that the only great migration occurred at the time of the collapse of the Roman Empire, there were several great migrations before that. For instance, the Turan people laid to waste Europe as far as France, though we have no written record of that period. But they must have stayed and mixed with the Germans and Anglo-Saxons; they must all have Turan blood in them – it helped to make them strong . . . And who knows how many great migrations convulsed the world before the Turans? There were no seas where you now see those islands between Asia and Australia; that was all one land mass. You could go on foot from America to Australia and Asia, to parts of the world which are now under water . . . Because you know, don't you, that the Earth is a ball of fire? Only a thin crust on top of it is earth. And wherever the fire burned out the earth collapsed; that was how we got the mountains and valleys and seabeds – because of course as the earth shrank the water ran towards the lowest ground. That was how the southern world sank, that was the Great Flood of the ancient epic poems and the Bible. But to get back to the Magyars, the Finns, the Ugors and all the rest, they still lived together at the time of the Greeks. Do you understand what I'm telling you?'

'Yes.'

'Well, look, the world of classical Greece came to an end when Alexander the Great came to power; by then the whole world was ripe for destruction. In Asia Minor you had the

Persian empire, then farther east you had the Indian empire. North of them there was the empire of the Mongols, and still farther north the empire of the Finn-Ugor-Magyar-Hun-Avar tribes. All these people had been living in the same place for thousands of years, but when Alexander the Great with his little Macedonian army struck out, he broke up all the eastern empires. He defeated Darius, he marched down to India, he was like a whirlwind striking a forest, burning, twisting, uprooting everything. Alexander died young, at the age of thirty-three, so the whole business lasted only a few years. But the news of his victories had a more devastating effect than his actual campaigns. The Mongols of the Gobi desert learned that the Persians were weak, that the world was full of opportunities for plunder, so they got on their horses to loot the riches of China and Persia. These wicked herdsmen acquired a taste for the best of everything; they no longer cared for work, all they wanted to do was to pillage and to kill. The Chinese were smart: they raised a hurdle the Mongol horses couldn't clear. They built a stone wall twelve metres high across their northern frontier – the Great Wall of China. It was an appalling labour – it took a hundred and fifty years – only the antlike Chinese would have been capable of it. No cavalry could leap over the twelve-metre-high wall. But the Mongols had tasted blood, they didn't want to go back to drinking mare's milk. So they turned around and headed west, because the riches of Europe had the same sort of reputation as the riches of China. And as the Mongols moved, everybody tried to get out of their way. The Finns left the Magyar tribes and headed north, the Lapps went even farther north, and to this day they live within the Arctic Circle.

'The Hungarians must have spent some time in the Arctic themselves, because Simon Kézai, the scribe of the last Árpád king, wrote in the twelfth century that at one time the Magyars had lived in a country where there was eternal fog and the summer lasted for only three months, and even then the sun shone for only three hours a day, from six to nine. Well, that's the weather in the Arctic Circle – the northern lights, the fog, the three-month summer. How would this scribe, living seven hundred years ago, have known about the weather conditions in the Arctic if he wasn't recording oral history, personal experiences passed down from mouth to mouth, from one generation to the other? In any case, even if the Magyars went up to the Arctic, they didn't dally there for long, they didn't like that kind of cold country. They thought they would be better off moving south. I must confess I approve of their judgment. So they rounded up their herds and grazed them down in the Urals and then down by the Volga. That was where they split up again.

'The old conservatives said "That's good enough land for us" but the cocky youngsters couldn't rest and went on, swam across the Volga, went down the Don River, swam across that too, got into the swamps near the Caspian Sea, then moved to the Black Sea, right down to the Crimea. They couldn't rest there either, they couldn't stay put in their skins, so they came to the Dnieper. That was when they made an alliance with the Greek Emperor and got beaten by the Petcheneg and driven farther west. Then it was just another step to the Carpathians. They came in, settled down, and here we are today. It's a beautiful country, a good place, if only you didn't have to work in it.'

Misi forgot all his troubles, all his sorrows, and laughed happily.

'Yes, it would be nice to rest a little,' said Mr Nagy with a grin. 'Haven't we fought enough? In two thousand years of history, counting the migrations and our time here, I doubt that we ever had a ten-year period without war. Except now. We live in the longest period of peace the Magyars ever had. Think of it, since the 1848 revolution we have had forty-four years of peace and there's still no sign of another war. It must be written into the history books, or as they say in Debrecen, we should write it into the chimney with soot.'

'And don't we have relatives in the West?' asked Misi.

'In Western Europe?' cried Mr Nagy. 'Where? You have the Latin nations, the Germanic peoples, the Slavs – total strangers, all of them. The French, the Spaniards, the Italians? We are not related. The Germans, the English, the Swedes, the Norwegians, the Danes, the Dutch – aliens, all of them. As for the Russians, the Slovaks, the Croats, the Serbs, the Romanians, our nearest neighbours, they are our deadliest enemies. We live here as in a cage. With whom could we make an alliance? The French, the Spaniards, the Italians? They may fight when their interests dictate, but afterwards they celebrate each other as dearest relations. The Germans and the English? They don't differ about anything except which should be first in the world. They would burn the whole of mankind for that, but otherwise they love each other. They have kindred languages and they think the same way. As for Russia, it's like a huge hen who wants all the little Slavic nations to sit under her wing . . . Whom could we join? We don't have a word, a shade of language in common, we don't share a drop of blood. The only thing we share with other languages is what we picked up from them to enrich ourselves, so we have many Slavic, Turkish, German, Latin words. We took them but then transformed them so much that their own mother couldn't recognise them . . . A Hungarian could learn any language in the world perfectly, but there isn't a single foreigner who could learn our language well enough to pass for a native.'

'That's terrible!' sighed the eleven-year-old, looking at the map. 'We have no relations.'

'Relations? Well, the Finns. Those poor people are far from us and they too live in chains, heavier than ours. And there are all those people in the east, Estonians, Zyrians, Voguls, Mordvinians, Cheremisses, Votyaks, Ostyaks, but that's like being related to Adam and Eve and the walnut tree.'

Imitating Mr Nagy's light-hearted tone, Misi said, 'My father says everybody is related – your mother and my mother are both women.'

'It's something like that. You can still find the Old Country on some maps, marked as *Ingria*, but it was destroyed by the Mongols during their westward drive. The eastern tribes were

swept away, scattered to the winds, robbed of all independence. Two centuries later King Mátyás[2] tried to find
them, sent out ambassadors to look for them; he wanted to
bring them to Hungary because there weren't enough of us.
But by then Russia had a firm grip on its empire and the
Orthodox Tsar didn't even allow the Hungarian ambassadors
to meet with their kith and kin; he didn't want them to have
any contact with each other. Then came Hungary's defeat at
Mohács,[3] the Turkish occupation for a hundred and fifty
years, and after that nobody thought of our eastern relatives
again. Not even Gábor Bethlen,[4] the Elector of Transylvania,
thought of looking for the tribes of the Old Country. He sent
ambassadors to the Sultan and could have told them to look
for our ancient relatives in the Caucasus and the Volga, but he
didn't think it was important. By then religious ties counted
for more than national ones. Bethlen's relatives were the
Protestant Swedes, not the pagan Hungarians along the Volga.
Gustavus Adolphus was his soul brother, not the chieftain of
the Cheremisses.'

The two students studied the map for a long time, and once
more Misi was overwhelmed by a sense of extreme solitude.
Hungary was painted red on the map, and he grew dizzy
looking at all the colours around it representing other nations
which seemed ready to devour it.

'We are threatened,' he said.

Mr Nagy was silent for a long while. 'Yes, our problem is
not to find our eastern relatives but how long we can survive,
how long Europe needs us. It is a beautiful country, Hungary,
but so far other nations have forgone the pleasure of
inhabiting this eternal battlefield. The country is painted red
on the map because it has always been a sea of blood . . .
True, life wasn't a bed of roses in Germany, France or
England either, but they could afford to fight with each other
because they could work and build a civilisation even while
they fought. But Hungary – we couldn't amuse ourselves with
theoretical arguments, we didn't have the luxury of hanging
and burning each other over scientific problems, we simply

had to lay down our lives in the Mongol, Turkish, German wars . . . Of course, the nations of the Balkans were even worse off, they lived in permanent servitude, they were the outposts of the Ottoman Empire. It was the Serbs, Bulgarians, Dalmatians, Romanians who had to provide the janissaries who made up the Turkish army. The Turks press-ganged boys in lots of fifty from the villages and trained them to be soldiers in their crack troops. In fact no native Turk could become a janissary. The civilian officials, too, even the heads of the Ottoman administration, came from the Balkans – few of the Grand Viziers were native Turks. In a sense the whole of the Balkans lived out its energies as the embodiment of Turkish power, attempting to conquer Western Europe . . . So we had our uses, as bastions against the onslaughts from the Balkans.

'But what will happen in the future? One thing is certain, our past usefulness won't count for anything in the West. We've got to be of some use, but what use, I have no idea . . . Wouldn't it be beautiful if we could all create something, make something which could be useful to the whole world!'

Little Misi was quite shaken listening to Mr Nagy. He had never thought of a nation counting as one, everybody sharing the same destiny, but now he stared at the twelve colours of the map as if twelve men were standing in front of him with bulging muscles, ready to fight with fist or sword. 'Why are we allied to Austria?' he asked.

'Allied?' asked Mr Nagy sarcastically. 'That Austro-Hungarian monarchy isn't a union, it is just the way Austria is trying to devour us. But their problem is that we're too big to gobble up. Look at the map, Austria is shaped like a big mouth. It's got its teeth into us, but we're too big a bite to swallow. It has no body, no belly to absorb us, just a mouth, a big, terrible, open mouth.'

'That looks like a mouth too,' said Misi, pointing to the half-circle on the map that was Romania, surrounding the eastern side of Hungary.

'Yes, that too is a biting dog. Its mouth is wide open to swallow Transylvania. We're surrounded, and the only reason it doesn't bother us is because we don't think of it. If we could only make alliances with nations beyond our threatening neighbours! Perhaps with the Germans . . .'

This was how two boys discussed politics on the second floor of the college, in the bleak dormitory with its whitewashed walls, in front of a school atlas, in 1892. They gazed at the map thoughtfully, looking for a way out.

'There's no way out,' said the older boy. 'We must await our fate. What will be will be. If Austria hasn't managed to devour us up to now, it certainly won't do so in the future – they're in bigger trouble than we are. If anything happens, its empire will blow apart, it will become three or four countries. Hungary will remain, with the Carpathian mountains protecting it, our two rivers, the Danube and the Tisza, tying it together. We must somehow survive until Hungary gets the chance to fulfil its geographic destiny and becomes the centre of Europe.[5] Look, we're at the very heart of Europe – from the east, from the west, from the north, from the south. This country is like a heart or a stomach (it's just as important as the heart), this country has the best future in the coming millennium. Distances will be eliminated by trains, mountains will be passed by planes – do you know that Jókai wrote in his *Novel of the Next Century* that the big battles of the future would be fought in the air? So being at the centre will mean something at last. Here is this blessed Great Plain between our two great rivers. It could be the garden of Europe . . . If we could only build a country of freedom, equality and brotherhood, as they tried to do in 1848. There was never a revolution in the whole world like that one, when the aristocrats and the gentry gave everyone the right to vote. But you wouldn't know about that, little brother.'

Misi listened intently. He didn't fully understand the arguments but he was caught up by the enthusiasm of the older boy, who meant to stop but couldn't.

'Our being Hungarians is no use to us abroad, it's a private matter. It's something like poor people's family feeling, so that

184

at home we can stick together because we all have to carry the burden of our isolation in the world. Nobody can escape the responsibility and the curse of being Hungarian. If our nationality means nothing abroad and can't help us to find friends or allies, we must find something else to tie us to the world. Do you understand? So when foreigners hear the word Hungarian they shouldn't think "Here's a little thief among the big thieves" but "Here is a serious good worker who can be counted on". They should think "Here is a country where talent can thrive" – they should be amazed: "Look, here is this tiny nation, and how many things it created! How much they suffered under the Mongols and the Turks, and yet they worked, studied and created as soon as they had a chance, and they knew how to be happy." That's the secret, we've just got to love work and study and build cheerfully. Whatever others can learn the Hungarians can learn too. They can learn it better, because there isn't a busier, more diligent, more useful nation on earth. That's the way. We have no problem in this country except politics.'

The bell rang in the courtyard and the older boy put on his hat and left. Misi would have liked to ask him what politics was, but by then he was gone.

For a while Misi leaned over the map with his chin propped on his hand. Hungary's beautiful round shield seemed to him brighter and brighter. His spirits rose and he went on writing his letter. He wrote about his life at the college, about his friends whom he loved, about his teachers; he praised them and glorified them all; he remembered only what was beautiful and good in his life; he felt that he was reborn and resolved that he would work and study and recite his lessons so well that he would astound the whole school. He felt as though he was the Hungarian nation surrounded by enemies, and was actually proud of the poverty and humble station of his parents, because he felt that he would gain strength from enduring every kind of trouble and misery. He felt that if he could fight his way through his troubles, then the whole nation would triumph.

When he had written his letter he put it in an envelope. He had two envelopes from home which his mother had put in his trunk. One had a grease spot on it and he was ashamed of it. He wondered whether he should tear it up but couldn't bring himself to do it; he felt that he must not hide his faults – let the grease spot be a warning signal that in future he should take better care of his things. He clenched his teeth, creased his eyebrows and looked into the distant future. Then he took out his Latin grammar.

He studied fervently until he heard the clock of the Great Church strike two quarters. It was half-past four and getting dark. Only then did he remember that he had to go to the old gentleman.

Bothered by the senseless reading, mouthing words about things he didn't understand, he was not looking forward to reading aloud. Even when he tried to pay attention and made out the meaning of the first few words, everything became unknown and alien by the second or third line. He had understood Mr Nagy very well, their discussion inspired him, filled his soul, even though he hadn't yet studied history. But he couldn't understand the articles in the newspapers, no matter how hard he tried.

'They still haven't drawn the numbers?' the old gentleman asked suddenly.

Misi's blood ran cold. He felt himself grow pale, and his tongue become rigid. He hardly breathed; he made no sound. But then he gained some confidence thinking that he was safe, the old gentleman couldn't see him. So he just swallowed and said the numbers weren't in the paper yet. That was partly true, because although the winning numbers had been printed in the newspaper, he hadn't seen them.

'They weren't?'

'No.'

'Damnation! What about today's paper?'

Misi scanned the paper. 'They're not there,' he said, relieved.

'What about the other one?'

Misi scanned that paper too. 'Nothing.'

'Well, let us go on.'

Misi read on but he was shaking inside. The old gentleman was too interested. He would ask others as well, and what would happen then?

He left the house feeling dejected. He wasn't well. It had been so nice earlier in the afternoon when he had managed to forget about the whole unpleasant business. He would have liked to believe that it was all over and done with. The ticket was lost, there was no way of bringing it back, and there was no point in worrying about it. It was nobody else's business, it was just his trouble, his worry . . . and the old gentleman's.

He walked back to the college with his head down and went straight to the dining hall, where Mihály Sándor greeted him, shouting, 'Nyilas! Orczy and Gimesi were up in the dormitory looking for you.'

Why would they be looking for him? The news frightened Misi, he was afraid that Orczy and Gimesi wanted to talk to him about the lottery. He sat down in his place and began to wipe his fork. They didn't wash the dishes very well in the kitchen and the boys had the habit of cleaning the cutlery with their napkins.

'Why weren't you in class this afternoon?' Mihály Sándor asked later as he reached across the table for the salt and paprika. He put a lot of salt and paprika on his bread. This was a common habit: it was how the students stimulated their appetite.

'Why wasn't I in class this afternoon?' repeated Misi, looking stupidly ahead of him.

'Yes. The teacher asked after you.'

'Today is Saturday, isn't it?' asked Misi, reddening. He had totally forgotten that there were classes in the afternoon. How could it have slipped his mind? That was all he needed, that he should forget things, especially classes.

He couldn't explain his absence to Mr Lisznyai the room

prefect either. In the end they decided that he was ill. Mr Lisznyai was very much annoyed and kept saying that he wouldn't have babies in his room; he had never heard of such a thing, a student forgetting classes! The boys sniggered.

Böszörményi outdid them all. 'It's a miracle that he doesn't lose his head!' he said sarcastically. 'He's lucky that it's glued to his neck!'

Misi felt that Böszörményi's jeering had special significance. In the dormitory no one had yet mentioned the lottery ticket, but he was sure that Böszörményi had stolen it just to make everybody say that he lost everything and could not be trusted.

In the evening he somehow managed to do his homework and write the composition they had to do for Hungarian literature class the next day.

'What should I write, what illness should I say you had?' Mr Lisznyai asked unhappily in the morning. The room prefect was *in loco parentis*; he had to write the note to account for the boy's absence from classes the previous afternoon.

'I don't know. Mr Nagy didn't go to classes either,' said Misi.

'The first hour was free for the eighth form,' said Mr Lisznyai. 'Come on, do you want me to write a note or not?'

'Yes, please,' Misi said in a small voice.

He thought that everyone in the classroom would laugh at him, but nobody even noticed him.

However, when Orczy came he beckoned to Misi from the doorway. 'I talked this business over with our cook,' he said. 'The question is whether your numbers came out in the Budapest lottery, or the Viennese lottery, or the Prague or the Brünn or the Linz lottery. Which one did you play?'

Misi was silent.

'Don't tell me you don't even know *that*!' sighed Orczy.

Misi didn't know.

'Because you won either one or two thousand forints. If your numbers came up in Brünn, you won two thousand for sure.'

Misi gaped with surprise: two thousand forints! That was something new. Two thousand! He couldn't even imagine so much money. At home his parents had bought their little house and garden for three hundred forints. Two thousand . . . It was like a tale from *The Thousand and One Nights*.

When Gimesi arrived he joined them straight away. He seemed to bear no grudge against Misi for the previous day's fight.

'Our cook says that Misi must have won two thousand, so help me God,' Orczy said. 'Half of it belongs to the old man, but even so, Misi has a thousand forints.'

Gimesi pounded the desk in his joy for his friend. 'Boy, that's something!'

'But my advice is that we musn't tell anybody,' Orczy said gravely. 'We must keep it between the three of us, because if the thief hears about it, it's all over.'

Misi looked at Orczy with new respect: he even knew that there was a thief?

The three boys put their heads together and talked in whispers. 'We have to make a contract agreeing to discuss everything with each other, and with nobody else,' Orczy advised. 'After class we'll go to the back courtyard and thrash out the whole business.'

'Agreed,' said Gimesi. 'But I propose that we should also involve Tannenbaum.'

'No, we don't need anybody else,' Orczy decided. 'Let's keep it among ourselves for the time being.'

'All right, it's all the same to me,' Gimesi conceded.

Orczy was the leader. 'We must make sure that nobody suspects anything!'

When the class was over they ran to the back courtyard.

At the back there was a small 'castle' made out of rotting old planks of wood: it was behind these foul smelling boards that they began their council.

'First of all we must ensure secrecy,' said Orczy. 'Let's elect our president.'

Gimesi consented. 'All right, I'll vote for you.'

'Me too,' seconded Misi, though he didn't understand why they needed a president when there were only three of them.

'Well, if you want me to, I'll take it on,' said Orczy. 'But only on one condition: if you swear on your honour that you will obey me in everything. You obey me blindly.'

'Right.'

'We mustn't be seen together, that might arouse suspicion,' said the president. 'But while you're in religion class I'll have a free hour, and I'll plan it all then, work out the basic rules.'

They shook hands on that.

Misi felt strange, even feverish; his heart beat uncomfortably at the thought that his trouble had become such a big secret thing.

During the next class the religion teacher's fine speeches were lost on Misi, who was quite beside himself. In his agitated state the only thing that struck him was the amazing behaviour of Gimesi, who was as carefree and natural as at any other time. He riffled through his notebooks, he sharpened his pencil, he laid out his books on the desk and then put them away; as always in religion class, he was in constant motion. Misi, on the other hand, sat in a daze, feeling a hot current running up and down inside him.

Orczy came to join them at the end of the class. 'Do you know what happened?' he asked, laughing. 'I was in the courtyard walking around the well and a theologian came up to me, took my hat and hit me with it. "Hey, why aren't you in class," he said. I told him I had no class because it was religion. So, he said, "You are a Jew," and he tried to press his thumb down on my head.'

The other two boys laughed uneasily.

'I'm not a Jew, I'm a Catholic, I told him. And he said, "Oh, I know your kind," and went away.'

'That's funny!' said Gimesi.

'Then one of the masters came,' continued Orczy, 'that old one with the white hair, the one they call Uncle Imre, and he told me, "Well, if you don't have a class, don't loiter outside, come with me up to the library." So he took me up to the college library, where there is nothing else but books. He gave me a good book, and I sat there and read. I'm going there every time I don't have a class.'

Misi looked at Orczy enviously. He would have liked to go to the library. My God, a room where there were only books! Misi couldn't imagine anything more glamorous.

'While I was in the library I thought everything through and I made up the basic rules of our association. Here they are, I wrote them down in three copies so each of us could have one.'

Basic rules of association! To Misi it was music. How could Orczy invent things like that? He looked up to him with respect, as to a superior being.

These were the basic rules:

1. Name: The Lottery Association.
2. The members are blood brothers.
3. There are no secrets between them.
4. The members of the Association are the President, the Secretary and the Recorder.
5. It is forbidden to betray the secrets of the Association to outsiders.

   This is all.

'I would like to be the recorder,' Misi whispered to Gimesi.

'And you should propose me for secretary, that's what I would like.'

'Gimesi should be secretary,' said Misi.

'You are the secretary,' argued Orczy. 'This whole thing is your secret.'

The other boys didn't know what to say to that.

'Isn't that so?' Orczy asked Gimesi. 'If it's his secret, he should be the secretary.'

Gimesi was getting annoyed. 'A secretary has to be able to keep secrets, and this one tells everything to everybody. I can keep secrets much better than he can.'

'That's true,' Orczy conceded. 'If he had been a good

secretary to himself, we wouldn't know anything about the ticket.'

'He's only fit to be a recorder and write down what others are doing.'

Misi wasn't offended. He laughed happily. Now he had something to write in his bound book of empty pages.

IX

*Only God knows what will happen. Misi is happy
that it is Saturday; he feels that his troubles must come
to an end with the end of the week*

Y OU STILL HAVE no idea who stole it?' Orczy asked
conspiratorially as he came into the class in the
morning.
'No.'
'Didn't you even think about it?'
'Well . . .'
'I already know,' declared Orczy.
Misi had been embarrassed by the previous day's foolish
business of electing a president; he felt that if anybody learned
about it he would sink into the earth. But now he was
surprised: the president already knew who the thief was! He
hadn't expected him to discover it so soon.
'I know how we can find him,' said Orczy triumphantly.
'You do?'
'We will make a list of all the boys in the dormitory.'
'All right,' said Misi without enthusiasm.
'Write down their names on a piece of paper, please. Right
now.'
Misi started to look for some paper but Orczy put a sheet of
notepaper in front of him. 'Write on this.'
It was very fine, thick, cream-coloured paper. Misi loved
beautiful paper and enjoyed writing the names on it. When he
finished he pushed it back to Orczy, who was telling a story to

the boys on the bench behind them but stopped immediately when he saw that Misi had completed his task.

'What form is Lisznyai in?'

'The eighth.'

'And Nagy?'

'The same.'

'What about Mihály Sándor?' Orczy stood up to look for Sándor, who as usual was not sitting in his place but wandering among the benches. He didn't talk to anybody, just stopped here and there and listened to what the boys were saying. Orczy beckoned to him and Sándor ran to them.

'You sit beside each other at the table, don't you?'

'Where?'

'In the dormitory. Tell me, is Misi tidy, does he keep his things in order?'

Sándor laughed. 'Well, he's not very orderly. If he was, he wouldn't have lost the lottery ticket.'

Orczy was silent for a moment. 'What lottery ticket?' He nudged Misi with his knee to warn him not to say anything.

'Well, he said last Saturday that he put one forint on five numbers, and now he can't find the ticket that he got at the tobacconist.'

'Incredible,' said Orczy. 'I guess you're right, he must have lost it.'

'It's possible, because whenever he looks for something he has to look in all his pockets, and even then he can't find things.'

Gimesi came into the classroom, walked around Sándor, who was standing in front of their desk, and sat in his place. He was in high spirits and his eyes were laughing. 'Now I will search his pockets,' he said.

'Please, do you have your mathematics homework?' Orczy suddenly asked Sándor.

'Of course.'

'Would you be kind enough to show it to me?'

Sándor ran for his notebook.

Orczy leaned towards the two other members of his

association. 'When I am interrogating someone, you must learn not to interrupt. Neither you, nor you,' he said, pointing to them in turn. 'So far Misi has behaved well, he hasn't said a word. The class must not learn that we are investigating, because if they do then everybody will talk and by noon even the masters will know about it. When the president is working, your job is to shut up.'

Gimesi nodded to signal understanding and obedience.

'I never put the lottery ticket in my pocket,' Misi protested in a whisper. 'I put it in my purse and never took it out. It got lost from there.'

Sándor came back with his mathematics notebook. Orczy looked at it as if it interested him and told him that his answer was wrong.

Sándor was astounded. 'Where?'

'You made mistakes in the multiplication.'

They discussed the mistakes and the ticket wasn't mentioned again. When the master came in Orczy put Misi's list under his notebook and studied the names. From time to time he turned to Misi. 'Is Mr Nagy the one with the hump on his back?'

'Yes. He is a very decent good man,' Misi said quickly. He didn't want Orczy to suspect Mr Nagy. 'He wouldn't steal from anybody.'

'We will see, we will see,' Orczy replied airily.

During break Orczy jumped about and played the fool and then entered into a deep conversation with Csicsó, one of the boarders from Misi's dormitory. Misi was anxious to learn what Orczy had found out, but though Orczy passed him twice he didn't even look at him. He laughed gaily and chatted with everybody else.

After the bell when they sat in their seats again Misi couldn't restrain himself. 'What did Csicsó say?'

Orczy laughed. 'I must warn you, it is forbidden to ask the president anything. But I will overlook it this time and tell you. Sándor and Csicsó are not suspects. They are two little donkeys. But I am going to grill Böszörményi during the next break . . .' He didn't say anything more but later during class he asked, 'What happened between you and Böszörményi?'

'What happened?' Misi asked guiltily, thinking of the pocket knife.

'Yes. There was something between you two.'

'There was nothing,' Misi said, afraid that the master would notice them whispering and call him up to the blackboard to question him about the day's lesson. But after a while he leaned closer to whisper into Orczy's ear. 'When I got my parcel Böszörményi ate my shoe polish. That's why he hates me.'

'Yes, yes,' said Orczy and laughed quietly, remembering the whole business about the parcel.

During the next break they played 'building a woodpile' in the courtyard. It was a beautiful dry sunny day – cold, but they were wearing their winter coats. All the boys were outside shrieking and shouting and running about. The game consisted of one boy wrestling another on the ground and a third jumping on them, shouting 'The pile is too small, let's make it higher!' Hearing the call, the boys came like bees from every direction and jumped on top of each other, and this little mountain of children grew and grew until the boy at the bottom of the pile started to cry. Then they all scattered far and wide, until they came together and started it again.

Twice Misi saw Orczy whispering with Gimesi. He felt awkward about spying on them, so he got into the spirit of the game and threw himself on the pile.

There was a lot of screaming; they made more noise than the sparrows on the bare branches of the trees. Misi got so excited that he hardly knew what was happening, until suddenly he became aware that there was nobody above him. He heard a voice shouting, 'Why don't you get up, you ruffian?' and felt the blow of a stick on his back.

'Who did that?' Misi shrieked furiously and looked back. It was Mr Hertelendy, the master with the waxed moustache and the terrible beard. He held up his crooked stick to strike Misi again, but he didn't. He never struck twice.

Misi was so scared that he could hardly stand up. His classmates were laughing at him for getting caught. Once Mr Hertelendy disappeared in the direction of the masters' room Misi laughed too and became so wild that he started to fight with three boys. Some restless fire lit up in his blood and he felt that he could wrestle the whole class, until he saw big Szegedi, whom Gimesi had head-butted to the ground on his account.

'You want a few blows, my friend?' Szegedi shouted. 'Come here, I will beat you up!'

Misi didn't accept the challenge; he turned and ran. As he passed the well he suddenly came upon Orczy talking to Böszörményi. He was even more frightened of them and turned again and ran in the opposite direction as if someone was chasing him. Then he changed his mind and ran into the building.

He was sweating and panting when he reached the classroom. The mayor's cousin Pista Simonffy, the gossip of the school, was just saying that Nyilas had kicked Mr Hertelendy in the belly because Hertelendy hit him with his stick. A heroic legend was born here, because Pista spoke with such a loud voice and such conviction that everybody believed him, even Misi himself.

'Well, he has a big belly, did you give him a really hard kick?' asked János Varga.

Misi laughed modestly and glanced at Imre Barta, the Hercules of the class, who was laughing too and patted him on the back. 'It was well done, comrade.'

That pat on the back felt very good, and Misi began to have a strange tickling sensation in his foot, as though he really had kicked the master.

'The best thing,' said Orczy, who had just come in and observed Hercules patting Misi, 'the best thing was that I got Jármy to start the woodpile and he has a gold watch. That gold watch was at the bottom and the whole school got on top of it.' The boys thought that was very funny and everybody who heard it laughed.

But what struck Misi was that Orczy got everybody to play woodpile but didn't play it himself. He got them all excited but he remained cool and calm, having a deep conversation with Böszörményi behind the well.

Böszörményi was a wild boy who liked fighting and never missed a woodpile, but he was in another class, and now Misi was convinced that Orczy had created the woodpile simply to make word of it spread and bring Böszörményi out to the courtyard so that he could interrogate him. Misi would have liked to know what Orczy discovered, he would have liked to hear their conversation word for word, what questions Orczy asked, what answers he got. He was tremendously impressed by Orczy . . . He wondered what Orczy would do in the next break. Would he tempt Andrási out from the other class? Misi was annoyed that he had allowed himself to be fooled as if he were a little boy, instead of watching what Orczy was doing. He decided that in the next break he would control himself.

Orczy said nothing during class; only once he asked for an eraser, and Misi was pleased that he could give him one, and that he had a fine first-class English Lion eraser, which he had bought that week. He was quite pleased that he still had so much money: he had one forint fifty kreutzers in his pocket, even though he had spent thirty-six kreutzers since the beginning of the month.

When the bell rang for break Orczy left the class in a hurry, putting on his winter coat as he ran along the corridor. Misi hurried after him but was too late; he hadn't put his notebooks away quickly enough. Yet he couldn't leave them lying on his desk – they would have been knocked off and everybody would have trampled on them. When he got to the courtyard Orczy was nowhere to be seen. Misi spent the whole ten-minute break looking for him. How clever Orczy was! And he was unable even to guess what Orczy was up to.

Gimesi, who had remained in the classroom, suddenly started to wonder what Misi and Orczy were doing without him and went out to the courtyard too. 'Where is Orczy?' he asked Misi.

'I don't know.'

'Aren't you together?'

Misi looked at him with surprise. He always supposed that Orczy was better friends with Gimesi and the two of them were keeping secrets from him. 'Well, you two were whispering in the other break,' he said.

'I wasn't whispering,' said Gimesi truthfully. 'Orczy said I should call Bay out of the building.'

'Bay from Böszörményi's class?'

'Yes.'

'What would Orczy want with him?'

'Does Orczy tell me anything?'

They exchanged glances to agree about Orczy and burst out laughing.

'He only asked me how I get along with Bay. I said we get along all right, we're cousins. Then call him out, Orczy said. I called him out, and then the two of them went off, whispering.'

'What were they whispering about?'

'How should I know? I don't have long enough ears. They stood there, I stood at that wall. I only saw Bay going back to the building. Then the woodpile started with Jármy again, I got into it, and then I saw Orczy talk with that tubby boy, you know, the one with a face like meat.'

'Andrási?' cried Misi. 'You mean Orczy has already talked with Andrási as well?'

'As well as who?'

Misi looked at the ground thoughtfully, sensing that he shouldn't say all that he knew. 'He doesn't even know Andrási and then he talks with him!' he lied, turning away a little. He decided that he was going to watch Orczy but would imitate him and take care not to tell anybody what he observed.

The booted porter walked past them. They guessed that he was going to ring the bell for the end of break.

'Do you remember when sausages and frankfurters were hanging from the bell?' asked Gimesi.

'Sausages and frankfurters! When?'

'At the end of the last school year, don't you remember? The eighth-formers who were matriculating decked out the bell with everything, even a ham and an orange, flowers, all kinds of things . . .'

'I don't believe it.'

'Don't tell me! I saw it with my own eyes. Just watch for it in June. When the eighth-formers have their exams, they will deck it out again. It's an old tradition of the college.'

Without meaning to, they walked towards the bell as they talked. It was fastened to the wall near the door of the eighth-form classroom. They watched the porter as he raised his short arm, grabbed the handle at the end of the thick wire that hung down from the bell and began to pull it.

They were just about to turn when to their great surprise they saw Orczy come out of the eighth-form classroom.

Orczy was surprised too, and for a moment they just stared at each other. Then Gimesi burst out laughing, while Orczy laughed silently. Only Misi remained serious. He realised that Orczy had been talking to the eighth-formers. He had visited his older brother, who was in the eighth form, and while there he had managed to have a chat with Mr Lisznyai and Mr Nagy.

'I must warn you that it is forbidden to spy on the president,' Orczy remarked offhandedly, then ran off.

Gimesi burst out laughing again, in his habitual way, which was with his head thrown back and his eyes closed like a rooster crowing at the sun. He got as red as a rooster's crest, too.

'President! That presidency went to his head. I am the secretary and I haven't got *that* much of a secret,' Gimesi said, showing the nail of his little finger.

Misi said nothing. He took Orczy very seriously. He was beginning to be afraid of him; he would uncover everything. He shivered as he thought of the rubbish bin and the pocket knife with its fish-shaped handle.

During the last class Orczy leaned toward him. 'Misi.'

'What?'

'If anyone asks you about the lottery ticket, you should say that you already gave it back to the old gentleman.'

Misi looked at him, taken aback. This was what he himself had told Orczy when Orczy first asked him about the numbers. He had thought of that; it was his idea not to confess that he had lost the ticket. He felt that Orczy knew everything now, and he cast down his eyes. Later Orczy whispered to him again. 'No matter how they question you, you must stick to this story, that you already gave it back.'

Misi nodded his head confusedly. But it seemed to him that there was a flicker of a smile on Orczy's face. It was a triumphant smile, and Misi began to suspect that Orczy had trapped him into a confession, learning from him just now that he had not given the ticket back to the old man. Angry that he had betrayed himself, he straightened up, bit his lip and looked darkly at his notebook, though he couldn't make out the letters and the sentences. He was boiling inside; he felt humiliated that he was such a child. Now he hated Orczy. He would have liked to push him off the bench. However, now he loved Gimesi very much. Poor little Gimesi, what a good little boy he was, how quietly he sat beside them, having no idea what was going on. Misi felt that they were living in an exciting crime story, but Gimesi, the third student in the class, this thin, puny boy, just sat there innocently with his smooth, white little face.

Misi wondered what else Orczy had up his sleeve. The next day was Sunday; there was a need for a conference. Perhaps Orczy would propose that they should meet at some mysterious place, under some tower or beneath a big tree in the forest. Later he thought that perhaps Orczy would invite them to his home. This made him remember the wax they had used to make the statues; he could still smell it. Then he thought of the tea they had, the white damask tablecloth, the fine painted china cups, and the beautiful blonde woman, and his face burned as he thought of the girl he had dreamed about.

At that moment he saw a piece of paper in front of him:

Tomorrow afternoon at our place at exactly four o'clock.

'Sign it,' whispered Orczy.

Misi didn't understand why he should sign it.

'Write your name there.'

'But why?'

Orczy became impatient. 'You have to sign it. It's a circular. Gimesi will have to sign it too.'

Misi signed his name and passed the note to Gimesi, saying, 'Sign your name.'

Gimesi signed without an argument. He passed the note back to Misi and Misi passed it to Orczy.

When the bell rang Orczy had already packed his things, as usual, and he left the moment the master stepped out of the room. He didn't even say goodbye to anybody.

Misi shook hands with Gimesi. '*Servus.*'

'*Servus.* Will you come to us this afternoon?' asked Gimesi.

'I can't. I would like to but I can't.'

'Why?'

'I have to teach.'

'Oh yes.'

Misi hurried away without saying goodbye. He wanted to imitate Orczy. In the past he had never been so mean; he was always the last to leave, letting everybody go ahead of him; he didn't keep any secrets – you only had to ask him and he told you everything; he always wanted to please everybody. But now something goaded him to be strong, to stand on his own and not let himself be pushed around.

He ran up the stairs two steps at a time and was quite out of breath when he reached the second floor. He was the first to get to the dormitory and took the key off the nail to open the door. He was pleased to be alone in the room; at last he had a minute to himself. He put his books in his drawer and took a deep breath. He wasn't thinking of anything but all his nerves were stretched to breaking point. Something was pulling him apart inside; he felt that his skin might rip.

Mr Lisznyai came in, without his overcoat; he never carried it inside the building. Then came the boys from the other class, Csicsó and Mihály Sándor. Misi was embarrassed; what if they realised that Orczy suspected them of stealing and had been interrogating them?

He hurried out of the dormitory and walked along the corridors to the old, unused part of the building where the windows, which had bars but no glass, faced the tower of the Great Church. A flock of shiny black crows was circling around the tower; he could hear their crowing. He put his arms through the bars. He would have liked to touch the birds, to rise into the air himself and fly away with them, and fancied that he was held back only by the bars on the window and the college walls. He felt as locked in as if he were in prison. It was so difficult to be without company even for a moment, yet he was all alone, without a brother, he could not pour out his heart to anybody. He grabbed the dusty iron bars and wished that he could be as strong as Sampson, shake the bars and bring down the whole building, let all the bricks fall on his head . . .

The dinner bell brought him to his senses, and he ran back to the dormitory. As he reached his corridor he saw the boarders pouring out of the dormitories, so he snatched up his overcoat and ran after them. Nobody seemed to notice him, nobody greeted him.

After dinner he hurried to the Doroghys', to his pupil.

As he passed the tall, sombre wooden gate, typical of the houses of Debrecen, imposing gates which hide barren, empty courtyards, Misi was buffeted by a gust of cold winter wind that took his breath away. He ran as fast as he could along the verandah to reach the protection of the house. As he entered the hallway, Miss Bella came out of the kitchen. She greeted him with a joyful cry and hugged him. 'God brought you, my dear!'

Misi laughed with delight. For a moment his face touched the girl's blouse; the warmth of her body melted the frost from his eyelashes. 'I kiss your hand, Miss Bella,' he said, trembling.

She held his face in her hands and leaned over him as if she wanted to tell him something, but she didn't speak, she only spread her sweet scent and showed her beautiful gleaming white teeth. 'Do you have a lot of homework?' she finally asked as she let go of him.

'Yes.'

'A whole lot?'

'Quite a bit.'

She laughed and turned her head, and gazed at some faraway place. 'Well, then, go in Mr Misi,' she said, and showed the way with a gesture.

Misi opened the door and went in. The mother was sitting in her usual place between three beds, in a shabby armchair with a table beside it. Misi greeted her in a quiet voice as he passed her. She didn't return his greeting but stared at him with her piercing eyes. She pursued him with her look until he escaped through the other door to the front room facing the street.

Only Ilonka, the youngest girl, was in the room, and as soon as she saw him she exploded in bursts of laughter. Misi was embarrassed and unhappy, finding himself alone with her. 'Please, isn't Alex here?'

The girl pressed her lips together to stop herself from laughing.

'Isn't he here?' Misi asked again.

At that she could no longer restrain herself and burst out laughing again. 'You can see that he isn't here.'

Misi blushed and she ran out, slamming the door behind her. If he had only been strong enough and had a long enough arm to reach through the wall or the closed door, he would have liked to grab her hair and shake her.

Perhaps she will call Alex, he thought, and sat down by the table, where the books were already laid out. He took out his pencil and began to draw lines at the edge of a notebook. It was warm, quiet and peaceful; he could hear the clock ticking in the other room. Suddenly he wrote:

Colonel Simonyi
in his brave youth
climbed the red tower

This poem had been moving about in his head for a long
time; he had no idea when he had first thought of these lines.
But he couldn't invent the rest. He never had time to think
about it. He wanted the poem to say that when young
Simonyi climbed out of the red tower to take some baby
sparrows out of their nest his friends dropped him but he
wasn't hurt at all. He wanted to make a ballad from the story,
something as good as 'Do not go up to Buda, good Hunyadi
László'.[1] One night in bed he composed the whole poem in
his head but he couldn't write it down and when he woke in
the morning he had forgotten it.

Suddenly he started writing it.

High was the tower
Its roof even higher,
covered with sparrows . . .

He was very pleased with that. He really hadn't expected it;
he hadn't even noticed that he was writing it down, because
he hadn't thought about it at all.

His friends pushed a plank
out from the tower.
He walked on it easily
high up in the air.
Goodbye, goodbye,
your obedient servant . . .

Oofff! He screwed up his face as if he had bitten into a
lemon. How beautifully it had started; he had thought the
whole poem would be that easy to write. But that 'Goodbye,
goodbye, your obedient servant'! . . . He had written that
down just out of silliness, because he couldn't think of

anything else . . . Now it was goodbye to writing poetry. How had he even imagined that he could write poems? 'Goodbye' . . . What would rhyme with goodbye? Oh my? Fly high? Good try? Don't cry? . . . Poofff.

> He stood on the plank
> ready to die . . .

He laughed sarcastically, he found it so bad.

> They pushed out the plank
> He stood on it high
> but he could not fly . . .

He gazed dreamily into space and then crossed out what he had written.

> The heartless rascals
> who held the plank
> were faithless to
> their brave young friend . . .

He crossed that out too.

Then a face bent over him. He recognised it from its warmth. It was Bella.

'Do you write poems?'

Misi tore the page from the notebook, crumpled it up and clutched it in his fist. Bella grabbed his wrist and, laughing, tried to wrest it from him. He defended himself with savage strength. She was far stronger than he was, but he curled up into a ball and pressed his fist against his chest. The girl grabbed him with both her arms and drew him against her to straighten him up. Neither of them knew how this wrestling began or why Bella had to have that poem, or why he couldn't let her have it, even if it cost him his life. They wrestled for over a minute in silence.

'Please give it to me, my dear little Misi,' Bella coaxed him when they separated. 'My golden lad, my only one, I will die if you don't give it to me.'

But Misi laughed triumphantly and put his fist in his pocket. His face reddened, his black eyes sparkled and grew bigger, and he just shook his head stubbornly and happily: 'No.'

'My dear little Misi, my sweet boy,' she said, stroking his face, 'you must give it to me, I'm so terribly curious about your poem, your lovely little poem, my dear darling good Misi, dear little Misi, give it to me my Misuka.'

'Out of the question,' said Misi. He had goose pimples from the joy of defying her.

'But my darling, you wrote it for me,' she said in a caressing, whispering voice. 'You know you will give it to me.' And she looked into his eyes, forcefully and strangely.

Misi wanted to laugh and tell her that writing a poem for her was the farthest thing from his mind, but – he himself didn't know why – he nodded that it was so: he let her believe that he had written the poem for her.

'What did you write, my sweet little poet? Did you write about rose petals, the scent of violets?'

Misi was flabbergasted. He really wanted to laugh. Rose petals? Was it possible to write a poem about rose petals? But he kept the laugh locked up inside him.

'If you don't give it to me I will be hurt, I won't forgive you.' But she said it cajolingly.

Again Misi shook his stubborn head.

'All right. I am angry with you.' She took out her needle-work and sat down behind the table by the window. 'I'm very angry,' she repeated, and didn't speak again.

Misi sat down at his place, saddened by the girl's seriousness. He came close to showing her the poem, but then Alex came in.

They didn't greet each other. Alex sat down across from Bella and noticed immediately that a page was missing from his notebook. He opened his eyes wide, he looked at Misi, he looked at Bella, but said nothing, just stared at them with a sour expression. Misi felt awkward about explaining what had happened, so he just started the lesson.

It was a difficult start, very disjointed, painfully haphazard work, but at one point Misi looked at Bella and their eyes met. The girl looked at him with such affection, so encouragingly, that some sweet warmth ran through his body. As if he had grown wings, every idea suddenly became clear to him, and he explained the rule of three very lucidly and succinctly. After that whenever he said something beautiful and true he always cast half a glance at Bella, and he always felt her caressing, kind, approving look.

He would have liked the afternoon to last forever. He had never felt so fresh, so wise, so amazing. Suddenly he could have taught anything. He embarked on the most difficult subjects and he was no longer explaining things to Alex, he had some higher purpose: he wanted to express himself in a majestic manner and use words which he had never dared to use before, such as 'the spirit', 'the sweet-scented flower' or 'poetic'. When Bella lit the lamp he fell silent and watched the flame of the match and the girl's dreamy, kind face. She had always been so lively, laughing, teasing, mocking, but now she was peaceful and kind; she really was a good sister. Misi had never felt so close to anybody apart from his mother. He was happy now; he forgot everything bad and ugly in life.

If only he could also forget that he would have to leave soon!

Today he was especially apprehensive about seeing the old gentleman. He tried to force himself not to think of the lottery ticket.

In the warm silence where only his voice could be heard he eventually lost heart and became dejected again. They were translating a Latin sentence, *the glorious origins of the Roman nation inspire every citizen*.

He couldn't help commenting: 'The origins of the

Hungarian people, on the other hand, do not inspire our citizens.'

Bella looked at him, surprised. 'Why not?'

'Because the Hungarians are such boors that they know nothing about their origins and they are not interested.'

'But why not, Misuka?'

'Because they think it's not worth their while. Because their ancestors were not great lords but poor shepherds, horsemen, peasants. And that's why they don't care about their relations either, because their relations in the east remained poor and are shepherds and herdsmen to this day.'

'What relations?'

'We too have relations! The Germans and the English, they know that they are related. The Italians know that the French are their relations. But the Hungarians don't know about the Finns or whoever.'

'They don't know about us either.'

'Because poor people don't keep in touch with their relatives. Only the rich do. Yet it's not only counts and princes who have relatives. Even poor day labourers have relatives, but they lose sight of each other because they can't afford to have anybody for dinner.'

'How do you know about our kith and kin?'

'I only know a little about them, what I heard from my mother and my uncle who is a professor, and from Mr Nagy, who talked to me about them yesterday, and our geography teacher. And I read the ancient Hungarian legends. When the Hungarians left Asia to conquer the empire of their ancestor Attila, many of them were left behind in the east and they were never invited to come to Hungary.'

'Why should they have come here anyway?'

'Because this was a great beautiful country. Wouldn't it have been better if they had all been together? But rich people don't want to know about their poor relations. A count with an estate may have poor relatives but he would never invite them.'

Bella looked at Misi thoughtfully. Misi was speaking with

anger and enthusiasm, with flaming eyes, as if he were confessing to her his most secret thoughts, as if she were the only
one who would understand him.

'That's true,' she said, growing serious, thinking of her
rich aunt in Budapest, 'the rich forget about their poor
relations.'

'We deserve to be ruined,' cried Misi. 'Wouldn't it be good
for us if there were Hungarians in the whole of this beautiful
country, if we had no Serbs or Austrians or other nationalities?
Those foreigners will never help us, they don't care what
happens to us. If there were Hungarians all around us, it
would be easier. But the Hungarians never thought of inviting
their people from the Old Country, because they didn't want
to share. They all wanted to be counts here, and it is not so
easy to lord it over your brothers.'

'People manage,' said Bella with a sigh, thinking of her own
family.

'That's true, I know that, too, because my family was
ruined,' Misi went on, getting more and more carried away.
'Our land and our two houses were auctioned off three years
ago, because the combine harvester got blown up and we had
to pay for it. That's when we moved to the village we live in
now. My mother has relatives there, in-laws, and they said,
come, join us, here you live as if in paradise. And when we
came they wanted to hire my father as a day labourer for
starving wages. They asked my mother to wash their floors
and didn't even think of paying her for it. When my mother
sews a skirt for a peasant girl the girl pays her twenty or
twenty-five forints, but when my mother made a skirt for my
Aunt Sára she didn't even give us a jug of milk, she paid us
with a compliment, telling my mother, "What clever hands
you have, Borcsa!" My mother hates that name, she has always
been called Borika at home, but my aunt calls her Borcsa, the
way the gentry call their maids, to make my mother feel that
she's an inferior person, no better than a servant. The poor
shouldn't go near their rich relatives because they will turn
them into servants, use them to do their washing-up. You

have to be well off to visit the rich, then they'll treat you with
respect, they'll try to please you.'

Bella understood, better than Misi, she felt, how true it all
was — but still! She watched the little boy with amazement;
her face was tender and sad. 'You are right, Misuka, a poor
girl can't go to them. She has to look rich, at least.'

Misi was silent for a while, thinking before he spoke.
'Imagine if somebody discovered some old parchments or
books which showed that at the time the Hungarians settled
here some of them went farther west and now they were the
inhabitants of France. Then the Hungarians would immediately start to talk and write about our great relations the
French, flatter them, try to get nearer to them . . . But our
relatives are only Cheremisses or Zyrians or Tartars who can't
do anything for us — it's better not to talk about them. That's
why I'm angry at the Hungarians.'

'Yes, that's what we are like,' sighed Bella.

'And yet, you know, it's possible that those Finns are better
and more beautiful people than the French. And if they had a
little luck they could be just as civilised, or more so. But the
Hungarians are not interested in helping a relative to become
educated or rich. My father doesn't have a single forint. He
has to work the whole day for thirty kreutzers, making sledge-
runners. If one of his rich relatives in the village would stand
surety for him we could get a combine and start something,
and in a year we could recover what we lost. They wouldn't
do that, of course. They prefer to visit us in their fur hats and
coats, those rich peasants, and drink the brandy my poor father
had to buy from his thirty-kreutzer wages. They do their best
to keep us poor. They're afraid we might acquire something.
They believe that if we were a bit better off they couldn't
tower over us like great lords.'

'You have to be rich to go near rich people,' said Bella,
adding wistfully, 'If I could be rich for just one day, I could
visit my relatives in Budapest, then everything would be all
right.'

She leaned forward over her needlework and with her big

dark eyes as black as coals and her fine, longing, noble face she seemed to Misi like a bird about to spread her wings and fly away. She was so strange, not at all like her usual self; it made such a deep impression on Misi that he would never forget that moment.

It took him some time to remember what he wanted to say. 'The rich Hungarians would never want to give a hand to the poor Hungarians. They would rather harm them than help them. There were times when we were a rich nation and we were never good, not for a moment, to our poor relatives in the east or in the north. We weren't interested. That's why we know nothing about our ancestors and that's why we don't have any allies. The Hungarians will never be a great nation. They are not like the Romans. The Romans were even fewer in numbers than the Hungarians when they started history: they amounted to no more than one city, and yet they could conquer the world. The Hungarians can't even conquer their own country. And no wonder! When the Romans set out to conquer the world, they let everybody join them – anybody could become a Roman citizen. The Hungarians would deny that their own brothers are Hungarian. Each one beats his chest and claims that he is the only true Hungarian. Who would want to be friends with us?'

'If only I had one really elegant, stunning, rich dress!' said Bella. 'Then I could go to my aunt, Princess Petky, and I could kiss her hand and tell her who I am.'

Distracted from his train of thought, Misi started again from the beginning. 'But Hungarian, German, French, English, Chinese, it makes no difference – our geography master talked about it the other day – we've all had the same skull for the past ten thousand years. *All* our bones have been the same for ten thousand years. The only thing that makes a difference is money.'

'Yes,' sighed Bella. 'Money is the reason for everything.'

'My father has to work all day in torn clothes, sweating, for thirty kreutzers. A teacher can wear nice clothes, doesn't get his hands dirty, all he has to do for his salary is go to school, just like a student. A rich person doesn't even have to do that much and he's still rich and has everything.'

Bella looked into the little boy's eyes expectantly. Out of the mouths of babes, she thought. 'I'm going to ask you something, Misuka. You must tell me what you really think. If somebody is really poor, unhappy, miserable, and has a chance not to be poor any more, to join the richest people and live in plenty and also help her family, her parents, would it be right for her to forego that opportunity?'

Misi thought of his parents and his younger brothers who were probably slithering about on the cold earth floor at that moment, the smaller ones wetting themselves and catching cold, with the wind blowing through the cracks in the door and the door frame with its thick white coating of frost. 'No, it wouldn't be right,' he said.

Bella bent her head. Neither of them talked for a while. Misi would have liked to speak, but his throat tightened. He remembered that he had held good fortune in his hand, the lottery ticket, and his share would have been a thousand forints. His family had been ruined for much less than that; everything they owned was auctioned off for six hundred forints. And he could have given a thousand forints to his parents! They could have lived like gentry; his younger brothers would have been little gentlemen, if only he hadn't lost the ticket! His lips trembled, he would have liked to tell everything to Bella, but he was held back by Alex. Alex didn't join in the conversation; he didn't understand a word of it, but he would have understood about the lottery ticket and would have regaled the whole class with the story. So Misi didn't speak. It was too late anyway. It was nearly five o'clock; he had to go to Mr Pósalaky.

With great noise, the oldest sister Viola burst into the room. It was mercilessly cold outside, and she brought in the freezing air with her. 'Now it's done, it's done at last!' she announced, 'I made ten forints' down payment for the land. But what it cost me talking all that time! These peasants are revolting.

How much I had to swallow, but it doesn't matter, now we have a piece of land big enough and good enough to feed us all the year around. Aren't you pleased, Bella?'

Bella straightened herself in her chair, then leaned back and closed her eyes. 'Should I be pleased?'

'Yes, yes, you ought to be very pleased!' Viola rebuked her and turned towards the boys. 'Well, how is it going? When are they going to hand out the report cards? When do they let you out for Christmas? The festive season is upon us! You've only two weeks left to show some diligence!'

Misi bowed his head; he had nothing to brag about. He doubted that Alex knew any more than when he had started tutoring him. 'We would need to study a lot more,' he muttered.

'Bella will help you. She will study with Alex.'

Bella didn't jump as she had the other time; she remained in her seat and was quiet, volunteering for duty with a 'Yes.'

'Yes, Bella, it's high time that you helped Alex, high time that you helped all of us a little!' Viola said accusingly, as she unwound the black cat fur from around her neck and took off her heavy coat.

'All right,' Bella replied almost inaudibly, 'I'll help you all, as much as I can.'

Misi watched her: there seemed to be tears in her eyes. The sight pierced his heart.

'Oh, Alex, if you can just get through the next seven years!' sighed Viola. 'Those seven years, oh God! They will be terrible, but never mind, I'm not sorry for myself, or anybody else, if only this boy will have a better life!'

Misi finally understood and was shocked. He foresaw that Alex would end up as a young dandy leading an easy life from the pain and sweat of his sisters; he looked at the lazy slob with loathing. He stood up. He had to hurry to the old gentleman, but even if he didn't have to, he couldn't bear to be with them any more.

'Oh, I almost forgot, this is yours,' Viola said and put two silver forints into his hand.

Misi took the money hesitantly: he didn't realise that he had been coming to the house for a whole month. He thanked Miss Viola shamefacedly, as if she had given him alms; he almost kissed her hand.

He was already in the hallway when Bella came hurrying after him. 'Won't you leave your poem with me?'

Misi had quite forgotten about it and his face burned when he remembered. He reached into his pocket and took out the crumpled piece of paper to hand it to her, but then suddenly he felt that it was a very bad poem and was afraid that she would think less of him and laugh at him if she read it, so he put the paper back into his pocket. 'I'm sorry, forgive me.'

Bella stroked his face and gave him a quick kiss on his forehead, which frightened him, and he hurried out of the door into the moonlight. He ran until he was out of breath. He found life very badly organised, without rhyme or reason. He didn't understand what was missing in him that he could make no sense of it. Why was everything upside down? There were so many wise people who could understand and explain everything; why should there be two families as unlucky as his own and the Doroghys?

He felt very close to Bella now. How good she was, how kind! He was profoundly moved by her curiosity about his poem. He regretted now that he hadn't given it to her. He had never experienced so much goodness from anyone outside his family. If the boys found his poem they would certainly make fun of him, but Bella, although she was a grown-up woman, had treated him as an equal all afternoon. What a pity that her family had lost their wealth. They were worse off than his family because they had lost more. Bella's grandfather had hired a whole train just for himself; no one in Misi's family could ever have done that.

Misi began to dream how nice it would be to have lots of money, enough to fill a basket. Or a whole room! Then he would buy back the whole Doroghy estate and give it to them as a present. But not to Viola, so that she could be even more shrewish and even more demanding and commanding! And not to their father, who would squander it on drink. And not to lazy, useless Alex, who deserved nothing but a beating. Nor to the giggling horror, nor to their mummified mother, but to Bella alone, so that she could rule over everybody and have beautiful clothes, a palace, servants, so that she could be the queen of the city, with the whole world trying to please her . . . But even then he wouldn't give her his poem. Not if she kissed him ten thousand times. He laughed to himself, tickled by the thought.

It would be good to have money. If he had a gold crown which he could spend as many times as he wanted because it always came back to him, then he would empty the shops of the city for Bella, send silk dresses to her house. No, it would be too slow paying with a single gold crown, waiting for it to come back each time. How much better if he would see in front of him right now, on the sidewalk, a big fat wallet stuffed with thousand-forint banknotes, which nobody was looking for! It would be even better if he could be like King Midas and whatever he touched turned into gold – no, only those things that he wanted to turn into gold. Then he could delight Bella with gold flowers. If he couldn't do that, he would be content to know where the ancient treasure was buried that was marked by a blue flame shooting up from the ground, as people said in the village. He would dig it out . . . Or if a beautiful fairy would come and tell him that he could have three wishes. Then he would make two wishes and his third wish would be three more wishes.

He found a thousand different treasures and gave them all to Bella. How hot her lips had felt on his forehead. Perhaps she had a fever, the poor girl.

He was so worn that he could hardly read the newspaper to the old gentleman. At the end of a column he was shocked to see a little news item about the lottery.

He was so frightened that Mr Pósalaky sensed something was wrong. 'What is it? What is it?'

'Nothing. The lottery numbers.'

'Well? Did our numbers come up?'

'No.'

'No? Damnation!'

Misi read out the numbers. 'Budapest: 5, 95, 4, 11, 92. Vienna: 12, 37, 43, 7, 88. Prague: 71, 7, 46, 83, 18. Linz: 34, 45, 76, 13, 2.' For some reason the winning numbers for the Brünn lottery weren't there.

The old gentleman was silent for a long time. Misi's heart was thumping so loudly that he was afraid Mr Pósalaky would hear it.

'Well, which lottery did you play?'

'The Budapest lottery.'

'And what were the winning numbers in Budapest?'

'5, 95, 4, 11, 92.'

'Not one of them is our number,' said the old gentleman angrily. He didn't want to talk about it any more. 'What else is in the paper?'

Misi read on hurriedly.

The lie made him quite happy. He could have laughed thinking how easy it was. Until then he had no idea how he would deny that they had won. If the old gentleman had kept questioning him he would have had to tell the truth. But how easy it was to lie! Just one word, that was all. What a fool he had been to worry about it so much, when it took so little to put it all behind him!

Mr Pósalaky didn't mention the lottery again. By the time Misi left it had got colder. He hunched himself up inside his coat and hugged it closer to his chest as he hurried on towards the college. He was contented and hungry. Yesterday had been a horrible day but today was all the better for that.

As he was about to cross the street by the Great Church he saw somebody out of the corner of his eye. At first he didn't think of any particular person, because he didn't usually notice ladies, but some unknown force drew his gaze to the woman.

In front of a shop window a young man and a young

woman stood talking and laughing and looking at the brightly lit display.

Misi stood rooted to the spot. The young man was the no-good János Török, and the young woman was Miss Bella.

If lightning had struck beside him he would not have been half as surprised. If the tower of the Great Church had raised its roof and bowed to the ground to greet him, he would probably have greeted it back politely, but this turned him into a tree. He was frightened, revolted and couldn't move.

The couple stood about five steps from him; he could hear Bella's familiar laugh. He heard her voice speaking lightly and cheerfully. 'I know your kind. The trouble is one cannot believe anything you say.'

'So help me God,' the young man swore in a deep rumbling voice, and leaned closer to the girl.

Bella made a gesture as if she wanted to walk on towards Misi, who was so terrified that she might see him that he ran like a scared little dog and looked back only when he had reached the darkness of the sidewalk by the Memorial Garden.

He could not see them from there and that upset him even more.

X

Misi wakes to a sad and difficult Sunday and looks into a dizzying future. Some unknown force pushes him forward onto a path which he would never have taken of his own accord

M ISI HAD GOT quite used to waking up in the middle of the night. He would look into the darkness and try to understand impossible things.

How had Mr János become acquainted with Miss Bella?

It had to be in an underhand way, because when Bella read Mr János's note she had said, 'gladly never'. She had no idea who he was and no interest in getting to know him. And yet she talked with him so freely, so gaily as they stood in front of the shop window. Misi would have liked to think that Mr János forced his way into the Doroghys' house and persuaded her with wicked lies to believe something horrible . . . And why was Bella so gentle and sad yesterday? . . . Tomorrow he would have to go to the Töröks' and tell Mrs Török that her son . . . No, he should tell Miss Török that her brother was about to do something evil, because he was an evil man.

Half-asleep, half-awake, he could see the scene in the Töröks' kitchen. He was telling them about Mr János. Auntie Török despaired, Miss Török cried angrily. Mr Török took his long pipe out of his mouth and, raising his thick grey eyebrows, told his son, 'I forbid you to put innocent girls in danger'.

Misi had no idea what that danger might be but he was heartsick for Miss Bella. She had been so sweet and melancholy yesterday. Thinking of it, he began to cry. He felt that something terrible, something unimaginable, threatened her. He was afraid; he didn't know what he was afraid of, but he was afraid.

He could hardly wait for the morning, for the sun to rise so that he could dress and go out and do something. He was in a rage with himself, with Miss Viola, Alex, their father, their mother, the giggling horror, Mr Lisznyai the room prefect, who was sleeping calmly, uncaringly, as if everything was all right. He was in a rage with the other boys, the college, the teachers, the Töröks, with the cold, the high fences, with fate, in a rage that he was still a boy, that he had to be so small and so weak. If he was as strong as Sampson then he would grab János Török, that show-off who always looked as though he had just come from the barber with his hair all oily. He would grab him and throw him against the wooden fence and make him wipe off the chalked message 'INFLUENZA FOR SALE!' with his nose.

That made Misi laugh. He chuckled to himself very contentedly, but carefully, without moving; he didn't want to wake up anybody. If he had magic powers he would fly through the walls and away from the college – still in his bed, with the eiderdown over him, because he could sense that it was very cold outside: he could feel the frost sneaking in through the cracks in the window frame. He saw himself flying in his bed over the other boys in the dormitory; one of them had kicked off his blanket and he reached down to cover him up. Then he flew through the back wall of the dormitory, over the roofs of the college, over the back courtyard, over the tiled roofs of the city, until he came to the Doroghys' house. Then he went into Bella's dark room . . . He had goose pimples from the pleasure of thinking about it. He would have brilliant light around him but it was only for him: others could see neither him nor his light; only he could see. And he would see poor, sad, sorrowful Bella lying in her bed, crying . . . That brought tears to his eyes too. Then this mirage faded and he saw himself in Mr János's room, hitting him in the face with his fists so hard that his nose swelled up and he looked so ugly that he couldn't go near Bella . . . But he should beat Mr János in such a way that he didn't wake up; he only felt that he was being beaten and knew who was beating him, so that he would always be frightened when he thought of Misi, Mihály Nyilas! Mr János wouldn't dare to go near Bella again, trying to make a fool of her . . . How he would jump on Mr János's belly, dance on him, hitting him with his heels and shouting, 'So you want that girl, you villain!'

He kicked his iron bed so hard that his feet hurt. What was worse, the bed creaked so loudly that it might have wakened somebody.

Then he thought about gold again. Oh God, how nice it would be to become rich suddenly, so that money went straight into his pockets from the pockets of everybody he met. Or when he passed the post office − there was lots of money there − the banknotes rose from the tills like butterflies and flew into his pockets. Or at his command the gold reserves of the Bank of England flowed through a mysterious pipeline to the potato cellar at home, where he used to collect frogs. Oh God, if only he had the money, he would give to everybody . . . Then he grew ashamed, thinking that he had been stealing, because all this money would be taken from somebody, and the postmaster would have to pay it back to the post office. What he wanted was power over gold that didn't belong to anybody; he wanted gold crowns to roll to him that would be lost otherwise. A wind, a special wind, would blow all lost money straight to him; all he had to do was pick it up. Or he had a magnet that drew it to him . . . Or all the unmined gold in the earth transformed itself into gold crowns for him and collected in a cave, and when he said 'Open, Sesame!' the rock rolled away from the entrance and he carried the gold away in his school satchel. Or maybe there was a room in the college with a false floor and under it a cellar full of treasure, and when he stamped his foot the floor opened for him. But only he could see it until he was ready to

let others see it too. Then he would give the college one
hundred thousand gold crowns for scholarships, so that every
student should get free books and be able to study without
having to pay tuition fees, and should get free meals too, and
better food and more of it, so that they would be in the mood
to study. But only the peasant boys, because the parents of the
gentry boys didn't send them to board in the college, or if
they did it was only for a year or two . . . And back home in
his village, that beautiful little village with all the walnut trees,
the best village in the world, he would give money to
everybody, as much as they wanted. And he would build
dykes along the Tisza to hold back the water, because every
year the river was coming nearer to the village; it had already
swept away half of the cemetery. He remembered his father
saying that the old cemetery was taken by the river when he
was a child. Once when he and some other boys were tending
horses on the banks of the Tisza they found an open grave
with a clay pot in it, and when he put his hand into the pot it
came out black as soot. Misi and his brothers laughed at the
story. Now he could see his father, smiling gently, sitting on
the bed. That was where he sat to tell them stories when he
was in a good mood because he had come home after being
away somewhere, or because it was Sunday morning and he
didn't have to work. On Sunday mornings he stayed in bed
and all the boys climbed on him and danced on his back and
on his outstretched arms. Misi could still feel the hardness of
his father's arms. Once his mother said, 'There isn't a
handsomer man in the world than your father. When he was
young his body was like glass and white as marble.' Oh my
God, how good it would be to roll about with him, to
snuggle up to his leg under the warm blankets. Sometimes he
shook them off like a big sheepdog shaking off his puppies and
sat up, beaming, to talk about his younger days. He told them
how he and some other boys who were tending horses on the
banks of the Tisza let the horses into a rich farmer's
wheatfields, and the man waited up for them night after night
with an axe and a pitchfork, but to no avail, because when he

was guarding his wheat in one field they herded the horses into another; when he was there, they were here, when he was here, they were there . . . Misi also remembered his father telling him about the time he and the other boys stole salt from a raft on the river. Later when the customs men came around the farmer who had bought the salt from them threw the sack into his well to hide it. And then for a whole year you couldn't drink the water . . . Misi could hear his father's dear strong voice. 'Ahhh, and you should have seen how many apples I rafted down the river to Szeged. You've never seen so many apples in one place. I sold them all and brought your mother cloth enough for three dresses and a basketful of money. I just poured it into her lap . . . Good God, how much I did in my life! What do all these donkeys know who never dared to stick their nose out of the village!' And there were the times when he came home and talked about *virtus*: how he had run into some men somewhere who thought they could push him around because he was short. Well, he showed them. He slapped those useless bullies so hard that they flew. 'That's true,' Misi's mother used to say. 'Your father has terrible hands, they are as hard as iron.' And his father laughed proudly.

Misi's skinny, weak little body was filled with warm happiness as he thought of home. He pulled the eiderdown up to his neck and pressed the warm corner of it against his face, making himself believe that he was hugging his father's dear warm body. And so he finally fell asleep, forgetting all his worries, all his troubles.

When he woke in the morning the other boys were washing themselves. They washed in line, first face, neck, chest, armpits, splashing water everywhere; afterwards an earthenware wash-basin was passed from boy to boy for the feet. The whole dormitory was soaked. They were surprised that Misi wasn't wakened earlier by all the talk and the noise of water sloshing around him, and laughed at him because he was the last to wash his feet and had to use the dirty water in the basin.

The bell was ringing for chapel and as Misi still wasn't ready the other boys went out, leaving him behind.

The sweeper – a boarder whose turn it was to sweep the dormitories that Sunday – came in and, stirring up the dust with his broom, told Misi to get out of his way.

'Leave me alone!' Misi shouted at him. 'I'll go when I'm ready.'

'Go, or I'll beat you with the broom!'

'Just you try, let me see you try!' Misi responded threateningly.

He had never been so aggressive, his schoolmate could hardly recognise him. 'If you won't let me sweep, then sweep yourself! I'm not going to stand around here waiting for everybody!'

'That suits me fine!' Misi retorted.

The other boy threw down the broom with its worn and broken twigs, put on his hat with a flourish and left.

That was better, Misi thought, at last he was on his own: he could dress slowly and comfortably. He would have liked to be handsome and elegant; he was annoyed about his worn brown suit, especially his detestable trousers which were neither short nor long. He wanted an elegant pair of breeches like Orczy's, which fastened below the knee with buttons. A pair of long trousers would have been even better, a pair of really long trousers which grown-ups wore. Even Orczy envied those; once he had complained to Misi that he had asked his parents to get him a pair of long trousers but they had said he couldn't have them until he got to the fifth form. It seemed nobody was happy with his clothes. Orczy had talked about the time he and Mr Gyéres were out walking and stopped at a shop window displaying suits and overcoats. Mr Gyéres looked longingly at a beautiful dove-grey spring coat and sighed, 'I could use a new coat' – but then added that it was all right, gentlemen shouldn't wear new overcoats. Orczy had commented to Misi that the Latin master's short brown overcoat was indeed quite shabby, but Misi couldn't see what he meant: to him Mr Gyéres always looked smart, too smart, disgustingly elegant. Misi's father looked better even in patched-up trousers and shapeless boots. He was the best-looking man in the village; he stood so straight, so brave, so strong, with such an open, clean face, that those big, dark, raw-boned farmers, no matter how they dressed up, were just peasants beside him. But right now Misi would have liked new clothes, new shoes; his shoes were scuffed, worn down at the heel and warped because of the way he walked. Once when they walked to the next village his father had told him, 'Watch your step! I'll break your ankle! You're kicking your feet as you walk.' Ever since then Misi had tried to keep his feet straight and watched everybody else to see how he should walk.

Dressing slowly, he had time to wish for everything. If only he had a pocket watch that would tick-tock in his pocket on the left side. Ahhh! that would be nice. But he didn't want a chain with it, dangling before everybody's eyes, like Mr Lisznyai's. He would wear it as Mr Nagy did, without a chain, and take it out and look at it every other minute.

In short, he wanted to be a grown-up. He was bored with this long-drawn-out business of childhood, which looked like it would never end. He thought his younger brother was right: he had kept asking all summer, 'Mother, how old am I?' 'You are seven years old,' they kept telling him for a whole week. The boy couldn't stand it and burst out, 'Will I always be seven years old?' Misi felt the same way: always a schoolboy, a little schoolboy, and around him all these donkeys who didn't mind being children and were complacent about going into the third form the next year and then into the fourth form and then into the fifth form and on and on to the eighth form. He had no patience for that. He wanted to be a man right away. He hated going to school; he wanted to know everything right away and understand it, without having to worry about Latin syntax and geometry . . . How those idiots could laugh! He could hear their clamour in the courtyard. How cheerful they were; life was all joy for them; they were happy about everything, even about Sunday. They rested and amused themselves; they thought even chapel was fun . . .

When he was finally dressed, in the same grubby clothes as on weekdays – only his underclothes were clean – he brushed himself and began to regret that he had so thoughtlessly accepted the task of sweeping the dormitory. Everybody else was already down in the classrooms; that was where they had to gather to go up to the chapel by classes. He would have to go on his own, trying not to be seen.

He had to ask the boy on duty to cross his name from the list of absentees, but once that was done he felt very comfortable in the chapel. He liked the high ceiling, the tall pews in which he got lost like a glove, and thought with awe that it was in this chapel, in 1849, that Lajos Kossuth[1] spoke about Hungarian independence. Kossuth stood in that very pulpit and spoke in his sonorous voice. If he could only have heard that speech!

Now it was the religion master preaching. Earlier the choir had sung and it had sounded so strange and mysterious, as if it wasn't human voices up there in the choir loft singing in four parts but the sound of distant trumpets. The religion master spoke just as he did in class, mildly and softly, only more slowly and nasally and half a pitch higher than normally.

After the service Misi looked at the inscription over the tomb of Professor Hatvani; he could never pass it without trying to read it, remembering the stories about Professor Hatvani, who turned four corn cobs into four fat pigs. When the farmer who bought them at the market in Debrecen took them home, the four fat pigs turned into four corn cobs again in his courtyard . . . Another time, when the Chief Constable of Debrecen saw Professor Hatvani walking on the highway and offered him a seat in his four-horse carriage, the Professor replied, 'I can't, I'm in a hurry.' With that he drew a six-horse carriage in the dust with his stick, took his seat in it and drove away, according to the Chief Constable himself, who saw him flying past in a gilded coach. The Chief Constable tried to

keep up with him but could not, and indeed when he reached
the city he saw the Professor leaning out of the window of his
house, puffing on his long pipe. Misi drew his hand over the
cracked marble as if he were touching the famous Professor's
cape, and then ran down the back stairs, jumping three steps at
a time, into the throng of students who were dispersing into
the courtyard.

Misi thought he would go to the Töröks' before lunch, but it
was already half past eleven and it wasn't polite to call on
people at lunchtime, especially as he had been there the
previous Sunday. They would immediately know that something was wrong. He started out after lunch, hurrying towards
Nagymester Street, but slowed down abruptly at the thought
that they were bound to be surprised, seeing him come again
so soon. He was thinking of not going at all; he didn't have all
that much time – he had to be at Orczy's at four. As he was
ambling along, running his fingertips over the planks of the
wooden fence, a thick, soft hand touched his shoulder. 'Well,
my schoolboy, my little tutor, how goes it?' Startled, he
looked up. It was Uncle Szikszay. Of course, the Szikszay
family visited the Töröks every Sunday afternoon. But now
the old man was on his own; there was no sign of his wife or
children. Misi thought of enquiring after them, but Uncle
Szikszay seemed to have forgotten about him, and they
walked beside each other in silence. After a while Uncle
Szikszay began to hum quietly to himself.

> Little dog, big dog,
> you bark too late . . .
> I'm with my sweetheart . . .

Misi was startled and looked at him. He was humming the
same song as Alex Doroghy's father; they were two of a kind,
those two good-time uncles, with their beards and their big
fur coats. Except that Uncle Szikszay seemed more human,
more ordinary, with his huge soft belly and his red nose and

his long sharp waxed moustache. As they went on he began to hum and whistle more loudly.

> Famous city built with bricks . . .
> tralala, tralala . . .
> My sweetheart lives here . . .

Then he gave a sharp, long whistle. Uncle Szikszay was in the habit of humming in the street, but now he sang and whistled so loudly that Misi didn't dare to look at him. He didn't want the old man to realise that he was making a spectacle of himself.

When they reached the Töröks' gate Uncle Szikszay went in first with Misi trotting behind him like a little dog, not looking a bit like a man appearing on the scene to wreak revenge and put things in order. He didn't hurry into the house; instead he went to the courtyard at the back and walked about a little before making his way to the Töröks' kitchen door. He was quite alarmed by his own courage and would have given a lot not to be there at all . . . He paused at the door, thinking that he might still disappear, but Uncle Szikszay had undoubtedly told the Töröks that he was there and they would be expecting him. If he ran away, what would they think? So he gathered his courage and went in.

Against all precedent, there was no one in the kitchen. But the door to the inner room stood ajar and there was a big discussion going on there. No, not a discussion but sobbing and wailing. Misi's blood froze. Uncle Szikszay was crying.

How was it possible? This man who was always full of good cheer and songs, who had just been singing in the street so loudly that his voice resounded through the whole city, was crying. In between the sobs Misi could make out a few words. Auntie Török said, 'But Lajos, Lajos, how could you even say such a thing?' And she wept and Miss Török wept too.

'Now I have no other choice,' shouted Uncle Szikszay. 'I cannot bear it. I would rather die a thousand deaths than suffer this humiliation.'

228

Miss Török shouted too. 'But Uncle Lajos, you must talk to that wicked man. You must try to soften him.'

'Never!' screamed Uncle Szikszay. 'Never!' And then he repeated it in a singsong voice. 'Never . . . I would rather die a thousand deaths . . . '

Now Uncle Török gave his opinion in his low, dried-out voice, but you could feel that he was more moved than the others with all their crying. 'There is no question of talking to him. There would be no sense in it. But you mustn't despair. There is no sense in that either.'

'But who am I? Lajos Szikszay!' Uncle Szikszay shouted at the top of his voice and pounded his chest so hard that it echoed. 'How dare they do this to me? I struggled and worked for twenty-five years in the service of this miserable city and they treat me like this?' Then he told them the whole story. The words poured from him. The Mayor was his bitter enemy and had been trying for a long time to push him out of his job, but couldn't get anywhere under the old Prefect because that man knew who Lajos Szikszay was. But the Mayor, the old fox, managed to blacken him to the snotty-nosed new Prefect, and now Lajos Szikszay was put in front of a disciplinary hearing and they suspended him, they fired him, all in one day, because when they audited the accounts the day before they discovered a miserable hundred and seventy-nine forints were missing . . . There must have been a mistake in the audit. Or – he wouldn't put it past them – they doctored the figures themselves to make out that there was a deficit. For a hundred and seventy-nine forints they swept aside the merit of twenty-two years service . . .

'And why? I ask you, Pál Török, why? Because a person's honour, a person's dignity mean nothing in this city. Here they need only servants who lick the feet of their superiors. They want only people who have no pride, who flatter everybody in authority and are ready to auction off a poor person's last pillow. I'm asking you all, why is this happening to me? It's because I wasn't born in Debrecen, I'm different from people who first saw the thieving daylight in this thieving city. I can't adopt their way of thinking, my religion is not the same as theirs. My *Our Father Which Art in Heaven* is not the same as theirs. Here every cow, every bull, every heifer, every colt, every pig, every armchair, every book has a stamp on it: CD, City of Debrecen. I couldn't learn this religion in twenty-five years; I'm not their property. Not me. Everybody knows what it means, CD, it means steal, steal, everybody knows, everybody practises it, only Lajos Szikszay doesn't, that's why he had to face a disciplinary hearing.'

There was silence for a while, then Uncle Szikszay began reciting his complaints in his sonorous voice. 'I took my job as comptroller seriously. How often I rapped the mayor's knuckles, asking him, What became of the city's fattened pigs? What happened to such-and-such funds of the city? What happened to the wheatstalks from the Great Forest? Where were the hides of the animals that died on the Plain? I . . . I'm the only one who knows that they wanted to turn the gasworks' fifty-year contract into a hundred-year contract, so that even our grandchildren would be paying for them. Even the Bavarian company that wanted the concession was more modest . . . Fifty years is enough, said I, Pósalaky is my witness. I saved the city money then. If people only knew, they would bless my name for thirty-six years. And now I am thrown out, my God, with six children, without anything, without a bite of bread, dishonoured, robbed of my good name, I can get myself a beggar's stick, and all this for a hundred and seventy-nine forints.' He slumped over the table with his head on his arms, sobbing so desperately that the table rattled.

'It's impossible, Lajos, it's impossible, my dear good Lajos,' cried Mrs Török.

'Impossible! That scoundrel had the face to tell me that if he wasn't the mayor I would be in prison on remand until they find out what happened to the money. Throw me in jail, Mr Mayor, I told him, throw me in jail, but throw me in a jail where they stab you in the heart without investigation. Unheard of! This man thinks he's the Doge of Venice, to wreck a life like that! To break it in two, to besmirch it, to poison it for generations. How will my son live down the name of a swindler, in this swinish city? All the thieving that went on here, which everybody knows about, now all that will be put down to me. People will point at me in the street: there goes the city's thief!'

He beat the table with his fists, now with one, then with the other. He beat it softly and rhythmically, and suddenly started to sing again:

> Little dog, big dog,
> you bark too late . . .
> I'm with my sweetheart . . .

Then he whistled the song right to the end without a false note. Still, his whistling was as ghostly as if it had been the last scream of a murdered man.

Misi listened with wide-eyed, horrified fascination to this appalling catastrophe of grown-ups.

'There is nothing left for me to do but hang myself. Or rip myself open. There is no other way out.'

'Lajos!' screamed both Auntie Török and her daughter.

'Don't get frightened, he's not going to do it,' said Uncle Török. 'He can't do it because he has six children to bring up, six small children who depend on him . . . For him, of course, the easiest thing would be to die. That is liberation. There is nothing better than death. The dead have no worries . . . But he won't do it, because he's a healthy man, he has a healthy soul, he is full of blood and strength, he is fit to work and willing to work . . . He can survive until his name is cleared, even on dry bread, even if he has to cut wood. He will survive because he is indestructible . . . I am different, I couldn't survive it . . . I couldn't . . . If such trouble befell me . . . I no longer have the strength to survive that sort of disaster. I cannot fight, I cannot struggle any more . . . ' His voice drowned in tears.

Nobody spoke.

Then he continued, choking. 'Look, I can't cope with this family. I have this wicked son, I can't stand him, I've despised him since he was sixteen years old. From that time I didn't talk to him, I ignored him, until this year. Now finally he's grown up, he's got a steady job, he does it somehow or other, I don't expect much of him but perhaps in time he will become a serious person, he will get married, his wife will straighten him out, and I thought, I am an old man now, why should I die a stranger to my son? But he's still a bad boy, irresponsible, a troublemaker . . . Now my wife can't abide him. She fought with me for ten years defending him, and now I have to argue with her for a bit of tolerance. Even that is too much for me . . . '

Uncle Szikszay began to whistle again.

> Famous city built with bricks . . .
> tralala, tralala . . .

Breaking off his whistling, he decided to help the Töröks. 'Look, my dear little Julia,' he said to Mrs Török, 'there is so much trouble in the world, don't add to it, make peace with your son.'

'My God, that someone should need to speak to a mother on behalf of her own child!' said Auntie Török, weeping. 'But I can't bear him, now that he's coming to see us again . . . He is *not clean*. He is my child, how did he get this way? Neither from me, nor my husband . . . he's so dirty . . . '

'How can you say that? He's always immaculate,' objected Uncle Szikszay.

'It's his soul I'm talking about. His soul is not clean. He's always hiding something. Just today he told us he's going away somewhere. But where?'

'He's going away on business, his company are sending him,' said Uncle Török.

'That's right, Papa, take his word for it. He can make his father believe anything.'

Misi couldn't stay in the kitchen; he was terrified that they would catch him eavesdropping. He should have shown himself a long time ago! And the news that Mr János was going away somewhere was like a bomb exploding next to him. He couldn't stay put. He tiptoed to the verandah door, closed it stealthily behind him and ran like a thief.

Misi had hardly got past the gate when he saw Mr János coming towards him. He was so shocked, he would have liked to become invisible, and quite forgot about his stormy fantasies of the night before when he had given Mr János a severe beating, having acquired great physical strength in his sleep. However, for the time being, in the cold light of day, it seemed wiser to lift his hat and offer a cowardly and respectful greeting to Mr János: 'I wish you good day.'

'Hey,' said Mr János in his usual loud cocky manner, 'come here, boy, hold my briefcase while I say goodbye to the old people.'

With that he pressed into Misi's hand a small black case. It wasn't a big or heavy case, but Misi felt so humiliated that he nearly dropped it.

'Take good care of it, mind you! *There's money in it!*' With that Mr János opened the gate to the courtyard. 'I'm taking the train to see your Uncle Géza,' he added before going in. 'While I'm inside, think of what message you want me to give him.'

Misi was left on the street, a pillar of salt. Finally he leaned against the wall and watched the dust on the road. He felt dizzy, and to tell the truth, the street was wide enough to make any boy dizzy: it was so wide that when Misi had lived at the Töröks' and watched the cattle coming back from the fields in the evening, he had thought they looked as spread out as if they were on the Great Plain. Two cowherds directed them with their long whips which could sting thirty or forty yards ahead. One of the cowherds had a brass trumpet and every morning at dawn he stood in front of the little shop opposite the Török house and blew his trumpet to signal the departure of the cattle. One morning Uncle Török opened the window and beckoned to the trumpeter: 'Come here, son!' He called him to the window and offered him a glass of brandy. 'This is for your trumpet-playing, you're very good at it. Did you learn to play in the army?'

'Yes,' replied the cowherd.

'I enjoy it very much. Every time you play your trumpet, I'll give you a glass of brandy.'

Well, at dawn the next day everybody in the street jumped out of bed: the cowherd blew his trumpet so enthusiastically that the pictures of Árpád raised on his shield shook on the walls.[2] In his nightshirt, barefoot and with his puffy eyes still full of sleep, Uncle Török opened the window, leaned out and gave the cowherd another glass of brandy. He did the same on the third day. The cowherd was amazed by Török's generosity, especially as until that time Török had done nothing but complain about his trumpeting. But at dawn on the fourth day Török gave nothing. His window did not open on the fifth day either. On the sixth day the trumpet did not sound, and the cleaning woman reported that the cowherd was angry and had sworn that the old miser wouldn't get another chance to listen to his trumpet playing for nothing . . . He went to blow his trumpet in front of Parraghs' mill, which was so far from the Töröks' street that not a single note reached them and nothing disturbed their early-morning sleep.

When Misi had lived at the Töröks' the previous year the whole household had laughed about this, and Misi, remembering it, couldn't help smiling too. He hadn't laughed or smiled for such a long time that he noticed the sensation of his cheeks folding into wrinkles.

What kind of money was in that briefcase? How could such a drinker, such a dandy get hold of so much money? The case burned Misi's hand as if it was stolen property. And why had Mr János entrusted him with it; why hadn't he taken it in himself? And he had threatened him, too, saying he would talk to Uncle Géza about him. It was sad to think he was such a bad boy that he had to be afraid that his uncle would hear about him. If he could be a bull, now! A big, black, sooty bull, like the one in his village that made people run into their houses whenever it ambled down the main street. Not for half the world would a child consent to stay outside, nor a grown-up either; it would have gored any man brave enough to show himself. Misi heard that the bull once gored a cowherd who had beaten it, and the cowherd was so badly injured that his bowels spilled out. Now Misi felt he was running down the street with Mr János's bowels dangling from his horns like sausages and trailing in the dust, like a dog dragging a stinking thighbone from the butcher's shop.

Mr János came out carrying a suitcase. He didn't tell Misi to hand back the briefcase, he just motioned to him to follow. That was a new humiliation, because it looked as though Misi was his hired porter, and Mr János walked so quickly that Misi had to trot to keep up with him. It was a good thing that he didn't protest, though, because Mr János had some big worry on his mind: his face was very dark and he was thinking, which wasn't something he was in the habit of doing.

But Misi decided that somehow he was going to forego the honour of carrying Mr János's case to the railway station. When he reached the college he said, 'Please, Mr János, I have to go back to the college.'

Mr János stopped and looked him over. 'Well, my boy, you're such a proud little fellow, you wouldn't accept a coin the other day. Here, I'll give you ten forints, will you take it?'

'No thank you,' Misi replied, and backed away as if Mr János had threatened to slap him; he even put his hands up to protect his face.

Mr János grabbed his arm, wrestled with him, trying to press the ten-forint note into his hand, then pushed him away with disgust. 'All right, go and pop, you little firecracker!' With that he picked up his briefcase and walked on towards the Great Church without looking back.

Misi watched him for a bit, then ran into the college. He was all stirred up; his whole body was trembling. He felt dissatisfied with himself. If only he had said one word! If only he had dared to throw one harsh word at the scoundrel, signalling his contempt. But no, he was as cowardly as a rabbit.

What should he do now? He had nothing to do in the college and he didn't want to go up to the dormitory; he would have to talk to the other boys. So he just raced along the corridors and stopped in front of the notice board, which no boy ever passed without looking at it to see who had got letters.

He saw his own name, and the notice wasn't for a letter but for a money order! He started trembling again, this time from joy.

He went into the porter's lodge, but no one was sitting at the desk. Several men were playing cards in the inner room, laughing and shouting; Misi didn't want to disturb them, so he just lingered in the doorway until one of the men turned to ask what he wanted.

'My letter . . . Please, my name is on the board.'

One of the men stood up — not the regular porter but another man — and after much rattling of keys and rummaging about gave him a pink form.

As Misi looked at it he recognised his father's writing and his heart began to hammer, because his father's forceful, impetuous, magnificent handwriting always electrified him. His characters looked like fresh wood shavings flying from his axe. Misi was happy that his eyes could roam between them. He could see his father's laughing face, his small moustache, his friendly blue eyes. When he read something his father had written, every letter in it made him laugh. When he read his mother's writing his heart contracted with guilt.

'You can pick up the money until three,' said the porter, taking his five kreutzers.

'Where?'

'Well, in the post office.'

Misi left the porter's lodge and read his father's note in the windswept corridor. It was brief:

My dear son, the money is for whatever you need.
Everything is all right here. Take care of yourself. Your
mother will send a parcel for Christmas. Kisses from your
loving Father.

'My dear son, the money is for whatever you need,' he
repeated in his mind, and his eyes filled with tears as he ran
out of the college. 'My dear son, my dear son!' he could hear
his father's brave sweet voice. 'Well, my dear son, buy yourself
a present!' But he had money, and he wasn't spending that
either. They had nothing at home, and he should buy things
for himself? Yes, if he could buy something he could send
home, that would be different. But what could he send them?
Only something useless. They should be buying things at
home, he didn't need anything. They should be buying meat
for the children, not just for Grandmother, they should get
sugar . . .

He ran as fast as he could and was at the post office in no
time. He went into the courtyard and saw the green post
carriages having their Sunday rest, without the horses. A
postman came out of the building with a pipe in his mouth;
he told Misi where he could get his money, adding. 'But
hurry, it's nearly three o'clock!'

It was only then that it struck Misi that he would be
spending Christmas in the college, because if his mother was
sending him a parcel, it meant that he couldn't go home. And
why? It must be that they didn't have the money for his fare.
They must be going without things at home . . . He would
send back the forints.

He went to the post office and through the bars, though he
could hardly speak for crying, he asked the only clerk on duty,
'Please sir, where can you send money?'

The clerk looked at the little boy with tears running down
his cheeks. 'Perhaps you want to pick up money?'

'No, I don't, thank you, I don't want to pick it up, I want
to send it back.' And he handed over the money order, feeling
sad that he wouldn't be able to read his father's writing

again. The clerk kept turning the paper around. 'Well, if you don't accept it, you must write here that you don't accept it.'

Misi took the paper and a pencil from the clerk and was about to write, but then he was suddenly taken aback. He should write to his father that he refused to accept it? What would his father say? 'The plague take this snooty kid. He's not accepting from his father?' Misi stopped crying to laugh as he heard his father's cursing voice. 'No, please sir,' he said awkwardly, 'I want to accept this but I also want to send them two forints.'

The clerk was a thin blond man in a uniform and Misi was already afraid that he would refuse him, because people in uniform were terribly strict. But in fact the clerk was beginning to take an interest in him and advised him in a kindly voice, 'Well, then, take this money they sent you and address another postal order.'

'Yes, sir.' Misi went to the table in the middle, which was quite black with ink-spots, and with the kind of broken pen that can only be found in post offices, with thick ink which gathered in a blob at the tip of the nib, he signed his name on the back of the postal order.

The clerk cut off the part with the signature and gave the rest to Misi, who was very glad to have his father's note back. He was given another blank postal order and wrote the address clumsily with the miserable post office pen; it looked so messy, he was ashamed of it. He also wrote a short message:

My dear good father, I thank you very much, just worry about me. I kiss your hand, Your loving grateful son Misi.

When he read it over he was alarmed to see that he had left out the word *don't*, so he stuck it in before *worry*. But he dawdled over the writing for so long that the clerk, in spite of being moved to sympathy for the little boy, observed in a voice like dried beans rattling, 'It's three o'clock, get on with it.'

Misi handed over the money order and wiped the ink from his fingers on the inner lining of his jacket. The clerk asked him for one forint five kreutzers. Misi took the money from his little purse and got a receipt. It was strange to see a stranger's hand writing down his father's name. He ran out happily with tears in his eyes. He would have liked to see his father's writing again, the way he wrote those big jumping letters, that *Mihàj Nyilas*. It made him laugh, the *j*. His father never made spelling mistakes, except that he didn't think much of the difference between *j* and *ly*, since they were pronounced the same way. He had never been so proud and happy in his life, and he ran all the way to the end of Market Street.

When he reached Railway Street, he stopped, remembering that he didn't have to be at Orczy's until four o'clock and it was only three.

So he walked more slowly towards the railway station.

The street was narrow here and led to a big square with a low one-storey yellow building in the middle of it. A small engine puffing smoke emerged from behind the right side of the building and then came to a stop. To the left of the station was an esplanade where the students liked to stroll now and then, especially in the autumn when the olives were ripe. Wonderful big olive trees stood in the square, and the students liked to chew on the dewy olives. The smell of the olives gave Misi a peculiarly pleasurable feeling; he liked it as much as he hated the smell of the acacia flowers. This alien tree which he had never ever seen anywhere else led his thoughts to other parts of the world under different skies. He recalled his Uncle Géza's words: 'What a pity that our father Árpád didn't lead his people beyond the Danube valley; a few more days of riding would have been sufficient, and we would be in Italy now and wouldn't need to heat our houses.' Misi smiled at that, because remembering snippets of conversation had the same effect on him as if he were listening to people actually talking to him.

The merciless, cold winter wind, which is meaner on the plains than anywhere else, flared up one minute, died down the next, and Misi drew himself together under his cape. He thought he might go inside the station to get out of the wind, although he didn't like to enter strange places that he had no business to be in. He could walk on the streets because it was common practice for people to walk on the streets whether they had to go somewhere or not, but it didn't feel right; he imagined that man should always work, that was what he was born to do, and from being with his father he had learned that when you have to do something you do it promptly, then start on something new.

He could feel his heart beating as he entered the station. A carriage happened to be standing in front of it; porters in striped jackets were taking a big trunk down from the box.

The main hall of the station had a high ceiling and in the middle there were glass windows with counters where tickets were sold. Misi mingled with the passengers, dazed by all the strangers around him, the echoing noises, all the hustle and bustle without pause or change, and by the terrible stink that came from the direction of the toilets, from the pink carbolic used to disinfect them. He went as far away from them as he could, towards the second- and first-class waiting rooms. He couldn't enter them, nor did he want to; railway clerks in blue jackets stood at the door asking for tickets.

But he couldn't resist peeking through the glass door. He found it very strange that people were constantly travelling. He felt the same way as when he looked at an anthill; he had no idea why all those creatures were scurrying about so relentlessly. These people were always travelling? That was their work, to travel?

Then he cried out loud. Through the glass door he caught sight of Miss Bella. He stood petrified, open-mouthed, staring at her.

But what if Miss Bella turned her head and saw him? There was a stir in the waiting room; everybody was getting up. The clerk started to ring the bells. In his fright Misi ran all the way back to the ticket counters.

He stopped there and pressed his hand, blue with cold, over his pounding heart. After a little while he pulled himself together and stealthily made his way back to the waiting room. Cautiously stretching his neck forward so that he could retreat in an instant, but also taking care not to look too conspicuous, he peeked through the glass door again. The girl was no longer there.

The passengers were pouring through the other doors to the platform. A railwayman was shaking his sharp-sounding bell and calling out a list of unintelligible names, the places where the train was going. Misi remained on the spot where he had been standing when he first caught sight of Bella; he stood there until the waiting room emptied completely. Beyond the glass doors facing the platform, he could see the train carriages moving, picking up speed and then disappearing in a blur. The station became quiet again, the porters came back from the platform counting their coins, and Misi watched them, and had no idea what he should think.

Then he turned around and walked slowly out of the station. Outside the wind hit him in the face; it was blowing again as if it had gone mad. He lowered his head, trying to hide behind the narrow rim of his hat, and his face hurt from the sharp stinging wind which almost blew him over. His eyes were watering by the time he crossed the station square and reached the shelter of the rows of houses; there the wind quieted down and he could progress more easily. 'But it couldn't be true,' he said to himself, 'I'm losing my mind, I think every girl is Miss Bella.' It was impossible that she should have been talking with Mr János last night and should have left town the very next day. She hadn't said anything about it to Misi when he saw her the day before.

But why should she have said anything to him? The previous year he had read a novel in an old bound volume of the magazine *Home and Abroad*, and there were such peculiar things in it that he couldn't understand them; he had thought, oh well, it is only fiction. The strange relationships between men and women were totally unbelievable. But now he began to sense that many mysterious things might be possible. True, Miss Bella had said *gladly never* . . . But who knew what it meant, perhaps it meant *perhaps, maybe, who can say?* . . . If she wanted to say *no*, then she could have said *no* . . . She could have sent Mr János packing. She could have told him to leave her alone, how dare he write letters to her, it was an impertinence, the plague take him . . . or whatever beautiful girls said whenever they didn't want to do something. But that was wicked, that *gladly never, never gladly* . . . Now Misi felt certain that they did meet and now they had eloped together.

He stopped in his tracks. Until then he hadn't thought of Miss Bella going away with Mr János, because he hadn't seen them together in the waiting room, but Mr János must have gone away on the same train. That was why he had gone to the station. Misi remembered that even then he had felt it wasn't right that Mr János should be going away with a briefcase full of money.

He felt that he would go mad thinking about it; he would have liked to cry, and did so instantly. Sudden tears ran down his face. Such a wonderful, beautiful girl, who was such a good girl yesterday and talked to him so nicely, and was so kind and friendly and not wilfully wild as at other times – that she should go away with such a dirty scoundrel . . . My God, what a misfortune!

He reached the Little Church, which didn't have a tower; it was half finished, like the bastions of castles in battle scenes. And there was Kossuth Street, where he had to turn right because it was a quarter to four and he had to be at Orczy's at four.

How terrible this afternoon had turned out to be! He resolved that he would never go back to the Doroghys'. Why should he? The only person who made it worthwhile to go there had gone; he despised the rest of the family . . . Poor girl, how sweet she was when they were together in the dark pantry and she said 'I wouldn't teach that donkey' . . . And always . . . And now she had gone away, and he would have to continue to teach that donkey, that stupid insolent pig, Alex.

Now he hated Orczy too. He was afraid that Orczy would

see that he had been crying, and he didn't want to tell him anything because he was certain that he would blab about it to everybody.

He stopped in front of the Orczys' apartment building; he wanted to wait a little to catch his breath and calm down. But when the church clock struck four he ran in, in the same way as he ran to the old gentleman at five.

Now he knew how to ring the bell, but when an old woman servant with a kind face let him in he didn't recognise the hallway and once more got lost among the many doors. Only the coat hooks on the wall were familiar. He was amazed to see that the velvet wall-covering under the hooks was green; he had remembered it as red.

The old woman looked him over, didn't say anything, and let him into Orczy's room. Again Orczy was in the other room with all the lights, but he hurried forward to meet Misi. 'Well, what should we do now?' he shouted excitedly and took Misi's hand.

'*Servus*,' Misi said mechanically, the way he had prepared the word beforehand in his mouth.

Orczy wasn't laughing, he was very serious as he said, '*Servus*'.

'What should we do about what?' asked Misi.

Orczy lost all his sang-froid. 'Our cook Fáni just came home. She went to the tobacconist after lunch, after washing up, and what do you think? Somebody picked it up yesterday afternoon!'

'What?' cried Misi, knowing what was coming.

'The winnings.'

Then they were both silent, looking at each other.

'The tobacconist told the person who came for the winnings on Wednesday that she would pay them only on Saturday. She wanted the delay in case someone else showed up. But the numbers were up in the window for four days and no one else came, so she paid.'

Misi clasped his hands and looked at Orczy, stupefied.

'And now neither my father nor my mother is here and I don't know what to do. Fáni, Fáni, come here!'

The old woman who had opened the door to Misi came in and started to speak with terrible despair, as if it had been her own money that was stolen. She wrung her hands, sighed and wailed. 'Oh my God, oh my God, if only the master was here. Oh my God, why didn't the little gentleman tell me in time? I could have gone to the tobacconist yesterday. Oh my God, this is terrible. The tobacconist is also beside herself. She doesn't know whom she paid the money to.' The old woman clasped her hands to her head and walked up and down. She was so desperate that her fright passed on to Misi, who only now began to feel that some calamity that cried to heaven had befallen him, if even strangers could be so horrified by it.

Then the old woman told him to sit down and he sat down and listened as she repeated the same story word for word, for the second or third time: how she had got to know the tobacconist, how often she played the lottery, how she had never won, she just carried her money there. True, she played only ten kreutzers at a time, playing numbers she dreamed about or picking numbers from a lucky box. At one time or another she had played all the lotteries, but she hadn't won on any of them, only once when she let her little niece pick the numbers, because innocent children had luck. That time the numbers came up, except that they played the wrong lottery, putting their money on the Prague one, and the numbers came up on the Vienna lottery.

Misi was silent; he couldn't say anything, and Orczy didn't know what to do either, he just kept jumping about and laughing and shouting 'Why doesn't Gimesi come? Why didn't he come at four?!'

They hadn't noticed how time was flying. When the clock in the other room struck three quarters, Misi jumped up. He had to go.

'A tall man with wavy hair and a waxed moustache took the money,' said Aunt Fáni, and Misi saw Mr János coming into the tobacconist, opening his briefcase, putting the money in it . . . And he, Misi, had carried that briefcase, he had held it in his own hand that day. He felt dizzy; he nearly fainted. He began to sob aloud and, ashamed of his sobbing, ran out to the hall. He could hardly put on his coat. The old woman wanted him to stay, Orczy wanted him to stay, to wait because his parents would soon be home and they would do something. True, he had called the meeting for four because he knew they wouldn't be home. He had wanted a presidential meeting; he hadn't foreseen, of course, how things would turn out.

Misi walked down the stairs trying to swallow his crying and wipe his tears away with his fist, then ran, turning right towards the theatre. He had enough presence of mind left to look at the poster: to his great surprise they were still playing *The Scamp*. Then he forgot about the theatre and ran across the public gardens towards Mr Pósalaky's house.

But how could he go to the old gentleman now, after all this crying? By now he must know that Misi hadn't read the winning numbers of the Brünn lottery, and he must have asked people about it. He too had an old servant woman, who deciphered his dream. By now she must know everything, because these old Debrecen women always knew everything, and she must be telling everybody that out of the five numbers four came out in Brünn and a whole briefcase full of money was paid to a thief.

When Misi reached the corner where he would have needed to turn left towards the market to get to the old gentleman's house, he couldn't bring himself to do it and hurried on towards the college.

Three boys were standing by the main gate, one who lived in the city and two boarders. They called him as he passed and asked him whether he wanted to go the theatre.

To the theatre? How could anybody think of asking him that when he had never been to the theatre?

'I don't want to go,' said one of the boys. 'I thought they were playing *The Red Purse* but it's something else. I have a ticket for ten kreutzers, if you want to go I'll sell it to you.'

All his life Misi had longed to go to the theatre, and he couldn't resist. He took out his purse, picked out a ten-kreutzer piece and gave it to the boy. 'But remember,' said the boy, 'you have to be there at seven o'clock, understand? And do you have permission to stay out late?'

Misi was alarmed. 'No I don't.'

'Then go to your class teacher. I saw him a few minutes ago, he's sitting in the Bull Café. Just show him the ticket and he'll give you permission.'

The two boys laughed but he took them seriously and turned around to go to the Bull Café. But when he got there his courage fell into his boots. He didn't dare to go into the brightly lit café, though he peeked through the window and could see Mr Gyéres sitting there reading a newspaper and smoking a cigar. There were other people there too and the café was flooded with light because all the gas lamps were burning. The gas lamps there didn't burn uncertainly, as they did in the college; they didn't flicker like butterflies: here the lamps were in glass globes and burned with a steady glow.

Misi turned around and ran away. He felt that he had to go to the Doroghys' and did not stop until he got there.

There too he stopped at the gate. His hand was on the latch but he couldn't bear to open it. What if Bella was home and looked at him, then what would he say, why had he come? But a group of men were coming towards him down the dark street and they weren't peasants but gentlemen. Perhaps there were some of his teachers among them, and they would see him with his hand on the latch, afraid to go in. And he couldn't run away either, because they would immediately recognise him and report him.

He was in a terrible fix. In his despair he opened the gate and went in. In the courtyard the watchdog started to bark; it was already unchained for the night. Misi was terrified of it because back in the village a little black dog had bitten him once, and the post office dog had bitten him too; he still bore the marks of it on his knee. He began to scream with fright and Miss Viola came out of the house and shouted at the dog. When she recognised Misi she was glad to see him and led him into the house by the hand.

'Well it's very nice that you came, my dear Nyilas, it was very kind of you, very very kind.'

Misi tried to smile but he was so pale that when he stepped into the lamplight they asked him what was wrong with him. The whole family was there, even the papa, who sat in his chair looking sad, ready to leave. He was just preparing his cigar.

'Well, Alex, now you should look for your games, for once you shouldn't study.'

Alex laughed but looked warily at Misi. He didn't trust this tutor; he was afraid that they would end up with a Latin lesson just the same.

Misi was hoping that Bella would appear from somewhere but she didn't. 'Bella isn't home,' said Miss Viola, as if she had sensed what the boy was thinking.

Misi nodded that he knew. At that Viola looked at him suspiciously. 'Did you see her somewhere?'

The question scared him.

'Where?' demanded Viola.

'At the station.'

'Where?!' shouted Viola, and they all looked at Misi. At that he reddened and recounted that he was out walking and went into the station, where he saw Miss Bella in the first-class waiting room, and later saw her getting on a train and going away.

Everybody got upset and looked at him as if he were an arsonist.

'She took the train?' Viola asked slowly, and leaned forward. 'She took the train? To where? With whom?'

Misi looked at them like a cornered animal.

A terrible hullabaloo started then.

'With whom did you see her? With whom?' Viola kept asking.

'I didn't see her with anybody. She was alone in the first-class waiting room. When I looked in the second time I didn't see her. The train was leaving.'

Viola picked up the lamp and began to search the cupboard, the beds, turned over everything and finally came back from the other room with a letter in her hand. She tore it open, tore the envelope to bits and then read:

Dear Father, I am going away today. Don't worry about me. I think I can help the family more by going away than by washing dishes all day to please Miss Viola. I kiss your hand. Bella.

Viola threw down the letter. 'The slut!' she shouted. 'And she has to travel first-class. First-class. We are keeling over from hunger here, we're getting as thin as reeds, and she's travelling first-class. Third class isn't good enough for her. Well, now I know what she is, this little lady.'

Misi sat quietly watching the family. The mother was silent, as always, but paler and more corpselike. Alex sat hunched over with his head down, practically under the table, and the youngest girl wasn't giggling. She was as scared as a cat; her face looked longer and she was much prettier than when she was giggling.

The father was savouring his cigar and smiling under his moustache, looking more cheerful than before. Finally he got up and said, '*Servus*, children.'

'And Father is going away! Father, how could you leave?'

The father looked at his eldest daughter with surprise. 'Why shouldn't I leave?'

'You leave us in the bottomless pit of despair.'

'But why in heaven's name are you so worried about your sister? I'm not worried about that girl. Didn't you hear that she travelled first-class?'

Viola looked daggers at her father. She became the archangel of moral outrage in this broken-down ruined family.

The father left and that took everybody's voice away. But

whom could they have talked to? None of them had anything to say to the other. For a moment it seemed that Bella was the one who had kept the family together.

As the minutes passed Misi thought more and more of the theatre, but he couldn't leave, he was afraid that they would say he came only to stir up trouble. So he asked Alex whether he had done his homework for the next day. Alex hemmed and hawed, confessing that he hadn't done the homework.

At that Viola jumped up and gave him a tongue-lashing. 'You *must* study,' she said. 'Even if that worthless slut has run away I am still here, and even if heaven and earth collapse, you must do what you have to do. And mind you, if this boy cannot teach you, I'm going to hire a boy from the eighth form who will teach you with a two-ended stick.'

At that the youngest girl started giggling. She thought the two-ended stick was meant to be a very great threat. With Ili giggling again it was back to business as usual, and so they took out the books for the next day's lesson. Which was lucky for Misi, because he hadn't studied anything himself for the past couple of days.

He stayed for supper. It was a very good supper; he didn't understand why they were always complaining about starving to death when they had such marvellous stuffed cabbage.

He left them at half past six and went to the theatre. It was an indescribable, magical fairytale evening: there was a hat shop or something on the stage with lots of white top hats and exceptionally beautiful girls with young gentlemen – the girls were the eloping kind. But he was distracted by the thought that Mr Gyéres would never have given permission for him to see such a shameless play and the college gate would be closed at nine o'clock. If he wasn't home by then he would be locked out and would have to sleep on the street. And he would freeze to death by the morning. Or if he rang to be let in it would be noted that he had stayed out without permission. The next day he would have to go to the Head's study, and that was the same as death.

So after the first act he slipped out and ran back to the

college, although it was only eight o'clock. Then he thought
again: everybody in the dormitory must know that he had
gone to the theatre, and what would they say if he came
home early? So he hid in the corridor near the chapel until
the gate was closed, and then waited until, with a great
hubbub, the boys came back from the theatre.

By then it was terribly late and Misi was chilled to the
bone. Shivering and with his teeth chattering, he slipped into
the dormitory. By then everybody was asleep but Mr Lisznyai
woke up and asked angrily, 'Where have you been, what were
you up to?'

'Mr Prefect, I was at the theatre.'

'Well, light the lamp.'

But Misi's hands were so stiff with cold that he didn't want
to risk breaking the lamp, so he asked permission to undress in
the dark. When he got into bed it took him a long time to get
warm; he was awake for an hour before his body thawed out
so that he could think. Oh my God, was the train still running
with Miss Bella?

XI

*The little schoolboy endures all the sufferings of
grown-ups who have to earn their bread*

AS HE WAS putting on his jacket in the morning Misi
found a ten-forint note in his pocket. He was about to
cry out from amazement but then caught himself.
Wondering how it had got there, he bit his lips and crumpled
the banknote in his fist. Ten forints! Almighty God! It flashed
through his mind that Mr János had tried to make him accept
ten forints when he gave back the briefcase. The thief was
trying to salve his conscience . . . He could certainly afford to
give away that much, the scoundrel!

Misi became so nervous that he was unable to collect his
books for school. The ten-forint note was burning his pocket,
his skin . . . He certainly wasn't going to give it back. He
would buy a pair of shoes for fifty kreutzers and spend four
forints going home for Christmas. It was high time he got a
new pair of shoes, because the soles of the old ones were
worn right through; if it rained or snowed he wouldn't be
able to go into the streets. His feet would get soaked, and he
had a lot of walking to do to get to Mr Pósalaky's, and the
Doroghys'.

The banknote wasn't safe in his jacket pocket. What if
he pulled it out with his handkerchief, just when he was
answering questions in class? Or at any time! Christ, what
would happen if someone saw that he had all that money! . . .
He transferred the crumpled note into his trouser pocket,
remembering only afterwards that he had no trouser pocket,

because once when he had no handkerchief with him he had torn out his trouser pocket and used it to blow his nose. He reached down for the banknote, which was already sliding down his leg, and caught it before it fell to the floor. He was pleased to have it in his fist again, but where should he put it? He thought of his drawer in the big table, but what would happen if someone rummaged in the drawer and found the money? The best thing would be to hide it in the false bottom of his trunk, but what if there was an official search because of the stolen lottery ticket? He couldn't hide it in a book; it might fall out or be forgotten. On second thoughts, the best thing would be to sew it inside his jacket: one of his uncles, a shoemaker, had brought his money that way when he came home on foot from Transylvania. But sewing took too much time, and he wasn't sure whether he could do it well enough; he had a needle and thread at home and once he had sewn his trousers when they were frayed at the edges, but it was poor workmanship, he could see that himself.

Then the bell rang for class. The boys were leaving the dormitory and Sándor called out to him. 'Aren't you coming, Nyilas?'

'I'm coming but I forgot something.' Misi opened his trunk and started to rummage in it, but in the end he didn't dare to leave the ten-forint note there. Instead he pushed it down into his vest pocket. It was such a small pocket that he had never put anything there before; there was hardly room enough for the banknote.

As he was going down the stairs he thought that perhaps it would have been better after all if he had hidden the banknote in his trunk, because if there was a body search, or if a corner of the note stuck out of his pocket, he could be in trouble. He kept putting his hand to his vest to check whether he still had the money there.

He took his place in class blushing and trembling, driven to distraction by the stolen money in his pocket. But what was wrong with that, the money was stolen from him! At least he had got ten forints back from his fortune.

Orczy came into the classroom and greeted him confidentially, whispering in his ear, '*Servus*, everything will be all right, the money will be found!'

Misi felt as though he had been struck by lightning. They would find the money? Then that ten-forint note in his vest pocket was in a very bad place. 'How do you know?' he asked Orczy, swallowing.

'My father went to the police,' said Orczy, and that frightened Misi even more. Cold sweat broke out on his forehead.

In an urgent whisper Orczy told him that his father was outraged and had said that however much trouble it took, he would have that thief arrested. He had already talked to the Chief of Police, who was 'in my father's hands', Orczy said: that man could fix anything, Misi had nothing to worry about.

'Well, and why didn't you come yesterday afternoon?' Orczy asked Gimesi cheerfully.

'Come where?'

'To our place.'

'To your place? Why?'

'Didn't you sign it on Saturday?'

'What?'

'The circular, of course!'

'What circular?'

'Didn't you have him sign it?' Orczy asked Misi, surprised.

Misi began to pay some attention to what they were saying. 'Yes, yes, he signed it,' he insisted.

'You mean that piece of paper?' asked Gimesi. 'I signed it, of course, but I didn't know what was on it.'

Orczy found this very funny, and even Misi smiled.

'Well, it was a presidential circular,' Orczy whispered.

'Why didn't you just invite me?' Gimesi flared up, red as a red paprika. 'It's so idiotic!'

Then the master came in and they couldn't continue their conversation. Misi sat in his seat dazed, numb, closing his eyes frequently. Saliva was collecting in his mouth and his throat tickled. He wished that he could get his half-share of the money Mr János had stolen. Would that be a thousand or two thousand forints? How much was in that briefcase he had been carrying for Mr János? How heavy was it? He tried to recall its weight on his arm; he thought it might have weighed as much as five kilos. Five kilos of banknotes . . . that must have been a lot of money. He wondered what a thousand forints weighed . . .

He suddenly woke up and looked around, surprised. How strange it was, here was the teacher on the platform; he had no worries, all he had to do was explain things. And here were the boys; they were paying attention or they were not, and they had no worries, they just had to be there, and someday somehow they would graduate. He felt he was the only one who didn't belong. His heart and mind were full of alien concerns; why was he sitting here with these children?

He leaned back in his seat and closed his eyes. He was so dazed that he almost fell asleep.

'Isn't that so, Misi Nyilas?' asked the master suddenly.

Misi jumped up, scared, having no idea what the question was about.

'It's nice to have a good little nap during class, isn't that so?' asked the master, prompting an outburst of general merriment.

Misi was ashamed, bowed his head and the master gestured that he could sit down. But Misi didn't notice that either. He stood with bowed head until the master walked over and, without saying anything, took him by the shoulders and gently pressed him down on his seat. Misi nearly burst into tears that the master was so kind to him, instead of telling him off and giving him a 4.

During break István the head porter came into the class-room and shouted, 'Mihály Nyilas!'

Misi was doing his mathematics prep, which he had never before left to the last minute, and was hurrying with it as fast as he could, trying to finish it before the master came in. Startled, he jumped up, and the rest of the boys fell silent. They all knew that Uncle István ran errands for the Head.

'Come to the Director's study,' said the head porter, who looked like a gentleman, so much so that many people mistook him for one of the masters. He walked very slowly and with his back bent, and his face was feverish all the time from tuberculosis. The boys said that he would have died a long time ago if he hadn't married a young wife. She would be the first to die, and if after her death he married another young girl, she would keep him alive until she died too. Misi didn't believe it; he had already heard the same story back home in the village and he thought that peasants' superstitions were just foolish nonsense. Still, Uncle István had acquired a mysterious aura in his eyes and he didn't want to have anything to do with him. Numb with fear, he left his exercise books and pen and ink behind and with unsteady legs hurried after the head porter. When he left the silent class burst into excited chatter; Misi knew they were talking about him.

As Misi entered the anteroom of the Head's study, where he had once spent a painful quarter of an hour, he was filled with dread, as if he had passed through death's gate. The head porter went on into the study, dragging him along; this time there was no question of waiting, and this frightened Misi even more.

The Head, with his frosty grey beard, sat behind his desk reading something in front of him.

'Sir, I have brought Mihály Nyilas.'

The Head went on reading; he had big round glasses on his nose. When Misi calmed down sufficiently to look around the room he saw two men. One was a tall, slim, fair-haired man in civilian clothes; the other was a gendarme in uniform. This was the first time that he had seen a gendarme at such close quarters; he had seen them in the railway station and in front of the town hall, but he had always given them a wide berth because they made him feel uneasy. Now those two men were watching him with such hard, piercing, searching looks. He averted his eyes, feeling dizzy and nauseated. God Almighty, those policemen had come for him!

He was no longer afraid of the Head; he looked up to him as his saviour. It steadied him a little to see that bearded bristly face, but he felt the policemen's eyes jabbing his side like needles.

'So,' grunted the Head, 'tell me, what kind of lottery ticket did you embezzle?'

Misi began to shake. He opened his mouth but no sound came out.

The Head pushed back his chair and shouted. 'Well, let's hear it, out with it, you scoundrel!' Then he thrust out his arm to point at the policemen. 'These estimable police officers came here to interrogate, to investigate. They broke into the College like Cossacks. Nothing is sacred to the law today, not even the College. They break through the walls, they threaten me with guns, they would shoot me if I resisted!'

'I humbly beg your pardon, my most esteemed sir,' the policeman in civilian clothes said very meekly, 'the Chief Constable humbly begs your pardon and begs you not to take our coming amiss.'

'What do you want me to take it for? A decoration?! This is how the College is honoured?' shouted the Head. 'Is the temple of the muses a house of thieves, robbers, murderers, that you should attack it with guns? You came here to crush the spirit of the youth in my charge?'

'I most humbly beg your pardon, but the latest ministerial decree . . . the Minister of the Interior . . .'

'I don't care a fig for your Minister of the Interior, your Minister of the Exterior, and if you want the whole truth, my dear sirs, I don't care a fig for Ferenc Deák[1] and his whole dirty deal with the Austrians . . . Here I embody the autonomy of the College. Don't you dare to touch it!'

'I humbly ask you, my esteemed sir . . .'

'Don't ask me anything! And don't provoke me, don't make me lose my temper. Two Goliaths have to come here with their shakos and swords, they have to break into the sacred halls of learning, for such a little lamb as this? . . . Well, here is this innocent mite. Take a good look at him. He's as big as a glove. Is he the one you want to gobble up? Do you know who this child is? This is an exceptional student, top marks in everything, he wins prizes, he is a boarder, he is a shining example of a puritan upbringing, honesty, trustworthiness, and you can raise your hats to him, my dear sirs. Now I have introduced you to the accused, and I bid you good day.' He waved them out of the room.

But the policemen didn't want to move. The one with the blond hair was shocked. 'I must ask you most humbly . . .'

'I already told you,' shouted the Head, springing up from his chair and striding out of his corner as if sallying forth from his castle, 'I already told you, don't ask me anything! Either humbly or non-humbly! Don't ask me a single thing in person. Don't question me! It is part of the autonomy of the college that the police can address me in only one way. In writing. Or is it the case that the gentlemen cannot write?'

'In view of the urgency of the matter . . .'

'There is no urgency! You should learn that in this life nothing is urgent except honour. Not even the Bach hussars[2] dared to touch the autonomy of the College. They took the nation's liberty, they suppressed freedom of worship, they censored what could be taught, but they did not meddle with the autonomy of the College. Do you know, my man, who Bishop Peter Balogh was? By God's will this Peter Balogh had a childlike mind, but by God's mercy he was a giant character. Do you know that when the leading ministers of the Protestant church gathered here in the Little Church for a council, the military commander of the city under orders from Vienna aimed his guns at the Little Church, surrounded God's house with his soldiers, entered the Church with his hat on his head and said, "In the name of His Majesty the Emperor, I disband this council." And our Bishop Peter Balogh replied: "In the name of His Majesty the Almighty God, I open this council." Now I bid you good day, my dear sirs, may God be with you.' The Head made a gesture of dismissal and turned his back on the policemen.

They shifted uncomfortably from one foot to the other for a minute or two, unable to make up their minds what to do, then with a cold goodbye slunk away.

When they left the old Head went back behind his desk and, sitting down, shouted 'István!'

The head porter came in.

'Call Mr Gyéres.'

A few minutes later the young Latin master came in. 'At your service, sir.'

The Head didn't look at him; he was absorbed in the papers in front of him. Then he looked up suddenly and asked in a gruff voice, 'Tell me, Mr Gyéres, do you know this student?' He looked at Misi.

'Of course I do, sir. He is my pupil in the second form.'

'What did he have to do with a lottery ticket?'

'Lottery?' asked Gyéres, surprised. 'I know nothing about it.'

'You don't know about it?!' said the old soldier, and shook his head. 'Well, my little son, tell him everything, because your form master knows nothing.'

At that Misi straightened himself and looked around a little. He had been so absorbed in the scene that had just taken place, watching the Head dressing down the policemen, that he had quite forgotten that he was the cause of it all. 'Please, sir,' he said, 'I read every day to an old blind gentleman and he pays me ten kreutzers an hour.'

'Do you? That's a fine thing,' said the Head, pleased and approving. 'That's three forints a month. That's a lot of money, a great help to your poor father.'

'And, please, sir, old Mr Pósalaky . . .'

'Pósalaky?' shouted the Head. 'The former town councillor?'

'Yes, sir.'

'So. Very good. Go on.'

'Old Mr Pósalaky, please sir, two weeks ago yesterday, Sunday, gave me a forint to put on the lottery, to play something he had dreamed.'

'He dreamed something?'

'Yes, sir.'

'Well, well . . . What an old fool . . . He plays his dreams on the lottery.'

'Yes, sir, because his laundress interpreted his dream into numbers.'

'His laundress? Arghhh, the devil take the old ass. In his old age he gets together with washerwomen to interpret dreams? . . . Well, did you at least win him a basketful of money?'

'No, sir, please, no,' lied Misi, shivering, with a smile on his face but deathly fear in his heart. 'I put the numbers on the Budapest lottery and they came out on the Brünn lottery.'

'Brünn,' barked the Head. 'Brünn, Budapest, Brünn, did he win or didn't he win?'

'He didn't win.'

'So. Of course he didn't win. Fools, fools . . .' The Head stood up and delivered, growling, a severe lecture on super-stition. 'My Mr Pósalaky lost a forint and for that the ass of a Chief Constable — he has always been a fool — sent me two policemen, two gendarmes, and overturned the College's autonomy . . . All right, go back to class, what do you have now?'

'Mathematics.'

'Run, don't waste time.'

Misi turned around happily and ran out. As he left the Head was saying to Mr Gyéres, 'On account of such an old fool and his washerwoman!'

Then István closed the Head's door.

Misi felt such a happy warmth around his heart that he started to cry, and he couldn't go to class until he had cried himself out in the corridor.

However, next day during class István appeared again. This time he didn't call Misi's name, just beckoned to him with his finger. Misi turned deathly pale and got up from his seat, far more afraid than he had been the day before. He was so scared that he tripped over Orczy's knee. Since the previous day all the boys had been talking about the lottery ticket and by now even the eighth form knew that somebody had picked up the money that the little student won.

Many thoughts raced through Misi's mind before he reached the Head's study. He hadn't gone to read to Mr Pósalaky the day before; since he had heard from the Head that Mr Pósalaky denounced him to the police, he hadn't even dared to think of going to the old gentleman. He was afraid of Mr Pósalaky, though he knew perfectly well that the Head was mistaken: Mr Pósalaky had no idea what was going on. Not only had he lost his lottery winnings but he was being talked about as somebody who would denounce an innocent boy. And it wasn't true; it was Orczy's father who had denounced him to the police . . . Since the day before, Misi hadn't said a solitary word to anybody; he had just been brooding by himself, hiding from human eyes.

This time they didn't let him into the Head's study right away, because they were holding a council.

At last they called him in.

The Head looked at him angrily. 'You bad penny, do I have to call you every day? Do you know this young lady?'

Misi realised with horror that Miss Viola was in the room. She was crying and wiping her eyes with a handkerchief and spoke quickly, as if trying to justify herself. 'Our whole lives are ruined and he must know something, sir, he must know something about my younger sister's affairs.'

The Head said nothing, just stared, amazed, at the little boy. Cowed by his piercing eyes, Misi gasped for air and began to stammer. 'Please, sir, Mr János ordered me to give a letter to Miss Bella. That's all I know.'

The Head got angry with him again. 'There is some trouble with you every day. Why do you get mixed up in everybody's business? How do you get to be a messenger between lovers?'

Misi trembled. 'Mr Gyéres ordered me to tutor Miss Viola's brother in Latin and mathematics.'

'You are tutoring?'

'Yes, sir.'

'Hmmmm . . . Do you get paid for it?'

'Two forints a month.'

'Well, well, so you are teaching too,' said the Head, quite pleased. 'Well, Miss, I don't see here any grounds for complaint. This little mite hasn't done anything. He's an exceptional student, the pride of his class. Besides, he receives a scholarship from the College. How can you make a complaint against such a boy? What does he have to do with the love affairs of grown-ups?'

'I beg your pardon, but I thought . . .' stammered Miss Viola, flustered.

'You shouldn't think anything. I'm certain that nothing untoward has happened. Just go home. Who trusts in God is never disappointed. Everything will turn out well, you'll see . . . People should leave my students alone,' he grumbled, as if talking to himself.

Miss Viola burst into tears. She turned around and left hurriedly with a hardly audible goodbye.

Misi remained where he stood. The bell rang and the Head looked at him. 'Well, you rascal,' he said threateningly, getting up from the desk and walking towards him. 'You are mixed up in everything. You bring me trouble every day. I'm being harassed by the whole world because of you . . . Do you have to carry love letters? I'm sure you aren't innocent in this business of the lottery either. I am telling you only this: if I have to call you in again, if I set eyes on your grubby little face once more, I won't even talk to you before I slap you so hard that you fly out the window . . . Get out!'

Misi turned around and, with his tail between his legs, hurried away. All the classes were in; the corridors were already empty. He began sobbing convulsively and when he got to the staircase where Petőfi's statue stood, he sat down on one of the steps and had such a crying fit that his whole body shook.

He felt that he couldn't talk to anybody, nobody would understand him.

As he heard steps approaching he ran up the stairs, though

his class was on the ground floor and he should have gone there. He ran up to the first floor: he wanted to hide somewhere but couldn't find a single corner. The corridors were open, windy and cold. He went up to the second floor by the back staircase and found himself in front of his dormitory. Taking the key down from the nail, he let himself into the room, threw himself on his bed and cried until he fell asleep from exhaustion. He didn't go to any classes in the morning. At noon he went down for his books but on the stairs he met Sándor, who was bringing them up.

'Where have you been?' Sándor asked.

'I'm sick.' Misi could see from Sándor's laugh that he understood what sort of sickness it was.

Misi went down to afternoon classes but the next day he decided to stay in the dormitory. He had resolved not to budge; with some kind of excuse he would stay upstairs. He had given up going to the old gentleman, he had given up going to the Doroghys', and now he didn't even have the strength to show himself in class.

But next day, as if the Head had sensed what he was thinking, Uncle István came up to the dormitory before the morning bell, and of course he came for him. Misi dragged himself after the head porter, more dead than alive.

The Head was always angrier in the morning than later in the day, and as István pushed Misi's poor, small, sweating head through the doorway, Misi obediently let himself be pushed. By now it was all the same to him.

The Head was pacing the floor in his study with a long cane in his hand. When he saw Misi he roared. 'You bad penny! What did I promise you yesterday? Am I never to have a moment's peace because of you? The whole college is turned upside down. Everything else has come to a standstill; we're all busy washing your dirty linen.' He beat the air over Misi's head with his cane. But even in his wild anger he felt sorry for the poor pale wreck of a boy, who was obviously beside himself with fright. 'Here is all this writing, the whole investigation.' He hit his desk with the cane and glared at the boy with bloodshot eyes. 'That's how you repay my kindness, you gallows bird? But now I will find out everything even if you don't talk.'

The Head paced the floor with pounding steps, then stopped suddenly and shouted at Misi: 'What in God's wrath is a lottery ticket?!' As Misi said nothing the Head went on pacing the floor. Then he stopped again. 'Why haven't you gone to read to Mr Pósalaky since Sunday?'

Misi said nothing.

The Head went on pounding the floor. 'This rascal turns everything upside down wherever he goes.' He pointed to his desk. 'Here is all this paper, the Töröks' family life, the tutoring with the Doroghy family, the woman who sold the lottery ticket, Orczy's father . . . I have a headache from it, I haven't been able to think of anything else for the last three days. An unscrupulous boy is ruining the whole reputation of my College.'

He started again on his angry walk. Then he roared: 'István! István!'

The porter came in.

'Where is that master?'

'He hasn't come in yet, sir.'

'What layabouts! He hasn't come in! If I can be here, why isn't he here? I'm going to create order in this unsavoury den of outlaws. I will leave – I won't be nurse to a lot of layabout teachers and blasted students. Put this whelp in the dungeon. But turn the key twice, because he's the sort of villain who would escape through the keyhole.'

Uncle István took Misi's hand. Misi went obediently, without a sound. He could already see the dark, dank, iron-barred cell where they would lock him up, and was terrified of the frogs and the snakes.

But István took him to the little room next door. It was the teachers' reading room but now it was empty.

'Well, sit down,' István said quietly and in such a kind voice that tears came to Misi's eyes.

'The Head isn't really angry with me, is he, Uncle István?'

István straightened his thin brown moustache. 'Well, we are angry enough,' he said quietly. 'But you mustn't lose heart, because our anger is not as dangerous as the goodwill of some other people.'

Misi went into another crying fit. 'Then take me to the dungeon if he is angry.'

'Dungeon?' said Uncle István. 'What dungeon? The detention cell was abolished ten years ago. There is no dungeon in the College of Debrecen. We just said it as a figure of speech. If you haven't done anything wrong you have nothing to fear. Let us just think of our mother and then no harm will come to us.'

Misi leaned over the table with his head on his arms. For a long time no one had talked to him with such soothing goodness.

'He is a shouting sort of man, our esteemed Head,' István continued quietly, 'but we will see . . . we will get to the bottom of it.'

The Head's roar was heard from the other side of the wall. 'István!'

The old servant hurried out.

Misi was left to himself.

He was so ashamed that he hunched up to make himself smaller. He was now in jail, in a dungeon, because after all they had locked him in. He was not in the classroom with the others, cheerfully studying, being called up by the master and acquitting himself well or not so well by giving excellent answers or good answers or at least satisfactory ones . . . Even the boys whose answers were unsatisfactory were clean, free people; only he was in the dungeon. They had put him in a cage; it was ridiculous and frightening; how could it be? He was a free person and they had caught him and locked him up and he could not go out? He looked around with new eyes. These were walls he couldn't break through; that was a window he couldn't jump out of; that was a door he couldn't open. He was dizzy, breathing heavily; his nerves were numb.

He felt like a butterfly that had lost its wings and turned into a caterpillar.

Exhausted, he leaned back in the big armchair and then shrank into a corner of it, and it seemed to him that he fell asleep.

When he woke, he felt that he was on a ship and the ship was sailing on the sea. He could see the great unending water all around him. It was not blue but grey-coloured like the Tisza River, and the ship was like a huge rowing boat. On the shore Indians were howling their battlecry and waving their tomahawks. They were painted red and their heads were the heads of his teachers. He could see the religion master, Mr Gyéres, Mr Báthori, Mr Sarkadi . . . The pilot of the boat was a rough, bearded old man. It was the Head, and Misi was very much afraid that he would kick him. All the Indians were aiming their arrows at the Head, who was roaring and tossing the arrows aside with his cane. Misi was crouched at the bottom of the rowing boat with Uncle István. And then he felt that he was out on the Sea of Life and would achieve great triumphs.

Then he stood proudly on top of a rock, like Sándor Petőfi's statue on the staircase, declaiming his poem about Colonel Simonyi who in his brave youth climbed up the red tower. But he couldn't remember any more of it . . . Then he was walking on the road with his father, carrying laths. 'Father, if the boys could see what I am doing!' 'What, my son?' 'That I'm carrying laths on the road.' 'Well, what would they say?' 'My classmates are such young gentlemen that they wouldn't dirty their hands picking up laths and carrying them on their shoulders. . .'

Then he heard birds chirping. He was in a beautiful garden, and it was his garden. A golden oriole was making a fuss in a tree. Misi laughed at the thought that he had such a beautiful garden with such a big walnut tree in it. And Bella was his wife, and the yellow-haired girl was his daughter, he was contented and happy, and he went into the Bull Café and ordered the waiter to bring him a lot of wine.

Everybody in the café looked at him with amazement. Then he was in the theatre, surrounded by actors in white top hats shouting, 'Viva Misi! Long live Misi!' and he wanted to recite his poem, Colonel Simonyi in his brave youth, but his tongue was heavy and he couldn't make a sound, and he felt miserable . . .

Then he was seized by a terrible fear because he was in a dark room and the door was locked, and outside witches were screaming. Invisible tittering ghosts came into the room, picked up his armchair and threw him into the air. His head was spinning and he began an unending fall into some horrible depths. He fell so fast that he lost consciousness, and then he hit the ground.

With a heavy heart he picked himself up from the floor and climbed back into the armchair, wondering why no one loved him.

All the boys were cheerful and contented; why couldn't they love him? He could die for a smile, if only they would laugh with him and hold out their hands. Why were all the boys and teachers so distant? And everybody! Nobody in the dormitory liked him. The blind old gentleman didn't like him either, never talked to him willingly, Miss Viola hated him, Alex loathed him, the Töröks didn't love him, they made fun of him, Auntie Török as well as Miss Ilonka . . . Miss Bella didn't love him, because if she had loved him she would have stayed and wouldn't have gone away with that evil man . . . Orczy didn't love him, didn't tell him his presidential secrets, Gimesi was the same, he didn't come to the Orczys' on Sunday . . . The Latin master didn't like him, he had looked at him so angrily the other day, and the other teachers didn't care for him either. The Head liked him the best, even if he shouted at him. But no, the Head didn't like him either, he was too much trouble. Nobody loved him, and why should they? Uncle István didn't like him either; he had passed on his death to him when he patted his head; that was what old people with consumption did, they gave their deaths to young people so that they, the old consumptives, could go on living.

Nobody loved him, nobody, only his father and mother. And he started to cry again.

He had time to cry and time to get over it.

How nice it would be, he thought, to climb up the Red Tower and throw himself down into the depths! Or to be a small child forever and go about barefoot on the cool earthen floor, hanging on to his mother's skirt and not knowing about anything.

He scowled, ashamed of his idiotic notions, and suddenly decided that he would not consider himself a student of the College any more. Here everybody insulted him and hurt him without any reason. Yes, he would not defend himself, he would not explain anything, every grown person should know that a boy like him . . . Those who thought ill of him should be ashamed. Police were looking for him as if he was a thief or a murderer. And Miss Viola had gone to the Head to accuse him. And the Head believed everybody. Yet he was an old man, he should know by now how to read people's character in their faces.

They were not going to trifle with him any more. When this business was finished he was going to get on a train and go home. He was not going to suffer any longer in the College of Debrecen.

He got up and went to the window. The courtyard was empty. He looked at the well. Now everything was hateful to him. It was beside that well that Orczy whispered with Böszörményi about his case, and to this day it hadn't occurred to Orczy that it was his duty to tell him everything. Now he hated the well, he didn't want to set eyes on it again, and he decided that he would never come back to Debrecen as long as he lived. He didn't want to hear about it either. There were schools in other cities too, and if his father wouldn't send him somewhere else to study, then he wouldn't study. He could become a poet without schools. Csokonai was expelled from school too. They rang the bells of Debrecen when he was expelled . . . Misi shivered, thinking that they might ring the bells of the College for him too, and then the whole school would know that he was expelled.

His eyes filled with tears. He decided he didn't care; it was enough that he knew he was innocent. At that moment other people's opinion counted for nothing with him. It wasn't important what grown-ups thought or said about him. What mattered was the truth . . .

What mattered was that he was involved in something big now. Being locked up was strange and marvellous! They *guarded* him, they would go after him with guns if he escaped. Grown men were racking their brains about something he was involved in, which he knew much more about than they did. Or at least he guessed more . . . Slowly, as a fog thins and drifts away, the despair lifted from his soul and he began to smile. He was pleased, because it seemed to him that he had broken through the barriers of childhood and entered into the adult world.

How he had longed for a pair of long trousers, for a pocket watch, for the respect of grown-ups, and now the possessors of long trousers, pocket watches and beards were preoccupied with him. He was beginning to like the whole business. It was as if he had a new strength in his hands and was squeezing the grown-ups. It was as if he was clutching the wasp on which the magic power of the seven-headed dragon depended.

The bell rang. He could see András, the little booted porter, pulling the bell, which echoed around the walls of the College. Soon the courtyard filled with students and Misi quickly drew away from the window; he didn't want them to see him in his prison – because even if it wasn't a prison, it was still a dungeon. He told himself that all this was nothing, it didn't count, justice was on his side, he had the upper hand and everybody would have to apologise to him, all those people who were now hurting him, including the Head. But it was no use, his face was burning with shame, because he couldn't explain to everybody that he was in the right. He couldn't explain to those who had locked him up, and the shame of it was so painful that his blood speeded up, started racing through his veins and he began to feel feverish again.

Oh, God, perhaps the gendarmes would march him through the streets with his hands tied behind his back! He remembered how one summer day he and the other children coming out of school at noon had seen four gendarmes with cock feathers in their hats and bayonets marching five men through the village because they refused to harvest for the count. He couldn't understand why the gendarmes should take the men away because they didn't want to harvest. Since then every time he saw a gendarme he felt that the gendarme was waiting for him and one day would get him too, because he didn't want to harvest for the count either. He wanted to work only for those he liked. He was a rebel before he knew the word rebel; he didn't want to be a slave, even before he knew what a slave was.

One warm summer evening two gendarmes halted their horses by the fence and one called out to Misi's mother in the courtyard, loudly enough for the neighbours to hear: 'Is Nyilas at home?' Misi's mother, who was sifting wheat through the big sieve onto a canvas, got so frightened that she dropped the sieve; her arms just lost all their strength. Luckily the wheat wasn't wasted; it fell on the canvas, not on the ground. Misi saw her turning pale and turned pale with her, but then she steadied herself and asked in a strong, resolute voice: 'What do you want with him?'

The gendarmes didn't say anything for quite some time. They were two big men on two big horses, hard, strong men with brown moustaches, holding the reins of their horses in their big black fists; they must have been good at slapping people when they caught their suspects. The neighbours all gathered to see Nyilas taken away, but then the older gendarme smiled, saying, 'We had a good time together in the tavern in Tarcal, and since we were passing by we thought we would look him up.'

Misi and his mother breathed more easily, proud that the

neighbours could hear that Father was a man who caroused with gendarmerie sergeants in the tavern.

'Tell him, Mrs Nyilas,' the sergeant added, 'that Sergeant Fazekas sends his greetings.'

And they made their big sorrel mounts jump and trotted away. But to this day joy and fright were mixed together in Misi's heart even about that friendly visit, for what if one day the men with tall cock feathers appeared as enemies, not friends?

Misi stayed away from the window until the bell rang and the boys ran back to the building; then he looked out at the empty courtyard again, alone with his thoughts. He had a painful hour to wait till the next bell, spending most of his time walking back and forth on tiptoe, taking care not to make any noise that could be heard in the next room. He didn't want to draw attention to himself; he didn't want them to think of him.

For fleeting moments his restless, exalted feelings turned into images in his mind. The great injustice that he suffered was contrasted with his future. For a moment he saw himself as a great and famous man, a tall, strong man, and decided he would wear a big beard, a long beard like the one Széchenyi[3] wore in the painting. Then all these people would be dwarfed by him, and would beg his pardon and say that he had always been their favourite student, and they would beg favours of him and, yes, he would help them, and would not even mention what they did to him.

Then he became dazed again and felt that he had the strength of Miklós Toldi[4] and in his thoughts, closing his eyes, he seized the door handle and broke it off so that it remained in his hand; then he kicked the door open, went through the hall to the Head's study and smashed the Head's desk to bits. In his hand the thick oak went to pieces like butter and all the masters were terrified and humbly begged his forgiveness. And he forgave them. Then he stood in front of them naked like Adam on a rock in a picture he had seen, with long floating hair and his arms flung wide, with nothing but a chasm and darkness beneath him, and he stood in front of God's throne with his pure body, and around him were scarlet poppies in a wheat field, and he was at home with his mother, a poor young boy again, and he put his head in his mother's lap and she whispered to him, 'Be good, my son, be good as long as you live, my little boy, be faithful unto death.'

Another hour passed and nobody came to open the door. He remembered a tale about a giant who carried off a mountain and his legs and his waist and his neck all got worn down and his skull rolled away with the last clump of earth. And then Jesus Christ came and picked up the diligent skull and said to it: 'My son, your sins are forgiven,' and kissed the dried old bone. Then the giant's skull turned into a white knight and rode into Heaven on a white horse . . . That was how he would be worn down by suffering, he would be reduced to a skull, but in the end he would be a famous man and people would marvel at him, and if he came back to Debrecen all the inhabitants of the city would come out to welcome him at the station. A five-horse carriage would be waiting for him, and he would be welcomed by the Mayor and the Bishop. He would be embarrassed and tell them that he disapproved of all the fuss they made about him. And he wouldn't recognise most of his classmates. They were such strangers in that class; they just sat there and studied, but what did they study? Studying now seemed to him such foolishness, studying hour after hour, learning lessons by rote, leaving out the passages that were marked not to be studied . . .

He wanted to know everything, and wanted to know it at once. He imagined that knowledge came from inside. If you wanted to know, you knew; all you had to do was open your heart and knowledge would come out of it. Then the ignorant would listen to his words and read his writing, because all he had to do was write, and whatever he would write, it would be the truth . . . When Colonel Simonyi was a boy he climbed up the Red Tower, and it was high, its roof was even higher, and full of sparrows . . .

Colonel Simonyi
stood on the plank
high in the air,
saw the whole earth
spread out beneath him.

He filled his chest
with little sparrows
wouldn't change happiness
with all the world.

Throw me down, no matter,
I have a thousand wings.
Wild, jealous earthworms,
you may gape after me . . .

He fears not the earth,
he flies up to Heaven,
who has a hundred thousand wings
beating in his heart.

He laughed and cheered, silently and with swelling heart, and
it seemed to him that he would really fly away. If the window
were open he would fly out, first to the tops of the poplars in
the courtyard, and he would flitter about with the other birds,
speaking to them not with a human stammer but with quick,
sharp, singing bird language. Blessed were those who had
planted the trees, and damned were those who cut them
down at the Simonyi dam . . . And then he flew away, away,
away, away . . . He filled his lungs with lots of air and felt that
he was floating through the brilliant blue sky. He even gave a
bird sound, saying 'tululullu'!

The door opened and the head porter came in and saw him
flapping his arms like wings and heard him saying 'tululullu'.
He was so ashamed that he lowered his head and covered his
face with his hands, saying, 'Oh my God!'

Uncle István said nothing but looked at him suspiciously as

if he had gone mad, and motioned to him that he should
come.

Misi followed him silently. But before his heart shrivelled he
laughed for a moment, thinking that he had become a great
poet. Only he should have written the poem down, because
he would forget it.

They didn't go to the Head's study but to a small, narrow
masters' room where five or six masters were sitting at a table.
Their chairs faced the door and they were so cramped that it
was evident the room was never meant for so many people.
They were all strangers to him; he knew them by sight but
none of them taught him. He looked at these faces: this was a
masters' court, he thought to himself, frightened.

He stood in front of them, pale and trembling. One of the
masters, who had grey hair and wore a pince-nez, said:
'Mihály Nyilas, student of the second form, reply to the
following questions. But I warn you that you must reply
honestly and conscientiously, because your life is at stake.
There are four groups of questions you have to answer. The
first one is how you came to be entrusted with buying a one-
forint lottery ticket for Mr Pósalaky, when you bought the
ticket, from whom, what numbers you played, and what
happened to the ticket.'

Misi goggled; he couldn't answer all those questions. 'Please,
sir, I kept the lottery ticket in my purse and then it got lost.'

'Is that so?' the master asked severely. 'It got lost? This
matter already belongs to the second group of questions, but
considering that we all understand the beginning of this affair,
let us move on to the second group of questions. How did
you come to know János Török? What did he promise you
for the ticket? When did he pay it to you?'

'To me?' asked the boy.

'To you, to you! I'm going to refresh your memory. Here is
János Török's letter in which he says that he bought the ticket
from you for ten forints and paid it to you when you carried
his briefcase on the way to the station.'

The room spun around Misi. He was pale and dizzy and stared at this man who was watching him with a teacher's severe, hostile look.

'Where is that ten-forint note?'

'He forced it into my pocket and I didn't find it until the next day . . . I sent it back to Uncle Török, because Mr János is his son.'

'Is that so? It's in your favour but it doesn't excuse the fact that you were entrusted with a fortune and you stole it. You sold it recklessly and for material gain.'

It was such a brazen lie that Misi couldn't even say that it wasn't true. His own lie, that he had already sent the money to Uncle Török, was a sacred thing: it calmed his conscience, because he had thought of doing it. But the lie that he had sold the ticket to Mr János outraged him and made him despair. If such a thing could be said then nothing made sense; he began to doubt that the sun shone and that stones were hard.

'Now let us move to the third group of questions. What happened in the classroom of the fifth form? How often have you been there? What did you do there? What are the texts of the songs abusing the masters? And what kind of bacchanal did you participate in there?'

Misi stared. In the fifth-form classroom? He had never been there. He vaguely remembered hearing that some of the boys gathered there on Wednesday and Saturday afternoons. That classroom was quite separate from the other ones, in the old part of the college, and it had an anteroom which excited the students' imagination as if it were the entrance hall of a romantic château. There might have been a rumpus there because once he heard that they drank wine. But they wouldn't have let him in even if he had wanted to go.

'Because,' the presiding master with the pince-nez continued drily, 'the general opinion here is that you sold that lottery ticket for cash, sold an uncertain winning for certain profit, so that you could contribute to the expense of these immoral gatherings.'

'Please, sir, I've never been to the fifth-form classroom and I don't know anything about it.' Misi's voice was so firm that the master dropped the subject.

'Let us move on then to the fourth group of questions. It has come to our notice that you kept sending money somewhere. To whom, how much and from what?'

The little boy's eyes filled with tears; his throat was tight. He looked at this bald, grey, hostile man. Was it possible that these people really didn't understand? Was it impossible for one person to understand another? 'Please, sir, I didn't hurt anybody and I didn't do anything to anybody.'

'This boy is incorrigible,' said another master, a heavier man. 'He even ate the shoe polish.'

Misi was about to burst into tears but this charge stunned him so much that he couldn't even cry. It was he who had eaten the shoe polish and not Böszörményi? He had eaten his own shoe polish? He looked at the man: he had a fleshy face, grey eyes and a chestnut-coloured moustache.

'These boys shouldn't be allowed to leave the College on any pretext whatsoever,' said another master. 'What were you doing on the street the other evening just when the lamps were lit? Watching the girls?'

Misi looked at the speaker. He was a fat, pot-bellied man who tipped his chair backwards with one of his arms dangling in the air and the other resting on his chest. He sat there like a sack, a thick-lipped, puffy little man, brown-skinned, with a tiny moustache, as repellent as a toad. Misi looked at him, mesmerised and appalled. He couldn't imagine what the man was thinking. Where had he seen him? He could neither cry nor laugh, just stared with horror and couldn't remember anything. And he couldn't take his eyes off the man. He was so horrified by him that he couldn't get enough of this horror.

Then the teachers began to argue among themselves. He couldn't follow them, he just stood there like an orphan. And he wasn't an orphan because they hurt him but because he didn't understand them. He understood them no more than they understood him. He thought to himself that it would be nice to tell them everything, but it was not possible, because then he would have had to praise himself. He would have had to tell them that he was better than the other boys, better than anybody, because not only did he not do anything wrong, he never even thought anything wrong about anybody or anything. How could he tell that to them? And perhaps it wasn't even true. Perhaps the masters were right and he was a wicked, evil person. He looked for the truth in his past, and then he decided that he would tell about the pocket knife he stole and that it was behind the rubbish bin on the first floor.

'But what an incorrigible, hardened boy this is!' the president was saying at that moment. 'He doesn't answer any questions, he is a dark, wicked soul, and instead of opening his heart so that we could read it as an open book, he caps his crime with silence. Speak! Come on, speak out!'

Misi had just been thinking, 'You will all come before me and you will kiss my hand when I am a famous man.' Aloud he said, 'Please, sir, I haven't done anything.' And when he said that and heard his own voice he was ashamed that he was speaking like a snotty child instead of doing something beautiful and great.

'How long have you been teaching at the Doroghys'?'

Misi thought about it. He couldn't remember. 'I got paid only once.'

'So, that's how you remember things, through the money? Very nice. Well, what is your salary?'

'Two forints.'

'A month?'

'Yes.'

'Are you tutoring a classmate of yours?'

'Yes.'

'In what?'

'Mathematics and Latin.'

'Nothing else?'

'No.'

'You don't tutor him in geography, Hungarian, other subjects?'

'No.'

'So as far as you are concerned he can fail in every other subject.'

Misi said nothing.

'Well, this is not strictly to the point,' remarked another master.

'It is very much to the point,' said the president. 'It gives us an insight into the boy's moral outlook. Selfish, demanding, with material gain uppermost in his mind . . . Come on, speak up! How did you get acquainted with the older sister of your classmate, what is her name, Bella? And what was your relationship with her?'

Misi raised his eyebrows. 'We were friends,' he said quietly.

'What do you mean, *friends*?'

'Please, sir, she is a very good girl,' said Misi.

'Good girl?!' the president cried. 'A girl who sank to such depths of moral corruption that she eloped with an embezzler? And that is a good girl for him? Well, go on, talk, talk, let's not have to drag every word out of you with pliers.'

Misi looked at the floor and said nothing. He felt that these men, however grown-up and wise they were, wouldn't learn anything. How could they learn to know a person when they tried to pry open his secrets with hostility and murderous intent? Oh my God, if there were only someone to whom he could pour out his heart, with nobody else there! He looked at the dusty window with a spider's web in the frame; it was as barren as his own life.

'If you would allow me, my dear colleague, to address a few questions to the lad myself . . .'

'Go ahead.'

'Tell me, my boy, tell me, my child,' said a black-bearded master, turning towards him, 'how could you have the impudence . . . Because it's not a slight matter, you know, that you should sell the lottery ticket for money, sell it for ten forints. You should have felt that it was not right. What were you thinking of? Did you think that the ticket wouldn't win?'

'But I didn't sell it! I didn't sell the ticket!'

'All right, good. You say that you didn't sell it. Then why did you lie to the old gentleman? Why did you tell him that you put the numbers on the Budapest lottery and not the Brünn lottery? And why didn't you read him the Brünn numbers?'

'The Brünn numbers weren't in the paper, sir.'

'Don't lie to me.'

'They weren't there.'

'Are you contradicting me? It would have been better if you hadn't sold the ticket, but you sold it, you sold it, you scoundrel. Don't lie to my face, you little scoundrel, because I will slap you, I will slap you so hard that your neck will break. How do you dare to lie to my face? What kind of boy are you? What does your father do?'

Misi was silent.

'Didn't you hear me? What is your father?'

'A carpenter.'

'Well, it shows. He was brought up to lie. He was drilled in lying. What kind of father and mother does a child like that have?'

At these words Misi froze. He clenched his teeth and gave the master such a burning look that it nearly scalded him. And the man who a few minutes earlier had tried to bribe him with honeyed words to make him testify against himself was so enraged by this look that he jumped up from his chair. 'You lowest of the low! You should be shaking before me, you wicked boy! I will tear your ears off, you . . .'

Misi stood there like an iron spike, with his nostrils flaring like a panting horse's. His white face grew whiter and it seemed that he was going to throw himself at the master at any moment.

'It is a totally rotten moral character,' said the president impatiently. 'I could see it at a glance. That is the only way we can explain this series of criminal acts committed by an eleven-year-old boy which would do credit to a clever hardened criminal.'

'It's a pity that he is such an outstanding student.'

'*Outstanding student!* What does it signify that he's an outstanding student?' asked the president. 'The mind can be God's gift or the Devil's. The question is what is in the heart, not what is in the brain. With a corrupt heart not even the cleverest man can be of use to his fellow men. But with a good and noble soul even the most simple-minded can be a useful member of society. It is not in the tradition of the College of Debrecen to turn out famous criminals. It is our tradition to educate faithful, worthwhile, moral and useful citizens.'

'I don't want to be a student of Debrecen any more,' shouted Misi.

This caused general consternation.

'You don't want to be a student of the College of Debrecen! You don't want to be a student of our college? First of all, it does not depend on you, my little friend. Secondly, you could be proud even on the gallows that once upon a time, even if just for a short while, you belonged to the College of Debrecen! . . . Rabble!'

In the master's voice there was such awe and such piety when he pronounced the words *the College of Debrecen*, he was overcome by such religious ecstasy that he stood up and the others involuntarily stood up too, as if they were bearing witness in the eyes of God to what a unique sacred place it was, the College of Debrecen.

This moment made an indelible impression on the boy. He had never experienced such exalted, incandescent patriotism, and like every true and strong feeling it also affected him. Suddenly he felt ashamed that he had lost even for a moment his sense of the beauty and magic of the great college.

But as the masters got up it was no longer a formal examination; they began to move about, come and go, talk in pairs, discussing excitedly and despairingly the declining moral standards of youth and the country's dismal future. 'Go out and wait,' said the president to the boy. 'We will call you when we need you.'

Then the boy turned towards the Head, who had been

present at the council without saying a word. 'Please sir, you do think I'm a good boy, don't you?'

The Head looked up, startled. 'Hmmmm . . . This is what we're trying to find out. This is what the professors are arguing about.'

The little boy bowed his head and went out, but his heart remained with the old soldier.

As Misi stepped out of the door, his ears full of the professors' excited discussion which broke out as he was leaving, someone came in the opposite door of the empty classroom. Misi was flooded with sudden joy and at first he didn't even know why. Then he looked again.

It was his uncle, Géza Isaák. He was wearing a big brown fur coat, a gentleman's fur coat, and on his narrow head there was a hard black hat. His big dark eyes looked around searchingly and when he recognised his nephew he hurried towards him with open arms. 'My Misi,' he said, and embraced him.

And the little boy who had spent so much time among strangers without hearing 'my Misi' began to cry and fell into his uncle's arms and pressed his face into his ice-cold fur coat.

He cried for a long time. It was inexpressible happiness to be able to cry so freely on the heart of his uncle, his idol, the pride of the whole family, his dear good Uncle Géza, whom he hadn't heard from for so long, whom he hadn't even thought about during his great trouble. And now he was here and would liberate him. 'They hurt me here, Uncle Géza,' he said in a choking voice.

And Uncle Géza stroked his head, kissed his forehead and looked into his eyes. His own eyes were moist, his big walnut-brown eyes, those dear, serious eyes. 'My dear Misi . . .'

'I don't want to be a student of the College of Debrecen!' shouted the child. 'Not any more. They hurt me.' He sobbed, he gulped, he hiccuped; his body was trying to get rid of the tension that had built up inside him.

His uncle pressed Misi to him, hugged him and squeezed him. He opened his coat to warm the shivering, trembling, pale, sad little boy, who was biting his fist so hard that the blood came, to stop himself from crying.

XII

*Misi gets a glimpse of his future. All his life he will
have to work in desperate crises, in the same sort of
extraordinary, amazing, chaotic circumstances as those
in which he wrote his first poem*

S TAY HERE, my boy,' said his uncle affectionately, 'I'm
going in there and I'll talk to them, don't worry, just
wait here.'

Misi sat down on a bench, trembling and shaking. He put his
hand on his forehead; he was feverish, his teeth were chattering.
Then to the rhythm of his chattering teeth he began to recite
his poem: 'Colonel – Simonyi – in – his – brave – youth –
climbed – the – red – tower . . . high – was – the – tower –
its – roof – even – higher – and – covered – with – sparrows
. . . he – walked – on – a – plank – high – up – in – the – air
– saw – the – whole – earth – spread – out – beneath – him
. . . he – filled – his – chest – with – little – sparrows . . .'

Then he stopped. It seemed to him that the poem was better
in the dungeon when he invented it. He had lost the poem:
there was a void in his life. It was unbearable and he tried again.
'How was it – how was it? That wasn't it – wasn't it . . . On
the prairie . . . falling among highwaymen, highwaymen . . .'
He liked that better, so he started it again. 'Tralalalalaa . . .'

> He filled his chest
> with little sparrows
> wouldn't change happiness
> with all the world.

He pressed his forehead against the desk in front of him and forced his brain to remember. He closed his eyes so tight that they hurt and clenched his teeth.

> He filled his chest
> with little sparrows
> wouldn't change happiness
> with . . . the whole college.

He laughed out loud. The verse was terribly wobbly – it had no rhythm, but the thought that he, the outcast, the insulted, tortured child, would not change places with the whole happy jumping cheerful college population . . . it wasn't a poem, but it was true!

The previous year when he lived with the Töröks, Miss Ilonka had told him the story about a landowner who teased his manservant, asking him 'Do you know what a poem is, Miska? You don't? Well, I'm telling you a poem:

> Listen to me, you foolish Miska,
> I am loved by your sister Juliska,

and he added: 'You see, you donkey, that's a poem, but it's not true.'

To which his manservant replied:

> Listen to me, master, sir,
> I am loved by my lady, the mistress,

and added: 'You see, sir, that's not a poem, but it's true.'

Misi had laughed a lot at this story whenever he thought of it, even though he didn't understand it, but now he felt that the line he had just written was the same. That he wouldn't change places with the college – it wasn't a poem but it was true. Resting his forehead on the desk in front of him, he chuckled about that so much that tears came into his eyes, and he suddenly became so hungry that he thought his stomach would fall out.

Then his poem came back to him.

> He fears not the earth,
> he flies up to Heaven,
> who has a hundred thousand wings
> beating in his heart . . .

Who cared whether he was going to be expelled or not expelled? What did it matter? But how could he have forgotten something so beautiful?

But how was the rest of it? He couldn't bring it back, as if he wasn't the one who invented it, as if he had just read it somewhere or had just dreamed it and immediately forgotten it . . .

Then he started to laugh at that too. What a silly thing to do, to write a poem and then forget it! Those earthworms in the other room had driven it from his head.

> Wild, jealous earthworms,
> you may gape after me . . .

There were lines like that in it. He dug a pencil out of his pocket but couldn't find any paper. He found a scrap and started to write on it but then he saw that it was his father's note that came with the money . . .

He put his forehead down on the desk again and collapsed as if he had turned to dust, annihilated. He suddenly felt his father's exhaustion, his father's fate, his misery, his misfortune. He suddenly had a sense of what it must have been like for his father when the combine harvester exploded and their house was sold at auction. He tried to curl up into a ball to make himself as small as he could . . . Now he was trudging along a dusty road in the heat; the hot dust of the road burned his feet. He was carrying food to his father. Sometimes the dust came up to his knees; his legs could hardly stand the heat . . .

In the cold classroom he felt as hot as during that hot summer day; he was even sweating . . . Then he heard a terrible cursing; his whole body was repelled by it. He opened the gate and saw the big black peasant raising his fist and shouting. There were two or three peasant women behind him in long black dresses with black shawls on their heads, egging him on, shrieking with all their might. And his father stood among these people. He was so small, so dispirited.

'God so-and-so' and 'God such-and-such' – curses came thick and fast in hostile, mean bursts like manure dropping. 'You took this job on for a hundred sixty forints. I already paid you two hundred ten. And where is the building? You don't have all the walls, you don't have the door, you have done nothing . . .'

When his father noticed him coming into the courtyard with the lunch pail he greeted him with a laugh, as if the abuse had been just a bit of wind not worth paying attention to. 'Now, Gazsi,' he said jokingly, because he gave all his sons different names, 'what did you bring me? Potato soup?'

'Chicken ragout,' said Misi.

'Ho-ho!' said his father, making a funny face. 'Chicken ragout! Wait a little, I'm going with you and we'll have a meal.' He was about to go to the back of the courtyard but the peasants, whose jabber had stopped for a moment at the child's appearance, started it again.

'Not a kreutzer! I'm not paying you any more. You cheated us, you robbed us, you thief!'

At that Misi's father lost his temper. 'Watch it, close your mouth, because I'll throw my axe into it. You will . . . You know what, I'm going to leave the whole thing and you can build it yourself. Let it fall on your head.'

'But you took on the job for a hundred sixty-two forints!'

'Go to hell with your hundred sixty-two forints. Where is that hundred sixty-two forints? You drank more of it than I did, because I paid for you when we drank a toast. You never paid me for so much as a glass of brandy. Your hundred sixty-two forints is in your house. There are the beams, there are the tiles, the bricks, there is the work. Die of apoplexy for your hundred sixty-two forints, you lice.'

'You agreed to do it, why did you take on the job if you couldn't do it at the price?' shrieked one of the women.

'What did I take on? Where is it, what I promised to do? You wanted walls twenty centimetres higher. You wanted a window ten centimetres bigger. You wanted a double door. You wanted a palace with high ceilings. I don't know why you wanted it, you're so bent, you couldn't even straighten your neck to see the roof of your house, you toothless old crone. Don't talk so much, go and die. An old woman like you doesn't need a palace, what you need is a coffin.'

By then there were a lot of spectators from the rest of the village, and they laughed appreciatively.

Misi's father took his hand and said, 'Let's go, let's leave this place.'

They went out to the street and from the street to the tavern, and by the time they got there his father had calmed down, since they could no longer hear the jabbering.

But Misi was trembling, his legs were shaking, his heart was throbbing. He thought that the peasants were right, his father had cheated them. Yet he had worked like blazes for them. Three men couldn't do as much in one day as he did in one hour. How he cut wood, how he raised things, how he threw things, how he ordered everything! He leaped about like flames; he had a kind of consuming fire in him. What did they know about work, those lazy slow-moving people, those peasants and those day labourers? How that day labourer stood there with a pipe in his mouth, hardly moving his boots, a little bit this way, a little bit that way. Was this a man? His father ran around the village ten times while his day labourers did a bit of insulating, spreading a basketful of earth on the attic floor. What beams he tossed up to the roof! In the morning there was nothing; by the evening the whole beamed structure of the roof was already in place. And what kind of time-wasters he had to contend with! . . . Those wicked peasants, they did not consider what the builder Nyilas put up for their money. The only thing they counted with their dull minds was the forints and the kreutzers. They wanted everything that came into their heads but they didn't want to give a penny more than was negotiated. The grasping misers! His poor father worked for everybody as a good worker would work for himself. That was all right, they accepted that, they laughed at that, glad that they had found a fool who would strain himself so hard. They paid and they saw that he didn't steal from the wood, the building materials, the labourers' wages, and didn't make money on his own work, yet when he got past the agreed amount because it wasn't enough for everything they wanted, they expected him to go back to his own village, sell his house, his clothes, his shirt, to pay for building their house . . . Now, in the classroom, thinking back on it, Misi was seized by consuming anger and unquenchable hatred. But he still thought that his father was in the wrong. He took his father for a dishonourable man. He thought yes, his father should build the house, it was better to be ruined than to break his word.

His father ate a few spoonfuls of chicken ragout with hearty appetite. 'Here it is, have some yourself,' he said, and pushed the pot over to Misi, who was reluctant to take it, made excuses: he wanted his father to have it for the evening or the next day. But his father said, 'Eat, you little squirrel, or I'll give it to that gypsy boy there.'

At that Misi started to eat in a hurry, because he knew his father would do what he said.

And now he too was in big trouble, the same big trouble as his father. There was a whole army of old teachers gathered together to abuse him, punish him, expel him. He wiped his forehead and said, 'Oh my God, oh my God!' In this sigh there was the greatest weariness, the weariness of struggling with other people's incomprehension.

What was it that prevented people from understanding each other? Why wasn't it possible for an honest decent man to live among mean and stupid people? . . . His father was set on fire by work, he worked for people as speedily as flames spread, he built them what they needed, and the end of his labours was always argument, criticism, dissatisfaction, protest . . . And what about Misi himself? Though he was just starting out in life, still a child, he dreamed of being useful to everybody, yet he had to live in the silence of his thoughts, already condemned . . .

No, this affair would never be settled. He would never be able to explain what had happened. If people lived in the dark, he could not light up their minds; he would be branded a thief for life, that was how people would talk about him. A thief, that was how they would remember him for as long as they remembered him at all . . .

He examined his pencil, which had six sides. It was short and worn, but he had carved patterns on two opposite sides – symmetrical waves, they looked quite nice – they marked the pencil as his own. Not because he wanted to recognise it if it was lost and reclaim it – if it was lost or stolen, he would not dream of asking for it back, he would not say anything, just as he had said nothing when he had seen his hat on the head of the young gardener – no, he had marked the pencil so that while it was in his possession, until it was lost or stolen, his pencil should be like no other pencil, so that he should have the only carved writing instrument in the world . . . He started to tap the desk with his pencil – Colonel Simonyi . . . stood bravely over the void . . .

No, that wasn't it, it was much more beautiful. How could he have forgotten it? He clenched his teeth, and thought losing his poem was almost like glory . . . That he lost the lottery ticket, that was nothing, let the devil take it, let the devil take the money, however much it was, let the devil take a whole briefcase-full of banknotes . . . but to lose his own poem!

He trembled from the thrill of having written a lost poem. If it hadn't been lost, perhaps he would have become famous, perhaps one day it would have been taught in the schools, and children would get 4 if they could not recite it. The masters would explain that 'a hundred thousand wings' should not be taken literally as so many sparrow wings, but as . . . something else . . . a what-d'you-call-it . . .

He heard voices from the other room; for a moment his heart contracted, though he didn't know why. He had no reason to despair; his troubles were over, his saviour had come, his Uncle Géza would take care of everything. It was no longer his worry what would happen; his uncle had taken the weight of responsibility from his shoulders. He thought his uncle's face resembled Christ's face; he had the same sort of gentle brown beard, and strong eyes which could see into people's hearts, and he could do anything. He would take it all on himself, like Christ; he would discover the crime, Misi's sin, and would show them that his sin was virtue . . . It was such a good feeling, to have the weight of responsibility lifted, it made Misi's soul rise in its glory. They had thrown mud at him, but now he was spotless and pure.

As the masters came out of their room he stood up, transfigured and shivering.

'Well, you poor little mite,' said the Head in his powerful soldier's voice, 'I always said all this foolishness was blown up from nothing. Look at him. He radiates honesty.'

Misi's eyes filled with tears.

'He is a good student, he is diligent, he earns money, his father can be proud of him. Everything is all right, my boy. Just carry on.'

Misi was red and pale and amazed, but the others still seemed to him dark, evil strangers, as if this lucky outcome was not to their taste. The master with the potbelly and potato head looked at him condescendingly and again Misi was mesmerised by his ugliness. He couldn't take his eyes off him; even when he walked off Misi kept looking after him so that he could despise him longer. And he didn't even know yet that this master was without any talent as a historian. He learned only later that this fathead wrote terrifying idiocies about Gábor Bethlen and viewed the world with putrid complacency, treating with contempt everything that was brain, heart and strength.

The president of the masters' court, however, had changed. He now looked at Misi with beaming goodwill. He was the kind of man who was harsh in his abuse and fulsome in his praise. 'Well, my boy, I have just one piece of advice for you. And that is what you read in the coat of arms of the college. *Ora et labora.* Do you know what it means? Pray and work. Don't forget it for a moment. Pray and work, and then God will help you. Well, now do you want to be a student of the College of Debrecen?' he asked and, adjusting his pince-nez, looked around his colleagues with the smile of someone who knew the answer was obvious.

But then some wild stubbornness lit up in Misi. He stiffened and his throat dried, and he replied hoarsely, 'I don't want to.'

This created terrible consternation in the whole company. The masters looked at the child, flabbergasted, especially the president of the masters' court, who couldn't open his eyes wide enough. 'You don't?' He raised his eyebrows as high as he could. 'And why don't you?' he shrieked.

Misi was silent. He almost shouted: *Just because!* Then his eyes met his uncle's, which were looking at him with surprise, seriousness, understanding, but also with warning and pleading. And then Misi's gaze remained in those dear brown deep heavenly eyes, as if his uncle was looking at him from another world, through fogs, through clouds, through past lives, and Misi softened and lost his strength. He felt that his will was broken, his wickedness and meanness were annihilated, and now he longed for goodness and patience. It was as if he were standing at the edge of a precipice, and so he said nothing, he only thought, repeating to himself: *Just because! Just because! Just because!*

'Let's not torture the child,' the Head said gruffly, offended himself. 'If he doesn't want to stay here, then he doesn't want to. The College of Debrecen is not the only place where a boy can grow up. Even a student of Sárospatak can become a man. Let the Mongols take him.'

At that Misi crumbled. He felt his uncle taking his cold hand and leading him away from the speeches and lectures and the unbearably clever people. He let himself be led blindly upstairs, downstairs, across corridors.

'Which is your bed?' asked his uncle when they were in the dormitory.

Misi went to his bed and stroked it affectionately. 'This is it,' he said, and touched it in the same way as a dead man waking at midnight touches his coffin. 'And this is my trunk,' he said, and put his hand on his trunk as if it was his tombstone. 'And this is my drawer,' he said, and put his hand on the corner of the green table, the graveyard of his student years in Debrecen. He opened the drawer to take out something, he himself didn't know what; his hand hesitated. Then he suddenly grabbed his bound book of empty pages; he was trembling, because he knew that he would write his poem in it . . . No, no, he wouldn't write it down, because then people would read it and talk about it and he would lose his secret. No, he didn't want that. And yet, he took from the drawer only this book. He didn't care for the rest, the 'Historical Portrait Gallery' or his paints or the incomprehensible book about Csokonai. He had only one treasure, the greatest possible treasure, this book of blank pages, white, pure, the symbol of his future life, the book that would never be filled because life could not bring enough great things worthy of it.

Taking nothing else, only that book, clutching it to himself, he went down the big staircase with his uncle. As they passed the giant double doors of the music room he could hear the rhythmical singing and his heart missed a beat. He would never go into that room again. He would not be a student of Debrecen any longer. He was choking from the hurt as he descended the steps, knowing that he would never climb them again, and at every step he dropped a tear as he descended deeper and deeper, lower and lower in the world, no longer a student of the College of Debrecen.

On the first floor the theologians were playing the violin

and the high, thin sound pierced his heart. Those poor screeching violins, those stumbling scales, made everything so peculiar . . . And he was no longer a student of the College of Debrecen.

Then as he and his uncle turned the corner of the corridor on the first floor, his eye caught the big oaken dustbin behind which Böszörményi's pocket knife would live forever. He tried to free his hand from his uncle's; he would have liked to kneel down as in church and lower his forehead to the floor as expiation of his sins, and he also wanted to scoop out the knife from the back of the dustbin to take it away as a memento that he was once a student of the College of Debrecen.

Lower down on the stairs he recognised the place where he had eaten a whole melon in the autumn so that he wouldn't have to share it with anybody, and on the ground floor the library of the eighth-form students where he had gone to fetch books for Mr Nagy. Oh God, Mr Nagy! The little hunchback, the good man who had taught him about the heroic origins of the Hungarian people. His heart contracted; he thought he would die as they stepped out of the gate, especially as just at that moment the college bell rang, the bell which rang when Csokonai was expelled.

But now the bell rang only for midday, and he was out of the college, jumping on the sidewalk. There he took a deep breath; his lungs opened and he filled himself with air. A moment before he had been a suffering little schoolboy of the College of Debrecen; now he was a liberated happy man among men. He flew across town, holding onto his uncle's hand. Then they reached the Pongrác shop, and he felt frightened; he felt that the Great Church raised its red roof as a schoolboy would raise his hat to catch a butterfly, and with a shout of triumph dropped it over him. Then he stopped in front of the old gentleman's house, and again in front of the dress shop where he had seen Miss Bella with Mr János. Then came the terrible barrenness of the Market Square, the shadow of the church tower leaning over him, the sound of the bells, and he felt dizzy and fell to the ground. As he lay on the icy sidewalk he didn't quite lose consciousness, he remembered how hot the asphalt had been when it was poured and that somebody had stepped on it with bare feet, leaving his footprints in it forever. Then he thought of poor Miss Bella . . .

Would the mark of his feet remain on the cold asphalt? . . . On the street of Debrecen? And he smiled.

He came to himself in bed, with bad and painful memories. He felt his lips were burning and his breath was hot; his blood was swirling like steam in a furnace, or in the combine harvester that exploded, which ruined them, took the walnut trees and plum trees which had given them jam for weeks, so that they became beggars and homeless people who had to be afraid of the gendarmes' cock feathers and the words *promissory notes* and the smell of brandy . . . And he was afraid that he himself would explode like the combine and would have to perish, because his father's misfortune was in his illness, and also the great misfortune of his ancestors, the serfs, who had landlords lying on top of them until the world exploded. Oh God.

When he got better his uncle brought him two red oranges and he held them in his hands. They were beautiful. He had never dared to buy them. He had seen them in the shop window – 'blood oranges' they were called – but he didn't have the heart to pay three kreutzers apiece for them . . . Uncle Géza also brought him flowers, and Misi remembered that he had been that sick once before, when the family were moving from the Tisza to the new village and he and his younger brother were staying with one of their uncles. They both got the measles, and the uncle wrote to Misi's father, 'Brother-in-law, your children are sick, come and get them because I'm not going to look after them!' He put it that cruelly, and Misi's father came. It was the same kind of big winter, and Misi's father just hopped into the room and made them a rattling toy from walnut shells. But he didn't take them away, because he didn't have a kreutzer. Did he have a kreutzer now?

Misi cried a lot, facing the wall.

One day when his uncle was out and he was alone, Orczy and Gimesi came to visit him. Misi was happy and got very excited. He was proud that he was lying in such a beautiful bed in a warm room in a hotel, and on the bedside table there were medicine bottles and glasses and a silver spoon. And he was sick!

'*Servus*, Misi.'

'*Servus*, Orczy.'

'*Servus*.'

'*Servus*, Gimesi.'

They all shook hands.

'Well, how are you?'

Misi shrugged. 'Oh, all right.'

'I read the letter that Mr János sent to the police,' said Orczy. 'Did you read it?'

'No I didn't.'

'Well, he confessed that he stole the lottery ticket from you.'

'When could he have stolen it?'

'When you were at his parents' place and showed it to him.'

Misi thought back. It was possible. Mr János asked to see the ticket and then didn't give it back to him!

'He wrote that he pushed the ten-forint note into your pocket when you gave his briefcase back to him.'

'Yes, I figured that out.'

'He got a hundred twenty forints from the tobacconist. He put the ten forints in your pocket and he spent forty forints on clothes for Bella, that's fifty; ten forints for other things, that's sixty; the railway tickets cost twenty, that's eighty; he gave ten forints to Bella when she went to call on her aunt the Princess, that's ninety; he paid for the fiacre, that was two forints, and he bought Bella a bunch of flowers for three forints, that's ninety-five. The rest he drank away, and with the last fifteen kreutzers he bought three stamps and confessed his crime to his father, to your uncle and to the police. And then he wanted to jump into the Danube, but he didn't because it was cold.'

Orczy and Gimesi laughed heartily but Misi was stunned and kept repeating, 'A hundred twenty forints? That was all?' He was terribly disappointed. Then what made that briefcase so heavy?

'It's all settled now, because they paid back the whole amount,' said Orczy. 'Mr Pósalaky received his sixty forints, and your uncle fifty forints – they counted off the ten forints you already got. Except that your Uncle Géza didn't accept the money, because the Töröks are poor and he said he owed them a great deal. It was Mr Török who paid back the money, to save his son's honour.'

Misi listened with a bitter taste in his mouth.

The three boys had a long talk. Gimesi told him that the whole college knew that he didn't want to be a student of the College of Debrecen any more, and they were all very impressed.

Then his Uncle Géza came home and asked the boys to leave, because if they stayed longer Misi would get feverish again.

Next day Miss Viola came to visit with Alex. She cried and apologised to Misi and even kissed him, saying that Bella 'sent a kiss to her poet'. (That made Misi blush.) Miss Viola also said that Bella had made her fortune; she was staying with her aunt the Princess and had already sent home a thousand forints. The aunt was very glad to see her and was very fond of her and promised to leave her the Egervár estate, because Bella very much resembled her own daughter who had died. The estate was nine thousand acres; their fortune was made. Alex would go to study in Budapest, and if he failed the year they would get a university professor to tutor him.

Misi listened to this as if in a dream, and he developed a high fever again.

It was another week before he could get up, and by then he had forgotten how to walk. He even laughed at it a little, how funny it was. He was as dizzy as a fly in autumn.

'When will we go back to the college?' his uncle asked unexpectedly one evening. 'I mean to classes,' he added gently.

'Never,' Misi said, lowering his eyes.

Neither spoke for a long while. The fire was blazing in the fireplace and outside the little steam tram was tooting.

'Then what will become of you?' asked his uncle quietly.

Misi didn't answer for a long time because he didn't dare to say what he had in his heart. He just hung his head.

'Well, what do you want to be, my dear boy?' asked his uncle.

'The teacher of mankind,' Misi said promptly.

There was silence for another long while.

'Teacher . . . You know, nobody ever became a teacher without studying,' said his uncle.

Misi got flustered, ashamed of himself for a moment. He knew that. He wanted to study, or rather, not so much to study as to know everything. He wanted to know everything that a human being could know. And he got worried that he would betray himself, his secret, what nobody had an inkling of, what he hadn't quite clarified even to himself, what he couldn't tell to anybody, except perhaps his mother: that he wanted to be a poet.

'Well, how do you picture that, my Misi?' asked his wise uncle in a kind of gentle, teasing tone. 'You just start out on the road of life and whoever comes along, you will start teaching him right away?'

Misi closed his eyes with a secret smile. 'Yes.'

His uncle, smiling, looked at him out of the corner of his eye. After a while he took his good-smelling cigar out of his mouth and said in a forceful, normal tone: 'Well, I think you should come to the school where I'm teaching. That would

be best. You'll learn the declensions and conjugations, everything you need to know, and then you can teach others.'

They sat in silence for a long while. Misi was crying quietly,
pleased and happy that this was how it would be. Then his
uncle asked gently, kindly, in such an encouraging voice that
it opened Misi's heart and spread it out before God: 'And
what is it you want to teach mankind?'

Misi stole a glance at him. His eyes filled with tears again
and he curled up like a little worm and said very quietly, 'Just
one thing. Be good, be good, be faithful unto death.'

He dropped his head. The room turned grey and mottled
like marble, and suddenly he was seized by an inexpressible
longing to leave that place and go to the school where his
uncle taught . . . his dear good uncle . . . Then he thought of
the sky.

Notes

Notes

1 Mihály Munkácsy (1844–1900). Romantic painter, the most celebrated Hungarian artist of his time. He studied in Munich and spent many years in Paris, where he enjoyed great success with his dramatic paintings such as *The Last Day of a Condemned Prisoner*, *The Death of Mozart* and *Milton Dictating* Paradise Lost *to his Daughters*.

CHAPTER III

1 Uncle Török. In Hungarian 'uncle' and 'aunt' are friendly appellations for any older man or woman, used in the same sense as 'uncle' by the Fool in *King Lear*. The words are also used in the modern English sense: Misi's 'Uncle Géza' is his mother's brother.

2 Sándor Petőfi (1823–49). The son of a butcher on the Hungarian Plain, Petőfi made his way to Pest and earned a living with his poems while still a student. His lyrical poetry encompassed everyday life as well as his countrymen's longing to rid themselves of serfdom and Austrian rule. Born six years later than Arany (see Chapter VII, note 2) but maturing earlier, Petőfi was the first Hungarian poet to breach the dividing line between popular and high culture; he appealed to everybody. *Liberty and Love* (a typical Petőfi title) mingles tender poems about the joys of going home to visit his parents, sitting in the kitchen with his mother and having his wife leaning against his shoulder, with calls for revolution and the hanging of kings. Loves, hates, affection, humour, ridicule, satire, philosophical reflections can all be found in his poetry, which has such force, such simplicity and melodiousness that there is hardly a Hungarian who does not know at least some lines of Petőfi by heart. Many of his poems turned into

folk songs even within his short lifetime. He gave meaning to the phrase 'incendiary poetry': his call to arms *Get on your feet, Magyar, It's now or never!* was the spark that ignited the March 1848 revolution. During the year-long war of independence he went into battle armed only with his notebook, and was killed on 30 July 1849 at the battle of Segesvár in Transylvania, his stomach ripped open by a Cossack lancer. In his death, Petőfi became the symbol of the nation's desire for freedom and democracy; his statue on the staircase of the Calvinist College of Debrecen is a declaration of national independence, a protest against foreign rule.

CHAPTER VI

1 Miklós Zrínyi (1508–66). In 1566 Count Zrínyi held out for weeks at his castle, Szigetvár, against a Turkish army led by Suleiman the Magnificent. When they ran out of food and ammunition Zrínyi and his men charged out of the castle and before they were cut down got close enough to the Sultan's tent to give him an attack of apoplexy from which he later died. The Turkish army withdrew and that part of the country enjoyed several years respite.

2 Ferenc Rákóczi II (1676–1735). Having lost his father in the year of his birth, Prince Rákóczi was heir to the independent principality of Transylvania and most of the lands of northern and eastern Hungary and was likely to be offered the crown. Emperor Leopold I of Austria, anxious to formalise his own claim to the throne of Hungary while a third of the country was still held by the Turks, sent General Carafa to seize the boy prince from the castle of Munkács. The Prince's mother, Ilona Zrínyi, the great-great-granddaughter of the hero of Szigetvár, held the castle against the Austrian troops for three years. In 1687 General Carafa took time off from the siege to capture and behead forty leading members of the Hungarian Assembly of Nobles who were suspected of intending to vote against the proposal that Leopold's descendants should be declared kings of Hungary in perpetuity. After the beheadings only one member of the Assembly of Nobles spoke against the proposal, and he died suddenly of unknown causes later that day. Emperor Leopold I was duly elected King of Hungary, but Ilona Zrínyi held out at Munkács for another year. When the castle was finally captured by treachery the twelve-

year-old prince was made the godson and ward of Emperor Leopold and sent to be educated in a Jesuit monastery in Neuhaus, while his mother and sister were shut up in a nunnery and the Austrian soldiery lived off his peasants' lands and livestock, raping the women and killing the husbands who objected.

Released from the tutelage of the Jesuits at eighteen and allowed to move to Vienna, Rákóczi developed a passion for cards, parties and hunting. He might have stayed at court like other Hungarian aristocrats who built palaces in Vienna, but at the age of twenty-two he returned to Hungary, and a few years later he led a war of liberation against Austria. The rebels fought from 1703 to 1711 but, lacking allies (Louis XIV kept promising help which never arrived), they were finally defeated and Prince Rákóczi had to flee the country.

All this is recounted in his two volumes of *Confessions and Memoirs* written in Latin and French. They also tell of the Habsburgs' subsequent reprisals and the rise of Count Eszterházy, who served the Habsburgs by pinpointing the noble families who might produce another Rákóczi. These families were wiped out, men, women, daughters as well as sons, to prevent anyone from claiming their lands or titles at some future date. Count Eszterházy was rewarded with some of his victims' estates. Though Prince Rákóczi died a poor recluse in exile, he continued to exert a profound influence on Hungarian history, tempting his country-men with the glory of fighting in doomed rebellions instead of choosing a life of ease and betrayal. Without his compelling example, for instance, it is impossible to understand the Hungarian communist officials and army officers, many of them educated in Moscow, who went over to the people in the 1956 uprising against Soviet rule.

3 Mór Jókai (1825–1904) wrote the same sort of dramatic, melo-dramatic, romantic, sentimental, rebellious, wordy prose works as Victor Hugo, and had the same sort of monumental impact in Hungary as Victor Hugo had in France.

CHAPTER VII

1 Árpád (c. 870–907) was elected chieftain of the seven tribes who settled in the Carpathian basin around AD 895. The Árpád dynasty ruled Hungary until the family died out in 1301.

2 János Arany (1817–82) was, apart from Petőfi, the most significant
and popular poet of the nineteenth century, the time when Latin
ceased to be the official language and the language of learning in
Hungary, and the fusion of the popular idiom and the educated
consciousness created a kind of verbal explosion. The richness and
vigour of this new language are most fully embodied in Arany's
ballads, his lyrical and epic poems, and his translations of all the
comedies of Aristophanes and three plays of Shakespeare. His
translations of *Hamlet, King John* and *A Midsummer Night's Dream*
are faithful yet have the full strength of the original – an
achievement due not only to Arany's genius but also to the fact
that Hungarian was then at the same stage of its development as
English in Shakespeare's time. Ever since Arany's translations,
Shakespeare has been Hungary's most popular playwright. Arany's
own poems rank with the poetry of Petőfi – and Endre Ady and
Attila József in this century – as the best loved and most widely
known in Hungarian literature; they are to Hungarians what
Verdi's operas are to Italians.

CHAPTER VIII

1 Hungarian speech is full of affectionate endearments (as well as
terms of abuse). 'My sweet good' is a common form of address;
indeed 'my dear good sweet' is even more common and usage has
rendered it a normal expression. However, these sound extrava-
gant in English and give the wrong impression of the emotional
content of the sentence. This translation has a couple of hundred
fewer endearments than the original, but it is a true English
rendering of the tone.
2 King Mátyás, Matthias Corvinus (1443–90), King of Hungary, the
second of János Hunyadi's two sons. His claim to the throne was
based on his father's great achievements. János Hunyadi (1408–56)
rose to be general of King Sigismund's army and won every battle
he fought against the Turks, successfully holding back the armies
of the Ottoman Empire which had set out on a religious war to
conquer the infidels of Europe. After the death of King
Sigismund, who had no direct successor, János Hunyadi was
elected Governor of Hungary; he was a popular national leader,
for all the serfs who joined his armies became free men. While
Hunyadi was fighting the Turks in the south, the Habsburg

Emperor Frederick III threatened Hungary from the northwest, and to protect his back Hunyadi made a treaty accepting the emperor's ward Ladislas V as the nominal King of Hungary, while retaining all administrative and military power as the country's Captain-General. His victory over the Turks at Nándorfehérvár, now Belgrade, on 22 July 1456 was celebrated all over Europe as a great triumph for Christendom; Pope Calixtus III decreed that bells should be rung in every church at noon till Judgment Day to commemorate it – a papal decree which appears to have been losing its force only in recent times. But the great victory left tens of thousands of corpses on the battlefield in the summer heat, causing an outbreak of plague which killed many of the survivors, including János Hunyadi himself.

His eldest son László (1433–57) inherited his father's popularity as well as the loyalty of all the commanders. However, the nominal king Ladislas V, or rather his backer, the Emperor, thought János Hunyadi's death would enable them to seize effective control of Hungary, and Ladislas issued a decree appointing his uncle Cillei as the new Captain-General. László pretended to comply and the king and Cillei went to the Hunyadis' stronghold of Nándorfehérvár, where László Hunyadi was supposed to make a formal renunciation of his father's powers. Instead, he killed Cillei and arrested the king, but freed him a month later after Ladislas made a solemn oath during Mass that he would not attempt to revenge his uncle's death and would never undertake any action against the Hunyadis. He also appointed László as the new Captain-General of Hungary, in effect continuing the same arrangement that had existed earlier with László's father: Hunyadi had most of the power while the king had the crown, Buda and northern Hungary. The following spring Ladislas V invited the Hunyadis to visit him. László unwisely accepted and went to Buda, followed by his younger brother Mátyás. There they were seized in their beds during the night and condemned to death in the morning. The public execution on 16 March 1457, on St George's Square in Buda, was a horrifying spectacle. The axe missed László's head the first time, the second blow was cushioned by his long, thick blond hair, and only the third blow cut into his neck. He still had the strength to get to his feet and run, but he was dragged back to the block and beheaded with the fourth blow. The reaction of the crowd prompted the king to spare the life of 14-year-old Mátyás, who had watched the beheading of his brother while waiting for his own execution. There was an uprising and within days the king had to flee Hungary to save his life, taking the boy Mátyás with him as prisoner.

Mátyás was still a prisoner in Prague a year later when he was elected King of Hungary in Buda in March 1458, and he had to be ransomed from Ladislas V's successor. However, he was crowned only six years later after winning victories over the Turks, the Bohemians, the Austrian Emperor and above all his own nobles. He was a liberal-humanist absolute monarch, with a formidable standing army which gave him the power to adopt policies far ahead of his time, liberating the serfs and granting them what today would be called civil rights. He married Princess Beatrice of Aragon, herself an educated woman, and together they turned Buda into one of the great humanist centres of Europe. Mátyás founded the University of Buda and the National Library. He was remembered as 'Mátyás the Just', and 'justice died with King Mátyás' became a common saying.

3 Battle of Mohács (1526). The second act of a great Hungarian tragedy. Upon the death of King Mátyás the nobles abolished the rights he had granted to the peasantry and reimposed serfdom, causing much suffering. In 1514 a peasant revolt led by George Dózsa, who had been elevated to the nobility for his bravery against the Turks, was savagely put down by the hereditary nobility, who effectively wiped out the country's foot soldiers, as well as roasting Dózsa on a white-hot iron throne with a white-hot iron crown on his head. (Móricz started to write a play about Dózsa in 1920 but decided that it would never get past the censor and wrote *Be Faithful Unto Death* instead.) Twelve years after Dózsa was burnt on an iron throne, the nobles' depleted army was annihilated by the Turks at Mohács in southern Hungary. It was the worst defeat in Hungarian history, and to this day Hungarians console each other with the saying, 'More was lost at Mohács'.

4 Gábor Bethlen (1580–1629). The Protestant Elector of Transylvania, where freedom of worship was law. Preserving the independence of Transylvania while the rest of Hungary was under Turkish or Austrian occupation, he also helped the Bohemians to defend themselves against Austria, and was a great

patron of the arts and sciences. He is the hero of *Transylvania*, the historical trilogy Móricz wrote after *Be Faithful Unto Death*.

5 The centre of Europe. Since Europe, extending from the Urals to the Atlantic, is neither a square nor a circle and spreads out in odd shapes in all directions, the location of its centre depends on who is doing the measuring. All Central European nations claim the centre for themselves.

CHAPTER IX

1 Misi is remembering lines from one of Petőfi's most popular ballads, 'The King's Oath', in which László Hunyadi is warned not to trust Ladislas V's oath and not to accept his invitation to Buda. See chapter VIII, note 2.

CHAPTER X

1 Lajos Kossuth (1802–94). Hungarian statesman and revolutionary leader. Born into an impoverished noble family, he studied law at Sárospatak and later became editor of the liberal newspaper *Pesti Hírlap*. His imprisonment for publishing the debates of the National Assembly in his newspaper – a crime against the state in Habsburg Hungary – made him a national hero. During the 1848 revolution he became Minister of Finance in the national government of Count Batthyányi, who advocated an independently administered Hungarian state within the Habsburg empire. Like the Soviet Union in 1956, Austria first recognised the government of the revolution and then invaded the country, whereupon Batthyányi resigned and Kossuth became Prime Minister. When the revolution and the independent republic were crushed by Austrian and Russian troops (sent by Tsar Nicholas I, a firm believer in the divine right of kings) Kossuth was condemned to death but fled into exile, escaping the fate of Count Batthyányi, who was executed even though he had not voted for the deposing of the Habsburgs. A great orator in several languages, Kossuth became a popular hero on a speaking tour of the United States and England, and lived for years in London, where he became a close friend of Mazzini. Revered in Italy for his stand against the Habsburgs, he died in Turin.

2 Árpád. Prints of Munkácsy's painting of Árpád being raised on a shield when he was elected leader of the Hungarians were the

most popular reproductions of the time. The original is in the parliament building in Budapest.

CHAPTER XI

1 Ferenc Deák (1803–76). Hungarian statesman. Leader of the liberal opposition in the Hungarian Diet, he became Minister of Justice in the first government of the 1848 revolution led by the moderate Count Batthyányi, and resigned along with him. He came back to prominence after 1861 as an advocate of home rule and was the author of an accord with the Habsburgs which allowed for autonomy on local issues but left the Austrians in charge of finance, defence and foreign affairs. This allowed Austria to drag Hungary into the First World War, in which it lost over a million dead and more than two-thirds of its territory.

2 Bach hussars. After the defeat of the 1848–9 revolution the policy of hanging and imprisoning Hungarian patriots was carried out by Alexander Bach, Minister of the Interior of the Habsburg monarchy. His reign of terror (1850–9) was called the Bach Epoch and his henchmen were called the Bach hussars.

3 Count István Széchenyi (1791–1860). Hungarian aristocrat, ranks beside Prince Rákóczi and Lajos Kossuth as one of the pivotal figures of Hungarian history and is often called 'the greatest Hungarian'. He spent most of his vast fortune organising the modernisation of Hungary in the first half of the nineteenth century. Among other things, he regulated the Danube and the Tisza rivers, built the national railways, introduced horse racing and the English method of horse breeding, spanned the Danube with the famous Chain Bridge of Budapest (the work of the Scots engineers Adam and William Clark), and founded and housed the Hungarian Academy of Sciences. He was a great reformer and innovator, not a revolutionary, but after the defeat in 1849 he was deemed too dangerous to remain at large and the Austrian government, anticipating the Soviet method of dealing with dissidents, imprisoned him in an asylum on the outskirts of Vienna, where he eventually committed suicide. Many Hungarian homes had a print of the engraving which showed him with a long beard, sitting in an armchair in front of his bookshelves in his room at the asylum in Döblingen; this is the 'painting' Misi thinks of.

4 Miklós Toldi, hero of Arany's great epic poem *Toldi*. Like Orlando in *As You Like It*, Miklós Toldi is a young nobleman whose older brother lords it at court and banishes him to the country to spend his life as a farm labourer. But, like Orlando, Toldi raises himself by his strength and heroism.

Central European Classics

This series presents nineteenth- and twentieth-century fiction from Central Europe. Introductions by leading contemporary Central European writers explain why the chosen titles have become classics in their own countries. New or newly revised English translations ensure that the writing can be appreciated by readers here and now.

The selection of titles is the result of extensive discussion with critics, writers and scholars in the field. However, it can not and does not aim to be comprehensive. Many books highly prized in their own countries are too difficult, specific or allusive to work in translation. Much good modern Central European fiction is already available. Thus, for example, the contemporary Czech novelists Kundera, Hrabal, Klíma and Škvorecký can all be read in English. Could one as easily name four well-known French, Dutch or Spanish novelists?

Yet, if one reaches back a little further into the past, one finds that it is the Central European literature written in German which has been most translated – whether Kafka, Musil or Joseph Roth. We therefore start this series with books originally written in Czech, Hungarian and Polish.

The Central European Classics were originally conceived and sponsored by the Central and East European Publishing Project. A charity based in Oxford, the Project worked to reduce the cultural and intellectual division of Europe by supporting independent, quality publishing of both books and journals in Central and Eastern Europe, and translations from, into and between the languages of Central and Eastern Europe. Sally Laird was Project Director at the inception of the series, and contributed much to its design. The publication of the classics is now being carried forward by the Central European Classics Trust. Besides the General Editor, its trustees are Neal Ascherson, Ralf Dahrendorf, Craig Raine and Elizabeth Winter, and the Secretary to the trustees is Danuta Garton Ash.

We hope each book can be enjoyed in its own right, as literature in English. But we also hope the series may contribute to a deeper understanding of the culture and history of countries which, since the opening of the iron curtain, have been coming closer to us in many other ways.

Timothy Garton Ash